Too Long In Paradise

Also by R. Lindsey

Cuddaby's Planet

NON FICTION

How Science Views Reality

TOO LONG IN PARADISE

R. Lindsey

QUODLIBET ROCK

Published 2019 by Quodlibet Rock

e-mail: quodrock@gmail.com

ISBN 978-1-9997097-8-5 (hardback)
ISBN 978-1-9997097-9-2 (paperback)

CONTENTS

The transmission from Earth, number 1/12546, began typically. There was an announcement of the death of the Palatine of Africa, followed by details and an obituary. Then came the regular population and energy budget statistics. Third item was a new story by one of Earth's authors.

It was during this part of the broadcast that something went wrong. When a piece of equipment breaks down, it attempts to emit a System Failure Signal. Sometimes the fault is bad enough to prevent that from happening. In this case, we distinctly heard the start of the failure signal, but it cut out almost immediately.

It was not a cause of concern to us. Such failures are likely once or twice per thousand years, and repairs would soon be put into effect. We waited patiently for Earth transmission 2/12546.

It never came.

"When you are at the summit, every path leads downwards."
Sheila Mress,
Chief Overseer of the Antarctic Council,
Sektaday 34th, 13162.

Part 1

Koltetra

1

I, Felip Varrandoe, have written this account of my recent past because I have been accused by the authorities on Earth of taking part in various acts of extreme violence, of indulging in reckless vandalism and, worst of all, of complicity in two murders, including the murder of one of my friends. It is only justice that I am given a chance to refute these charges. I do so in what follows. Some of the events I shall relate will undoubtedly disturb any civilized person (as they disturbed me) and I apologize in advance for that. But I am determined to tell the truth.

I will not waste the reader's time by giving a full account of my life to date (even if I could remember it, which I can't) despite this being the practice in modern autobiographies. Instead I shall start at the point where I became involved in the historic expedition to Earth. I was at that time living on Koltetra, Earth's fourth interstellar colony, and serving as a Congressman. It was this role that led me to become deeply involved in the events which set the expedition in motion.

It is, then, on my home planet back in the year of human civilization 13046 that my story begins....

*

Earth is revered on Koltetra. It is the birthplace of life; the cradle of humankind; the 'Old World' where perfect knowledge and perfect technology have led to the creation of a perfect society. It is a planet whose inhabitants live out their days in mutual respect and harmony, where war and disease and poverty have been eradicated, to linger only as mere ghosts of a long-distant past in textbooks and novels and works of art. It is a blue and beautiful oasis in the void, on which the dreams of billions of human beings across the millennia have been turned into reality. It is a world of universal happiness, unchanging, eternal. It is paradise.

But somehow some kind of irrecoverable fault must have developed on the perfect world. A logical contradiction, I know, but undeniable. Earth transmission 1/12546 took fifteen years to reach Koltetra, arriving in 12561. And then silence. The years passed.

At first, with each new day we expected to hear again the voice of the Old World reassuring us that all was well, and explaining what had caused the break in communication. But all we heard was more silence. Our astronomers turned their telescopes Earthwards. They saw exactly what they had always seen. At all wavelengths Earth and its sun looked entirely normal. Thus, as the years became decades, and the decades a century, arose the most baffling mystery of the Tenth Civilization.

It may perhaps seem surprising that beyond telescopic observation none of the New Worlds actually did anything to resolve this mystery. On reflection though, it becomes obvious why. The problem is simply that the distances involved are prohibitive. Koltetra, for example, is fifteen light-years from Earth. With two exceptions all the other New Worlds are even further away. This remoteness of the various inhabited planets from one another means no travel ever takes place amongst them — at least not since the colonial voyages from Earth that brought the New Worlds into existence. Of course, all of us have the knowledge of how to journey between the stars; it's just that we haven't the inclination or the equipment to do it. In any case, physical movement between worlds is unnecessary. Transmission of data at the speed of light is the fastest and most efficient way of keeping in contact, and that's the method we use. I think our name for the resulting network of communication — the Galactic Information Grid — is a little grandiose given that we humans only inhabit a tiny part of the galaxy, but never mind. It reminds us of our aspirations.

All this is so much history. Unfortunately I am myself no historian, an ignorance compounded by my being an immortal, which means I have a great deal of difficulty remembering long-past happenings. So, for my own reference and for those of my readers who are similarly placed, I will set down here a few historic events of relevance to the account which follows in this document, together with when they occurred.

  7042 — The Koltetra colony is founded.
  7350 — The Tenth Civilization begins (nominally).
12546 — Earth leaves the Galactic Information Grid.
13063 — The Koltetrian mission to Earth sets off.
13162 — The Koltetrian mission reaches Earth.

My personal involvement in the mission of 13063 began in 13046, exactly five hundred years after Earth became silent. For irrational reasons people always seem more aware of anniversaries which end in a couple of zeros, and this one was no exception. It was consequently a year which played host to one of the major debates of Koltetrian history thus far. On one side were those who wanted to send an exploratory mission to Earth; on the other were those who saw any such thing as an untimely extravagance.

Leading up to this debate, and providing it with some of its force, were messages which Koltetra had received from the nearer amongst the other New Worlds. They had all independently come to the conclusion that it was time the questions about Earth's silence were resolved and that it was Koltetra which should carry out the investigation. Taking distance and available resources into account, my home planet was undeniably the best placed.

Whether we should rise to the challenge at this moment in time had deeply divided our society. At root, the dispute revolved around the question: 'Why now?' We had, after all, never felt impelled to take action before. It would be fair to say we were concerned by the Earth mystery, but not concerned enough.

As was to be expected, the matter duly came before Koltetra's Ruling Congress, of which I had the honour to be a member. The opponents in Congress to the proposed expedition to Earth were led by one Madam Magrit, our finest orator and a worthy champion of any cause. She and I were occasional adversaries in the debating chamber, so I can bear personal witness to her first-rate intellect, her wit, her reluctance to compromise and her determination to win.

Speaking in the Congressional debate, Madam Magrit expressed the view that 'now is not the time'. She forcefully asserted that (as we were all aware) the main constraint on the rate at which Koltetra is progressing is shortage, not of personnel or raw materials, but of energy. Unlike Earth, with its huge surplus, we on Koltetra endure a shortfall. There are countless projects waiting to be implemented, each clamouring for limited energy resources. Each, when complete, will provide major benefits for our citizens. Yet if energy was to be diverted to the construction of an interstellar vessel, who would benefit from that? No one. Far better to press ahead with climate control, tectonic plate de-stressing, the integrated memory system and the magrider network (to name but four).

The counter argument put by the pro-expedition

faction — amongst whom I was numbered — was simply that finding out what had happened to Earth would be worth a modest delay in our progress. Future comfort could, in this one exceptional circumstance, stand aside for present curiosity.

It was not a proposition to which Madam Magrit and her supporters could be reconciled. The debate ended therefore without a consensus. When that happens we don't settle the issue with a majority vote, as is the practice on Earth. Instead, Koltetra's Congress is presided over by nine Adjudicators — our wisest, most humble and respected of citizens — and they are called on to decide who won the argument. Their opinion is then put to a referendum of those citizens who watched the debate and have read the adjudication. On this occasion we weren't kept waiting long for their verdict. It was the following morning when the Chief Adjudicator announced that he was instructing the Executive Director of Koltetra to put in hand immediately preparations for an expedition to Earth. Seven Adjudicators had come out in favour, with two undecided. The subsequent referendum duly endorsed their decision.

*

Not surprisingly, the building of an interstellar ship is a long job. We had none of the necessary equipment, nor any existing vessel to use as a model. The liner that had brought our forebears across the light-years had long ago been dismantled and recycled into other applications. Our engineers had to reacquire forgotten knowledge and relearn lost skills. I think we initially underestimated how difficult a task we had set ourselves.

To the technical difficulties were added political ones. Several attempts were made to delay or even scrap the ship during the seventeen years it took to build. As a Congressman, I was able to give my strong support to those seeking to fend off these unwelcome moves, and I like to think I contributed in a small way to ensuring the project reached fruition.

Sittings of Congress notwithstanding, I had many opportunities during the years of construction to ascend into orbit and see how work was progressing. The man in charge of the fabrication phase of the project soon became a friend of mine, tolerating with great patience my frequent enquiries about how things were going. His name was Karter and he looked on the slowly maturing ship as a child over which he could claim a kind of fatherhood.

Eventually, at long last, the years of building approached their end and attention turned to selecting the five people who would make the journey to Earth. The notion had been growing in my mind for several years that I should be one of them. Being a Congressman was becoming a bore, I felt my life needed a new direction, and I was emotionally committed to the project. Three good reasons for putting my name forward. To help matters along, I resigned from Congress in order to have no existing commitments to bar me from being considered. The other possible barrier to my participation in the mission, my wife, was not, when I broached the subject, disposed to object to our separating. Like me, she was an immortal, and had lived longer than she could remember. We had been together for over sixty years and I suppose she felt as much in need of a change as I did. When the time came, our parting was amicable and only briefly a source of sadness.

As I had hoped, the Executive Director regarded my request to join the expedition to Earth favourably. Being a recently retired Congressman gave me a social standing that the people of Earth (assuming there were any) could be expected to view approvingly. And also, there weren't that many volunteers. It would take a hundred years to cross the fifteen light-year distance separating Earth and Koltetra, making the round trip a two hundred year voyage. A lot would happen on Koltetra during those two centuries — exciting developments that were not lightly to be missed. And of course one's family and friends would either be dead or, if they were immortal, have completely changed by the time one returned. There were very few Koltetrians with a degree of commitment to the expedition sufficient to overcome such strong disincentives. As a result, the volunteers for the five places on the voyage numbered less than a hundred. It was not unexpected then that I got the assignment.

To those who don't know about interstellar travel, it comes as a surprise how simple the travelling part of the job is. There was little training. We learnt about the ship and that was more or less all. Even learning that much was primarily intended to overcome fears arising from the journey rather than to instil essential knowledge. Strictly speaking, it would have been good enough just to show us around and then send us on our way.

Apart from what we were taught about the ship, our training mostly covered what we were going to do when — not if — we got to our intended goal. Thinking on that score was rudimentary precisely because what we would find on our arrival was the very mystery we were going there to solve. We did, however, have two basic plans.

Plan One assumed that Earth had been overwhelmed by a calamity of such magnitude that nowhere habitable remained. In that case we were to make observations and measurements from the ship, supplementing them if possible with sorties to the surface and anywhere else that interested us. What we discovered, and our conclusions if any, were to be reported back to Koltetra on the ship's soliton transmitter, following which we would make the return journey home.

Plan Two assumed a somewhat lesser calamity, leaving Earth inhabitable and therefore presumably inhabited. This would give us a much easier time, for all we'd have to do would be to make contact with the survivors, hear from them what had happened, and report accordingly. After that, we had the option of detaching the soliton transmitter and leaving it behind so that Earth could use it to re-join the Galactic Information Grid. It would be the civilized thing for us to do. Return to Koltetra would then proceed as under *Plan One*.

Simple really. Foolproof. Provided the ship avoided any calamity of its own during the voyage, success was guaranteed. Indeed, technically it wasn't even necessary for us five astronauts to be aboard. Hybrimorphs could do the job just as well. But we were going along for a very good reason. Almost everyone on Koltetra expected *Plan Two* to turn out to be the appropriate one, and that meant we would be met by people. It would be an insult to Earth, and highly uncivilized, if Koltetra's representatives were not human. After all, when two long-separated friends greet one another, they do so by embracing physically. You might well reappraise your relationship if the so-called friend required you to embrace his hybrimorph instead.

When the ship was complete, we spent a while familiarizing ourselves with it, and then were given thirty days to put our affairs in order. I passed much of the time touring my favourite sights.

There are many beautiful places on Koltetra: the Valley of Eternal Summer, the site of our first local climate control system; the Siren Hills, where the wind blows constantly through subterranean caverns to play strange, eerie music; Jathra, a mountain range with countless outcrops of glass-encrusted rocks which glisten in sunlight like a sea of diamonds.

And there is my favourite, which was the place I travelled to last of all on my final complete day on Koltetra: the Falls at Ikterun. No geographical feature on Earth or any of the other New Worlds can match this most famous of Koltetra's sights. It is quite simply the most spectacular waterfall human eyes have ever beheld, where the waters of our largest river plummet over a cliff into the sea nine hundred metres below at a rate of over fifty thousand tonnes a second.

For me, the Falls at Ikterun were where the tiny world inside my head and the vastness of the universe met as nearly as it is possible for them to do. To stand on one of the observation platforms close to the foot of the Falls, with the thunderous roar in my ears, the upward-rushing fog of cold, dense spray on my skin, and the sharp sensation of ionized air in my lungs, was to experience, through my utter insignificance beside this colossus of natural violence, a most profound peace. Many were the occasions I had remained on that platform, unaware of the passage of time, unaware of the growing ache in my feet, unaware of the cold seeping into my body, until eventually, sometimes only after several hours, the cries of my physical self made themselves heard and I would tear myself away to come back to the unpeaceful, and sometimes stressful, lesser realities of everyday life.

I took my leave of the Falls at sunset. It was an emotional experience, for into my mind, unbidden and unwelcome, came the accursed thought which was my reason for visiting Koltetra's beautiful places. It wasn't that I was going to be away a long time. As both the outward and return journeys would be spent asleep, my conscious separation from Koltetra would only last for as long as we took to unravel the mystery of Earth. Nor was it that I expected many of 'the sights' to have changed beyond recognition by the time I got back; they wouldn't, since they are protected by law. No, it was the fear that I might die on the journey as I hurtled at a hundred thousand kilometres a second between the stars. It was easy enough for Fabrication Overseer Karter to dismiss the notion that an accident could happen; that anything irrecoverable would occur. Every Koltetrian — except the five who were to make the journey, that is — was totally confident about it. But somehow it looks different when *your* life is the one at risk. When you ask someone else to trust his continued survival to the thickness of a thread, that thread appears a lot stronger than when he asks you to do it.

It was an irrational fear. Not all the perfect knowledge and the perfect technology of the Tenth Civilization, though I believed in them totally, could drive it away. It provided a salutary reminder of the perfidy of the human mind. Science, all-conquering invention of that very mind, can prove there is nothing to be afraid of. But when it comes to the test, we are afraid nonetheless.

2

Before I and my four fellow travellers made our final ascent into orbit, there was a ceremony to endure. The Chief Adjudicator and the Executive Director jointly officiated, and both made speeches, the contents of which were markedly similar. Both told us they hoped our long voyage would be a safe one, and how they trusted we would do our best to carry out the duty we had voluntarily accepted; namely, to inform the New Worlds about the fate of the Old. A considerable number of Koltetra's people were watching. I suspect they were unsure, most of them, whether to pity us astronauts for our folly, or to admire us for our personal sacrifice in the cause of civilization. Probably they thought about us in both ways at once. If that was so, they reflected my own feelings.

The Executive Director added a touch of poignancy by noting that, as a mortal, he would never know the outcome of our voyage. "At fifty," he said, "I am already half way through my life, so I shall have died many years before you reach Earth. I will never hear your report from there; nor will I be around to greet you on your return. No matter. It is enough for me to know I have set you on your way and contributed to what I believe to be potentially the most momentous undertaking of this century, and the most important I have been privileged to direct. If I was cursed — or blessed, depending on your point of view — with immortality, I would doubtless regard this venture as no more than a forgettable waymark along an endless road. As it is, I can truly consider it my crowning achievement. And now I place it in the hands of you astronauts. You take with you the curiosity of all the citizens of Koltetra; nay, the citizens of every New World. I am as confident as I can be about a voyage of this nature that you will succeed in your mission."

One of the five brave adventurers was then called on to reply. As a former Congressman well practiced in speechmaking, my colleagues nominated me. Rather unfairly, really, because in Congress one speaks to the point. Verbosity is not welcomed, least of all by the Adjudicators, who silence wafflers without mercy. They had never silenced me for that offence. Yet in the circumstances of the departure ceremony, waffle was just about what was needed. When you came down to it, the only things to say were thank you and goodbye. Somehow I managed to pad that out to several hundred words. The Chief Adjudicator must have been wishing he was back in Congress by the time I finished.

Then, not without some relief, my four companions and I got into the ferry and bade farewell to the surface of Koltetra. We ascended on a dissipating beamtrack until reaching an altitude of about a thousand kilometres, after which the beam was too weak to guide us. We continued upwards using chem-ion thrusters.

It took us three hours to reach the dock in which the ship resided. The dock was a hollow sphere four kilometres across, rotating slowly so as to give the inner surface a centrifugal gravitational field. There were two shells to the sphere, between which was an air-filled environment where the construction workers lived and carried out some of their functions.

We left our ferry at one of the dock's poles, making our way into the air-filled section. From there we were conveyed in a car 'down' to the equatorial region of the sphere where the gravity was as strong as that on Koltetra's surface. ('Down', I can mention, is always perpendicular to the axis of rotation. That means that as soon as you step away from the stationary entry point at the pole, you begin to slide 'down' what appears to be initially an almost vertical sloping surface.)

Fabrication Overseer Karter was already present in the dock, and joined us for the final stage of this opening part of our journey. He led us to one of the interior equatorial ports, where we boarded a small magrider with him. It followed a beamtrack connecting to the ship. The floodlit vessel looked tiny at a distance of two kilometres, lying at anchor in the centre of the dock.

"Beautiful, isn't it?" Karter said. "I shall be sorry to see it leave."

We watched the ship grow slowly larger as we drew nearer and nearer to it.

"Absolutely flawless," the Fabrication Overseer continued. "We've tested every part of it, and not an atom out of place."

We caught briefly the reflection of one of the dock lights in the very steep-sided conical panflector.

"Just look at that," said Karter. "That panflector shield will protect you against every conceivable collision, up to rocks the size of a house. We've never made anything like it here before. So just you make sure you bring it back. I'm looking forward to playing around with it."

"What about hitting rocks bigger than a house?" asked Roshan, staking her claim to be the most morbid of the five of us.

"It's impossible," replied Karter. "Anything that large will be detected in advance by the flight controller and avoided. You really are completely safe. Collision mitigation was an overriding concern when we drew up the design."

The magrider moved into the underside of the panflector cone. We passed first the vacuum impeller and then the helium annihilator and the two spherical fuel tanks supplying it, one containing two hundred and fifty tonnes of helium, the other containing two hundred and fifty tonnes of anti-helium. Finally we arrived at the accommodation area.

There were three docking ports giving access. Two were already occupied by ferries: ferries which we would use to travel to the surface of Earth. The magrider locked to the third.

The cabin door of the magrider opened and we floated weightless into the ship's operational deck.

"This is as far as I go," said Karter.

I forced a smile. "We'll see you in two hundred years' time."

"I'm not doubting that for a moment, Felip," he replied. He hugged each of us in turn. Nothing more was said. He re-entered the magrider and the door closed.

We watched his craft on the external monitors as it returned to the dock wall. Then followed a quick, and quite unnecessary, check of the operational equipment. The ship's soliton transmitter was fine, the space-to-ground radio was fine, the two ferry attachments were fine, the internal and external sensing and control systems were fine. Mother's monitors showed she was alive and well and functioning optimally. It was mildly comforting.

"Well, it looks like everything is in order," said Ruth. "Shall we head out?"

It wasn't a rhetorical question. Even now, any of us could withdraw if we wanted to.

"Come on," I said. "Let's get it over with."

Vallensel, it was, who gave the commands. "Tell them we're ready to go, pilot, please."

[N.B. *His name not being in use on Earth, Vallensel has asked me to point out it is pronounced with the stress on the middle syllable.*]

There followed a machine-language blip as the pilot

signalled to the dock, and then several more blips as various messages passed back and forth. The great door at the pole of the dock began to open.

Once our passage into space was unbarred, the pilot fired the ship's chem-ion thrusters. Very, very slowly we began to move towards the exit, creeping forwards at a few metres per second into genuinely outer space. The manoeuvre took twelve minutes.

As the foot of the panflector cone, where the external sensors were located, passed out of the interior of the dock and into sunlight, the external monitors were momentarily transformed into sheets of blinding white. Then the sensors adjusted to the new light level and we could see again, albeit in a dazzled way.

The pilot took a few minutes to get its bearings, then turned the ship to point in the desired direction and increased the power output of the chem-ion thrusters. It took twenty minutes for us to reach Koltetra's escape velocity, and a further fifty to reach the escape velocity of Koltetra's sun. Then the thrusters shut down and the pilot activated the vacuum impeller. We found ourselves almost weightless as the ship began to accelerate at an almost imperceptible sixty-seven millimetres per second per second — producing a linear gravitational field of less than one per cent of that experienced on the surfaces of Koltetra and Earth.

We must have watched our home planet gradually receding for about two hours altogether. By then it was over two hundred thousand kilometres away.

There were times during preparation for the flight when I had yearned to leave my home. I had thought Koltetra boring. Lacking uncertainty. Koltetrian society was like someone heading from *A* to *Z* down a well-trodden road. There would be no unexpected obstacles that could block our relentless progress. True excitement,

I thought, came from trying to reach a doubtful goal, rather than merely striding boldly towards a certain one.

But as my beloved world hung apparently motionless on the monitors, my thoughts were the very opposite of those earlier ones. So much was happening there. Everything was changing, maturing, blossoming. And I thought of how much had already been done. When the colony had been founded six thousand years ago, Koltetra had had only primitive xenobacteria in its oceans and no life on land at all. Its atmosphere had possessed only a trace of xenobacterially produced oxygen, otherwise being almost pure nitrogen. Half the planet at the poles had been ice-bound. But look at it now! Atmosphere engineering had been the key. We had built up carbon dioxide levels by chemical processing of carbonate minerals, and thereby warmed the planet; and we had dumped colossal quantities of oxygen into the atmosphere — oxygen which we had extracted from oxygen-rich rocks — supplemented in due course by photosynthesizing organisms regenerated from the archives and introduced into the oceans. It took three thousand years before the first Koltetrians could walk on their home planet without the use of breathing apparatus. But we did it! And now Koltetra has a balanced community of living things, albeit a poor one by Earth's standards, both in the oceans and on the land. Yes, I was proud of what we had done there. There were fishes in our seas; the deserts had been turned into forests and pastures; human settlements were found in many parts of the globe; magrider beamways straddled the continents; we had partial climate control; and four hundred solar flux converters supplied us with energy. All this in a mere six thousand years. Give us another thousand, I thought, and Koltetra would achieve perfection: the ultimate stability of a mature Tenth Civilization. The final goal. Permanence. Perhaps then we'd build a full-scale interstellar liner and become the first New World to found a colony of its own. It would be Earth's first grandchild. I wouldn't miss that for anything.

It was distressing to contemplate being away for so long. The world that had hitherto given my immortal life its purpose was being torn from me. I was aware that that old perfidy of the human mind was taunting me in another of its guises, for here I was, barely at the start of a journey I had enthusiastically chosen to go on, already longing to get back. I promised myself that, whatever we found on Earth, I would return and see the work on Koltetra completed.

"I've had enough of this," said Vallensel, interrupting my train of thoughts. "It's making me sad."

No one argued.

"Shall we go to sleep?" he asked.

Again no one argued.

"Monitors off, pilot, please," he commanded.

The external monitors went dark.

We followed him up a floor. This was the recreation deck, but we were only supposed to use it while in orbit about Earth. Right now, we could stay there, awake, for as long as we wanted, but there really wasn't any point. We'd get awfully bored.

The floor above the recreation deck was 'Mother'. She was probably the only one of her kind in the galaxy: a vacuum-dwelling, biologically closed, human-support system. Being inside her was not an experience I particularly relished. She was entered through a kind of sphincter, a ring of muscle tissue that was normally tightly closed but which relaxed enough when touched to allow us to pull ourselves through it.

One's first impression of being inside Mother was of floating in a tubular corridor a couple of metres in diameter. The walls were translucent and outside them one could discern bright spots like artificial light perceived through thick fog. The result was a dim, milky sort of twilight. One was also struck by the warmth, by the musty smell, and by the faint background noise, not unlike a whisper too indistinct to be understood.

We drifted along the corridor until we came to Mother's central part, and the reason for her existence: the sleeping chamber, or womb. In here the milky light was tinged with violet produced by several luminescences clearly discernible beyond the walls of the chamber. These lights were feed-spots: places where a tiny fraction of the helium annihilator's energy output was released into Mother's bioplasm for her to harness. Through photosynthesis she was able to use the energy to keep herself warm and to constantly repair and renew herself. And being a closed system, that energy also enabled her to convert her waste products — urea, carbon dioxide etc. — back into nutrients. In effect, she had a self-contained nitrogen cycle, a self-contained carbon cycle, and so on. All driven by energy from the feed-spots.

The womb was the warmest part of Mother, being at a little below the temperature of blood, and also the noisiest. The whispering had an almost urgent quality to it. The size of the womb was sufficient for the five of us to be in it together without feeling cramped or having to stoop. In the lining of the womb were five grooves, each big enough for a person to lie in. These were our 'beds' where we were going to sleep away a century.

There was a small pit adjacent to each bed where our clothes were to be stuck. (The pit was sticky necessarily, of course, because we were practically weightless.) Once we were naked, we each selected one of the shallow grooves (also slightly sticky) and lay in it.

This was the moment that really tested your belief in Tenth Civilization technology. Slowly the walls of the chamber contracted, closing in on us. Closer and closer, until I could feel the warm, moist surface touching me. First my legs, then my arms and abdomen.

A teat formed in the roof of the womb, now just a few centimetres above my head. I took it into my mouth. Almost at once, a warm, sweet fluid began to flow out of it. It was the sedative that would render my body chemistry quiescent until Mother decided otherwise. I had twenty seconds left. When that time had passed, I would be asleep and the chamber lining would descend the final few centimetres, coming into intimate contact with every square millimetre of my body, from the top of my head to my toes. For the next century, I would receive oxygen through it, food and drink through it, excrete through it, knowing nothing beyond the occasional dreams Mother would let me have.

I thought of the journey ahead. For fifty years we would continue with our feeble rate of acceleration, building our velocity cumulatively to a third of the speed of light. By then we'd be at the midpoint of our voyage and it would be time to start slowing down. The vacuum impeller would reverse its polarity so that instead of reducing the vacuum density behind the ship, it would increase it. In terms of speed, the journey would then be symmetric; half of it spent accelerating, and half spent decelerating. By the time we reached Earth our speed would once again be effectively zero.

(It's a technically complicated matter but, basically, reducing the vacuum density creates a negative — that is, repulsive — gravitational force, while increasing the vacuum density creates a gravitational force that is attractive. Since changes in vacuum density are invisible, to naïve observers it would appear we were breaking one of Newton's laws: that of conservation of momentum. Actually, though, we were emitting undetectably weak gravitational waves in the backward direction to match our increasing momentum going forwards; or conversely, emitting gravitational waves in the forward direction as we reduced our momentum during decelerating.)

I was becoming drowsy and too relaxed to worry about dying on the journey. I wondered if my companions, Jannet, Roshan, Ruth and Vallensel were asleep yet. It was my last thought. A hundred years passed before I had another.

Part 2

The Mayor's Earth

3

Mother wasn't exactly polite when it came to waking us up. She used a series of mild electric shocks. It was enough to bring forth protests, but Mother did have a point. When you're warm, relaxed and comfortable, waking up, far less getting up, comes very low on your list of desires. The people who gave Mother her genes obviously knew that well.

The sleeping chamber had returned to its original size before we were woken, enabling us to get up and dress. After that, we made our way to the operational deck. Our limbs were stiff and needed a lot of stretching. I hoped it turned out Earth was still inhabitable; I felt the urge to go for a stroll somewhere.

The operational deck lighting came on as we entered the room. Everything seemed okay.

"Any internal faults to report, pilot?" Vallensel asked.

"None at all," it replied.

"Have you informed Koltetra of our safe arrival?"

"Yes. A soliton message is on its way."

"What about external faults? Have we sustained any damage outside?"

"Four optical sensors have been destroyed by micrometeors, and the vacuum impeller has developed a slight leak."

"Do we need to worry?"

"No. I only require ten of the sixty optical sensors to perform my functions, and the vacuum impeller will not fail at this rate of leakage in less than three thousand years."

"What's the date and time?"

"It is nine minutes after seven o'clock in the morning,

Salem Meridian Time, on Quinday 28th, 13162."

"Excellent. Let's have the external monitors."

The blank screens were instantly transformed into a space panorama not unlike the one we had left behind, in that there were two main astronomical bodies in view. One was a sun, its brilliance clearly greatly reduced before being relayed to us. The other was a greyish world which was obviously airless and lifeless. It was not what we were expecting to see.

"Where are we, pilot?" asked Vallensel, slight alarm in his voice.

"We are at our destination," the pilot replied, not very helpfully.

"What is the planet we can see on the monitor?"

"That is Earth's moon."

"The moon!" said Ruth in awe. "So that's what it looks like. What a pity 'Kol' only has tiny moons. I've never seen anything remotely so beautiful as this!"

"Where is the Earth?" Vallensel asked.

"It is in line with the sun," the pilot replied. "If I shield out the sun, you will be able to make it out. Do you wish me to do that?"

"Yes please, briefly."

The sun went dark as if being eclipsed. As our eyes adjusted, we could make out the faintest white crescent slightly to one side of where the sun was.

"Well, that's a relief," said Vallensel.

I noticed Ruth was frowning.

"What's the matter?" I asked her.

"Why are we so close to the moon?"

"I assume we're just passing by."

"I don't think so," she said. "I think we're in orbit about the wrong world."

That was definitely not as it was supposed to be. According to both *Plan One* and *Plan Two*, which the pilot was fully aware of, we were to go into Earth orbit on our arrival.

"Pilot," said Vallensel, "are we in lunar orbit?"

"Yes."

"Why is that?"

"I was directed here."

"By a signal from Earth?"

"Yes."

"Human or hybrimorph?"

"Hybrimorph."

"That's something, anyway," I said. "At least the automatic systems are still operational. Which probably means there are people too. Any disaster which wiped out humankind would almost certainly have wiped out the hybrimorphs as well."

"It's still odd, though," Ruth remarked. "Why direct us into lunar orbit?"

"How many signals have you received from Earth, pilot?" asked Vallensel.

"Just the one. Plus a confirmation."

"How long ago?"

"Four hours."

"And you've told them we're alive and awake?"

"Yes. I sent that information as soon as the sleeping chamber confirmed you were fully reanimated."

"But there's been no reply?"

"No."

We looked at one another, nonplussed.

Jannet expressed what we were all thinking. "They park us in a lunar orbit, a lunar orbit of all things, and then make no attempt to welcome us. Why aren't they saying hello? What's the matter with them?"

"Perhaps they're waiting for us to start the dialogue," I suggested.

"We'll soon see," said Vallensel. "Ask them to open

an audio-visual channel of communication with us, please, pilot."

We heard the blip of a machine-language message as the pilot obeyed. A full five minutes passed with no reply.

"It looks like I was wrong," said Vallensel eventually. "We won't 'soon see' after all."

"I suggest we transfer the ship into Earth orbit without permission," I said. "Assuming they're just impolite rather than dead, if they can't be bothered to send us any further orders, I don't see they've a reason to complain. What else can they expect us to do?"

On this suggestion, however, I was overruled. The other four thought we should wait a while longer; at least for one complete circuit of the moon, which the pilot said would take five and a half hours.

And so we watched the lunar surface as it passed beneath us. Superficially there appeared to be nothing wrong. We were able in the course of the circuit to make out all twenty-six of the lunar cities, including the capital, Chaytambeor, pride of the Palatinate of Luna, beneath its great array of domes. Neither it nor any of the other cities appeared non-functional. The flux receivers that supplied Luna with energy looked in order. But we could see no signs of movement; no obvious activity.

Sun and Earth both dropped below the horizon at about the same time, with the result that we had only stars for company as we crossed the night-time side of the moon, but we were able to detect the cities on the dark side by means of their beacon lights, which were working normally.

Back in daylight, still with no message from Earth, Jannet and Ruth began arguing about whether the moon remained inhabited.

To me it was a pointless dispute, so I interrupted them

and said: "There's only one logical way to settle the issue. We need to use one of our ferries to go down and investigate."

"I agree," said Jannet.

"You'd rather do that than transfer unilaterally into Earth orbit?" Vallensel asked me.

I shook my head. "I don't know. *Plan One* and *Plan Two* don't seem to cover the situation we're in. My main concern is that we don't float here doing nothing."

"We'll go down," said Vallensel. (He could speak authoritatively not because he was in charge — he wasn't — but because democracy ruled on board. His vote made it three out of five in favour.)

We decided, just in case Earth got round to talking to us, that Roshan and Ruth would remain with the ship. It was thus Jannet, Vallensel and I who set off for the surface of the moon in one of our ship's two ferries.

Our first surprise, and very discouraging it was, was that the ferry could pick up no trace of a beamway. Not so much as a beamtrack. The entire descent had to be made using chem-ion thrusters to break our fall and to steer with.

"It fits," said Jannet. "We've seen no sign of any traffic on the surface, nor anything coming from Earth or going to it. There's nobody here."

I found myself experiencing a strange sense of unreality. If there had been any evidence of a cataclysm I could have understood the absence of people. But there was nothing wrong. Where was everybody?

We decided to head for Chaytambeor, on the grounds that if humans remained anywhere on the moon they would be there. As we approached, the ferry pilot struck up a machine-language dialogue with the city's flight controller.

"I am in receipt of a standard flight-control

communication," the ferry pilot informed us. "I will allow it to guide me down."

We drew steadily nearer our goal until the dome array, looking like a collection of giant mushrooms whose curving tops had fused together to completely seal in what lay beneath, loomed over us. A vacuum door opened in the city's outer wall and we entered. Still, except for the absence of people, everything seemed normal.

The ferry came to rest in the centre of Chaytambeor's enclosed ground-station, looking solitary on that vast pad. A tractor set off from the edge of the pad, connected itself up and conveyed the ferry through one of the airlocks. The air pressure outside the ferry was rapidly increased to normal.

"This is all automatic," said Vallensel. "There's no one here. It looks, Felip, like your speechmaking talent isn't going to be needed."

The three of us disembarked and stood on the hangar floor, stretching our limbs and looking about. The air smelt clean and pure, the lighting was working normally, and the temperature was what you'd expect it to be. There was no sound. Silence hung over the place like death. A shiver ran down my spine.

Another hybrimorph appeared, heading towards us. This one was a city coach. As it drew up to us it announced: "Welcome to Chaytambeor. Please be seated. I will convey you to off-world reception."

We obeyed in the fading hope it wouldn't take us to just more hybrimorphs. But it did. Reception was empty except for a couple of chefs and a collection of guides.

A number of illuminated signs directed us to this place and that: ring-road, accommodation centre, bodily waste depository, and so on. Exactly what one would expect. All utterly normal.

One sign promised more than the others, indicating the route we should take if we wanted to visit the visuary. I pointed it out to my companions. They agreed it was worth a try.

The vehicle we were in refused to take us, however, saying its job was to convey people from the hangar to off-world reception; we should ask a guide. So we got out of the coach. We decided, however, not to avail ourselves of hybrimorph services, preferring to walk instead. We assumed the visuary would be close by, and reckoned the stroll would do us good. And the weak lunar gravity would help to prevent the exercise from becoming too arduous.

We followed the occasional 'this way' arrows in silence. Silence was somehow appropriate. We saw no one.

Presently, Vallensel tapped me on the shoulder. "We've got company," he whispered.

Looking back down the wide, gently curving corridor along which the latest arrow had directed us, I saw a hybrimorph, human in size but with wheels instead of legs, and with a trailer attachment at the rear on which were several seats: one of the Chaytambeor guides. We stopped and regarded it. It too stopped.

Vallensel commented: "It's probably following us in case we get tired or lost. Let's see what it does."

What it did, after a pause, was to approach us.

"Can I be of assistance?" it asked in the usual sexless voice one associates with hybrimorphs.

"We're going to the visuary," Vallensel said. "It's not so far that we need to ride, is it?"

"Two kilometres," the hybrimorph replied.

We exchanged glances of mock horror.

"Then take us there," Vallensel commanded, and the three of us got into the trailer.

The guide was not designed in an aesthetically pleasing way, at least not in my judgement. It had two faces, one looking forwards in the direction of travel, the other face looking back at the passengers with a fixed, whimsical expression on it. That backward-looking face for some reason made me feel I was being scrutinized. I didn't like it.

The guide picked up speed and settled down to a steady twenty kilometres an hour.

"At least something remains of civilization," said Vallensel. "It's an awfully long time since I walked as far as two kilometres in one go. I'm glad you're not expected to here."

"I once walked over five kilometres," said Jannet with a wistful look on her face.

"Whatever for?" I asked.

"I felt like it. Out in the Wild Country, it was, some way to the north of Jathra. You can walk for days without seeing a living thing."

"What was it like?"

"The Wild Country? Haven't you been there?"

"Not the Wild Country. Walking five kilometres."

"Absolute agony. My whole body ached for a week afterwards. Never again."

"I suppose they wouldn't have minded quite as much here," commented Vallensel. "Not with the gravity being so much less."

I noted his use of the past tense in referring to the moon's inhabitants, but made no comment on it.

The guide took a sharp right turn through a tall archway into a very large room. The ceiling was at least a hundred metres high at its highest point and dome shaped. Around the walls and spaced at intervals throughout the room were standard visuary booths. We alighted from the guide and went into the nearest one.

Nothing happened. No sexless voice asked us what we wanted to know.

"Perhaps it's switched off," I suggested.

"Let's ask the guide," said Jannet.

We returned to the guide, waiting dutifully where it had stopped, and asked it how to turn the visuaries on.

"You can't," the guide replied. "They have been decommissioned."

"What? All of them?" I exclaimed.

"Yes."

"Why?"

"I don't know."

Jannet tutted and said: "That's one piece of civilization that lingers on. The brainless hybrimorph that'll do what you tell it even though it's a waste of time."

"I am not brainless," said the guide. "I have a cerebral cortex of five hundred square centimetres."

"Do you now?" said Jannet. "Then why didn't you tell us this place is closed down?"

"You didn't ask me."

"Civilization lives!" exclaimed Jannet.

"Where can you take us," Vallensel asked the guide, "that's still actively functioning?"

"I can take you back to off-world reception or, if you have authorization, to any of the maintenance facilities."

"What about the intercity beamway stations?"

"They are not actively functioning."

"Can you take us to any people?"

"No."

Considering the information we could have obtained from the visuary had it been working, it was most frustrating having to switch our questioning to the guide, but it was all we had. It and its five hundred square centimetre brain!

"What happened to all the people?"

"I don't know."

"How long has Chaytambeor been decommissioned?"

"I don't know."

"Are the other lunar cities uninhabited too?"

"I believe so."

"How far back in time does your memory go?"

"My indelible memory contains data from the day I was commissioned. My delible memory covers the last twenty-eight days."

"So you can only tell us no one has lived here for at least four weeks?"

"That is correct."

"What about traffic from Earth?" I asked. "Is this place ever visited?"

"You are here," the guide replied politely, clearly uninformed about where we had come from.

"We're not from Earth," I corrected it.

"Apart from you, I am not aware of any other visitors in the last few weeks."

"Are there any hybrimorphs in this city whose knowledge extends further into the past than yours?"

"There is the Plinth of Names."

"Of course!" exclaimed Vallensel. "I should have thought of that. Take us to the cemetery."

We re-boarded the guide and it set off for its new destination.

"Simple," Vallensel explained. "Chaytambeor is still functional, right? People could live here if they chose. It hasn't been overwhelmed by some disaster such as was speculated about on Koltetra. So the question is: where have the people gone? I can think of only two possibilities. Either they all died, or they evacuated to somewhere else. The Plinth of Names will tell us which."

As Vallensel spoke, the guide carried us out of the

visuary building — or more accurately, the network of buildings — we had been in, and we found ourselves crossing one of Chaytambeor's open spaces. Above us, over a kilometre up, was the roof of the city. The city's 'official' time was obviously close to sunrise or sunset, for the roof was a deep blue colour, simulating a twilight sky, while the 'sun' was out of sight behind some buildings. Apart from the spaceport to our rear, which was ablaze with its interior lighting, almost everywhere else was in darkness. The guide turned on its headlamp.

We soon left the open space and entered what appeared to be a residential dormitory. There was a central street running down the whole of its length, flanked on either side by dwellings, some made of duram, others alive like Mother. None showed any signs of recent habitation.

After a quarter of an hour or so, we emerged into another, much larger open space. Lighting levels had become noticeably higher during our time in the dormitory. So: sunrise rather than sunset.

"Where are we now?" asked Jannet.

Unlike our earlier enquiries, this question was exactly the sort guides are designed to deal with.

"We are in Yupee Park," the guide began. "This park covers nine point six per cent of the city, a total of over two hundred square kilometres. To our left is Neil Armstrong Hill, the only piece of natural lunar terrain remaining inside the city. To the right is Yupee River."

Behind us, the false 'sun' rose partly above the buildings which had been obscuring it. The effect was very realistic. One could even feel the heat from it on one's skin.

Presently we passed between two pillars joined at the top to make an arch, and found ourselves in an area of lawns and flowerbeds and a number of bushes. Over in the distance, a hybrimorph was engaged in watering. The guide came to a halt and announced: "This is the cemetery. All humans are authorized to enter this maintenance area. But I am not. I can take you no further."

We alighted and walked for a short distance along a path surrounded by almost overwhelming (for a Koltetrian) floral displays. After a hundred metres or so, at the end of the path, stood the Plinth of Names.

"At least this hasn't been decommissioned," said Vallensel quietly.

"They wouldn't," I commented. "The hybrimorphs have no power to; and the humans would have had no wish to. Not a shrine. It wouldn't be civilized."

There was a pause. We were intruders in this place.

Vallensel took the lead. He stepped up to the Plinth and touched the surface lightly. The faint glow from inside grew brighter. A female voice — not the usual sexless one — spoke. "Can I help you?" it said.

"When did the last person die here?" Vallensel asked.

"Tersaday 38th, 12712."

"Four hundred and fifty years ago," I heard Jannet whisper.

"Did many people die that year?"

"No. Just two."

"May we have the number of people who died each decade before that, starting with 12710 and working back?"

I recalled that the population of the moon as last reported over the Galactic Information Grid had been forty million, of which one tenth had lived in Chaytambeor. Given a typical balance between mortal and immortal members of the populace, one would expect around one hundred and fifty thousand deaths per decade in the city. The figures quoted by the Plinth of

Names for the decades before 12712 were far lower than that. We had to go back over one hundred years before the number of deaths approached the expected size.

Vallensel stepped away from the Plinth. The internal light returned to its former dimness. Looking at Jannet and me, he said: "It was an evacuation. It has to have been. The number of people declined year by year until there were none left. The only alternative is that the mortals all stopped breeding and the immortals all committed suicide. I don't find that credible."

I found myself agreeing with Vallensel. Barring fatal accidents — which plainly couldn't explain what had happened in Chaytambeor — the only way an immortal dies is through suicide. I simply couldn't believe every immortal in the city would choose to take their final decision in the space of a single century. Any more than I could believe that the mortals would unanimously stop having children.

"Evacuation," said Jannet, "if it took place, was presumably to Earth."

"Quite," I agreed, recalling my original rejected proposal. "I suggest we return to the ship, and if there have been no further communications we'll just have to risk upsetting the flight controllers by going into Earth orbit without their permission."

We got back on board the guide, waiting patiently for us at the cemetery entrance. By then it was full daylight and everything stood out very clearly. I was aware of a faint breeze blowing. That was one of the greatest advantages of living in an enclosed city like Chaytambeor: total weather control. Doubtless an air circulation system was operating every bit as efficiently as the water system that kept Yupee River flowing through Yupee Park.

The guide was instructed to convey us to the ground-station, and it did so, taking us through the park and the dormitory and along the street of unlit buildings.

I tried to imagine how these places had been hundreds of years ago, thronging with people. Some individuals would have been going about business. Others would have been enjoying themselves. Hybrimorphs would have milled around, doing the jobs humans either couldn't do or else didn't feel like doing. It would have been a city of bustle, of noise, of human speech, of vitality — a city whose present state would have been unthinkable to its inhabitants.

But the empty, dead reality perceived by my senses refused to let the illusion take hold. I had never seen Chaytambeor when it was the capital of Luna. At no time had it ever been more for me than what it now was: a place kept going by hybrimorphs for no other reason than that no one had decommissioned them. It made me wonder if perhaps the last humans in Chaytambeor had left their city running because they expected it to be inhabited again one day? Or was it simply that they had been unable to bring themselves to carry out that final act of decommissioning? Whatever the answer, the city was no place to tarry in. Suppose Earth was like this? I, at least, would be desperate to return to Koltetra if it was. Loneliness is not for me.

In due course we found ourselves standing once more in off-world reception. The guide waited, silent, stationary, in case we wanted to be shown somewhere else, watching us with its aggravating, whimsical expression that in happier times might have passed for friendliness, but now seemed mocking and out of place.

"Let's get out of here," Jannet said. "This place is giving me the jitters."

As we left the reception area, I looked round at the guide. It was parking itself once more in the slot it had occupied ever since it had been commissioned. It would wait there with infinite patience until its turn came again to show someone else around. Perhaps it would wait forever. I realize hybrimorphs don't experience emotions in the way humans do, and that it is therefore stupid to identify with them, but I couldn't stop myself feeling sorry for that guide. In principle Chaytambeor would remain operational, repairing its faults indefinitely as they develop, until five billion years hence when the sun becomes a red giant star. And that lonely guide would wait all that time for the visitors who never came. It was so futile, and futility always makes me sad.

Leaving the city was the reverse of our arrival, and we were soon space-born. The descent to the surface, our time spent there, and the ascent back into orbit had taken a total of five hours, so we found our ship was some distance away. The ferry pilot took us up to an altitude somewhat greater than the ship's, where we could wait for the ship to catch us up. Above us, the sun blazed impossibly brightly, making the blue and white crescent Earth almost too insignificant to see. Below us lay the grey moon, its fine city of Chaytambeor dominating the lunar landscape.

"What a waste," said Jannet. "A feat of technological engineering like that just.... abandoned. What a waste!"

It expressed how we all felt. Chaytambeor, the ultimate contradiction: a perfect city and no inhabitants.

Three quarters of an hour later we saw our ship coming up behind us. When the time was right, our pilot dropped us down into the ship's orbit and we rendezvoused without any fuss.

As soon as the ferry had sealed itself to the airlock and we had the hatch open, it was apparent something had happened. Roshan and Ruth were looking pleased. It transpired that during our exploration of Chaytambeor a message had been received. Our vessel was to transfer to Earth orbit at our convenience. We would be given further directions when transference was underway.

It was good that the triumph of patience over rudeness had been rewarded. Our decision to obey orders and remain in lunar orbit had obviously provided Earth with enough time to sort itself out. They could be forgiven, I suppose. We were the first incoming interstellar ship Earth had ever had to deal with.

But the real significance of the message lay not in its contents, but in its source. Yes, it had been a hybrimorph sending instructions in machine-language. But those instructions came under the authority of the Mayor of Jerusalem, no less. Which meant human beings still lived on Earth. It looked like it was going to be *Plan Two* after all.

4

We needed no encouragement to get the ship underway. The pilot switched on the chem-ion thrusters and began the transfer to Earth orbit.

We had just passed the gravitational zero point between Earth and moon when the next lot of instructions came through. They were no machine-language blip this time. The image of a man appeared in the receiver. He was sitting behind a desk, facing directly towards us. He looked entirely normal; the setting looked entirely normal.

"Hello there," he said. "I'm glad to see the five of you made it."

The first thing I notice about anyone is their age. If they look older than late twenties, they're not immortal. It is, I'm told, common for that to be the first personal characteristic to be checked. Psychologists explain it as a seeking for group identity. This man was either immortal — one of 'us' — or genuinely young. Aside from that, he was unremarkable.

Transmission between ground and ship was using a standard ribbon-signal, so identification formalities weren't necessary in either direction. I — spokesman as usual — simply replied: "We're as glad to see you." I diplomatically refrained from asking why it had taken so long.

He smiled. "Think yourselves lucky. Usually they have a 'morph doing this job. But once in a while they let good old human me loose in here. Space traffic control is my hobby, you see. It's a nice way to pass the time."

A remark like that made me ninety-nine per cent sure he was an immortal.

"Right now," he said, looking at something out of our sight, "your approach is faultless. It's been decided to bring you into way-station six, which means you'll need to re-align about three degrees northwards. I'll just send you the instructions."

We heard a machine-language blip, followed by our ship's pilot's acknowledging blip of reply.

"That's great," said the space traffic controller. "We've arranged for the station to put out a dissipating beamtrack for you. You should be able to lock onto it about a thousand kilometres short of target. Is that okay?"

"Certainly," I confirmed.

"Once you've docked, you'll have to wait a while, but I expect you won't mind. When you've been travelling for a hundred years, what's a few more hours? Anyhow, we'll be sending up a ferry to collect you."

"There's no need," I said. "We have our own. We'll come down in that."

"I'm afraid you can't," said the controller. "You may be carrying diseases, as may the air in your ferry. I've been told there'll be a need for decontamination."

Roshan giggled nervously. I didn't have to look at the others to detect their annoyance. It is not civilized to greet visitors with an insult.

"We have no communicable diseases on Koltetra," I remarked calmly, thinking but not saying aloud that he must know that.

The man smiled again. "I don't suppose you do. It's some sort of regulation, I think. Probably been in force for millennia. One of those rules nobody got round to changing." He looked at us intently. "Just imagine you're wrong, though. With the health of an entire world at stake, we'd be foolish to take any chances."

On the floor of the Koltetrian debating chamber, I would have argued. Firstly, we weren't carrying any diseases. Secondly, even if we were, it would be a minor inconvenience for the people of Earth to eradicate whatever we might introduce to them; hardly a threat to their safety. And thirdly, to suggest that Koltetra was so barbaric it might send unclean representatives to another world was undiplomatic, to say the least. All these arguments passed through my mind, as did the decision not to pursue them. This was not, after all, the Koltetrian Congress in session. Acquiescence struck me as the best option in the circumstances.

"We shall use your ferry, then," I agreed. "I assume it will arrive shortly after we dock."

"Em.... no, actually. It's likely to be about thirty-six hours before it collects you."

"Thirty-six hours!" exclaimed Vallensel.

I motioned for him to leave it to me, and remarked: "That's quite a long time."

"I'm sorry," said the controller, looking embarrassed and probably starting to wish he'd chosen a different day to pursue his hobby. "That's how long I'm told it'll take to rig up a decontamination unit on board. Nobody bothered to prepare for your arrival."

The poor man realized, even as he spoke, that he had insulted us yet again, for I saw him wince slightly. Nobody bothered, indeed! "That's all I've got to say for now," he finished, in a lame kind of way.

"Good day to you then," I said neutrally.

His image faded from the receiver.

"Gibbering automaton!" was Jannet's verdict.

Simultaneously Vallensel said: "Decontamination! I can tell you I've been verbally abused more than once in my life but no one's ever accused me of being contaminated before."

"Don't let them upset you," I advised the pair of them. "It will distort your judgement."

It was a remark intended to calm everyone down, and it had the desired effect. The fact was, we were all angry. If the ship had had the ability to secrete Trangas, it would have come in useful at that moment. Unfortunately it didn't, so we had to stay level-headed the old-fashioned way, without assistance.

"This is madness," Vallensel remarked more coolly. "We cross fifteen light-years, at vast expense to Koltetra, out of concern for the wellbeing of Earth. And what do we find when we arrive? No overwhelming catastrophe. Not even a little catastrophe. But seemingly total disinterest in us and our mission."

"It's probably because there aren't any precedents for this sort of thing," I said, looking for excuses. "They've never had a visit from one of the New Worlds before."

"Why should not having a precedent be a problem? They obviously knew we were coming. That means they've had eighty-five years to prepare. And as for diseases, there's not been a single communicable disease on 'Kol' for — what is it now?"

"Four thousand two hundred years," said Roshan.

"Exactly. They are deliberately insulting us."

"I certainly get the feeling we're not completely welcome," I said. "But look. We came here to find out why Earth left the Information Grid, and we haven't even begun finding an answer to that question. All we know is that it wasn't any kind of disaster. So I suggest our best course is to keep calm, keep polite, and wait patiently until they're ready to talk to us. Ultimately we're in their hands. In the meantime, let's show them that Koltetrians haven't forgotten the basics of civilized behaviour even if Earth has."

My suggestion was agreed to without dispute and we settled down to make the best of our unexpected situation.

46

*

Transference to Earth orbit took about four hours. On arrival, our ship locked onto the dissipating beamtrack put out by way-station six and rode it to one of the poles of the satellite. The polar door opened and the ship's pilot manoeuvred us in.

Seen from the outside, the station was a lot bigger than the one we had left Koltetra from. I guessed its mass as several billion tonnes. That was not in itself surprising, since one tended to assume that whatever Koltetra had, Earth was sure to have the same thing scaled up, either in size or number. No, the surprising thing was what we saw inside the way-station. Or rather, what we didn't see. As the ship moved slowly through the polar aperture, we noticed the interior was unlit. We confidently expected the lights to switch on at any moment, but they didn't. When the polar door closed behind us, we found ourselves in total darkness.

"Oh, this is too much!" said Vallensel. "They expect us to sit in this thing for a whole day without light? And where are the operating personnel?"

"I believe this station's derelict," said Roshan.

"That's what I was thinking," I concurred.

By now it was late evening. There was nothing more that could usefully be done for the moment, and we were getting tired. We passed the night sleeping on the recreational deck.

Next morning, partly out of boredom and partly out of irritation with Earth, we decided to take a look around the station, using one of the ship's ferries to transport us. Ruth wondered if somebody ought to stay behind in case Earth sent any more messages, but no one was inclined to volunteer. We weren't expecting to hear anything further, the pilot could deal with routine signals, and we'd come to the view that if Earth wanted to talk to us, they could wait.

We got into the ferry and detached it from the ship. Using the chem-ion thrusters sparingly, we set off for the station's equator ('equator' being defined by the polar door we had entered through, there being little else to distinguish one part of the interior from any other). For light we used the ferry's headlamp.

When we arrived at the inner wall of the station we changed our direction so as to perform a complete circumnavigation. The station appeared to be in perfect condition. Nothing broken, no dust, no decay. We could see through windows into the space between the station's inner and outer walls, and deduced from the way the beam of our headlamp cut into the blackness that where people had once lived and worked there was now no air to support them.

"This place has been completely decommissioned," said Jannet quietly. "It's even worse than Chaytambeor. No humans. Not even hybrimorphs. There's something badly wrong here."

Ruth, however, was not of that mind. "I don't see why," she said. "I presume this station's been abandoned because it's no longer needed. That's all. Nothing sinister."

At that moment, before an argument could develop, we came to an open airlock leading directly into the formerly inhabited part of the station. It was big enough for the ferry to pass through, and Vallensel was in favour of going into the station — that is, going between the inner and outer walls — by means of it. He was in a four-to-one minority on the issue, though, because it was impossible to tell from our restricted vantage point just how decommissioned the station really was. Might the airlock door close behind us, thus trapping the ferry?

Outvoted on that idea, he suggested as an alternative that we could leave the ferry outside and explore 'on foot' (so to speak). The ferry carried five vacuum suits, so the option was viable. Roshan, Ruth and I were against the idea, which effectively made it Jannet's decision, for Vallensel agreed it would be unwise for him to go alone. Jannet decided to accompany him.

They were gone for nearly an hour. It was a subdued two explorers who re-entered the ferry. Their reaction to what they had encountered confirmed to the rest of us that we had been wise not to go with them. In truth, they had learnt nothing. It had just been a dispiriting way to pass the time.

"No air, no life. Workshops, living quarters, tonnes of machinery in perfect condition. It's an operational way-station. But it's dead." So reported Jannet.

We took our ferry back to the ship and awaited the pleasure of Earth. We listened for news, but made no attempt at communication. We were not disposed to contact our hosts. The feeling of all of us was that it was up to Earth to make the next move, though if they kept us waiting much beyond thirty-six hours we'd give them our opinions of their conduct. The trouble was, there was actually nothing we could do. The only real protest open to us was to go home, and we weren't ready to contemplate doing that yet.

We got our next contact precisely on time — after exactly thirty-six hours! Just as we were waking up after our second night on the recreational deck, the way-station's polar door opened and in came a passenger coach. It obviously had the key to turning on the lights, for the interior of the way-station was suddenly filled with brilliant illumination.

"I've been thinking," said Vallensel as the coach was

connecting itself to the spare attachment at the base of the ship. "Perhaps a couple of us ought to remain on board."

"What for?" asked Jannet.

"Just a feeling I've got. I don't trust these people. They're behaving in an unfriendly fashion. It would be sensible to take precautions until we know why."

"Are you suggesting they'd harm us?" asked Ruth. "That they'd perpetrate an act of barbarism?"

"Maybe."

To me, the suggestion was preposterous. I said: "This is Earth. This is the Tenth Civilization. It's absurd to suggest they might engage in hostilities. If they want to get rid of us, all they've got to do is tell us to go away."

"Look," Vallensel persisted, "all I'm saying is...."

"All you're saying is ridiculous," interrupted Ruth. "As Felip has just pointed out, this is the Tenth Civilization. It's perfect. It is absolutely impossible for a perfect society to revert to barbarism."

"If it really was perfect."

"What do you mean by 'was'? A mature Tenth Civilization is immortal, just like the five of us are as individuals."

"How do you reconcile that with Chaytambeor?"

"Chaytambeor was evacuated. An evacuation is not an act of barbarism. They doubtless had a good reason to abandon the city. And you said yourself it was left in faultless condition. Barbarians would have wrecked it."

"I still think we should be cautious," said Vallensel, holding to his argument. "Something's wrong here, and to assume there's nothing malevolent about it is risky."

"But that's the whole point," Ruth retorted. "As I've been implying, *nothing's wrong*. If you come across an uninhabited house, you don't conclude the owner has turned into a brute. He's merely gone to live somewhere else."

"If nothing's wrong, Ruth, why have we come here?"

I could see Ruth and Vallensel were becoming angry so I, diplomatic as ever, interposed myself between them. "It's a pity the two of you were never Congressional representatives. You've made me realize how difficult the job of a Koltetrian Adjudicator is. I can't decide which of you has the strongest argument. You've both made valid points. So, suppose I go along with Vallensel. The question then is: who's going to stay behind? Can we have a couple of volunteers?"

Silence. Vallensel was clearly not about to put his own name forward! Nor was anyone else prepared to give up the chance to visit the Old World.

"Well, that settles that," I said.

There was nothing unusual about the coach Earth had sent up for us, which was surprising bearing in mind the fuss that had been made about decontaminating us. Possibly they had thought better of it. Whatever the case, the coach lacked any equipment for that purpose. Instead, it consisted of a large living room with comfortable seats to travel in, and with big artificial windows to provide panoramic views. We were disappointed to find the coach contained no human passengers; only the usual hybrimorph pilot, who was pleasant enough in a hybrimorph sort of way.

The coach separated from our ship without delay and moved slowly to the polar door. As we crossed the threshold into space proper, the way-station's lighting switched off, leaving our ship to await our return in darkness. Then the door closed.

It struck me, as our beautiful interstellar craft disappeared from view, how much Earth's disinterest in it had to say about the relationship between Earth and Koltetra. On Koltetra, that ship had been an outstanding achievement, a wonder of technology. On Earth it rated nothing better than to be shut up in a disused old way-station with not so much as a second glance. And why should I expect anything different? Earth had dispatched vessels a hundred thousand times bigger to found the New Worlds. Koltetra was still a baby compared to Old Earth. I had a feeling that fact was going to be brought home to us forcibly over the coming days.

The coach commenced its descent to the ground using chem-ion thrusters. In the days when way-station six was in commission it would have been possible to follow a beamway, the satellite being geo-stationary and therefore easily connectable to a terrestrial terminus. But those days had gone.

At the start of our descent, the Atlantic Ocean was below us. It was early morning down there, and almost half the globe was in darkness, but we could make out two of the palatinates: Europa in the far north, and Africa in the near north and centrally. Cloud patterns over Europa were too oblique to make sense of, but over northern Africa there was a perfectly formed cyclone bringing rain to the surface a few hundred kilometres inland from the Atlantic. It was heartening to know that the climate control system was functioning normally. It bore out Ruth's assertion that nothing was wrong, and made Vallensel's worries about possible danger seem needlessly alarmist. Normality was what we wanted to see, and normality was what we saw. Our trust in the Tenth Civilization began to recover from the doubts that had been growing since we awoke from our century of sleep.

We passed over night-time Latica, then back into daylight over the islands of southern East Asia lying to the north of Oz. The first we saw was Sulawesi, then Borneo, then Sumatra. After that we made contact with the Ultima Salem to Melbourne beamway. The coach switched onto it, slowing to sub-sonic speed and proceeding as a conventional magrider towards the terminus at Ultima Salem.

We clipped the southern tip of the 'V'-shaped part of Bharat and shortly after, following another ocean crossing, watched West Asia's rich land of forests and meadows pass beneath us as our altitude gradually decreased.

At last, Ultima Salem came into sight.

"They got the destination right, at least," said Vallensel, once it was clear we were indeed going to land in Earth's capital city. "I was expecting them to dump us on a desert island."

"Or in the ocean, maybe," said Ruth with a hint of mock malice.

We watched the gigantic city unfold before us, becoming ever more detailed as we neared the ground. It is at least ten times larger than the chief city on Koltetra. Seeing it at first hand, it was easy to understand why it is acknowledged throughout the planets of the Tenth Civilization to be the finest and greatest city ever built by humankind. The architecture is of immense beauty, but what really impressed was the knowledge that well over ten thousand square kilometres of terrain had been reformed to give Ultima Salem the contours it now possesses. Rivers had been diverted, mountains had been levelled, an enormous lake had been created. The local geography had been completely transformed. The warriors of the three ancient religions which had fought for thousands of years for possession of this land would not recognize it now.

The beamway terminus came into sight.

"Not long to go," said Vallensel. "Let's see how rude they are face to face."

The coach dropped the few hundreds of metres

remaining and settled onto the ground. The pilot then drove it over to one of the reception buildings. The door of the coach opened. We got up stiffly from our seats and walked out.

Thus it was, at just before 15.00 hours Salem Meridian Time on Findelasemana 28th, 13162, that Earth's first New World visitors set foot on the founding planet of the Tenth Civilization.

<h1 style="text-align:center">5</h1>

We emerged from the coach directly into the reception building, the door of the one tightly abutting the door of the other. The room we found ourselves in was comparatively small and, contrary to our expectations of a welcoming ceremony and a large audience, occupied by only one human and two sentinels. The latter two hybrimorphs were an even bigger surprise than the lack of formality. Evidently, Vallensel's distrust of the people of Earth was reciprocated. I personally considered it yet another insult that they should have suspected our party of being hostile. None of us would ever have hurt the lady the sentinels were presumably there to protect.

She was short, youngish, though probably a little too aged to be an immortal, with long hair curling down over her shoulders, and a very beautiful face. Perhaps too beautiful, for her appearance struck me as somehow nondescript and not greatly interesting. Her smile was unmistakably friendly, which offset to a degree the effect of the sentinels at her side.

"Welcome to Earth," she said. "We are honoured that you have paid us a visit."

It was spokesman time again. I chose my words carefully, not wishing to begin with complaints, but neither wishing to let our treatment of the past two days go completely unremarked. I said: "Your words are reassuring. We had been uncertain of our welcome. I trust we can look forward to a pleasant stay."

Her smile never even flickered. "Of course you can. I must apologize for our slow response to your arrival. The truth is that until you had actually got here your visit was accorded a low priority. Nothing was put in hand until we knew for sure that you had survived the journey. There didn't seem much point."

"That falls a little below our expectations. We had hoped the first New World colonists ever to return to Earth might be received with more enthusiasm."

"Oh dear," she said. "Is a Culture Secretary enthusiastic enough for you?"

"Culture Secretary?"

"I am the Mayor of Jerusalem's Culture Secretary. My name is Annalivia."

The woman had a certain bland charm about her which made it very difficult to say anything which could conceivably offend.

"I am sure the Mayor has sent along his most able — and enthusiastic — representative. It's a pleasure to meet you, Annalivia." I stepped forwards. "I'm Felip Varrandoe." She followed my lead, and we touched. "And these are my fellow travellers." I introduced Jannet, Roshan, Ruth and Vallensel. Each in turn greeted her in the customary way.

"About the decontamination...." I began.

"Forget it," she said. "The Mayor has issued a special exemption for you."

"A pity he didn't do it beforehand," muttered Vallensel slightly too loudly to be ignored.

Annalivia showed no sign of being perturbed. "To be honest, the decontamination law of 6306 was a useful excuse while we sorted out your reception. I do hope you weren't insulted."

"Only by the fact you didn't simply tell us the truth in the first place," said Vallensel.

"I'm very sorry, Vallensel," Annalivia apologized. "Would you believe that yesterday I was attending a Palatinate conference in Delhi? So partly the delay in receiving you was due to me being in the wrong place."

"Think no more of it," I said quickly before Vallensel could come up with another rejoinder. "What's the plan now?"

"Now? Well, as you can imagine, the Mayor has a very busy schedule and won't be able to see you until the day after tomorrow. In the meantime I've been asked to extend all hospitality. For the rest of this afternoon I thought you might like to see some of Ultima Salem."

"That sounds like a good idea," I agreed.

"There's a standard tour you can go on. I'll be happy to act as your guide." She gestured to a door helpfully labelled EXIT. "Follow me then. We're too late in the day to see all the main sights, but I'll show you the most famous ones that lie between here and where you'll be spending the night."

She led us through the exit and out into the open. The two sentinels followed at a distance. A guide somewhat differently designed to the one that had conveyed us around Chaytambeor drew up, and we got aboard. Our hostess instructed it to take us to the Lake of Life.

We pulled away from the terminus. The sentinels, left behind, watched our departure passively.

Thus we found ourselves seeing perhaps the greatest of Ultima Salem's wonders: an entirely engineered lake. Annalivia acquainted us with the facts as we crossed from one side to the other. A body of water three hundred kilometres long and thirty wide, it's kept filled by a syphon connecting to the Narrow Sea. (It is of course the biggest syphon ever built!) And not 'just' a syphon. The Lake of Life is pristine fresh water, whereas the Narrow Sea is salty. Consequently the water has to be desalinated as it passes through the syphon, and Earth has for that task the largest desalination plant in the inhabited galaxy, one which consumes about seventy per cent of the energy coming into the Eilat flux receiver. Furthermore, the lake exists in a geologically salt-rich terrain — it does, in fact, replace a much smaller, toxically saline 'Dead Sea' — so, to keep it fresh, the lake floor was sealed using a silicon-gold polymalloy. I found the whole thing staggering. Koltetra has nothing remotely capable of competing with such a marvel. I allowed myself to be breath-taken while the guide carried us at a sight-seeing, slow speed over the sun-sparkled surface.

We were travelling towards the west, and after crossing the lake found ourselves ascending a line of hills running north-south.

And then, directly ahead of us was the Yarway Pyramid. Despite the sun being in almost the same line of sight, the east facing side was a wonderful blue colour, due to its reflecting the cloudless sky. As Koltetrians we had only a passing idea of the reason for the pyramid being there. Annalivia told us it represents the purity of the Tenth Civilization. Three of its four triangular sides have engraved in them a six-pointed star, a vertical cross, and a crescent moon, these symbolizing the impure past. The fourth side is unsullied by symbols: the pure present. The Yarway Pyramid is two kilometres high and covered by a panflector, which accounted for the brilliance of its reflections of the sky.

Once again I was staggered by the technological achievement.

We were of course aware of Earth's marvels, but Annalivia was able to add the details and the history that we didn't know about. For example, concerning the pyramid she said: "You may be wondering where the Jerusalem is that the Mayor is supposed to be mayor of. It's under the pyramid, buried along with all the madmen who died fighting over it."

As we left that colossal monument to the Tenth Civilization behind us, Annalivia asked if we wanted to see anything else before going for a meal and settling down for the night. We consulted amongst ourselves and decided we were in need of sustenance.

"Right," said Annalivia, her eternal smile broadening for a moment on her faultless face. "We'll leave Parliament and Mem and the other things till tomorrow. The guest apartments at Ashdod next."

The guide set off, continuing to follow a broadly westerly course in pursuit of the setting sun, now only partially visible above the skyline.

Overhead, a star appeared in the blue sky. It grew steadily brighter until it shone with all the illuminating power of a second sun.

"We only want eight hours of near darkness in Ultima Salem," explained the ever-smiling face. "That means there's a need for a few hours of artificial lighting. That second 'sun' up there is actually an array of spotlights attached to the geo-stationary way-station four complex. It meets our requirements excellently."

We sped on, passing by many houses, some made of duram but mostly alive, and all of them set in an idyllic garden of orchards and lawns and flowerbeds. Then, near our destination, we came to Ghedera Park with its stunning display of a thousand fountains, including one which throws a column of phosphorescing water two hundred metres into the air. It is, we were told, best seen after dark. I could well believe it.

Just past the fountains, while still in the park, we topped a rise and saw in front of us, dwarfing the Lake of Life, a large expanse of blue water, turning to comparative blackness beyond the range of the orbiting spotlight 'sun'. This was the Mednean Sea, yet another of Earth's marvels: specifically, the largest expanse of water with a controlled sea level on any inhabited planet. Annalivia explained that there are two dams, at Gibraltar and Suez, restricting the inflow of ocean water so as to keep the sea level constant.

Ashdod, in effect just an outlying part of Ultima Salem, turned out to be a collection of buildings lining the waterfront. The guest apartments, where it was intended we should reside during our time on Earth, occupy pride of place, looking across a hundred metre wide strip of sand to where the Mednean waves lapped gently up the beach. It was a very tranquil setting.

We chose a duram apartment block as our base in preference to the living structures simply because duram was what we were used to. (The widespread liking for organic dwellings shown by the people of Earth is not echoed on Koltetra. The majority of Koltetrians live in duram houses.)

Having settled in, we ate a meal, during the course of which we told Culture Secretary Annalivia about Koltetra. Quite early in the conversation, I remarked that a lot of what we were recounting she could have learnt from the Galactic Information Grid.

"I know," she said. "But it's better hearing it from you. I like the small personal details. You don't get them from the Grid."

"So you're still listening to Grid transmissions?"

"Of course."

"Do you know *why* we've come here?"

"Yes."

"Can you tell us what we want to know?"

"I think it would be best if you discuss directly with the Mayor why Earth no longer transmits into the Grid. It would be unacceptably presumptuous of me to answer for him."

"Okay," I said, and let the matter drop. The Mayor's explanation, when we got it, would be good enough for me.

After the meal, Annalivia and the others took themselves off to the story salon to be entertained. The idea didn't appeal to me. I wanted to think. So I excused myself and went for a stroll down to the water's edge. As I had hoped, the beach was deserted. The only human being I could see was a few hundred metres away, exercising a couple of dogs from a landau.

Despite the artificial sunlight, there was a feeling of evening in the air. Mist had formed over the sea. The slight breeze was cool. I realized the orbiting spotlights provided no heat.

I walked a short distance along the sand, disturbing a number of small, whitish birds which took off at my approach and wheeled away across the water, issuing shrill alarm cries. A magrider flew overhead, on its way, no doubt, to the beamway terminus.

My mind was filled with a confusion of thoughts that needed sorting out. To begin with, there was the inferiority I was feeling. Koltetra couldn't match any of the engineering feats we had been shown this day. We had the knowledge and the technology, but we simply didn't have enough energy. Compared to Earth, Koltetra was still a primitive place. Frontier country. We had four hundred solar flux converters to Earth's six thousand, but I doubted if any of them could deliver more than ten per cent of the energy that each of Earth's did. It was hardly surprising I felt inferior. Koltetra was inferior, and that was the end of it.

And yet, in a baffling way, I was almost proud of that inferiority. Why? I admired Earth; I was jealous of Earth. I didn't want Koltetra to be inferior. How could I feel pride that it was? Given the choice, I thought to myself, between living on Earth and living on Koltetra, which would I opt for? I had no hesitation in answering Koltetra. It wasn't merely that Koltetra was my home. It was more than that. But try as I might, I couldn't discern what that 'more' was. All that happened was that my thoughts kept returning to what I had seen. Massively engineered landscapes, panflector pyramids, controlled sea levels, artificial suns. Such things struck me as too self-indulgent. Yet, ultimately, is not self-indulgence what civilization is all about? It was a conundrum, and I was not enough of a philosopher to solve it.

What about the reason for my being on Earth? The scenes we had encountered in Chaytambeor and on way-station six seemed to belong to a different galaxy. What had they to do with the affluence, the warm permanence, of Ultima Salem? How could such stark contradictions exist so close together? Here and now, Ruth seemed correct to assert that there was nothing wrong. Out in space, it was Vallensel's contrary assertion that held sway. Which of the two did I really agree with? One of them had to be wrong. I reckoned the afternoon we had spent in Ultima Salem was a powerful antidote to Vallensel's view. And yet.... And yet....

The daylight suddenly dimmed for a second, before returning to full strength. Naturally I looked up, but there was nothing unusual to see.

A woman's voice called to me above the bubbling sound of the ripples. It was Annalivia.

We walked towards each other.

"I thought I'd better warn you," she said as she came up to me. "When the light flickers like that, it indicates nightfall in three minutes."

"Thanks," I said. A reflective mood was on me and I was in no rush to go indoors.

She stood beside me, smiling as ever. "Have you enjoyed your first day on the Old World?" she asked.

"Very much. It's been fascinating. You know, you can look up Ultima Salem's famous sights in a visuary, but it lacks something when you're not actually there."

"Yes. I think it's that, in a visuary one can see the scene, feel the wind, hear the cries of birds, and so on, but one never interacts with them except passively. You can't change anything. You can't participate."

As she spoke, the smile slipped from her face and I became aware of a vivacity in her eyes that had not been there before. I looked at her curiously. The smile fell instantly back into place.

"You've enjoyed yourself," she said unvivaciously. "That's the main thing." The light began to dim. "Time to sleep. Tomorrow I'll show you Ultima Salem's main visuary. I guarantee it's faster and more comprehensive than anything you have on Koltetra."

"I don't doubt it."

The artificial sun switched to its nocturnal lighting illumination level, shining with about twice the brilliance of the full moon, which latter was to be observed in the south-east. Away from those two bright lights, the stars could be clearly seen. I paused to look.

"You won't find Koltetra's sun up there," Annalivia said gently. "Not at this time of the year."

"A pity," I said, and shivered. I let her lead me back to the waterfront buildings.

And so I spent my first night on Earth, sleeping peacefully in the guest apartments at Ashdod on the shore of the Mednean Sea.

6

Next morning we went on a tour of more of the sights in the company of Culture Secretary Annalivia, using our assigned hybrimorph guide for transport. We were taken first to the Dam at Suez, travelling slowly so that we could enjoy the scenery on our route.

There can be few more impressive sights on Earth than that dam. From our viewpoint on the Mednean side, it had the appearance of a wall many kilometres long and a hundred and fifty metres high, running between two distant pieces of rising ground, one off to the east, the other to the west. Issuing through a row of sluice gates some way up its side was a sheet of water which flowed down fifty metres into the river. The roar that it made, and the dazzling whiteness at the foot of the dam, brought back memories of the Falls at Ikterun. The scale of the two waterfalls was vastly different, of course, but what the Dam at Suez lacked in size it made up for by being human-made.

Annalivia introduced us to the dam keeper, a clearly mortal individual nearing the end of his days, who was delighted to give us a guided tour, telling us the facts: Ninth Civilization construction, nearly seven thousand years old, used, along with a matching dam at Gibraltar, to restore the old pre-Warming sea level in the Mednean lands. The rest of the world may still be living with the consequences of the Seventh Civilization's suicidal heating up of the planet, melting the polar ice caps and raising global sea levels by eighty metres, but the Mednean coastline is back where it belongs.

Our next port of call was the main public visuary, located in the centre of Ultima Salem. What made this visuary hugely superior to any of the best visuaries on Koltetra is that this one is tied into the Mem system. Mem knows *everything*. Physics, biology, history, ancient languages, art, psychology. There is nothing in the universe that could be known from the vantage point of Earth that Mem doesn't know. Total knowledge. And hooking Mem into the visuary system means you can see, feel and experience absolutely anything. You can learn as much as Mem knows, subject only to the limitation of having such a tiny brain (compared to Mem).

We were each invited to select a visuary booth and go inside. For my part I began by looking at the First Civilization, that of the Nile, watching it develop from its beginning in the year 1 to its end around the year 1000. I toured irrigated fields, met the pharaoh, watched the river-ships, saw the battles being fought, and so on.

And then it occurred to me, perhaps a trifle vainly, to ask about the voyage I had just made from Koltetra. Mem knew about it, of course, but my enquiry produced nothing more than the bare fact of the journey. That was distinctly odd. No reconstruction, no depictions of sleeping inside Mother, nothing about the travellers.

Feeling uneasy, I decided to be bold and ask about the reason why Earth had left the Galactic Information Grid. It was arguably an undiplomatic thing to do, but Annalivia hadn't placed any restrictions on the topics we could raise with Mem.

However, somebody else had. Mem asked me for a security code. I didn't know one, and was told that in consequence the information would be withheld. To be denied knowledge was a new experience for me. It made me even more uneasy.

Frustrated in that direction, I tried a different tack by asking about Chaytambeor's depopulation.

Mem replied: "The settlement in Chaytambeor was

progressively evacuated at the request of its inhabitants. Net emigration began in the decade 12510 and reached a peak in 12623. Last emigrants left the city in 12712. The city remains commissionable at short notice, but apart from two brief resettlements in 12844 to 12847 and 12901 to 12909 no one has expressed any interest in living there permanently since the evacuation. Chaytambeor is visited by several thousand people every year out of curiosity."

"Why did everybody want to leave?" I asked.

"The populace preferred to live on Earth," was Mem's unhelpful reply.

Plainly, attempting to anticipate our meeting with the Mayor was not proving successful. I asked a few more general questions and then left the booth.

Outside, I was confronted by a displeased Vallensel and an Annalivia lacking her usual smile. Jannet was off to one side, pretending to be somewhere else. Roshan and Ruth were still in their visuary booths.

"Did you ask any questions about the current state of Earth?" Vallensel asked me angrily.

"A few, yes."

"And were they answered?"

"Mostly."

"Mostly! Well, I'll tell you what I was told: I needed a security code."

"Yes, I was told the same at one point."

"I was told it a lot. And I mean a lot. Like when I asked why sentinels accompanied the Culture Secretary when she greeted us, and how long security codes have been required, and what it is that Earth is intentionally hiding from us. And when I ask the lady here, she smiles sweetly and says the Mayor has ordered her not to tell us. So I've just told her a thing or two. The setup here is normal on the surface, that's sure enough, but underneath something's rotten, and they mean to keep it hidden. They needn't think, though, that I've crossed fifteen light-years and left everything I value behind to let them treat me like a contaminated criminal."

"You're behaving like one," Annalivia interjected, with no smile at all and showing more spirit than I had until then credited her with.

Vallensel swung back on her, about to tell her another thing or two.

"Okay, Vallensel," I said firmly before he could do any more damage to relations. "Let me handle this. Would you grant me a quiet word with you in private, Annalivia, please?"

The smile returned. She led me into one of the visuary booths. Before I followed her in, I looked back at Vallensel, still close to erupting. I was not pleased and made sure he received the message.

In the dim light of the booth, I could see Annalivia had regained her normal composure.

"I apologize for my friend," I said. "He's not always as self-controlled as he ought to be."

"I've known worse," she reassured me. "I'm surprised, though, that Koltetra has sent us a malcon."

"Er.... Have we? What's a malcon?"

"You don't know?"

"No. It's not a word we use on Koltetra."

"How surprising. A malcon is someone displaying an overdeveloped aggressive drive. Quite inappropriate for the Tenth Civilization. Most people with that character defect manage to keep it under control and be good citizens despite themselves; but some — the ones we call malcons — don't control themselves. They're regular nuisances. They cause nothing but trouble, and the worst of them go about wrecking things for the sake of it. As you will understand, they're very unpopular."

"I don't think Vallensel is a malcon," I said, paying regard to my role as a diplomat. "He's just rather abrasive sometimes."

"You're being a diplomat, Felip. Abrasive; aggressive. What's the difference? Vallensel strikes me as a malcon in manner even if not in deed."

"I suppose so. But in this instance he does have a point. Superficially we're being treated courteously, and my thanks for that, but we're clearly not being trusted. All this Mem security code nonsense. Since when has it been polite to deny people knowledge? If we were asking how to commit murder, I could understand being refused an answer, but our questions are quite proper. Why won't Mem answer some of them?"

"The Mayor decided it would be better if certain kinds of knowledge possessed by Mem were security classified for the duration of your visit. I don't doubt he'll explain it when you see him tomorrow."

"Okay, let's not argue about it now. I'm sure we can manage to wait one more day."

With that, we got up and left the visuary booth. The other members of the Koltetrian party had emerged by then and were standing about. Vallensel had fortunately cooled down.

"I'm sorry about losing my temper," he said to Annalivia.

"That's all right," she replied with her usual smile. "You couldn't help it."

"No, I suppose not," said Vallensel, disarmed.

We left the visuary and, after a discussion, decided that the final place we'd visit that afternoon would be the Museum of Ancient Art, located in a suburb of Ultima Salem called Bethlehem.

The Museum was entirely indoors, housed inside a gigantic conical hill. The interior was cool and very dry, spotlessly clean and bacteria free. It was the most tranquil place we visited, and also the most crowded. Many people were peacefully contemplating the art.

In order not to disturb the silence, we were each issued with an earpiece through which a commentary could be heard. The tour starts, logically enough, with the First Civilization, and then proceeds through the Egyptian, Mesopotamian, Greco-Roman, Medieval, European, Industrial, Recrudescent and Interstellar Civilizations. It also covers in their correct places in the chronology the art of parallel civilizations in places such as East Asia and Latica. It was fascinating to see how art developed across the civilizations, or occasionally, as in the case of the Seventh Civilization near its end, regressed into stupid ugliness. The whole thing was marvellous. We had nothing like it on Koltetra.

Right at the centre of the museum we came across the music chambers. Again, this was a novelty for us Koltetrians. We had no idea what to expect.

Annalivia led us into one of the chambers and asked if we had ever heard ancient music.

None of us had.

Her smile broadened and I fancied a trace of impishness about it. "I like Wagner," she said, and then to the chamber: "Play us...." She named a piece of music whose title I no longer (mercifully) recall.

Instantly, the chamber displayed an image of a collection of people, men mostly, dressed in a black and white uniform. All were clutching various objects, in the main made of metal and wood as far as I could make out, and of outlandish shapes. The illusion was created that we appeared to be looking down on them from across a large hall.

The black-and-white assembly directed their attention to one of their number, standing in front of them and clutching a short stick. His role, it transpired, was to coordinate the others. He did this by means of a form of sign language which reminded me of someone trying to dance with his legs tied together. To be honest, though, I had little time for the dancer, for the music — I'm being diplomatic here — was 'difficult'. Out of solidarity with the others, I managed to endure it for a good five minutes. But then Roshan lost her nerve and fled the chamber, giving the rest of us the excuse we needed to do the same. Annalivia came out last of all. She was greatly amused.

"Didn't you like it?" she asked innocently.

"That was the musical equivalent of drinking a cup of grit," said Vallensel with his usual tact.

"It is an acquired taste," Annalivia admitted.

"Give me Direct Interaction every time," said Vallensel.

"I didn't know you malcons made music," commented Annalivia.

"We what?" asked Vallensel.

"It's a long story, Vallensel," I said, seeing trouble on the horizon. "I'll tell you about it later." And then to Annalivia: "You see, Vallensel's not so negative. He could certainly outdo Wagner."

"Hmm. Well, just you remember, poor old Mr Wagner didn't have D. I. Back in the Seventh Civilization, the only way he could get music from his brain to other people's was by writing it down like words and then getting a gang together to make the music by vibrating things. Considering the difficulties he faced, I think he did a splendid job. You've got to get acclimatized to it, though."

We readily agreed about that.

We re-boarded our guide and were about to move off when another guide blocked our path. It contained a single occupant, a youngish woman, possibly immortal. She seemed quite excited.

"Are you the party from Koltetra?" she asked us.

I was about to answer, but Annalivia spoke first, confirming we were.

"Oh wonderful, wonderful," said the woman. "What an amazing world Koltetra must be to have sent you all this way. And now I've seen you with my own eyes. Such a privilege!"

This was more the sort of greeting I'd expected back at the beamway terminus when we'd first encountered Annalivia, who now said: "They have yet to talk to the Mayor. I'm sure he will make that point when he greets them officially tomorrow."

That, if I wasn't mistaken, was a diplomatic way of telling the woman that if she wanted to form a queue to speak to us that was fine, but the Mayor had first place and the woman would have to wait her turn.

"I understand," the woman said, instantly restraining herself. "Carry on," she commanded her guide.

The guide began to move out of our way, and at the same moment the woman, who had stood to address us, started to sit down. Somehow she overbalanced, tried to steady herself by partly rising to her feet, and managed thereby to fall out of the guide — no mean feat, considering there was a bar designed to prevent exactly that from happening. The hybrimorph came to an emergency stop.

This time my reaction was faster than Annalivia's. And Vallensel's. He and I both got off our guide, but I reached the woman first.

I heard Annalivia say: "No," but by then I was about to help the woman up.

She allowed me to assist her to get to her feet, grasping my extended hand. Something hard was pressed into my palm. Our eyes met and there was trouble in hers. Trouble or a warning.

"Are you all right?" I asked with genuine concern.

"I don't know. My wrist...."

"Would you like me to summon a medic?" Annalivia asked.

"No thank you. I think it's just bruised."

If the fall hadn't shaken her up, she was very good at maintaining a pretence. I watched her get unsteadily back on her guide.

"I'm sorry to have troubled you," she said to Annalivia. Then, this time sitting firmly in her seat, she ordered her guide to be on its way. Vallensel and I watched her recede into the distance, and then re-boarded our own guide.

"You know what?" said Vallensel. "That fall almost looked deliberate. Poor woman obviously couldn't resist New World charm."

"It looked genuine enough to me," Annalivia responded. "She'd hardly risk breaking her bones just to have one of you help her up. You aren't that charming. Anyway, if she's so desperate to have a word with you, she only has to wait until tomorrow. Once the Mayor's spoken to you and got the protocol out of the way, I expect you'll be comparatively free to talk to other people."

I caught Vallensel's eye, undetected by Annalivia, in time to stop him rising to the unintended provocation. That big word 'comparatively' could wait for the Mayor. Having another row with Annalivia would get nowhere.

I made no attempt to examine the object in my palm. It was a disc about the size of a fingernail, and sticky enough to remain where it was without me holding it in place. As I'm not given to gesticulating, it was easy to keep it hidden.

We returned to the guest apartments at Ashdod, where we had an evening meal. Afterwards, as on the previous day, I strolled down to the water's edge in the light of the artificial sun. Again I was alone except for a person, perhaps the same person, exercising two dogs from a landau a few hundred meters away.

I examined the disc surreptitiously. I don't know why I was so cautious about it, except that it seemed appropriate. The whole melodramatic business made me feel I was being watched. The disc was clearly an audio device of some kind, for there was a speaker membrane imbedded on one side. I pressed the disc into one of my ears and seemingly activated it, for I began to hear a recorded message. It was a man's voice.

"My name is Kway Myer and I wish to talk to you. I trust my unconventional approach has not caused you offence. If you are aware of the extent to which you are being guarded, you will not be surprised. I am, you will gather, nothing to do with the Culture Secretary, or anyone else in the government. If my information about the reason for your journey to Earth is correct, I believe you will find what I have to say interesting. More interesting, anyway, than anything you'll hear from the Mayor. You will not be able to get away until after your audience with him. If you are dissatisfied with what he tells you — and I am almost certain you will be — request to visit Garden Island. Ensure you come alone. I stress 'alone' because it is most important. When you arrive, get a guide to take you to Mount Troodos. I will meet you there. Lastly, do not tell anyone about this message. My survival may depend on your secrecy. Do not come to Garden Island if the secret becomes known. Now squeeze this call-button between your fingers. That will erase it."

I replayed the message twice and then squeezed the

disc as directed, dropping it onto the sand where I could bury it with my foot.

I had the feeling I'd fallen into water too deep to stand up in. I had no desire to go against the authorities of Earth or to offend them. By that reasoning, I should report the message to Annalivia. Yet the truth was apparently being hidden from us by those same authorities. Then again, my highest loyalty was morally not to the Mayor or Kway Myer, but to Koltetra. What would my own people have me do? I had to make up my mind based on almost no knowledge of what was going on; of why there were secrets; of who Kway Myer was. I wasn't used to that kind of decision; it was uncivilized. I longed to be back in Koltetra's Congress, where knowledge is paramount and there are Adjudicators to settle disputes. In the end I decided to wait and see, and to stay silent in the meantime. Keeping secrets could cut both ways.

I didn't go in when the artificial sun dimmed to bright moonlight, but sat on the sand listening to the gentle rhythmic whooshing of the ripples as they ran up the beach. I had learnt a lot that day and needed to think. In a way, I was like a medic examining someone who was superficially healthy but who might have some deep-seated malaise. I had to search for clues and discard those that were irrelevant. I thought of the evacuation of Chaytambeor; the abandonment of way-station six; the self-indulgence; the secrecy; the cool reception we had been given. How did all these things fit together? Or were some of them irrelevant clues to be discarded? And what about Kway Myer? Did Earth's attitude to him — what did he mean, his survival depended on secrecy? — have anything to do with the mystery? If Earth was indeed 'ill' (so to speak) how could I distinguish causes from symptoms? Oh for the simplicities of *Plan One* and *Plan*

Two. Unquestionably I was out of my depth in deep water.

I sat musing and, to be honest, getting nowhere until I was quite chilled. Then I got to my feet, stiff-legged, and walked back to the apartments. It had been a tiring day.

7

I awoke early on Segunday 29th while the sun was still behind the hills of Ghedera Park. A thin, low-lying mist carpeted the ground and stretched out over the sea. The sky was cloudless; the air felt fresh. Courtesy of the climate control system, it was going to be another fine day. Thoroughly appropriate, I thought, for our meeting with the most important man on Earth.

After breakfast we were each given a wash by one of those cleaning organisms that totally enfolds you and leaves you smelling like a garden of flowers. That was the final preliminary before our guide carried us across Ultima Salem to the Mayor's residence, not far from the Yarway Pyramid.

The building, architecturally very Seventh Civilization to look at, is impressively large, and made, not of duram or organic material, but of bricks. Its façade must be nearly two hundred metres across and twenty high. There is a wide, hinged entrance door positioned centrally, above which is engraved a six-pointed star — a motif I recalled from the Yarway Pyramid.

We passed through this entrance and found ourselves in a grandiose hall. I remarked the ceiling far above our heads, the marble floor, the two flights of stairs, and the balconies around the walls. There were also a number of sentinels watching us. Koltetra's Executive Director had no need of sentinels in his abode; why did the Mayor of Jerusalem? Was it another symptom?

Annalivia walked alone through another hinged door over to our left, reappearing a few minutes later to beckon us into the presence.

And so at last we came face to face with the man who

could answer our questions, Earth's head of government. He looked young, which probably meant, considering men under forty years of age are not normally wise enough to assume positions of power, that he was an immortal. His height, inasmuch as I could judge it — he was sitting — was rather greater than average, perhaps on account of some genetic intervention desired by his parents. He sat in a large chair shaped like a hand. The thing was plainly alive and reacted to changes in his posture in a comfort-maintaining way. There were five similar chairs in the room, grouped together and facing towards the Mayor, and these we were invited to occupy. We did so. Annalivia stood to one side of the great man and introduced us.

"Well," he said, turning his eyes from one to another of us, "you've come a vast distance. I hope you think it was worthwhile, considering there is nothing here for you to discover." Fleetingly a frown appeared on his face. "Koltetra informed us repeatedly you were on your way. And...." He paused, staring at the wall behind us. "And here you are."

There was an awkward silence. Before we had set off that morning it had been agreed I would be our spokesman. I was not inclined, however, to respond to the Mayor's unusual opening remarks until it was clearer what line he intended to take, so I cast about for some trivial comment to fulfil the needs of the moment.

"You know," he said suddenly, "I've been Mayor now for...." He looked at Annalivia. "How long is it?"

"Four hundred and twenty-three years, Sire."

"Are any of you immortal?"

I told him we all were.

"You'll understand then," he said in an oddly indifferent sort of way. "Ah, what a burden immortality is. Having a body that continually renews itself is fine enough — nobody wants to become feeble — but when your brain does it too.... I can't even remember my mother's face any more. Or her name. Or where I was born. At least mortals only die once. We immortals die all the time. A memory here, a memory there. New memories come, old memories go. On and on. Isn't that right?"

"Yes, I suppose it is," I answered.

"Suppose? What do you mean, 'suppose'?"

"I mean I've never thought of it quite how you express it."

"How old are you?"

"Five hundred and six."

"How do you manage to remember that?"

"I make an effort to relearn it every so often, like I have to relearn all the other things I don't wish to forget."

"The curse of immortality," he said reflectively, looking at the ground beside his chair.

Immortals have two ways to get out of living forever. One is the unforeseen accident. The other — by far the most common way — is suicide. Some immortals just get sick of living. Possibly every one of us will eventually, but as we're not all dead yet nobody can be sure. The Mayor, I reckoned, was close to ending the uncertainty in his own particular case.

"I suppose you want to ask me some questions," he said without enthusiasm.

That was the cue I had been waiting for. "If you wouldn't mind," I said.

He raised an arm limply like one prepared to acquiesce in an unpleasant duty.

"Mayor, when we left Koltetra we had no idea whether life still existed on Earth. Neither we, nor any of the other New Worlds, had had any response to our messages of concern for five hundred years. We wish to

78

know why Earth left the Galactic Information Grid."

"Five hundred years. As long as that, hmm? That's another thing about being an immortal. You lose track of time. Mem," he shouted, addressing a Mem terminal somewhere in the room, "how long ago did we drop out of the Information Grid?"

"Six hundred and sixteen years, Sire," Mem replied.

"You see. You've lost track of time, just like me."

"I was forgetting the hundred years it took to travel here from Koltetra, Sire," I remarked defensively.

"Oh, don't you worry about all that 'Sire' stuff. That's only what you're supposed to call me. She should have told you that," he said, indicating Annalivia. "But I really can't be bothered with it. Mem does, of course. Mine's a voice Mem recognizes individually. It knows who the boss is. It keeps no secrets from *me*."

He looked me straight in the eye as he spoke. There was provocation in his face. I made no response.

"No," he sighed. "You call me what you like. I don't care. That's what immortality does to you. One day the thought takes hold of you, not as a fancy idea, but as a conviction in the depths of your being, that there's no point. No *point*. Then you stop bothering to remember how old you are and relearning all those precious memories. There's no point. Isn't that so?"

I shook my head. "I've always enjoyed my life and I look forward to a lot of living in the future. I don't worry about the point of it. I just make the most of a precious gift. I don't think I'll ever regret being an immortal."

"You will. One day you will. One day you'll curse your parents for bringing an immortal child into the world. And what about being sterile? How do you like that?"

We were getting further and further away from the purpose of the meeting, but what could I do?

"I think sterility is a fair price to pay for being immortal," I replied.

"Fair!" he exclaimed, suddenly becoming animated. "I'm the Mayor of Jerusalem and I can't have children. What do I care about fairness? Your parents get you made genetically pure when you're no more than a fertilized egg. That's fair enough. Every child has a right to be born free of defects. But do they stop there? Oh no. They have to add the genes that make you immortal. Nobody asks your permission, mind. It's your mother's and father's idea because they don't want you to grow old the way they are. But what do they know of immortality? And when I want children the doctors say to me: 'Sorry, Sire, we regret to inform you that the sperm and eggs of immortal people are sterile'. Is that my fault? Is that fair?"

"There's always cloning," I said in a misguided attempt at sympathy which only succeeded in making him angry.

"I wanted a son, not a belated twin brother," he retorted.

Another awkward silence descended on the meeting. The Mayor stared vacantly at the floor by my feet. My colleagues exchanged glances of the 'what do we do now?' kind.

"Sire, you have not answered my question," I remarked as the silence lengthened from awkward towards embarrassing.

He looked at me blankly for a moment. "What was it?" he said to Annalivia.

"Mr Varrandoe asked why we left the Information Grid," she replied.

"Mem," the Mayor shouted, "why did we drop out of the Information Grid?"

Mem responded: "The immediate cause was a

catastrophic system failure. A fifty-week repair was required and immediately put into operation by the service hybrimorphs. However, before repairs were completed, Parliament voted to suspend temporarily all work on the damaged transmission equipment. That parliamentary vote has never been revoked, Sire."

"Ah, so it wasn't my predecessor's idea. It was that bunch of jabberers down the road. Still, he must have approved. That's the best thing about being Mayor. Parliament can vote about this matter and that, but nothing becomes law unless I agree to it. Not that I argue much with them these days. As I say, there's not a lot of point. I trust that satisfies you, Mr Varrandoe."

"Not completely, Sire. The decision of Parliament to suspend the repair work seems rather unusual. What was their reason?"

He eyed me like I was an irritating dog. "Mem," he shouted, "the Parliamentary vote you just mentioned: what was the reason for it?"

"It was decided Earth had nothing to say that warranted proceeding with the repair, Sire."

"That's your answer, Mr Varrandoe. If you've nothing worth saying, don't bother to say it. So we don't."

"I find that hard to believe, Sire."

"That's your problem, Mr Varrandoe, not mine."

"Surely you would have been justified in at least communicating your continued existence."

"From your point of view, perhaps. Not from ours."

I had no doubt I was being told the truth. Yet it beggared belief that the Old World, a society at the apex of human perfection, an ideal planet venerated throughout the inhabited galaxy, could have such a seemingly low opinion of itself. Unfortunately, short of arguing with the Mayor, I could see no way to pursue the line of enquiry further. I decided to change the subject.

"Can you tell me," I asked, "what my and my colleagues' status is on Earth? Are we welcome to stay?"

"Status? Status? I suppose you're uninvited guests. I have no objection to your remaining on Earth as long as you keep the peace."

"Are we free to go as we please?"

"Where did you have in mind?"

"Nowhere in particular. But I get the feeling that until now we've been under guard."

He stared at me coldly and said nothing. I don't know whether he was trying to reach a decision or just hoping I'd speak again and possibly let him off dealing with my remark. I waited to find out.

"You have been escorted, that is all," he said at last. "If you have no pleasure in being accorded that privilege, it can easily be withdrawn."

"We are all very grateful for the attention paid to us by your Culture Secretary. It has been a most enjoyable two days. But we do not wish to be a burden on anyone's time."

"I am happy that it should be so. What's more, I think it is better that it should be so until you leave."

How, I wondered, could we investigate the mystery of Earth more deeply if we were permanently chaperoned? I could see no option but to try harder. "Your wishes are paramount in this matter, Sire, but I respectfully request you allow us to go exploring unsupervised."

It was a cat-and-mouse game the Mayor and I were playing. He had only one reasonable sanction against us, which was to expel us from Earth back to our ship. We had no sanctions against him at all. The big question was how far I could go before provoking him into using his one sanction against us. If I got it wrong, we'd find ourselves returning to Koltetra with our mission incomplete.

The Mayor neither acceded to my request nor refused to grant it. Instead he broached a related topic. "I will consider what you have asked for. But before I can reach a decision, I need to know your plans. The question you came to Earth to answer has been answered. You can have no further interest in staying beyond personal pleasure. When do you intend to leave?"

"My colleagues and I haven't really discussed that yet. There is much on Earth we'd like to see. Much, as you say, that would give us personal pleasure. Which is why I request permission to roam unaccompanied. We would like to be free to explore your ancient and historic world. I would guess, were we granted that freedom, we should hope to set off for Koltetra again within a dozen weeks."

"I do not expect to have to repeat my instructions, Mr Varrandoe. For the time being, you will continue to be escorted. That is my decision. Your request to be freed from what you evidently regard as a tiresome restraint I will give my attention to in due course. I will agree to no more than that."

"Thank you, Sire. Might I then ask that we each be accorded the choice of going to different places from one another, even though that necessitates you providing more than one escort for the five of us?"

My request was made with the call-button message from Kway Myer in mind — come alone to Garden Island he had said — but I could have done a better job of leading up to it. As it was, the Mayor decided I was being uncooperative.

"No, you might not," he said. "You came together. You're going to leave together. You can stay together while you're here."

I dared not argue further. Any self-preserving mouse knows when the cat's patience is coming to an end.

The Mayor leaned back in his chair and regarded me defiantly.

"As you wish, Sire," I said. "We shall stay together."

"I expect there is much to do on Koltetra. You're probably all very busy building things and full of the stupid idea it's getting you somewhere, are you not?"

"We have about a thousand years of development ahead of us, yes, before we reach maturity as a civilization."

"It surprises me they can do without the five of you. Or that you can bear to be away for so long."

That wasn't even a subtle hint.

"I suppose," he added, looking into the distance, "your ship can't accommodate more than five occupants."

"No, it was designed for five."

"That's a pity. I can think of several residents of Earth we'd be better off without. I'm sure they'd be a lot less troublesome on Koltetra than they are here. Oh well."

Suddenly he nodded to his Culture Secretary.

"The Mayor is very busy," she said.

We rose from our seats and returned with Annalivia to the guide waiting for us out in the wide hall. For once she wasn't smiling.

"If you find me undesirable as an escort, I can arrange for someone else to take over," she said.

"We could not have asked for a more pleasant, more competent escort than you," I assured her. "I have no doubt we all agree it was our very good fortune to have you looking after us these last few days. As long as we have to have an escort, I hope sincerely it will be you."

There were murmurs of agreement from the others. The smile returned. Somehow her face looked wrong without it.

"That's all right then," she said. "What I suggest we

do for the remainder of this morning is have a look round Parliament since it's only a short distance away. This afternoon we can go back to the apartments at Ashdod and I'll tell you about some of the other things you might be interested to see that are away from Ultima Salem. You can decide your itinerary for yourselves. I really don't want to restrict you, but the Mayor's decisions must be respected. If you act responsibly, he might relent on your keeping together and being escorted, so we needn't plan too far ahead."

And so we went to the Parliament building. Practically everyone knows about it. It is, quite simply, the largest genetically formed organism ever created. It's a rather Mother-like structure, though much more massive and containing as its centrepiece not a womb but a debating chamber somewhat larger than that on Koltetra. However, Koltetra's building is made of duram and so needs continual maintenance by service hybrimorphs (and occasionally still by people). Earth's, in contrast, maintains itself by way of photosynthesis, plus its own water supply pumped from the Lake of Life.

The debating chamber — it was deserted during our visit — had eleven banks of seats of the kind we had sat on during our audience with the Mayor. The seats were arranged in a semi-circle, each bank being occupied by representatives of one of the palatinates. "Running clockwise," Annalivia said, "the representatives of Africa sit over there, then come those of Europa, Rossiya, West Asia, Bharat, East Asia, Oz, Antarctica, Latica, Merica, and Luna. The Mayor and representatives of Ultima Salem sit on that raised platform facing everyone else."

"Luna?" said Vallensel. "Nobody lives there any more. What's it doing with representatives?"

"It used to be inhabited," Annalivia replied.

"How quaint," said Vallensel. "The moon's been

deserted for half a millennium and it's still represented in Parliament."

"No one's got round to changing it," said Annalivia. "It's not important, anyway. Parliament hardly ever meets these days. There's nothing much for them to decide about. Nothing ever happens any more."

"What *is* important to the people of Earth, Annalivia?" I asked.

"Being happy," she replied, smiling. "We're happy here. That's what civilization is all about. On Koltetra you're still working towards the state where there is complete contentment. On Earth we've got there. Happiness is the only important thing. What does it matter if no one lives on the moon any more? What does it matter if the moon continues to be represented in Parliament?"

"What does it matter if Earth leaves the Galactic Information Grid?" I thought aloud.

"Exactly," said Annalivia.

"As far as I can tell, the Mayor isn't happy," commented Jannet.

"He used to be," Annalivia replied. "His trouble is that lately he's lost interest in being Mayor. And maybe in being anything. It happens to immortals. It could be corrected with medical treatment, but with one or two exceptions, compulsory treatment is expressly against the law, and very few immortals in the Mayor's mental state ever ask for treatment voluntarily. I think it's true to say that immortals may be genetically built to live forever, but emotionally they eventually become as mortal as the rest of us."

After having a tour of the Parliament, we returned to Ashdod where we spent the afternoon as planned, talking about what we'd like to see if we went further afield.

We broke off for a while to go bathing with the

assistance of a bather-hybrimorph, a sort of aquatic, floating guide. It was a great novelty — in my opinion one of the best — because Koltetra has nothing like it. Afterwards we dried out in the sun, while the light breeze kept us cool and the antics of the various birds picking their way along the water's edge kept us amused. Overhead, seagulls wheeled and soared and called to one another with their raucous cries. It was beautifully relaxing, to the extent that our discussions of the future were conducted in a very dreamy way. We watched the occasional magriders passing above us, the brilliant sparkling of sunlight on water, the tiny crustaceans that would spring out of the hot sand for no discernible reason. An atmosphere of sublime peace settled on us.

It was easy in that balmy state to see why the people of Earth were so complacent. They wanted for nothing. An over-aggressive malcon might become troublesome or destructive, but if you weren't afflicted by such redundant emotions you had everything you could ask for. They had built paradise here and were basking in its treasures, as was their right.

Although I felt like joining them that afternoon, there was too much on my mind to permit me to do so. Kway Myer had said I wouldn't be satisfied with the answers I got from the Mayor. He was right. The Mayor's explanation was true but incomplete. I still didn't know what lay behind the secrecy, the unfriendliness, the insistence on our being escorted. Perhaps Kway Myer could enlighten me. I mulled over how to meet him, while listening vaguely to the touring plans being discussed by the others. All I could think of was to sneak out before dawn and get the guide to take me to the beamway terminus. From there I might be able to travel alone as instructed to Garden Island. The main difficulty was that I didn't know the location of the place. If I asked

Annalivia, she might enquire where I had heard the name and why I wanted to go there. It would probably be self-defeating. In the end I decided to bide my time, even though it worried me Kway Myer's patience might be limited. I didn't know how long he'd wait on Garden Island before concluding I wasn't interested in talking to him.

The next morning I rose before dawn and carried out a trial run. I found the guide ready and waiting. Leaving it where it was, I made my way into the open. A chill hung in the air. Everything was damp. The moon, off to the south-west, cast its light across the sea. Almost directly overhead, the spotlights of the artificial sun provided a brighter, but still dim nocturnal greyness to everything. There was no one about. Nor was there any sound to hear; not even from the sea, which was completely calm. The silence and the tranquillity were rather lovely. I shivered and returned to my bed.

Stage One of my defying the Mayor and taking unauthorized leave to visit Garden Island was feasible, anyway.

8

It had been unanimously agreed the previous afternoon that one of the things we were most keen to visit was some of the hardware associated with the climate control system. As Koltetra is still very primitive where mastery of the weather is concerned, it would be interesting to see what the finished product looks like. Consequently, after breakfast we left the guest apartments and set off for the beamway terminus to begin what was, to my concern, a three-day trip.

We spent the first day in mid Atlantic, touring one of the plants that control ocean temperature. It was astounding to realize that the amount of energy beamed from the orbiting solar flux converters to Earth's ground-based flux receiving stations is so huge that it would rapidly heat the planet to such a degree that the oceans would boil. Hence the need to control ocean temperature. Ocean refrigeration plants, sea-to-space infra-red beamers, sea-floor conduits, conveyor pumping stations: this was climate engineering at its grandest.

The first night was spent on a group of islands called the Azores. We had a storm pass over as we were preparing to sleep. It was explained that every time rain is wanted in southern Europa, the Azores have to put up with a gale for a few hours as the rain-bearing cyclone is generated.

The second day was, if anything, even more astounding than the first. We learnt about control of the atmosphere. We saw in operation jet-stream decussation channelers, Coriolis vortex triggers, solar radiation deflectors, high-altitude cloud generators, low-altitude cloud generators, and so on.

Our second night was spent at the Climate Global Monitoring Centre located in the Alps of Europa. It was there, on our third and final morning of this trip, that we were given a question-and-answer session with Earth's top climate engineer. Then we flew back to Ultima Salem, arriving at the guest apartments at dusk.

It was decided over the evening meal that we'd go nowhere the following day, taking a rest from globetrotting. That suited me excellently. I had made up my mind to attempt to get to Garden Island, wherever it might be. If no one was planning on going anywhere, I wouldn't mess up their day, I wouldn't be missing anything myself, and with luck they'd get up that much later in the morning, thereby giving me more time before my absence was noticed.

Prior to retiring for the night, I went for my usual stroll down to the sea. It was dark by then, and the man exercising his dogs had gone. I was sitting on the cold sand, listening to the wavelets on the beach, when someone walked up beside me. I turned, expecting it to be Annalivia, but it was Vallensel. He sat next to me without saying anything. His fingers scooped up a handful of sand which he threw casually seawards.

"They're humouring us, you know," he said at last. "Keeping us busy. Lots of things to amuse ourselves with so we won't raise the difficult questions."

"Are they?"

"Yes. And don't insult me by pretending you haven't noticed."

"I thought the Mayor gave an answer to everything I asked."

"Everything you were allowed to ask. But why the secrecy? Why is he unwilling to let us move around unaccompanied? And as for that nonsense about the people of Earth being so happy they can't be bothered to transmit into the Galactic Information Grid, I don't believe that. They *actively* halted repairs to the system. That is not the action of a contented community. It's the action of.... well, a community that's got something wrong with it."

"I broadly concur with your reasoning. What do you think we should do about it?"

"I don't know. Beat it out of them."

"Don't be absurd."

"Haven't you ever felt so frustrated you want to hit somebody?"

"I agree it's frustrating. But hit somebody? When was the last time you spilt someone else's blood?"

"I can't recall ever having done so."

"That doesn't surprise me. I don't think you honestly want to start beating it out of them at all."

Vallensel sighed. "No, you're right. But we can't go on like this. What are we supposed to report back to Koltetra? Everyone on Earth is happy so it's all okay? We'd be ridiculed."

"I agree with you. But there's no desperate hurry. Sometimes you can't blast your way to the solution to a problem. Sometimes you have to creep up on it. This is one of those occasions. We have to plod. We'll get to the answer eventually."

"Perhaps. One other thing: why did you ask the Mayor about us not keeping together? I didn't get the reason for that."

"It was just an idea."

"I see." He was silent for a few moments and then said: "Are you up to something?"

What could I say? To lie was unthinkable, yet I had decided against involving anyone else in my escapade, partly out of deference to the wishes of Kway Myer, and partly out of the belief that the Mayor was less likely to order our immediate expulsion if only one of us was guilty of disobeying him. It meant there was nothing I could say in response to Vallensel's question.

When I didn't answer, he got to his feet, briefly squeezing my shoulder as he did so, as if to steady himself. It was paradoxically like a weight being partially lifted from me. I knew my silence had told him what he wanted to know as well as dozens of words could. And I knew from his gesture that I could count on his support. Vallensel may have been prone to aggressive behaviour, but he was also the shrewdest, the most dynamic, and the most strong-willed member of the expedition. Right then, I was very glad he was with us. I only hoped, after tomorrow, that the feeling would still be mutual.

*

I rose an hour before dawn while the waning half-moon was still well up in the sky. The artificial sun, dimmed to its night-time illumination level, easily outshone its natural companion. There was a warm wind blowing from inland out over the sea. The world felt sleepy and not yet quite refreshed for the coming day.

The guide which had been assigned to us I found parked in its usual place. I instructed it to take me to the beamway terminus. It obeyed without question.

For all my nervousness about getting caught, the plan, such as it was, went smoothly. Nobody saw me leave. Nobody tried to stop me en route. I passed through Ghedera Park — yes, the phosphorescent fountains were glorious in the near darkness — and half an hour later crossed the Lake of Life. As I skimmed the waves, the artificial sun switched off completely. Its night-time's work was done, for in the east the sky had turned from black to a greenish-blue. It was a lovely sight.

Quite soon, I thought, the others would be waking up. My absence would rapidly be noticed. Probably they'd assume I'd gone for a walk down to the sea. How long before they realized I hadn't, and discovered the guide was missing? And how long after that before they concluded I was defying the Mayor by travelling alone? What would Annalivia do? There were Mem input terminals in the guest apartments which would enable her to inform the Mayor (and the rest of the world) of my action. The Mayor would give orders to have me found. But how would the sentinels know where to look? They'd certainly know what I looked like, for I had been seen by a number of them since arriving on Earth. They'd remember my face; it was one of the things they were good at. But where to search was another matter. Were they clever enough to guess correctly? Might there be resident sentinels at the beamway terminus who could detain me when I showed up there?

As so many questions ran through my mind, I began to think myself a fool. I didn't stand a chance. There were too many unknowns. And I became convinced there would indeed be sentinels at the terminus. Of course there would be. They'd see me, and that would be the end of my escapade. There'd be no Garden Island and no second opportunity. But then, if I didn't make the attempt there'd be no Garden Island meeting anyway. I was going to lose whatever I did.

By the time I got to the beamway terminus I was convinced the place would be swarming with sentinels and they'd just about bury me. In reality, it wasn't. As I entered the main building, I could see only two of them. Both were standing motionless, apparently in a quiescent state and totally indifferent to my presence.

Doing my best to look relaxed, I quickly located the information booths and entered one with much relief at getting out of sight. I asked about what I wanted to know, and received in reply a helpful list of magrider flights to Garden Island. Confirmation was duly forthcoming that a place could be reserved for me on the first of them, a freighter with a few spare passenger seats. I made the booking, giving my name when asked. The flight, I noted, was of only thirty minutes duration, meaning Garden Island was quite nearby.

Departure time was still a quarter of an hour away when I left the information booth. I sat on a seat in the waiting area trying to look calm, sneaking a glance every now and then at the two sentinels. They remained inactive.

There were several other people in the same general vicinity as me, presumably waiting for flights of their own. It was regrettable there weren't more of them; I'd have felt less conspicuous. Sensible people, I thought, would still be at home having breakfast. These few were the most that could be expected.

Never in my life have fifteen minutes taken so long to pass. I imagined what Annalivia was doing, what the Mayor was doing, and what the sentinels were bound to do at any moment. But nothing happened.

An incoming freighter arrived, and several fully-laden, hundred-tonne fetchers turned up almost simultaneously and began climbing aboard. This was my flight. I rose from the padded duram seat I had been sitting on against the wall, and started walking towards the craft. As I did so, one of the sentinels came to life and headed in my direction. My body felt as though all the energy was draining from it. A sense of disappointment and helplessness overwhelmed me. I didn't run; there was nowhere to run to.

As it got to me, it raised an arm and clamped its grip round my wrist. "Felip Varrandoe?" it said.

I nodded.

At that moment, there was a loud bang. I, and the sentinel, and the few other people, and the various hybrimorphs dotted about, all turned together towards its source. Smoke was rising from the other sentinel, which had been standing by the main entrance. Its back was ripped open and bits of its innards were dripping stickily onto the floor. It was quite dead. A young woman, seemingly unaffected by the event, was walking towards me. There was something familiar about her. Who...?

"Put your fingers in your ears," she said to me, with a calmness one more normally associates with someone telling you the time of day.

She slapped the remaining sentinel, the one that had a hold of me, hard on its back. It let go of my wrist immediately and made a distressing effort to remove the little limpet-like device the woman had stuck there. I plugged my ears. As I did so there was a second, louder bang. The sentinel's chest bulged outwards and its head jumped up slightly from its body. The air was suddenly filled with the stink of burning. Before I had time to react to the gory details, the woman took me by the hand.

"Come on, Felip," she said with the utmost lack of urgency. "We mustn't miss our flight."

She led me, as in a dream, onto the freighter.

*

I slumped into a seat on the passenger deck. My heart was pounding; my hands shook out of control; I was close to fainting. Looking through the small window by my side, I could see a fair amount of the terminal building. The people were still stunned, immobile as I would have been but for the woman's intervention. The hybrimorphs, in contrast, had resumed their business.

Both, in their different ways, were refusing to take in what had happened. So was I.

The freighter's hybrimorph pilot was no exception as regards behaviour. Receiving no instructions to the contrary, it set off at its appointed time. As the freighter rose out of the terminus, I turned my eyes from the scene on the ground, and regarded the woman who had caused it and was now sitting next to me.

I estimated her age as late twenties. The skin of her face was perfect, a shade lighter than my own. Her eyes were a gold-flecked green, and her collar-length hair was light brown. She didn't strike me as pretty so much as attractive in a serious kind of way. She was looking at me with a neutral expression.

"I'm sorry if I frightened you," she said.

"That's okay," I replied automatically, though it wasn't. My mind was still in turmoil. I had just witnessed an act of anti-social violence like nothing I could recall ever seeing before. The image of those two disembowelled sentinels persisted vividly in my mind.

She continued to look straight at me but said nothing more.

"That was madness," I said eventually.

"I don't agree, but I'm not going to argue. Kway will explain."

Mention of that name caused something to connect up in my head. The woman in the Museum of Ancient Art; the one who had fallen out of her guide; the one who had passed me the call-button with Kway Myer's message on it; that woman and this one were the same person. I forced a smile and said: "How's your wrist?"

"What? Oh that. It's fine now. Just bruised like I said at the time."

"That was quite a trick, falling out of that guide."

The woman grinned. "I practiced that trick, as you call

it, for several hours before doing it in front of you. Good, eh? It fooled your chaperone and that's what mattered."

I smiled a bit more naturally. The way this person was talking didn't match up with my preconceptions about what lunatics were like. But then I'd never actually met anyone afflicted in that way, so I wasn't sure.

"It didn't fool Vallensel, one of my companions," I said.

"Did he say anything to the Culture Secretary?"

"Yes, but she didn't believe him."

"No surprise there."

"How did you know we'd be at the Museum of Ancient Art?"

"I didn't. I'd been following you around all day, awaiting an opportunity."

The pounding in my chest was becoming less vigorous and my hands had regained their usual steadiness. Self-control and confidence were re-establishing themselves. My thoughts turned to the civilized norms of behaviour.

"I'm Felip Varrandoe," I said.

"I know," she replied as we touched hands lightly. "I heard the sentinel when it spoke to you. I'm Kerra Dyanie."

"I'm pleased to meet you, Kerra," I said, adding with a frown: "I think."

Outside, I could see we were heading roughly north. The coastline of the Mednean Sea was approaching our flight path obliquely. As the terminus receded behind us, my curiosity began to assert itself.

"Did you follow me to the terminus this morning?" I asked.

She shook her head. "It wasn't necessary. If you wanted to go to Garden Island, you had to go to the terminus. All I needed to do was stay close by and wait. I had hoped my involvement wouldn't be required. But never mind. I assume they wouldn't let you go off on your own."

"No. I had to make a dash for it."

"You didn't do so badly. The authorities always react very slowly. No planning ahead. You nearly made it." She paused. "I must say, though, you're going to have to put up more of a fight or they'll make a puppet of you. When the sentinel asked if you were Felip Varrandoe, you could at least have denied it. And it's no good going twitchy just because I decommission a couple of 'morphs. These things are sometimes necessary. You'll have to get tougher."

My doubts about the woman's sanity began to re-surface. For one thing, I would never lie except in extreme circumstances. Indeed, I can't remember ever having done so. Nor would any civilized person. Dishonesty is counter-productive and a betrayal of oneself and those misled by it. For another thing, she hadn't 'decommissioned' the sentinels; she'd destroyed them. And it wasn't 'necessary'. All that would have happened is that I'd have been returned to Annalivia at Ashdod and not got to meet Kway Myer. Certainly nothing so bad as to justify unleashing such criminal violence. I had little doubt, given Annalivia's assertion that some malcons were so aggrieved that they wrecked things for the sake of it, that Kerra Dyanie was just such a malcon. Annalivia's dislike of that group of individuals was beginning to make sense. If they were all like my present companion, no wonder they were unpopular.

While I was thinking these things, I stared at the reassuring world outside the freighter. The craft was over the sea now, with the land disappearing beyond the eastern horizon.

I was glad we were the only two humans on board. It

was easier to talk. But even then, a certain fear —
hopefully hidden — kept me from expressing my
opinions too starkly.

"These explosive things," I said with caution, "do you
always carry them around with you?"

"Only when I'm on a mission," she replied. She
reached into her pocket and pulled out half a dozen.
When she tried to put one in my hand, I thought for a
moment she had become homicidal. My whole body
flinched involuntarily.

She looked at me with contempt. "They're quite safe
until they're activated. Are all the people on Koltetra as
easily frightened as you?"

"I was taken by surprise," I said, picking one of the
little limpet things up, holding it in the palm of my hand
and pretending to examine it while my mind got over its
latest shock.

I had no wish to be associated with such evil devices
and surprised myself by daring to say: "I want you to get
rid of these things. Now, please."

"And how would you suggest I do that?"

"Well, at least put them back in your pocket. And
leave them there. I don't want you blowing up sentinels
when we arrive on Garden Island."

"I won't have to," she asserted confidently. "No one
will have alerted the sentinels."

"They won't?"

"Listen. When you take people by surprise, when you
shock them, they don't see what's happened. Their minds
freeze. None of them will realize what part I played in the
affair at the terminus. Nor will they attach any
significance to our boarding this flight. A sentinel would
have, of course, but there weren't any commissioned
ones within seeing distance. We'll be all right."

I wondered how easy she'd be to restrain if we

weren't 'all right'. Could I pinion her arms in such a way as to keep her hands out of her pockets, where she now returned her awful arsenal?

Fortunately it didn't come to that. Her prediction proved correct. There were no sentinels waiting for us. Indeed, the Garden Island terminus had no sentinels on duty at all. We were just two ordinary people taking possession of a guide and sallying forth.

I presumed we were now going to head for Mount Troodos, where Kway Myer would be waiting. I hoped most sincerely that he didn't turn out to be anything like the mad criminal woman I was currently with. Somehow, though, I had a feeling he would indeed be like her.

I found myself seriously regretting my decision to accept the invitation to this meeting on Garden Island. But there was no way I could back out of it now.

I reckoned my immediate future was going to prove.... challenging.

9

The small beamway terminus at which we arrived was located in the centre of the island, on the outskirts of a town, which we went round. We then headed a little south of east towards the rising sun. I noted with alarm but without comment that there was no sign of a mountain ahead of us. Weren't we supposed to be going to Mount Troodos?

It quickly became apparent Garden Island was aptly named. An enormous variety of plants covered the ground in profusion, all carefully tended by an army of hybrimorphs. Indeed, as Kerra Dyanie informed me, there are more hybrimorphs per square kilometre on Garden Island than anywhere else on Earth. All dedicated to horticulture. The perfumes emitted by the countless flowers made travelling round the island into a wonderful olfactory experience.

After a time we came to a ruined Ninth Civilization coastal village. There were no flowers here, but two parallel rows of flat-roofed stone-and-duram buildings divided by a dusty street. Despite the lack of inhabitants, the place was free of debris. Hybrimorphs obviously kept it tidy even if no one had lived there for a very long time. An open-air, miniature Chaytambeor, I thought.

On Kerra Dyanie's orders, the guide halted in the middle of the village and we got off it. Unbidden, it selected a nearby alcove against which to park itself, thus getting out of the way of any passing traffic.

A man emerged from one of the doorways about fifty metres away. I was ordered to wait where I was.

The man and Kerra Dyanie jogged towards each other and embraced. It was more than the greeting of friends. I found myself shocked to realize they were emotionally attached. Somehow it hadn't occurred to me any man would get involved with a woman so clearly unsound in mind. Unless, of course, he had the same illness.

I wanted to get away from these people. To be honest, I was very scared of them. What if I made a run for it? Would they 'decommission' me perhaps?

But it was a different consideration that held me to the spot. It was plain Kerra Dyanie had no part in the perfection of the Tenth Civilization. That she could exist at all on Paradise Earth was a sign of something seriously amiss. I didn't know whether she was a symptom or a cause of Earth's hidden malaise, but it seemed likely she and the malcon fraternity were connected with it somehow. It was my duty to Koltetra to follow this clue up, even — and I trembled at the idea — if it put me in personal danger. I can't help being frightened, I thought grimly, but that doesn't mean I have to run away.

I watched the two of them talking for a few minutes. Their discussion was obviously about me, judging by the way they looked in my direction repeatedly. At last, the man shrugged and they walked over to where I was standing.

"This is my husband, Kway Myer," said Kerra Dyanie.

He and I exchanged no more than a nod of mutual acknowledgement. I was subjected to an unblinking stare which I responded to by looking away. I felt very uncomfortable.

"Wait here," he said to his wife. And then to me: "We'll talk up on the roof. This way."

He acted like a man it would be unwise to argue with. I followed him meekly.

He led me into one of the houses. Large, single-floored affairs they were, with rooms off a central corridor and a flight of stairs on one side leading to the flat roof. I followed him up.

There were no chairs to sit on on the roof, so I copied his example and squatted cross-legged.

"What do you think of this as a place to live?" he asked, looking around him.

"Pleasant scenery. Perhaps a trifle primitive," I answered diplomatically.

He didn't smile. That, I think, was the thing which most unsettled me about him. He had the air of one in a state of permanent displeasure with the world. It spoilt what was otherwise a perfectly normal face. Apart from that, the only noteworthy aspect of him was his size. He was my height and looked late twenties in age — and immortal? — but was considerably bigger than me. Underneath his clothing, I suspected he bore a closer resemblance to some of those Fourth Civilization nude Greek statues in the Museum of Ancient Art than to a modern Tenth Civilization man whose greatest physical exertion is unlikely to be more than a stroll of a few hundred metres.

"Primitive, maybe," he said, "but it suits me. No sentinels, the only hybrimorphs are gardeners passing through, and the few people who come here are on the way to somewhere else and don't stay. Nice and quiet. Exactly how I like it."

I didn't know what to say to that, so I said nothing.

"Quite right," he said. "We didn't come here for a social chitchat. I'm afraid we have a problem, you and I."

"Do we?"

"What do you think of us, Kerra and me?"

"Er...." I said, while groping for some tolerably inoffensive words to use.

He subjected me to another intense stare and waited.

"You won't hurt me if I'm honest with you?" I asked.

"I'm not here to hurt you, you idiot. I'm here to persuade you."

"Okay. I don't know about you, but I think Kerra is.... lacking sanity."

"Why?"

"Sweet reason, she blows hybrimorphs up! That's why. She's got bomb-things in her pocket."

"If you were me, what would you do about her?"

"I'd get her treated so she can be cured."

"Suppose I tell you there's nothing wrong with her."

"How can you say that?"

"Easily, if I agree with her."

"But that'd make you...." I trailed off, because I knew exactly what that would make him. And he was less than a metre away from me, and stronger than me, and we were alone.

"And *that*," he said, "is our problem."

Another silence and another unblinking stare.

"You're obviously impressed with Earth's perfect system of things," he said eventually.

That was a safer topic of conversation. "Very much so," I agreed.

"And that's what you'll report back to Koltetra?"

"Partly."

"So you concede you've not got the whole picture?"

"Yes, I concede that."

"And you came here hoping to learn what was missing from your picture?"

"Yes."

"Okay. I'm going to tell you. All I ask is that you keep an open mind. There is a sub-population on Earth — you will probably have been told we're called malcons — who are not happy with the Tenth Civilization. We disapprove of it, and it disapproves of us. To you that sounds like we 'lack sanity' as you timidly put it. But it

104

doesn't follow automatically that malcons are the ones who are wrong. We have good reasons to be opposed to the Mayor and his perfect system.

"Now, I'm not a philosopher. And I'm not eloquent. But there are malcons who are. They want to talk to you; to give you a reasoned account of how they see the situation on Earth. They are very wise, very intelligent people. If you want to complete the picture you came from Koltetra to build up, you have to talk to them. Will you accept their invitation to meet with them?"

"What would be the point? It cannot be rational to oppose a perfect civilization. It *does* follow automatically that malcons are wrong. In fact it means you must be insane, if you prefer that word to 'lacking sanity'."

"If we're so wrong, listening to us will provide you with a factual basis for that conclusion. Your report to Koltetra will at least be able to tell the New Worlds why we're insane; what form our insanity takes. Wouldn't that be valuable?"

His logic was irrefutable. "Yes, it would," I agreed.

"Good. But unfortunately there are complications. The Mayor will not want you to meet these people. In fact, though it may not be obvious to you, you Koltetrians are being guarded precisely to prevent any such meeting taking place. Now, because you've spoken to me, we're of the opinion that if the authorities find out, they'll evict you straight back to Koltetra. That was why our meeting here today had to be secret. On your return to Ashdod you will need to tell them you had an irresistible desire to see Garden Island. Don't mention Kerra and me. We don't want them to send you home just yet."

"You want me to lie?"

"Felip," he said angrily, "I don't want you to lie. But if you hope to get to a full understanding of what is going on here, you *have* to. Telling the truth to the authorities will have consequences that are undesirable from your point of view. Anyway, you didn't tell anyone about my call-button, did you?"

"No."

"Then don't tell anyone about meeting me. What's the difference?"

Again the logic was irrefutable. "Go on," I said.

"About the invitation. The people who want to meet you can't come to you. Not here in the north. You'll have to go to them. It will be very hard for this to be discreet. At the least you'll have to disappear for a few days. But don't worry about that. Once we have your agreement, those sorts of things can be arranged. So, as I say, it's up to you. You can come along and hear them put their case, or you can walk away. I can only advise you to accept the invitation. I promise no harm will come to you if you do."

"Who are these people you're talking about?"

"The Council. A kind of government."

My reaction to yet another insane statement was not well concealed.

"I'm not going to plead with you, Felip. Don't believe me if you don't want to. All I can say is that I'm not mad, and I'm not making this up. Will you accept the invitation?"

Neither of us spoke for a few seconds. He got to his feet. I did likewise.

"So it's no," he said.

"I'm not sure."

"I suppose there's no need for an immediate answer. I'll tell you what. Think about it. If you decide to meet the Council, call into the Ultima Salem visuary. Someone will keep a watch on the place. If you turn up there, I'll assume you want to go ahead. Then leave it to us to get you and the Council together."

"I'll bear it in mind."

I followed him out of the house. He went into a huddle with his wife for a few moments, and then she summoned the patiently waiting guide. She and I were soon speeding back to the Garden Island terminus.

After a few minutes travelling as we had on the outward journey — mostly in silence — Kerra Dyanie said: "Can we have an agreement, Felip?"

"What sort of agreement?"

"This meeting between you and Kway didn't go how we wanted."

"It didn't go how I wanted either, so we can agree on that."

"You think we're mad, don't you?"

"Yes."

"That's what I want an agreement about. You see, we think you're a weak, timorous, unimaginative fool. Will you agree to suspend your judgement about us if we suspend ours about you?"

"If you can tell me what purpose would be served."

"Easily. Freedom of communication is one of the definitive characteristics of civilization. Correct?"

"Yes."

"We, that is those of us critical of the present order on Earth, want to communicate, but access to the means of communication is denied to us. We cannot join the Galactic Information Grid because the authorities would deny us that right even if this planet was still broadcasting. You offer us the chance, via your ship, to communicate. As a civilized person, you cannot refuse us. After all, if what we say is such anathema, no one will pay us any heed and no harm will be done. We ask for a hearing, that's all. Don't judge us before we've stated our case."

I shook my head. "I don't understand you, Kerra. One

minute you behave like a psychopathic vandal; the next you talk like a normal person."

She looked at me. I don't know the best way to put this, but I was suddenly very aware of her. Of the wind ruffling her hair as the guide drove us amongst the flowers; of the sunlight reflecting off the silver buttons on her suit; of the shape of her; of how close she was to me. For all my effort, I could see no evil in those gold-flecked green eyes.

Perhaps she read my thoughts, because she said: "They were only sentinels, Felip. I would never kill a human being except to preserve my own life."

"It's not just the sentinels. It's carrying those explosive things at all."

"What would you do if you found a friend of yours barring your path? Someone who claimed he was justified in doing so because he was perfect. But equally someone you believed to be profoundly mistaken."

"I'd reason with him."

"And if he refused to listen?"

"Anyone who was perfect would have to listen. You can't be perfect if you deny reason."

"But he has to deny it. To claim perfection is to claim no possibility of being wrong."

"Then I don't know what I'd do."

"I know," she said. "You'd get frustrated. Eventually you'd have to decide whether to give in or to force your friend to get out of the way. Kway and I have chosen force."

"That can't be right, Kerra. Perhaps it's you who are profoundly mistaken. Perhaps your friend is right to block your path."

"You think I don't know that? On my blackest days I'm almost convinced of it. But most of the time I believe in the choice I've made."

I looked away and said nothing. It was self-evident to me that violence in a modern society is never justified. What Kerra Dyanie did or did not believe about herself made no difference to that simple truth.

"The trouble is," she resumed, "you have a set of standards of behaviour that blind you to the reality of what is happening on Earth. At this moment, you deduce Kway and I are a disorder of the Tenth Civilization, when in fact it is the Tenth Civilization that is disordered."

"The two of you are right and the whole of civilization is wrong?"

"That's how it looks to you. But what do you expect? You're a product of the Tenth Civilization. You've never known anything else. You're indoctrinated to believe in its perfection, its ultimateness. Any action which damages it, like what I did at the terminus this morning, is a form of barbarity to you. How could you perceive it to be otherwise?"

"I take your point."

"About the future. We don't want them tying your feet together any more than is unavoidable, so please don't tell anyone about meeting me and Kway. For your own freedom of action if not for our safety."

"Your safety?"

"Yes. If the sentinels ever caught us, they'd have to kill us. Kway would never allow them to detain him alive."

"Stop it, Kerra," I said angrily. "You just about convince me you might be worth listening to, and then you come out with a mad thing like that."

"Forget I said it. It won't happen. We're too careful. Remember you were supposed to go to Mount Troodos when you got to the island?"

"Yes."

"That was a decoy. If you'd given the call-button to

the Culture Secretary, she'd have sent sentinels to a place we were nowhere near. It's all part of anticipating the future. Plan for the worst, allow for it, and it won't take you by surprise. That's how we manage to keep clear of the authorities. They don't plan ahead. Why do you think you were able to get to the Ultima Salem beamway terminus this morning? Because no one had asked themselves in advance what they'd do if you went absent without permission. It's always the same. React after the event is the only strategy the authorities know. As long as that remains the case, Kway and I will not be detained."

"The two of you will be leaving Garden Island straight after me, then?" I said.

She nudged me with her shoulder and grinned. "So you aren't such a fool. You'll have to admit we'd be unwise to rely on your silence. Besides, it's not safe for us in this part of the world."

I forbore to mention it wasn't safe for the world either.

Evidently she'd had enough of serious talk, for she changed the subject abruptly. I was astonished to hear her telling me about the plants we were passing. She knew which ones were natural and which ones were designed by geneticists; which ones had survived the Warming and which ones had been recreated from the archives.

She stopped the guide a few hundred metres from the island's beamway terminus.

"By now," she said, "sentinels will be looking for you over half the planet. It's better I'm not seen with you. I hope we hear from you again. Perhaps a few weeks in the company of your bland secretarial guardian will persuade you to give us a hearing."

"Don't count the days," I advised her.

"I won't," she agreed.

I stood watching her recede into the distance for some

time. I was very confused. I could still see the mutilated sentinels; the casual way she had produced the explosive devices; the contemptuous look in her eyes; could still hear the mad things she and her husband had said. Yet she was also the woman who had asked some very pertinent questions, and who had put her point of view with all the eloquence one would expect from an inhabitant of a mature civilization.

I had come to Garden Island for answers. But I had found only another puzzle. The enigmatic Kerra Dyanie.

10

On entering the terminus building, I made my way to the information booths to discover when the next magrider flight to Ultima Salem was due out. Shortly afterwards, I was aloft over the Mednean Sea, and so returned to the beamway terminus at Ultima Salem that I had departed from two or so hours earlier.

It was as I walked into the waiting area that I was approached by a sentinel. It locked its handcuff onto my wrist and asked if I was Felip Varrandoe. This time there was no one around to blow it up.

The sentinel commandeered a guide and ordered it to take us to the guest apartments at Ashdod. It was still only mid morning when I was reunited with Annalivia and my fellow Koltetrians. I didn't exactly get a hero's welcome from any of them.

"Where have you been?" demanded Annalivia, her usual smile remarkable for its absence.

The sentinel could have answered for me, but I knew it wouldn't unless it thought I was lying.

"I went to Garden Island," I replied.

"Garden Island? Of all the stupid things! Why didn't you just ask? Then we could have all gone."

"I wanted to go alone."

"You know the Mayor forbade that. Have you any idea of the trouble you've caused?"

"I'm sorry."

"I hope 'sorry' is enough. I shall have to report your conduct. Don't be surprised if the Mayor orders all of you to be expelled from Earth. As it is, in the meantime a couple of sentinels will accompany us whenever I take you anywhere in future. They will also be on guard at night to stop any further disobedient escapades."

It was a case of Kerra Dyanie's 'react after the event'.

The smile partially returned to Annalivia's face as she said: "What are we to do with you! This was meant to be a day of rest. I trust you will enjoy what remains of it."

The sentinel let me go on Annalivia's orders and my four colleagues and I ambled down to the sea. Annalivia stayed behind to make her report to the Mayor. Two sentinels positioned themselves prominently, one at each end of our section of the beach. More than once that day, I saw them warn people away from us.

I was severely condemned by my companions. They considered, with justice, that I had made our task that much harder. The main point they made was that we were never going to be able to find out anything if nobody was allowed near enough for us to talk to them.

Vallensel put his own argument, saying: "If we made no progress, I was prepared to get away from that Culture Secretary, illegally or otherwise. But you said yourself we should be patient. By moving so soon, you've made it impossible for us. We shall be supervised to death from now on. Assuming, that is, we aren't put back in Mother and told to go home. What made you do something so reckless?"

All I could say was that it hadn't seemed reckless at the time, plus how remorseful I felt. It wasn't that my comrades were untrustworthy, so much as that the sentinels were not far away and I was unsure how good their hearing was. To tell the others about all that had transpired could well be to announce it to the world.

Anger, once expressed and accepted with contrition, soon dissipates. We whiled away the afternoon in as pleasant a fashion as any other passed on the Old World.

For me though, it was a time of unease, despite my outward relaxation. It was clear to me that my duty as a citizen of the Tenth Civilization was to assist the authorities to detain Kerra Dyanie for her crime at the beamway terminus so that she could be cured of her vandalism. Yet I kept quiet about her and her husband. Why? I reasoned it was simply that I didn't know what was going on. In such circumstances, it is better to wait on events than to act precipitately. It was a matter of not closing off any options; in Kerra Dyanie's words, of keeping my feet as untied together as possible. Assuming, of course, that I hadn't already done irretrievable damage in that respect by venturing alone to Garden Island.

I was very quiet that afternoon. The others interpreted my withdrawn state as an expression of guilt, which suited me, though they were wrong. My silence was born of a distracting conundrum, not self-reproach.

*

The next day we embarked on another jaunt, this time to the island of Sumatra. Departure was, as usual, from the Ultima Salem beamway terminus, and took us to Rajalan, the only town on the island.

Sumatra, as everyone knows, is where Ninth Civilization geneticists recreated the plants and animals of the immediate pre-human period in Earth history, before primitive tribespeople wiped out the megafauna that roamed the planet alongside them. And Rajalan is the human haven inside this zoo of large, and in some cases ferocious, animals. It is indeed a well-protected haven, being surrounded by a high wall.

We went into the terrain next day in a specially designed Sumatran guide, bright blue in colour (to look unappetizing to predators) and armour plated (for any predators who don't get the colour message). During our

114

foray into the prehistoric wilderness, we managed to catch sight of quite a few large creatures, especially including a sabre-toothed tiger, a herd of colossal elephants and a monster like nothing I'd ever seen before. This last creature, I was informed, was a gryposuchus. A reptile almost ten metres long — we have no reptiles on Koltetra — it was the largest crocodile that had lived on Earth in the last five million years.

That day was the last carefree day of our stay on the Old World. We forgot about the Mayor and the problem I had caused. Unfortunately, the Mayor hadn't forgotten about us. After the evening meal on what was supposed to be the first of three full days on Sumatra, Annalivia received a communication from her master. The Mayor of Jerusalem had decided not to overlook my transgression in going to Garden Island unaccompanied. The visiting Koltetrians were no longer welcome on Earth. We were to return to our ship and go home at the earliest opportunity.

It utterly spoilt an exciting day for all of us. Even for Annalivia. And especially for me.

*

It was a subdued party which travelled back to Ultima Salem on the first flight the following morning. And no one was more subdued than me. I was to blame. By one impetuous act from which almost nothing had been learnt, I had ruined everything. I could hear it now. Our report would have to state that due to unauthorized action by Felip Varrandoe we were expelled from Earth before our mission could be completed. We would only be able to report that the people of Earth are alive and happy and living in paradise. In response, someone would ask why Earth had left the Information Grid. To which our reply could only be that Earth's transmitter broke and they decided not to repair it. I knew what Madam Magrit would say to that. She'd tell us we were incompetent imbeciles who'd wasted the fortune that had been spent sending us to Earth.

Incompetence, when I thought about it, was exactly what it was. How could we go home with a story like that? True, we could add that the Mayor was given to pathological secrecy, which was some excuse for our failure, but it left unresolved the question of what he was hiding. I could also contribute my personal knowledge of the destructive malcon subculture personified by Kerra Dyanie and Kway Myer, but I didn't know whether that was relevant, nor, if it was, how it fitted in with everything else. If only I hadn't been in such a hurry. If only I had taken the advice I'd so glibly given to Vallensel. Instead I had thrown away a huge amount of Koltetra's valuable energy for almost nothing. Madam Magrit was too civilized a person to indulge in recrimination, but she'd consider me responsible. And I'd have to agree with her.

Because we'd travelled west across several time zones, when we arrived back in Ultima Salem it was still only the middle of the afternoon. There had been a discussion amongst us during the flight about what could be done about our predicament. Basically it came down to two options: acquiesce in our fate; or apologize to the Mayor and appeal to him to reverse his decision, at least in respect to the 'innocent' four of us, and suggesting that I alone should be exiled to Mother where I could wait till the others had completed our mission. My view on the choice I didn't express. I reckoned my behaviour had disqualified me as a source of advice. Roshan and Ruth were in favour of apology and appeal. Jannet and Vallensel thought that'd be wasting our time. Vallensel particularly was dismissive of the idea, saying we might as well appeal to a tiger not to eat animals.

As we disembarked from the magrider at the Ultima Salem terminus, he even went so far as to remark to Annalivia: "Why don't you put us on a ferry right now and have done with it?"

"You can go straightaway if you want to," she replied, "but the Mayor would like to say goodbye officially."

"Why the sudden politeness?"

"I expect he's worried you'll go spreading calumnies about Earth across the galaxy. He probably intends to ask you not to." Annalivia showed not a trace of embarrassment as she said this.

"The nerve of you people!" said Vallensel angrily. "You treat us like we're the worst thing to happen since the Warming, and then expect us to go away reporting nice things about you. That's not how it's going to be. I shall tell the truth."

"And so you should," retorted Annalivia. "I think, though, you're being unfair. I've done my best to make your stay on Earth a pleasure."

"It's not you I'm annoyed with. It's your boss. If you ask me, he's been looking for an excuse to get rid of us ever since we arrived."

Annalivia finally lost patience with Vallensel. "If I was asking you, which I'm not, it'd only be as a preliminary to advising you to get that aggression of yours treated."

"Right. That's it," said Vallensel, foolishly giving some justification to Annalivia's remark. "I've had enough of this degenerate wreck of a planet. And the Mayor and his secretaries. This charade is making me sick. Let's go now."

"No," I said hesitantly.

They all looked at me.

"I'd like to pay another call on the visuary first," I explained.

"Why?" asked Annalivia.

For the first time I can remember, I invented a lie. It surprised me how quickly and easily I could do it. "It's just that it would be interesting to see some of the sights we won't be able to visit now in person. You know, places we'd planned to go to before the Mayor made his decision."

"You can see them on Koltetra," said Vallensel unhelpfully. "We've got visuaries at home too, remember."

"Yes, but not tied into a Mem system as universal as Earth's."

"I've no objection as long as you stay together," said Annalivia, adding, with her eyes fixed firmly on Vallensel: "And behave."

"Well, I object," protested Vallensel, excelling himself. And then he looked at me and got the message I was desperately trying to send him. "On the other hand, I'm prepared to be magnanimous," he said.

Annalivia looked from him to me and back again. Evidently she'd detected something of the message. She said: "We can call into the visuary on our way to the guest apartments. It's only a little off our route. But I want an assurance from each of you, especially you two," — she nodded at Vallensel and me — "that you'll not act in any way I or the Mayor might disapprove of."

All five of us assured her. In my case, it wasn't the whole truth. But then, I wasn't going to do anything active. Kway Myer had said that if I called into the visuary, he'd assume I wanted to meet his malcon friends, and would make the arrangements to bring that about. He'd be the one taking action, not me.

In retrospect, I can see that that request of mine to

visit the visuary marked the most decisive fork in my road of life. Had I kept my mouth shut, my future would have been totally, completely different from that which I now behold. Yet at the time it seemed such a trivial thing. And I don't really know why I made the request. As I had understood it, the contact at the visuary was intended to be similar to that at the Museum of Ancient Art; merely a means of arranging a meeting. Neither Kway Myer nor I had known then that I'd be on my way back to Koltetra within hours; that there'd be no time left for meetings. The only option open to his so-called 'government' that I could see was for them to turn up and knock on the door of the guest apartments at Ashdod this evening while I was still there and ask to be allowed to speak with me. But there was no possibility that Annalivia and her sentinels would agree to that. It was hopeless. But when there is no hope, you clutch at the least thing. Roshan and Ruth clutched at the idea of an appeal. I clutched at contact with the malcons. I had nothing left to lose. And with that gesture of despair I sealed my fate as surely as if I'd put a gun to my head and vaporized it.

11

We called into the visuary as agreed. I conjured up some of Earth's greatest waterfalls — there, at least, Koltetra beat Earth into a clear second place — visited the Sixth Civilization university where Isaac Newton had resided around the year 4700, and finally toured the abandoned atmosphere engineering plants on Venus, which planet the Ninth Civilization had for a time tried to convert into a second Earth. Not all human endeavours had successful outcomes, not even with the technology now at our disposal.

At any normal time, using the finest visuary in existence would have been a sheer delight. But this was no normal time, what with my guilt about the failure of our mission, and my edgy anticipation of receiving a contact from the malcons. After an hour, I could bear sitting about no longer and left the booth. Outside, the others were waiting for me, and engaged in a trivial conversation about the visuary's architecture. I was also concerned to note that the sentinels in attendance had increased to seven in number.

"The lady thinks you and I are planning something," Vallensel muttered to me.

So Annalivia wasn't incapable of anticipation. Kway Myer had misjudged. Not even Kerra Dyanie with her explosives could get to us through that cordon.

"Nobody has tried to speak to any of you, I suppose?" I asked Vallensel, risking the sentinels overhearing — though I couldn't see it would make any difference if they did.

"No. Were you expecting someone to?"

"Not specifically. It's just that if anyone wanted to

talk to us unofficially, here and now is likely to be their last opportunity. Put it down to wishful thinking on my part."

Vallensel knew me well enough not to be satisfied by that answer. But he also knew when it was unwise to pursue a matter. He nodded and looked away.

Annalivia said to me: "Have you seen all you want?"

I confirmed that I had.

We re-boarded our guide, two sentinels accompanying us. The other five could not be accommodated and were left behind. We drove out of the visuary and onto the open road. The malcons I had clutched at were noticeable only for their absence. Our other last hope was gone too, for Jannet informed me that during the time I had spent in the visuary booth Annalivia had been in contact with the Mayor, who was adamant in his determination that the next time he saw us it would be to wave goodbye.

We headed west towards Ashdod. The Mayor's unreasonableness had angered everyone except me — I was past being angry — such that they expressed their view freely that I could feel absolved from blame for our expulsion.

"He was going to throw us out anyway," said Jannet, speaking for all of them. "You were just a convenient excuse."

I was forgiven. My mood lightened.

Annalivia, conversely, was in a state I had not seen before. There were times when she had been cross, and there were times when she had been happy. Now I suspected there were tears close to the surface. The others thought so too, for they carefully avoided saying anything to her; Vallensel especially. It was a rotten business all round.

By the time we reached Ghedera Park, the sun was setting. The number of people out in the open was markedly less than earlier. Traffic on the road was also light. Most Salemites would be indoors, preparing for the evening meal. The notion must have occurred to Annalivia, for she asked us if we had any special requests for our last dinner on Earth.

Her question eased the atmosphere in the guide quite a lot, mainly because it enabled us to express to her, without saying anything directly, that we in no way held her to be responsible for our plight. We discussed food for a time, she describing various Earth delicacies, and we saying yes we ate that on Koltetra, or no we didn't but it sounded revolting anyway, or no so let's try it. By the time we topped the final rise in the park and were able to look down on Ashdod and the Mednean Sea, we had drawn up a list of three things to put on the menu.

The discussion we were having was quite engrossing, with the result that no attention was being paid to the scenery. We had been along the road several times and were familiar with it. It came as a surprise, therefore, when the guide suddenly told us to brace ourselves, and began to decelerate rapidly.

We looked up from our discussion. Ahead of us we could see, almost incredibly, an aircraft settling down in the roadway a couple of hundred metres beyond our position. The guide came to a halt at the same moment as the aircraft's chem-ion thrusters cut out, dropping it with a considerable jolt the final metre onto the surface.

"Have they crashed?" said Roshan, bemused.

No one answered her. Aside from the fact that crashes are extremely rare — we hadn't had one on Koltetra in nearly a thousand years — the landing appeared deliberate, which crashes aren't.

The two sentinels on board with us simultaneously commanded the guide to reverse.

The door of the aircraft opened and three men jumped

out. The guide began to accelerate backwards as ordered. One of the men raised his arm. There was a brilliant flash, followed instantly by a clap of thunder. The guide jerked upwards, tipping crazily. Momentarily we were jolted senseless.

My wits returned almost at once. I was incredulous. Someone had just discharged a gun in our direction. Either he was a skilful shot or we were lucky to be alive.

Our guide had, not surprisingly, come to a halt. I waited for someone to tell me what to do. The three men were standing like statues by their aircraft, also waiting.

Another guide pulled up alongside ours — one that had been heading for Ashdod behind us. There was a single passenger inside it. Just another person on the road, I thought. But there was no 'just' about what he did next. He leapt from his guide, ran across to ours, and attempted the same trick Kerra Dyanie had at the beamway terminus three days earlier. He reached in and slapped the sentinel nearest him on its back, sticking one of those little explosive devices to it. Unfortunately for him, the other sentinel was close enough to pick it off rapidly and throw it outside. It hit the ground and detonated.

In the instant before — or maybe after, I can't recall — the man shouted: "Get out! Get out!"

His forcefulness, and the shock of the explosion, ensured we obeyed. Annalivia, Vallensel and one sentinel got out on the side the man was standing on. The rest of us, not accidentally, alighted on the opposite side.

The sentinel nearest the man made a grab for him. He fell backwards to avoid it, but sentinels are designed to cope with attempts to escape. It caught the man's upper arm in its clamp.

Everything was happening very fast. And yet in a way it was also like slow motion in which I was merely a spectator. These events were nothing to do with me. I registered the fact that our guide was dead, its front partially vaporized and gouged open, but I reacted like I would to a dream. It couldn't be real.

"Seize him," Annalivia called from the far side of the dead guide. The sentinel standing next to me gripped my wrist. I just looked, stupefied.

The man who had jumped from the aircraft and fired the gun was suddenly running towards us. He was still a hundred metres away when he veered off to the side. He crouched and fired at something behind us. The power setting was much higher. Thunder rolled around for seconds, and I felt the heat from the blast.

Turning to see what he had shot, I saw another guide had come over the brow of the hill, also heading for Ashdod. I glimpsed it for only a fraction of a second, for then thick black smoke from the road ahead of it, hit by the energy bolt from the gun, obscured the view. There was a thud as the poor hybrimorph, unable to stop in time, crunched into the hole in the ground. It was only shallow but I pitied the passengers.

By the time the smoke had cleared — a mere few seconds — the passengers were out of the guide and moving rapidly away from it. They weren't human. The five sentinels I thought had been left at the visuary must have been following us, like the man with the explosive device, now under restraint.

The gunman, once he had identified the five sentinels as such, never gave them a chance. He let rip with an energy bolt that dwarfed his previous efforts into insignificance. The ground over which the sentinels were running was instantly white hot. A blinding curtain seemed to have been drawn across the road at that place. There was a roaring sound like a jet of gas burning under high pressure, quickly drowned by a deafening clap of thunder. A shock wave surged outwards, knocking us all off our feet.

As I rolled over, winded and slightly scorched, I realized the sentinel holding me had released its grip. It got back on its feet well before I could, and would have grabbed me again, but for the gunman. He shot it on the spot. This time he used almost no power at all, which was fortunate as otherwise he would have killed me too. The effect of the gunshot was the same as that produced by the explosive devices. The sentinel became flaccid, its chest cavity open and smouldering.

Towards the brow of the hill, a new cloud of smoke and dust was rising in great gyrating whorls. There was a large crater in the road. No one would be travelling along it again until it had been repaired. Of the five sentinels and their unlucky guide there was nothing left.

The man with the gun ran up to us. "Which one of you is Varrandoe?" he shouted.

I tried to say that I was, but the words wouldn't come.

He seemed to know anyway. "Get to the aircraft," he commanded, sounding very agitated.

I stood quite still. It wasn't that I didn't want to obey him. I couldn't. I was paralysed with shock.

I was aware Vallensel and Annalivia had come round to my side of the vehicle.

Annalivia stepped between me and the gunman. "Go away," she said to him. It was a command, not a plea.

"This isn't a discussion, lady," the gunman replied. For a dreadful moment I thought he intended to shoot her. But instead he grabbed her left shoulder with his left hand and pulled her across in front of him, causing her to fall over. "I'm from Kway Myer," he said to me, not giving Annalivia another glance. "You want to talk, move!"

I still didn't react.

"Felip, who are these people?" said Vallensel urgently.

Somehow, the question didn't register.

"Felip!" he practically screamed, shaking me roughly.

"I.... They're...."

"Just him or can we all come?" said Vallensel to the gunman.

"Not her," replied the gunman, indicating Annalivia. "The rest of you I've no instructions about."

"Right," said Vallensel. He grabbed my arm and shouted: "Come on," to the others.

At that moment, the sole surviving sentinel with its vigorously resisting prisoner came round from the far side of the guide. The shortcoming sentinels have is an inability to change track. The poor thing was utterly beyond its parameters. (I know the feeling.) The gunman shot it like it was a normal thing to do.

With Vallensel's encouragement, I ran to the aircraft and got on board. Vallensel was immediately behind me, followed by the gunman. Then came the two others who had jumped from the aircraft — the reserve team, I would guess — and the man with the explosive device. Lastly, Jannet. We were airborne almost at once.

As we ascended, I looked back at the scene we were leaving behind. The disc of the setting sun, half below the horizon, cast a lurid glare across the landscape. On the road, I could see two guides side by side, our dead one and the one that had followed us from the visuary. Annalivia was on her feet beside them, Roshan and Ruth close by, the two 'decommissioned' sentinels standing motionless. Further away, there was a grotesque gash across the road, where now another guide from Ultima Salem had drawn up.

Strangely, though, it wasn't the appalling vandalism which commanded my attention the most; it was

Annalivia. The last I saw of her, she had raised her hand to impose some order on her dishevelled hair, watching us flying away as she did so. My heart went out to that woman. She was a gentle, peaceful, civilized person, someone I would always remember for her smile and her happy disposition. She would never hurt anyone. How obscene that she should have witnessed such madness. Her world had no place in it for the kind of terrible deeds that had been done this evening. And yet she had stood unprotected in the face of insanity and defied it. I had little cause to admire her for anything else, but I admired her for that.

Farewell, Annalivia....

Part 3

On the Run

12

I noted from the sliver of sun still above the horizon we were travelling in a south-westerly direction. And with that, I fully regained my senses and turned my attention to the present and the new predicament I was in.

Aside from Jannet and Vallensel and me, there were five people in the aircraft. Four I had already seen in action. The fifth had obviously remained inside throughout the operation.

"Hello, Felip," she said. "It looks like we've horrified you again."

Of all the ridiculous times to notice it, I was suddenly aware the woman's nose was not perfectly symmetrical, but leaned very slightly to the left of her face. The odd workings of my brain gave me something, however banal, to be amused by. I managed a slight smile.

"Hello, Kerra," I said.

"You've got some explaining to do, Felip," Vallensel said severely. "Who are these people?"

"I don't know the others, but this is Kerra Dyanie." I then introduced Jannet and Vallensel in turn.

They acknowledged her warily.

Perhaps I wasn't so stunned by this second display of unrestrained force, or maybe having two of my companions with me kept me calmer. Whatever the reason, I was much less disturbed than on the previous occasion or, more accurately, I recovered faster. And disgraceful though it was, I was actually pleased about it. Confound me, I wanted to impress that woman with the serious face, the fair hair, the gold-flecked green eyes, and the not-quite-symmetric nose. Even if she was badly in need of psychotherapy.

"Names are a start," commented Vallensel, "but that's not the kind of 'who are these people?' I meant."

"We're people who aren't content with the state of affairs currently prevailing on this planet. We want to change things," said Kerra.

"Change through destruction," said Jannet. "That's a novel concept."

Kerra disagreed. "Actually it's not novel at all. It was a way of life for the first seven civilizations."

"Yes, and where are they now?" Jannet retorted.

"Where we'd like the Tenth Civilization to be."

That was too much for Jannet to accept in one go. "You're mad," she said, in a tone of voice suggesting disbelief that she could have heard the words Kerra had just spoken.

Recalling my own bad start with Kerra, and the agreement I had made with her before leaving Garden Island, I interjected: "Look, Jannet. You think she's mad. I think she's mad. But she doesn't. And neither do her friends. I suggest we suspend our judgement."

Kerra responded in kind. "Why, Felip," she said with a mischievous grin, "you might even not be an unimaginative fool like I thought."

When she was being sane and intelligent, it was very hard not to be attracted by Madam Dyanie. In an indefinable way, her smile was much deeper than anything Annalivia was capable of.

"Garden Island!" exclaimed Vallensel, who was definitely no fool. "That's what the Garden Island business was about. It was a meeting you went to."

"Yes," I confirmed. "It was our second meeting." I smiled knowingly at him and waited for a response.

He looked at Kerra more closely and quickly made the connection, saying: "I should have guessed. You were the woman in the Museum of Ancient Art. I said at the time you fell out of that guide deliberately. What were you doing? Passing Felip a message?"

Kerra laughed and said to me: "Your friend Vallensel is a smart man."

And then, between us, Kerra and I recounted the story: of her husband Kway Myer's call-button now buried in the sand at Ashdod; of the incident at the Ultima Salem beamway terminus; of my meeting with Kway Myer; and of the arrangement I'd made with him about making contact at the visuary.

Once our shared narrative was concluded, Kerra proceeded to describe her side of things after we parted. "Kway and I went over the water to Anatolia straight-away," she said. "We intended to stay there for a couple of weeks, and then, if there was no word from the visuary, we'd go back home. It would have slowed our reaction time should you have made contact after that, but if you'd left it more than a few weeks we could fairly have assumed you were in no hurry. Then we heard from one of our people in government circles that you were being ordered out. Kway wanted to prevent that by force, but our Council said no, not unless you asked for help. So we planned your rescue and hoped you'd show up at the visuary. Once you did, it was simple. One of us escorted you from behind so that we could pick you out from the air. The rest you witnessed. It went quite smoothly, considering."

"If that was smooth," commented Jannet, "I dread to think what you're like when you get rough."

"So what happens now?" I asked.

"Now," Kerra replied, "comes the difficult part. That Culture Secretary will alert everyone in sight. The Mayor will be roused from his torpor and order you Koltetrians to be recovered, and us malcons to be detained."

"Malcons?" Vallensel interrupted. "That's the second

time I've heard that word. Will someone please tell me what it means."

"A malcon," Kerra elucidated, "is someone who isn't satisfied with what society has become. Someone with enough drive in them to take action to change what they don't like."

"On a developing world such as Koltetra," I added, "it's people like you, Vallensel. On a stable world like Earth, it's Kerra and her friends."

Vallensel actually looked shocked. I could understand his reaction, for it was quite disturbing that while he was closer behaviourally to Annalivia than to Kerra, emotionally he was Kerra's kinsman, not Annalivia's.

"You were explaining what happens next," I said to Kerra.

"I was about to say that from this moment we can all consider ourselves to be hunted. Every sentinel in the world will be searching for us. Or more precisely, for you three Koltetrians. They won't have much idea what we Earth people look like. The Culture Secretary's word-of-mouth description of two of us won't be much use."

"What'll they do if they catch us?" asked Jannet.

"To you? Nothing. You'll just be expelled. To us? Psychotherapy. They'll turn us into a collection of happy, contented nonentities. I tell you, I'm an immortal, so I've a lot of life to lose, but I'd rather die than let them do that to me."

I thought she was being unfair to people like Annalivia but it wasn't a suitable time to discuss it. Anyway, I was more concerned with the immediate future. I didn't like the idea of being hunted. "I wish you two would stop interrupting," I said to Jannet and Vallensel. "I want to know what's going to happen."

"Sorry," said Jannet.

"The plan is this," Kerra resumed. "At the moment,

we're several kilometres out to sea. In a few minutes' time we'll re-cross the coast and that'll bring us to the main road connecting Ultima Salem to Suez. We're going to set down there. Kway should be waiting for us with a guide which we can transfer to. Then we'll make for Suez; and thereafter, Cairo. Once we've got that far, they won't be able to track us because we'll be lost in all the other traffic. A friend in Cairo will shelter us for the night. What we do tomorrow, and in the following days, depends to a great extent on how soon the Mayor loses interest in recovering you."

"What's this about tracking?" asked Vallensel, interrupting again.

"If the authorities aren't already, they'll soon be monitoring our course by satellite," Kerra explained.

I frowned. "I don't think I understand this. You say we'll be hunted, right?"

"Yes."

"Then it strikes me you're placing a lot of trust in the Mayor calling it off. Suppose he doesn't. We can only run and hide for so long."

"You don't know the Mayor. Once he's sure you came with us voluntarily and weren't abducted, he'll soon decide you aren't worth the bother. That's how it always goes with him. You'll see."

"I presume," I went on, still trying to get a proper idea of what the malcons had planned, "that once the fuss has died down, the intention is that your Council will come and talk to us."

"More or less. They'll explain to the three of you what, in their opinion, is wrong with Earth. Once their dialogue with you is finished — by mutual consent, of course — you'll probably want to re-join the two Koltetrians who stayed behind with the Culture Secretary. The Mayor will then send you home. What

you report to the New Worlds will be your affair. That's
how we see it. One thing, though. The Council won't be
coming to talk to you; you'll be going to talk to them."

"I suppose that's okay. Are they far away?"

"Antarctica."

"Oh! Er...."

"What Felip means," said Vallensel impatiently, "is
what has Antarctica got that Cairo hasn't?"

That amused look appeared on Kerra's face again.
"The Mayor's writ doesn't run in Antarctica. We're all
so-called malcons down there." She suddenly became
exasperated. "Can't you get it into your stupid heads the
Tenth Civilization is in decline. It's crumbling. Decaying.
All we malcons are doing is helping that process along.
And in Antarctica it's already finished."

I was utterly horrified. "Do you mean to tell us you've
destroyed civilization completely in Antarctica?"

"Oh, Felip, Felip," she said. "We're doing better than
that."

I knew in that instant what she was going to say next.
Once more I found myself thinking she was a raving
lunatic, for she was going to tell us, not that they'd
destroyed the perfect civilization, but that they'd replaced
it. And she did.

"In Antarctica," she said without affectation, "we're
building the Eleventh."

*

There was no time to argue about her absurd proposition,
for the aircraft was already descending, and we had to be
briefed on what to do.

"We're going to come in fast, and land fast," Kerra
instructed us. "As soon as the thrusters are off, I want the
three of you out of here. Get away from the aircraft as

quickly as you can. At least far enough the thrusters won't burn you when they're turned on again."

"Ready?" said the man who had fired the gun, as the aircraft completed its descent.

Kerra nodded.

The chem-ion thrusters cut out, to be followed by a nasty thump as the aircraft dropped the distance remaining onto the surface. The abuse that poor aircraft suffered!

"Move!" shouted the gunman. He, Kerra, Jannet, Vallensel and I jumped to the ground and ran. The aircraft was underway again in less than fifteen seconds.

"What about the other three?" I asked, as we watched the craft receding into the almost completely dark sky.

"They'll continue on course until they reach the outskirts of Benisef. Two of them live there. The third will make his way back to Ultima Salem in the morning," Kerra answered.

"Do you reckon that little manoeuvre worked?" asked Vallensel mysteriously.

"The chances are about even," Kerra replied.

"Chances of what?" I asked.

Vallensel couldn't resist showing off. "The idea behind getting the aircraft away from here so quickly is that the surveillance satellites might not register the stop at all. With any luck, they'll think we're still on board, on our way to Benisef. Right, Kerra?"

"Of course. Now it's almost dark, surveillance will be by infra-red emissions. Infra-red resolution isn't nearly as accurate as optical. They might just interpret our brief stop as a misreading caused by atmospheric turbulence. It'd be unwise to depend on it, but every ploy helps."

A guide, bathing the ground around it in a pool of light, was approaching us. Kway Myer was on board. We were soon on our way to Suez.

Kway and Kerra kissed and then he asked the gunman if there were any problems. The gunman told him there weren't.

Kway looked at my fellow travellers. "Who are the other two?" he asked.

"Vallensel and Jannet," Kerra informed him. "Koltetrians."

"Good," Kway commented without enthusiasm.

Feeling comparatively secure at last, our party began to be less tense, but nobody said anything much. The gunman was introduced as Rivien; a man of few words, it would seem, for he was most untalkative. We elicited from him that he lived in a town called Fayoun. After that, the attempt at conversation was abandoned through lack of support.

The landscape provided no stimulation. It was dark now, and away from the guide's illumination of the path before us there was nothing to see except occasional lights in the distance where people were spending the evening in their houses. The noise of the wind buffeting the guide was the only sound. A number of vehicles passed us, heading for Ultima Salem, the glow of their lights disappearing rapidly as they receded into the distance. Far behind, we could glimpse off and on the headlight of another guide travelling in our direction, but it got no closer.

We passed to the south of Suez, taking the road which runs along the top of the dam, and so came to Cairo. The city was lit up by twenty or so lamps, each mounted on a mast of considerable height. They made it seem like daylight.

We drove through the modestly busy streets for quite a long time. The roadways were narrower than those of Ultima Salem, and the dwellings closer together. The place felt old.

The mast-mounted lamps dimmed just as we crossed a bridge over the River Nile, changing to an illumination level like the one they have at night in Ultima Salem. It was thus in semi-darkness that we arrived at the house of a lady called Beverly.

All of us, except for the gunman Rivien, who departed in the guide, I assume on his way to Fayoun, entered the abode. We found Beverly inside, a mortal woman aged about fifty.

"You are welcome," she said politely. And then to Kway: "It'll be a bit cramped with the five of you, but you'll be safe as long as you keep indoors."

"We'll do that," Kway assured her. "I hope it won't be for more than a few days."

"How are you going to get the Koltetrians away?" she asked.

"The Council will send up an aircraft once they've been informed our guests here are out of the Mayor's hands. Rivien has gone to make the arrangements. We'll be collected by him when the time is right."

Beverly showed us round her home. It was one of those organic affairs that are not popular on Koltetra, and it was quite a while since I'd been in one. There was a food preparation and eating area, a bathroom, a bodily waste depository, and three other rooms that could be used as the fancy took you. The largest of these she reserved for herself; the second largest was allocated to Kway and Kerra; and the smallest, somewhat perversely, was to be used by us three Koltetrians.

We were provided with a meal of fruit, vegetables and beef, after which we went to bed.

As I waited for sleep, I felt a strange, unsettling mixture of triumph and foreboding; triumph because I was at last free from the Mayor's suffocating restrictions; foreboding because of the search being mounted to find us, which meant we were restricted still, albeit in a different way. In effect, the three of us had swapped the comfortable cage the Mayor had kept us in for the far more uncertain and potentially hazardous cage that went with living as fugitives. I could convince myself that the change was necessary, but not that it was an improvement.

I did not sleep well.

13

Next morning, straight after waking up I tried out the bathroom, but it really wasn't to my liking. The thing enfolded you rather like Mother's womb and sort of slurped you clean. The experience was supposed to be very sensual, but it just didn't strike me that way.

We spent the day lying low, excepting Beverly, who went to work, being a fairly high-ranking official in the local administrative office of the Palatine of Africa in central Cairo.

Beverly's house had a Mem terminal, but we Koltetrians were told not to use it. This was because of our accents. Nobody else on Earth spoke with the vocal intonations that we did, and Mem would identify us easily and would be sure to pass our location to the authorities. As a result, there was almost nothing for the three of us to do except speculate: about whether we'd be apprehended and, if so, what would happen to us; about what we'd find in Antarctica if we weren't detained; about the insanity or otherwise of the malcons; about what we'd report to the New Worlds in the light of the past twenty-four hours; about what we'd do when we got home. The consensus amongst us was that we were not prepared to believe the Tenth Civilization on Earth was falling apart. That was impossible simply because the system was capable of indefinite self-repair. It couldn't degenerate any more than immortal humans could. We put Kerra's remarks about an Eleventh Civilization down to her need to justify her colleagues' (and her own) violent behaviour, and not therefore to be taken seriously. But we couldn't deny that malcons were an unexpected flaw in the perfect system.

To find out more on the issue we got Kerra, on our behalf, to ask Mem about malcons. Mem was very enlightening. Uncomfortably so, in fact.

"The malcon problem," Mem explained, "has its roots in genetic intervention, also known as genetic pure-ing. This is the process whereby any defective genes present in an embryo are repaired or replaced shortly after its conception. It has resulted in a present-day human population which is free from the scourges of earlier eras; all babies are born fit and perfectly healthy.

"A question arises, however, as to whether aggressive behaviour is normal or abnormal. The prevailing view is that aggression has no role to play in a mature Tenth Civilization, and that emotions which lead to it, such as anger and frustration, can therefore rightly be regarded as aberrant. There has consequently been a tendency for the brain structures responsible for these emotions to be genetically altered so as to greatly reduce their influence on the way individuals behave. The result has been a trend towards a populace which is not only perfectly healthy, but also one which is happy and contented; a society of people who are mentally as well as physically in a state of faultless equilibrium.

"Unfortunately, this trend is no more than that, which means a sizable remnant population still exists whose brains continue to respond to the social environment in aggressive ways their ancestors would recognize, but which are not appropriate to modern times. This has recently become a cause for concern.

"The reason for this is that society has begun to polarize between those most prone to behaving aggressively and those largely incapable of it. Individuals capable of aggression at present constitute about six per cent of the population, and most of them manage to control their aggressive tendency. However, a small minority — referred to as 'malcons' — do not do so. They are sufficiently aggressive in their day to day lives as to be disruptive to the rest of society. It is this minority which is causing the social polarization.

"The growing alienation of the malcon community is continuously exacerbated by the fact that, whereas non-aggressive parents always choose to conceive non-aggressive children, malcons have stopped availing themselves of this option. Their undesirable behavioural traits are thereby being passed on to future generations, thus perpetuating the polarization.

"Because of their disruptive nature, malcons are now under great social pressure to submit their embryos to that part of the genetic intervention process which will remove the anti-social component from their mental make-up. It is considered by the government that the law guaranteeing total parental control over genetic intervention may eventually need to be amended; that is, that malcon parents might have to be compelled to conform to modern social norms regarding child conception. Similarly, existing malcons, particularly those who are immortal, are being constantly urged to seek treatment at psychotherapy centres where their aggressiveness can be cured."

Mem fell silent. We looked at one another uneasily. I, for one, was shocked.

Vallensel said: "So it's not just me who's a potential malcon. I'd say we all are."

"Almost everyone on Koltetra is capable of aggression," Jannet remarked.

"But we're not like Kerra and her friends," I protested.

"Not yet," said Vallensel.

"Let's think about this," said Jannet. "A malcon becomes aggressive as a result of frustration or boredom or dissatisfaction with life. That's a defect — if I may so call it — which would only reveal itself once a society has achieved stability. Until then, aggression is an essential part of progress. But when progress attains its goal, aggression has no target. The obvious solution is to remove by genetic pure-ing the emotions giving rise to it. That's plainly what they've done on Earth. It's the sensible, reasonable thing to do. The exceptions, the people left out of this process, including immortals born in earlier times, then find themselves becoming misfits. Life would appear aimless from their point of view. At least, that's how I would feel about Koltetra if it was in the same state Earth is in."

"Right," agreed Vallensel. "If you're a mild case, you learn to live with it. You presumably end up listless and apathetic. If you're a more severe case, you opt either to have your mental outlook altered by psychosurgery or you become a malcon. Aggression can't be constructive any more because there's nothing left to construct, so it must be eliminated or it turns to *de*struction instead. Hence the kind of insanity we witnessed yesterday."

"Worrying, isn't it?" I said. "A thousand years from now, we three will be considered anti-social Koltetrian malcons."

"I shan't," said Jannet reflectively. "I'll be one of the listless, apathetic ones."

Whatever any of us was to become, we agreed the malcon problem was something the New Worlds urgently needed to know about, though what action they'd take to deal with it we couldn't imagine. Unfortunately it left unexplained why Earth had dropped out of the Galactic Information Grid. How could anyone seriously believe the malcon problem was something 'not worth saying'? Or was the malcon issue what the Mayor was trying to hide? That would explain his desire to send us home as soon as he could. But then, what would make him want to hide such a thing? A complete solution to the Earth mystery continued to elude us.

Beverly came home from work early in the evening to report that all was much as expected. She told us: "There's a panic on to find you. There are sentinels swarming all over Benisef, looking. People are being asked to report any strangers who seem suspicious. Quite a number of malcons in Ultima Salem and Benisef have been detained in order to be questioned."

"I don't like the sound of it," was Kway's comment.

Beverly said: "It's accepted the Koltetrians went of their own accord. I assume the Mayor's just feeling unusually incensed that his orders have been disobeyed."

"What about Roshan and Ruth?" I asked. "Is there any news of them?"

"Yes. They've been moved to Malta. That's a small island in the Mednean Sea. The Palatine Office in Cairo has been informed they are officially unwelcome foreigners. Unofficially, I've also heard they've been placed under sentinel guard so that they can't talk with anyone. It all adds up to imprisonment."

"Imprisonment!" I exclaimed. "Can the authorities do that here?"

"The Mayor can do anything he likes. The fact that he normally doesn't shows he's quite upset."

"Relax," said Kerra. "He just wants to know where they are. He doesn't want them absconding like you three. They'll be let out once the fuss has died down."

Nobody seemed all that reassured, not even Beverly.

There followed a second night in Beverly's house, as we continued to hide from an unexpectedly determined Mayor.

The next day started much as had the preceding one (though I avoided the bathroom). We were just beginning to adapt to the lethargic way of life when events took an unexpected turn: Beverly's son showed up. He was a nice lad who had his own dwelling, but he wasn't a malcon. Beverly's husband of the time, long since gone, had prevailed on her to do her duty and bring a happy young man into the world, and not another malcon like herself. She regretted it, but to me it seemed the sane thing to do. Malcons were not appropriate on Earth any more.

The trouble was, Beverly's son wanted to know who we were. She told him, lying to him in a most uncivilized way, that we were just some government officials. He stayed only briefly but it was enough to scare Kway and Kerra. They decided to leave at once.

Kerra was sent out to obtain a guide. As soon as she returned, we bade farewell to our Cairo hostess. The lady wished us an uninterrupted journey, and assured us, in response to our concern, that we hadn't got her into trouble.

"Kway has to be cautious," she explained, "but I'm not in any danger. My son is no fool. The search for you is being concentrated around Benisef because that's where the aircraft you escaped in was tracked to. But Benisef is not that far from Cairo, and you are strangers. He'll probably look you Koltetrians up in a visuary and behold: they're living with me. He won't say anything, though. He knows I'm a malcon and, bless him, he feels sorry for me. He'd never do anything to harm me, any more than I would to harm him. I trust my son with my life, even if Kway can't. And mustn't. I'll be all right."

We set off for Fayoun, where Rivien lived. Kerra informed us the place was a small town on the edge of the Sahara Reserve, which was the location from where our flight to Antarctica was to commence.

"We often make flights from there," she explained. "It's one and a half million square kilometres of wilderness where all the world's surviving desert plants and animals are preserved. Too big for the sentinels to police effectively. We pick a different location each time, more or less at random, to fly to or from. Rivien or one of his friends is notified in advance to arrange transport. That's important, for it wouldn't take you long to die if you were stranded in the place. It's kept very hot and dry."

We travelled to Fayoun overnight, arriving at dawn, just as the thin crescent of moon was overwhelmed by the brilliance of sunrise. We slunk into Rivien's house in a most conspiratorial manner. It was not the sort of time of day when a person would normally receive visitors and we had to hope nobody was awake to notice.

Rivien greeted us fresh from his bed, with very little clothing on. I couldn't help noticing how much more muscular he was than Koltetrian men. He and Kway were alike in that respect, providing some evidence for my developing view that muscle enlargement was a defect associated specifically with Earth-dwelling malcons.

We had done our best to sleep in the guide en route, but it wasn't easy when there was nowhere to lie down. We were in consequence grateful for the opportunity to complete our slumbers on Rivien's living room floor.

When we awoke at noon, we discovered Rivien was about to go off somewhere to sort out details of the flight to Antarctica. He promised it would not take long to get things settled. We were assured the 'Council' moves a lot faster than do Earth's official authorities.

While Rivien was absent, we asked Kerra about the people we were being taken to meet. (Kway had no interest in talking to us about such things.)

"This Council's a kind of government?" I suggested.

"That's correct. They run Antarctica."

"On behalf of the Mayor?" asked Jannet.

"Definitely not. We're not a palatinate. Fossilized relics, they are!"

"You mean to say you were serious about the Mayor having no authority in Antarctica?" I said.

"You mean to say you didn't believe me?" Kerra rejoined.

"So how many people live in Antarctica?"

"Several millions. Everyone a malcon. Several millions more of us, like Rivien and Beverly, live in the palatinates. Then there are a further forty million self-suppressing sub-malcons who won't have anything to do with the Council. They accept the Mayor's rule and pretend we rebels don't exist."

"Which category do we come in?" asked Jannet.

"That's up to you. You're here so there's hope yet. Meet the Council. Hear what they have to say. Then you can decide for yourselves whether you sympathize with us or not."

"Suspended judgement," remarked Vallensel.

"That's right," said Kerra.

While we waited for Rivien to return, we watched the coming and goings in the locality. Rivien lived in Fayoun, it seemed, mainly to facilitate his anti-social malcon activities, there being little else to do in the town. A few of its inhabitants supervised hybrimorphs servicing the Sahara Reserve, and a few chose to do actual physical work, mostly growing things, but the majority were idle, and happily so. I could understand how a malcon in such an environment might become frustrated. Not that it excused gun-wielding behaviour.

Rivien got back in the afternoon with the news we had been waiting for. The Council did indeed move fast. An aircraft would collect us two hours before midnight from a location two hundred kilometres south-south-west of Fayoun. Regretfully, however, he also brought other less welcome news. Apparently the Mayor was still as determined as ever to reacquire us. Instead of scaling down the search effort, he was, if anything, stepping it up.

"I don't know what's got into him," commented Kway, who was clearly worried by the development. "He's never reacted like this before."

"It has rather wrecked the plan," Rivien stated.

"How's that?" asked Vallensel.

"Basically, transporting you to Antarctica was intended to be a straightforward business. The Council was going to send an aircraft once everything had quietened down, and fly you direct. That plan has had to be scrapped. The idea now is to get you away from Africa as quickly as possible. The trouble is we can't take you straight to Antarctica. The Mayor reckons that's where you're headed — rightly — so he's decided to try his hand at anticipating the move. Most of the sentinel-aircraft at his disposal are being sent to operate from Patagonia, Capeland and Oz. The skies are being packed down there. Anything flying out of Antarctica is being followed, and anything flying towards it is being forced down and inspected. We're having to send a man overland to Santiago to pick up an aircraft from there. And that, I'm sorry to say, is where you'll be flown back to. We'll have to get you from Santiago to Antarctica some other way."

"Oh, that's just brilliant," said Kway, who clearly meant the exact opposite.

"Can't you bring the Council to Santiago?" I asked.

"As a last resort, we might."

"Why don't you just blast the opposition?" Jannet asked Rivien with a cynical edge to her voice.

"We don't do that unless we have to. The Council doesn't like it. I don't like it. Anyway, as the sentinels know we're armed, they can shoot back in certain circumstances. I wouldn't want to get you three damaged. That would upset just about everybody."

Because of the distance to be travelled over what was casually described as rough terrain, our party left Rivien's house in late afternoon. It was a good thing we did, for the terrain was very definitely rough. We followed a track for a while and then, as night fell, began travelling completely off-road. The guide did quite well in the circumstances but it bumped about severely, its speed much reduced.

In the light cast by the guide's headlamp we could see the landscape consisted chiefly of rock and hard-baked mud, and dust which had accumulated to form large drifts. There were sparse scrubby plants but nothing that could have sustained a human. I mused on whether, had I never absented myself to go to Garden Island, we might have ended up being shown this strangely unearthly place by Annalivia in daylight, instead of unintentionally by Rivien, Kway and Kerra in the dark.

It was a little before ten o'clock when the guide came to a halt.

"This is the place," said Rivien.

The guide's headlamp was left on so the incoming aircraft could spot us.

Presently, there appeared in the sky something resembling a shooting star, coming from the south-west.

I was astonished to see Rivien draw his gun. He walked away into the darkness.

"Just anticipating," said Kway.

The aircraft slowed when almost vertically over us and was soon hovering. The guide was instructed to turn off its lights, plunging us into darkness. A minute or so after that the aircraft was down.

A man got out carrying a torch, and came trustingly

over to us. He shone the light — rudely, I thought — in our several faces.

"We meet again, Kway," he said.

"You're late," was Kway's response. The strain of being responsible for conducting us to Antarctica, and for our safety in the interim, was not improving Kway's already humourless disposition.

"Only a few minutes. These are the Koltetrians?"

"They are."

"Ah! And the beautiful Madam Dyanie."

"This is too hot a place to hang around in. Let's be on our way. You can pay my wife compliments later."

We began walking towards the aircraft.

"What about the guide?" said the man. "Aren't you going to send it home?"

"No."

The man glanced blindly into the darkness and nodded. "It'll be a shame when we lose you, Kway. You're one of the best."

"You won't lose me."

"It comes to us all eventually. One day you'll get careless and forget to have someone in reserve hidden away out of sight. One day you'll do that and it won't be me landing here but a sentinel-aircraft."

"True enough if I was mortal, but I'm not. We immortals don't get careless because we don't get old."

"No, you lose interest instead. It has the same result."

We climbed the steps into the aircraft.

Rivien remained hidden to the end. We flew off, leaving him to take the guide back to Fayoun in time for the dawn.

14

The flight was a long one taking about ten hours. It benefitted from the fact that our pick-up site was only a short distance to one side of the Ultima Salem to Santiago beamway. As a result, it was necessary to use chem-ion thrusters for very little time. The bulk of the journey took advantage of the aircraft's magrider attachment to follow the beam.

"Do you think this flight is being monitored?" Vallensel asked at one point, shortly after we'd taken off.

"What makes you think that?" said Kway.

Vallensel, I admit, was more in tune with the malcon way of thinking than I was. "It seems to me, if your use of Saharan locations is common, that the authorities probably know of it. Bearing in mind we were last seen heading for Benisef, which is in the same general area as the Sahara Reserve, an aircraft landing there might attract attention. Indeed, if I was the Mayor I'd have ordered the Sahara Reserve to be closely watched."

Kway responded: "So you think this aircraft may have aroused suspicion?"

"Yes, I do."

"Especially," I said, joining in to prove I wasn't that far behind, "since it came from a location in the southern hemisphere and is now returning in that direction."

"You're both correct," Kway agreed. "It means it's possible — though unlikely — that a sentinel-aircraft will be directed to escort us. But there's a worse difficulty to deal with. There'll be resident sentinels at the Santiago terminus, and they'll have been alerted to look out for you three as a matter of course. The question is, what do you suggest we do about it?"

Of course, Kway already knew what he was going to do about it. He was just amusing himself.

"I hadn't thought of a sentinel-aircraft escort," said Vallensel. "Can we get rid of it without landing?"

"No," Kway replied, "but it's not a problem. As long as we don't go anywhere near Antarctica, it'd only follow us. There would be no benefit in forcing us to land before we get to the beamway terminus. So what about Santiago?"

"We detach from the beamway and land before we get to Santiago," Vallensel said.

"Very good. Where?"

My turn: "I don't know the local geography, but somewhere to the north."

"Why to the north?"

"Less suspicious. It's not in a direction we'd be expected to take if we were trying to reach Antarctica."

"But what if they assumed we'd try not to look suspicious? If we headed north, might they not say to themselves: 'These people are trying not to look suspicious. That *is* suspicious'. Perhaps we should head south."

Kway smiled faintly at my nonplussed expression.

"Don't tease him," said Kerra. "At least he's trying."

"It's a complicated business outwitting sentinels," Kway sighed. "The point is, if this aircraft is being tracked, nothing we do will allay their suspicions short of our landing at Santiago and being seen not to be the people we in fact are. Clearly that's impossible so, yes, we must land short of Santiago, but it makes little difference where. Providing we don't have a sentinel-aircraft in attendance, what we've planned is to detach from the beamway before it crosses the Cordilleras, and set down at Arenalez."

"Arenalez? Cordilleras?" said Jannet, bemused.

"Latica has a range of mountains running along its western coast," Kerra explained. "They're called the Cordilleras. Santiago lies west of the mountains, between them and the sea. Arenalez, on the other hand, is a small town to the east of the high ground."

"And if we have an unwelcome escort?" Vallensel asked.

"Then we have to land near a larger town, decommission as many sentinels as possible, and get in amongst the general populace where we can lose ourselves, much like we did in Cairo."

We discussed the geography of southern Latica for a while, and it was clear Kway and Kerra knew it well. They acknowledged it to be the best travelled route between Antarctica and the rest of the world. This was particularly so of the land to the east of the Cordilleras, known as Patagonia. They anticipated it would be by way of that country that they'd take us to our meeting with the Council. It was clear they knew what they were doing. My optimism was growing that the Mayor and his sentinels were not going to be able to stop us.

The aircraft dropped us close to Arenalez, and was then flown off by the man who had brought it across to the Sahara Reserve. Presumably he took it back to Santiago. He had remained almost completely silent during the flight, seemingly lost in his thoughts. An anonymous man whose identity remains unknown to me to this day.

Owing to our westward movement, it was still the middle of the night locally, with the result that the five of us had to make our way round the periphery of the town not only on foot but in the dark. Having to walk was a sign that Kerra's much vaunted anticipation wasn't always as infallible as one might have expected. There really should have been someone to meet us. But as

Kway dismissively explained, when a trip is organized in a hurry there are times when improvisation is necessary.

It was a kilometre and a half before we came to some unoccupied dwellings. The distance was more than I was accustomed to covering unaided, a situation made worse by the uphill nature of the ground.

"If bringing an end to the Tenth Civilization means enduring this sort of physical punishment," said an annoyed Jannet quietly to me, "I'm against it. This is plain brutalism. I shall be aching for a week."

I knew exactly what she meant. Kway and Kerra, on the other hand, seemed not to notice the arduousness of the trek.

The dwelling Kway chose for us was a duram one, obviously a house that was regularly maintained, but equally obviously in a block that nobody used any more.

"We'll be safe here for the rest of the night," he told us.

"I take it you don't know anyone in Arenalez," commented Jannet.

"Not that I can rely on," Kway admitted.

We paid a price for Kway's lack of contacts in that the house was bare; there was no food.

As in Cairo, it was Kerra who was sent out early next morning to obtain a guide. I wondered about that.

When the opportunity arose, I asked Kway: "Why is it always Kerra who goes out for the guide and not you?"

"She's not known to the authorities as someone who's committed serious crimes. I am. They'd detain me if I was seen in public."

"Serious detainable crimes? Such as?"

"One day maybe, I'll tell you. But not now."

I got the unmistakable impression I was to leave well alone, so I did.

Kerra returned in about an hour, having walked

several kilometres into the town to get a guide, and we left without further ado, setting off for the south. Our guide was soon cruising down a wide road in the presence of a fair amount of traffic.

After a quarter of an hour, we came to a food warehouse. It was well stocked, with the usual fetchers coming and going. We took the opportunity to load the guide with a good supply of things to eat and drink: bread, cheese, vegetables that could be eaten raw, fruit, some delicious, pre-cooked pork, and bottles of sweet-milk. Hardly able to restrain ourselves, we pulled off the road a few kilometres further on and had a belated breakfast. The ache in my stomach was quickly dispelled. I only wish the ache in my legs from last night's long walk could have been got rid of as easily.

Despite the discomforts, it was good to be alive that morning. We dawdled over breakfast, using it as an opportunity to take in our surroundings. The sky was cloudless and the scenery magnificent. Our altitude was quite high, the road being one tracing the foothills of the Cordilleras, and this resulted in a rather low air temperature, but the sun was more than powerful enough to compensate. It was a day of bracing freshness, invigorating as nowhere else I had visited on Earth. On one side of us were the mountains, a chain of snow-covered peaks (it being the middle of the winter in the southern hemisphere), the highest ones also wreathed in cloud. Well below the snow-line, the slopes were planted with trees, doubtless harvested once every hundred years or so. Where we were parked, the trees stopped many kilometres short of the road, to be replaced by moorland which, even at this time of the year, was dotted with flowers. On the other side of the road, the moor extended to a distant ridge which cut off our view of what lay beyond. Only the wind disturbed the silence.

"It'll be like this on Koltetra, one day," I remarked.

There was peace here, and for a while I forgot the trouble we were in. It was a pity we couldn't have stayed longer. But there was no avoiding it. Breakfast over, we resumed our journey southwards.

In spite of two more stops to eat, and others to relieve ourselves the old-fashioned way, and occasionally to look at items of interest that we passed, we made good time, averaging over two hundred kilometres an hour. By mid afternoon we were half way to our destination. We expected to arrive at the southern tip of Patagonia a few hours after nightfall, when doubtless the Council would use the darkness to get us undetected from there to Antarctica.

As we progressed, I found myself becoming increasingly uneasy about the world outside our warm and comfortable guide. The density of the population noticeably declined: dwellings became fewer; towns smaller; and the quality of the road led me to believe it was less frequently maintained than I would have expected. Other traffic decreased in quantity until ours was often the only vehicle in sight. Also, puzzlingly, the temperature fell more than I would have thought it should. Although the mountains on our right were no longer so high, the snow extended further and further down their slopes. This was not what I would have expected with an operational climate control system, working as it does by preventing more than minor differences in temperature from occurring over the globe as a whole. In a curious way, the developments as we neared journey's end didn't seem natural — not natural to the Tenth Civilization, that is. Yet in other respects everything remained unremarkable. The land below the snow-line continued to be organized and productive and unblemished. I decided it was the imminent prospect of meeting more people like Kway and Kerra that was making me wary.

Kway, who I was expecting to become more relaxed as we got nearer to malcon Antarctica, instead became increasingly tense and was clearly worried. Kerra was the same.

"You might as well know the situation," said Kway at last. "There are a lot of malcons in this part of Latica, so it made sense to get you down here, rather than lie low in Arenalez. That much we've done. But now we've got to southern Patagonia, there are two options open to us. One is to make a dash for the south coast and hand you over to the Council there. The other is to go into hiding with one of the local malcons and wait until the Mayor reduces the search effort being made to find you. We've been ordered to try for the quick handover. But the prospects of success are not good."

"Why's that?" asked Jannet.

"Think about it," said Kway dismissively.

I thought. The answer was pretty obvious. The Mayor had packed the skies around Antarctica with sentinel-aircraft. And there we were, quite possibly the only guide on the road, heading south. If so much as one sentinel-aircraft flew overhead, and it decided to intercept us to check on who we were, we were lost. Detention would inevitably follow — unless Kway and Kerra decided to let loose the insane side of their nature, which was an even worse prospect. Who knew what the consequences of that would be?

For a while the gamble appeared to be paying off. The sky began to darken as night drew on, the sun having dropped behind the mountains. Our southward progress continued uninterrupted. The forests became more omnipresent, reaching down to the road and off into the distance on its other side. That was to our advantage as it provided us with cover. A sentinel-aircraft would have to pass almost directly over us before it could see the guide.

It was when we emerged from the forest onto an open stretch of road where the trees had recently been harvested that our luck ran out. Kerra touched Kway on the shoulder and pointed south-eastwards. Naturally we all looked. There, like the first star of evening, was a shining point of light. It had to be stared at for several seconds before its motion was discernible. It was following a westerly course.

"One of yours?" I said optimistically.

"No," Kerra replied. "One of the Mayor's."

"Do you think it can see us?"

"Don't you have sentinel-aircraft on Koltetra?"

"A few."

She sighed. "Yes, it can see us."

"Surely it'll take us for local people going about our business," ventured Jannet.

"If this was Capeland or Oz it might. But not Patagonia. There's only one beamway connecting to Antarctica and we're heading straight for it. Added to which, we're probably the only vehicle travelling south between the Cordilleras and the Atlantic. If they're stopping aircraft and inspecting them, it wouldn't make sense for them not to want to inspect us."

"You'll have to destroy it then," said Vallensel, revealing once again his affinity with the malcons.

"It's not that simple," said Kway. "They're all in communication with one another. Destroy one sentinel-aircraft and others will home in on the area like bees to a hive. They'll be on us long before we reach the south coast."

"So destroy them all," said Vallensel. I felt ashamed of him.

Kway shook his head. "It wouldn't work. After the

first one, they'll be empowered to shoot back. Besides, they're not that easy to bring down. The Mayor lost a few in the past to us, so he had them panflector shielded. It means you can't vaporize them any more. Instead, your only hope is to hit them at close range and square on. That can destabilize them enough to push them beyond their aerial stability limit. If you're lucky."

"Surely you anticipated we'd be spotted," I said in exasperation.

"Naturally. Unfortunately, if there's no plan-able way out of a situation, anticipating it doesn't do much good."

My confidence in Kway's infallibility was rapidly dissipating. "So what are we going to do?"

"I don't know. Just keep your eyes open. Dwellings, caves, other traffic, anything we might turn to our advantage."

The guide forged on. The 'star' moved slowly across in front of us and I began to wonder if we were being too pessimistic. Maybe it would take no notice of us. And then it altered course. Kway took a gun out of his pocket. Not again, I thought miserably. Not again.

"It'll be over us in five minutes," said Kway. "Grab as much to eat as you can. We may not get another meal for some time."

"They won't starve us if we surrender, will they?" asked Jannet in amazement.

"Just do it," Kway ordered in reply.

Easy for him to say. Speaking personally, I'd suddenly lost my appetite. I stuffed as much as I could into my pockets, and contented myself with chewing nervously on a bit of the pork.

Minutes passed. The 'star' grew brighter and higher in the sky. Ahead of us, the harvested area of forest was coming to an end.

"We'll have to take to the trees," said Kway. "You

can carry on alone, Kerra. They don't know you. Act the innocent. You should be all right."

Because the aircraft was approaching us at an angle, it was briefly lost from sight as we re-entered the forest.

"Stop!" Kway commanded the guide. And then he ordered us to get out.

The four of us leapt to the ground. The guide, with Kerra still on board, accelerated away. We retreated into the trees.

"Keep together and head uphill," Kway told us, before setting off in a different direction.

"What about you?" Vallensel called after him.

"My wife comes first," Kway replied over his shoulder.

We watched him head along the fringe of the forest that bordered the road, sprinting after the receding guide.

"Come on," said Vallensel.

Jannet and I followed him unhappily.

15

And I thought the hike around Arenalez had been bad enough! For a start, it was nearly dark, making it difficult to see where we were going, the trees cutting out most of the available light. Added to that, it wasn't just uphill; it was rugged, rocky, strewn with small branches and sticks, and slippery where dew had settled.

A number of birds high up in the trees were frightened by our passage and set up a lot of flapping and alarm cries. It was one of these that brought us to a halt. There was a raucous screech and Vallensel, momentarily distracted by it, misjudged his footing. He fell to the ground, letting out a screech of his own.

The damage proved to be superficial, merely a grazed ankle, but it triggered a decision to go no further. After all, Kway and Kerra would need to come back and find us once the sentinel-aircraft had flown on its way. It would be unwise for us to go far from the road.

As we sat on the damp, nastily hard ground, the birds began to calm down. At the same time, I became aware of how cold it was. The wind, though fairly light thanks to the trees, was blowing from the west, down off the snow-capped mountains. I was surprised such a wind would exist in a climate controlled environment. It served no obvious purpose. Except, that is, to evaporate the sweat from our faces and add to our discomfort.

We waited, expecting at any moment to hear the sound of gunfire, but it didn't happen. However, it wasn't a reassuring silence. Somewhere close by there was an animal making a noise somewhere between a dog's bark and a kind of howl. I looked about for a suitable lump of wood to use as a weapon.

"Really!" said Vallensel, sensing my and Jannet's fear. "This is Earth. All the dangerous animals are held in reserves like Sumatra. Besides, the three of us should be able to chase off anything we don't like the look of. I doubt very much if there are any carnivores in Latica bigger than a human."

"To think we could have been sleeping peacefully in Mother on our way back to Koltetra," said Jannet dejectedly.

It grew completely dark. A few stars appeared, but were quickly hidden by a bank of cloud rolling off the mountains. Aside from a whole collection of scary night-noises, and the wind swaying the tops of the trees, there was silence. No gunfire, no sound of Kway coming to retrieve us.

I was getting very cold and had to resort to working my hands under my jacket in an attempt to warm them up. For the first time, it occurred to me we were in real danger. I couldn't see us surviving the night if we remained in the open.

Jannet shivered and voiced the same fear. "What happens if Kway Myer and Kerra Dyanie have been detained? We'll freeze to death in this wind."

Vallensel agreed. "We can't stay here. We've got to find some sort of shelter."

"What do you suggest?" I asked.

"Let's go back to the road. We might be able to see the light of a dwelling."

We got stiffly to our feet and set off downhill. We all slipped on the damp ground and lost our footing more than once.

It was while I was picking myself up after my second fall that I thought I heard something. We stood motionless, straining our ears. Faintly came the sound of a human voice. It was Kway calling us.

We three yelled back more or less simultaneously. The relief was tremendous. I could almost feel the warmth inside that lovely guide, surely not far away.

Ten minutes later, after much shouting back and forth, Kway located us amongst the trees.

"I was getting worried," I said as he did so.

"It's under control," he replied.

"Is Kerra okay?"

"Yes. The sentinels allowed her to resume her journey. Their aircraft flew off towards the mountains."

"I'm glad about that. I can't wait to get back on board."

"Don't be stupid, Felip. Kerra's gone."

"What?"

"We had no choice. After the aircraft had departed, she doubled back and we had a quick discussion. Racing for the south coast wasn't working. The chances were heavily that we'd be spotted by other sentinel-aircraft along the way and maybe next time we wouldn't be as lucky as we were on this occasion. So Kerra's travelling on alone. She'll tell the Council where we are. It'll be up to them to send us a rescue party."

"So what do we do now?"

"Now we get out of the forest and find some shelter. Follow me."

Kway gave us no time to argue. We hurried after him as he set off downhill, all of us afraid of being left behind.

"This is ridiculous," muttered Jannet as we scrambled our way towards the road. "These people have lost their minds!"

Once out of the trees, Kway trotted away southwards along the road with us three lambs in tow. Keeping pace with him warmed us up, but forced us to find reserves of energy we had no idea we possessed. The thought kept coming into my mind that this just wasn't civilized.

After half a kilometre or so, we came to a place where there were no trees on the left side of the road. Kway stopped and waited for us to catch him up.

"This is about the best location," he informed us. "I noticed it when discussing our next move with Kerra. It wasn't so dark then. There are no trees here because of the slope of the ground. It's quite steep. We can camp at the bottom."

He led us down a slope which was a lot more than 'quite' steep. We slid rather than walked, the ground being covered in a layer of loose, friable rock. The bottom of this escarpment was perhaps fifty metres below the level of the road. Once we were all assembled on more nearly flat ground, Kway told us to search the sky for any sign of a sentinel-aircraft.

We obeyed. Overhead it was uniformly black and overcast. There was nothing to see. Kway drew his gun and aimed it obliquely at the rock face. We lay down on the damp ground and shielded our eyes. He fired. For a quarter of a minute, microsecond pulses blasted the base of the escarpment. Waves of heat surged over us. Thunder filled the air.

When he was finished, we stood up to look. A cave-like depression had been dug into the rock face. Its interior still glowed redly in the dark. It was good to see Kway could use a gun for the sort of purpose for which it had been invented. Even if his terrestrial engineering hadn't been authorized!

An hour later, we had ourselves well organized. Under Kway's direction, a considerable quantity of dead wood from the nearby parts of the forest had been gathered, as had a collection of modestly-sized stones. Mixed together and piled up in the entrance to our cave, wood and stones made a useful barrier against wild animals and the wind.

That only left the cold to trouble us. Kway heated the back of the cave with occasional discharges from the gun, using a low power setting. That didn't completely solve the problem of the chilling environmental temperature, but it helped enough that we were no longer in danger of dying from it.

"Ironic, isn't it?" said Vallensel, as we sat munching the food we had brought with us from the guide, and looking out beyond the fortified entrance at the darkness beyond. "This is how people used to live before civilization had been invented. We came all the way from Koltetra, using perfect technology, to spend a night like this. I wonder what the folk back home would think if they knew."

"They'd be disgusted," said Jannet. "I wish I'd stayed behind with Roshan and Ruth."

I couldn't honestly blame Jannet for her less than enthusiastic attitude. She was reacting to our plight in much the same way as I had reacted to the Garden Island episode.

Kway had no sympathy for her. "If you don't like it, you're free to leave. I never invited you on this trip. It was your decision."

"How long do you think we'll be here?" asked Vallensel.

"It depends on the Council. It could be several days."

"We'll starve!" I exclaimed.

"No we won't. I've lived off the land before in places like this. It was part of my training. I'll see you're fed."

"You know, Kway, you were born seven thousand years too late," said Vallensel.

"Meaning what?"

"This world doesn't need people of your kind any more. In some ways you're like a wild animal, cunning, always alert, depending on foresight and experience for your survival. Those are things the Tenth Civilization has no need of. Today's Earth calls for gentle people content to idle the time away. You just don't belong to it."

"So you say," said Kway without interest.

Vallensel continued: "Couldn't you persuade them to equip a new colonial expedition? You malcons could go somewhere you'd be useful instead of destructive."

"And run away?"

"It wouldn't be running away. When my ancestors set off for Koltetra they weren't running away. They wanted to be in at the start of something new; to play their part in human destiny."

"Well, good for them."

"It'd be good for you too. You're like a fish in an evaporating pond. You'd be much happier in a new pond."

Vallensel had finally gone too far.

"Happiness," Kway said angrily. "That's all you ever get from the Mayor and his cronies. Nothing matters so long as people are happy. I even know malcons up north who feel guilty because they can't be happy all the time. They think of themselves as defective, like someone who wasn't made genetically pure. A few get to hate what they are so much they voluntarily submit to psycho-surgery. Voluntarily! Well, let me tell you, I think the fools who are contented come what may, they're the defective ones. They're the ones who should leave Earth, not me. They can go and be contented in hell. I'm not leaving this planet, and that's that."

There was silence for a few minutes.

"The funny thing is," Kway resumed more calmly, "that's where they are all going: to hell."

"What do you mean?" I asked.

"Do you know what the population of Earth is?"

"About nine hundred million."

"It was when Earth left the Information Grid, but it's not now. In the early days of the Tenth Civilization it stood at one and a half billion. There were settlements on the moon and Mars and several of the gas-giant satellites. But they were all abandoned. And for why? Playing their part in human destiny lost its appeal. Why would anyone choose to live on some unfriendly outpost of civilization when they can be cossetted on Earth? And now they're so happy they can't even be bothered to keep up the numbers. We're down to seven hundred million now, and falling by about a million a year. That's why there are so many unoccupied dwellings around. So you see, we so-called malcons only have to be patient. One day it'll all be ours."

"You seem to be saying that a degree of unhappiness is essential for long-term human survival," I remarked, as the import of what Kway had just said sank in.

"Not only human survival. Any conscious species. That's why the Tenth Civilization is in decline. They're too busy being happy to care. And that's why I'll see them all in their graves. Because I'm not happy and I do care."

I found myself recalling my first reaction to Earth, the day of our arrival, after Annalivia had shown us the sights of Ultima Salem. What had I thought then? Self-indulgence? Yes, that was it. And there, I realized, was part of the answer to the mystery of Earth, expressible not as disconnected thoughts, but coherently. It wasn't that the mature Tenth Civilization was imperfect. Far from it. It was as perfect as the laws of physics and biology and ideology allowed. On Earth they had built, and on Koltetra we were building, the perfect machine. And thanks to genetic pure-ing we were making humankind into the perfect pilot for the perfect machine. A pilot so flawless he had nowhere to go except into a slow collapse towards oblivion. Humanity on Earth was collectively dying of happiness. This, at last, was a message we could convey to the New Worlds. I felt that Koltetra's efforts in sending us across the light-years had no longer been wasted. I wondered, though, what the New Worlds would make of our discovery. Just how do you avoid the consequences of attaining perfection?

<h1 style="text-align:center">16</h1>

We passed the night awake. It was too cold even to doze, and the back wall of our cave needed to be re-heated every fifteen minutes or so.

Kway was of the opinion we should sleep amongst the trees by day, when it was comparatively warm, and spend the nights in the cave. Other than that, he reckoned we'd have to be patient. By now, Kerra would have told the Council where we were, so it would only be a matter of time before they organized our retrieval, but Kway had no way of finding out how or when rescue would come.

"Wouldn't it have been a lot easier if Kerra had come back for us?" asked Jannet. "I accept we couldn't have continued southwards, but heading north shouldn't have been a problem."

"And go where?" said Kway.

"I don't know. Anywhere would have been better than this."

Vallensel then said: "It seems to me you've misjudged the Mayor's reaction to this escapade of ours."

"Yes, we have," Kway agreed. "We misjudged badly. I don't know what's the matter with him. By now everything should have quietened down. It's nothing for you to worry about, though. Ninety-five per cent of keeping ahead of the authorities is being careful. The other five per cent, when you make a mistake or they don't respond according to plan — as in this instance — is being lucky. I've always been lucky. We'll be okay. But I suspect we're going to be cave-dwelling for a few days. The sentinel-aircraft patrols will be making it difficult for any rescue from Antarctica to be mounted at the moment."

The thought of spending several more nights in the cave was ghastly. Unfortunately there didn't seem to be any alternative.

At the first hint of dawn, Kway quickly made a start on getting things organized, thus giving us less time to feel sorry for ourselves. We evacuated the cave, removing as many traces as possible of our presence. We then climbed up to the road, crossed it and entered the forest on its far side, keeping a watch for sentinel-aircraft as we did so. If they noticed the cave from the air and investigated, they'd find no one.

We were set to work gathering vegetation to make ourselves a kind of mattress each to sleep on. Kway disappeared into the trees, to return after an hour or so with a dead animal over his back; a vicuna he called it. By then we three were decidedly grumpy on account of hunger and sheer discomfort. Our muscles were simply not used to the demands being placed on them, and we were all suffering from numerous aches and pains.

What Kway did with the vicuna was appalling. He not only admitted to having killed it by vaporizing its head with his gun; he now proposed to eat it. We watched in boundless disgust as he dislocated and skinned with a sharp stone one of its hind legs. It was a laborious process. Despite doing his best to avoid it, he got blood on his clothes. Finally he had us gather enough sticks and twigs to light a fire, and cooked the meat. That was marginally less disagreeable in being a passive business, but the smell of wood smoke, burning blood, and cooking flesh mingled to make a most unsavoury aroma — one I had never smelt before and will never forget.

When the meal was ready, hunger overtook our natural revulsion, but none of us was delighted with what we were doing. Of course we'd all eaten meat before, but on Koltetra it's always cultured, as it is on Earth, and never the real thing. It was a first time for all three of us, and Jannet particularly took her offering ungratefully.

"I'll share it with you this time," said Kway, "but if I get no help with the other leg tonight, you can all go hungry."

I fervently hoped the Antarctic Council would get to us before then.

In mid morning, the cloud cleared. The sun was unable to penetrate to the floor of the forest, but it nonetheless warmed the air. We slept on our damp leafy mattresses until evening. Needless to say, no one from Antarctica put in an appearance.

"Two of you get the meat ready for cooking. The other one can come with me and gather wood for the fire," Kway commanded when we had all woken up.

It wasn't much of a choice. Gathering wood was less degrading but was nastier in terms of physical discomfort, which sleeping on the ground had done nothing to cure.

At first Jannet refused to do either task.

Kway told her that in that case she could start walking straightaway. "You should come across someone who'll feed you in a manner more to your liking in a hundred kilometres or so," he said.

Jannet expected me and Vallensel to back her up, and perhaps I would have done if Vallensel had, but he didn't. To my surprise, Vallensel took Kway's side. He picked up the sharp stone and began working on the vicuna's other hind leg.

"Well?" said Kway looking at Jannet.

Suddenly it was me he was looking at. I knew what was required.

"You'll find it easier to get the skin off this thing if I hold it," I said to Vallensel, and squatted down beside the carcass.

"Atavists!" Jannet said with disgust, but she followed Kway, all the same, into the trees.

"Do you know what?" Vallensel remarked after they'd gone. "That's about the rudest thing I've ever been called." He grinned. "Poor Jannet. You can have a go at this in a minute."

I can't say I enjoyed the business. My thoughts kept drifting to Koltetra and whether we'd be wiser not mentioning this part of our stay on Earth when we made our report. But they also drifted to Kerra and the amused expression she'd have on her face when told of my efforts carving up a dead vicuna. It made me question my peculiar psychology. I clearly wanted her approval and I couldn't imagine why.

As evening drew on, we cooked the vicuna's other back leg, ate it, and then returned to our cave. Kway insisted on bringing the remains of the animal into the cave with us.

"Leave it outside," he said, "and it'll not be there in the morning."

Once it was dark, we settled down to endure another chilly night, heating the back wall from time to time and staring out into the darkness. Astonishingly, the cloud became so low during the small hours that we found ourselves enveloped in a cold, drizzly fog. Kway was pleased about that because it meant we could be less vigilant. Aerial detection of our cave was no longer a worry. But the damp which swirled around us added yet more to our miseries, making us wet as well as cold.

Those hours waiting for the dawn were the most despondent I had yet spent on Earth, shivering with the chill, with nothing to see, nothing to say, and with only the sounds of Patagonian night animals to hear. This was desolation far worse than Chaytambeor, or even Koltetra's Wild Country.

In the morning we transferred from cave to forest as on the previous day. Vallensel and I went out collecting firewood while Jannet assisted Kway in extracting more edible bits from the vicuna. We cooked and ate the meal, and then slept.

I was awakened early in the afternoon by a hand covering my nose and mouth. If you've got to wake someone up silently, I suppose that's a good way to do it, but frankly I didn't like it. The hand, of course, belonged to Kway.

"There's a guide pulled up on the road," he whispered.

Vallensel and Jannet were woken the same way as I had been, and then we all crept down to the edge of the trees. There was no guide in sight.

"Gone," said Kway. "Wait here."

He entered the trees and a short while later appeared some distance away on the road. Then back into the trees. When he returned to us he was carrying a large sack.

The contents proved to be a quantity of food, a malcon call-button and (blessed discovery!) four thermaks. We needed no bidding to put them on. It was lovely to be warm again.

Kway listened to the call-button and then passed it round so the rest of us could hear it. It was a brief message from the Council, telling us we'd be retrieved by a 'snap air pick' — whatever that was — at dusk.

It turned out the 'snap air pick' was an aircraft which came from over the mountains when it was nearly dark, landed extremely quickly, got us all on board in a few seconds and took off again. I noted it was heading in the wrong direction: northwards. The pilot was a hybrimorph and couldn't explain why it was taking us away from Antarctica, but we judged our reaction from Kway's behaviour. He was plainly not concerned.

174

Ten minutes into the flight, the aircraft veered suddenly west for perhaps a kilometre, set down, and we were ordered to get off: a 'snap air drop' I suppose it might be called. The aircraft then flew rapidly away.

We were not alone. It had deposited us by the side of an east-west running road and there was a guide nearby with a human driver. The four of us got on board and the guide set off, heading west.

The driver introduced himself as Dalkayel, and he had some bad news to give us, though I'll allow him credit that he led up to it gradually. He began by asking if we were the three Koltetrians.

Kway, who had obviously met Dalkayel before, confirmed we were.

"I'm pleased to meet you," Dalkayel said to us. "The Council will be relieved to know you're safe. There was some concern you might have been detained. The situation down here is almost impossible at the moment. You can forget about reaching Antarctica by conventional means. Kerra Dyanie was stopped twice more after leaving you. The second time, she was 'offered' — that's a euphemism, by the way — a lift to Puerto Cothani. The sentinels actually escorted her into the beamway terminus there and watched her leave for Antarctica. So heading south by road is out. As is flying there. Every aircraft is being intercepted and searched. The Council's Conflict Management Superintendent calls what's going on a 'blockade'. Apparently that's the name for a technique they used in the Seventh Civilization to further disputes."

"The Mayor's gone mad," said Kway in a matter of fact tone of voice.

Dalkayel laughed. "He's certainly making life difficult. It's a long time since he's deployed sentinels in Puerto Cothani. I know it's in Patagonia, but it's practically Council territory."

"So what does the Council want us to do?"

"It's the west coast route for these people. I'm to take them through the mountains now. Once the Council knows they're safe, collection will be arranged in a day or two. You're all welcome to stay at my house in Zagossa until then."

"Thank you."

"Do your friends know about the language here?"

"No."

"I expect you all speak English on Koltetra," Dalkayel remarked.

I confirmed we did.

"Well, in Latica the first language is Spanish. Nearly everybody understands English but they don't tend to use it in their homes. So keep your mouths shut in public and don't use my Mem terminal. You'll arouse suspicion if you do. We don't get many strangers in this part of the world. Not west of the Cordilleras. It's too cold and windy."

The road we were on was taking us higher and higher into the mountains. Very soon the guide was enveloped in thick fog, making it impossible to see anything more in the darkness than the snowdrifts by the roadsides.

Dalkayel, quite a contrast to the other malcons we'd met, was very talkative. He chatted to Kway about the latest news from Antarctica, about the people and events in his town, family news, the things he had done recently, and the things he was still doing. Amongst all this gossip, I managed to insert a few questions, enabling me to acquire a few useful snippets of knowledge. Apparently, the malcon population in the southernmost parts of Latica is proportionately higher than anywhere else in the world (except Antarctica), many malcons choosing to live within reach of their fellows in the southern continent while nonetheless retaining their links with the Tenth

Civilization. This has resulted in an erosion of the Mayor's power this far south. The island of Tierra, at the very tip of Patagonia, now accepts the authority of the Antarctic Council, as does much of the land on the west coast south of about latitude fifty. But not Dalkayel's home town of Zagossa, which is at latitude forty-eight.

During one of the breaks in Dalkayel's discourse, Jannet asked why the Mayor permitted the people of Antarctica to get away with their defiant behaviour.

"What would your Mayor on Koltetra do in that situation?" asked Dalkayel.

"He wouldn't have to do anything," Jannet replied. "No one would ever consider refusing to accept the authority of the Executive Director. It's unthinkable."

"It used to be unthinkable here too. But now it's happened, what action is the Mayor supposed to take? He can't detain an entire continent."

"He could at least isolate it."

"He has. There's only one commissioned beamway connecting to Antarctica, the one running from Puerto Cothani. All the other ways in and out are primitive or inconvenient. Very few people enter or leave the continent regularly. He's also denied anyone in Antarctica access to the Mem system, and little in the way of supplies are imported or exported. That's isolation, I'm sure you'd agree."

"But it's not complete," Jannet persisted.

"Again, what's the Mayor supposed to do? The only grounds for coercion on Earth are to prevent activities which are detrimental to others. If I do something which causes my neighbour distress or discomfort, a sentinel can use minimum necessary force to make me desist. I presume it is the same on Koltetra. But if I choose to make a journey to or from Antarctica, in what way am I distressing or discomforting anyone?"

"I would have thought Kway distresses a lot of people," Jannet remarked, unexpectedly boldly.

"Which is why I'd be detained if I ever met up with a sentinel," said Kway, not taking offence. "Dalkayel distresses no one, so he can go where he pleases: to Ultima Salem, to Luna, to Antarctica, to anywhere."

"Who do we Koltetrians distress?" I asked pertinently.

"No one," said Kway. "If you really wanted to travel openly to Antarctica, the Mayor would probably be unable to stop you by legal means. But then, as your two colleagues who got left behind are finding out, in practice the Mayor doesn't always bother about legality."

"Are you saying he can break the law?"

"That's right."

"If Koltetra's Executive Director did that, he'd be dismissed instantly."

"The Mayor can't be dismissed," said Kway. "If he breaks the law, the offended person can bring the case to the attention of Members of Parliament. They're able to collectively overrule the Mayor if he can't justify his actions. The chances are, though, they'd find in the Mayor's favour. They always do, these days."

"Surely the people here don't think that's a good state of affairs," I said in amazement.

"They're happy with things the way they are," said Dalkayel. "The only ones who'd complain are malcons, and the great majority has no sympathy whatever for that group of people. It's a happy, contented, totally benevolent world they run up there. Perfection itself. Who'd want to change that?"

Malcons could be very perplexing at times. They asked such difficult questions. If everyone except a small anti-social minority was contented, surely it would be madness to change things, for change could only be for the worse. Yet in spite of the contentment of the populace, the situation seemed unsatisfactory. It made me question the purpose of human life and human civilization. What could it be if it wasn't to make all people as happy as possible? I didn't like contemplating such questions; I had never had to do so before. Perhaps, I speculated vaguely, that's another aspect of the malaise afflicting Earth, and that would one day affect Koltetra too; that people don't think about difficult questions.

We climbed for quite a time, the guide going very slowly because of the condition of the road and the poor visibility. After several hours the road began to descend to the strip of land west of the Cordilleras. Fog blanketed the entire journey until we emerged from it quite suddenly a few kilometres before reaching the coast. The darkness was very intense. There were stars in places but most of the sky was cloudy. There was no moon. The blackness revealed nothing except, by implication, how deserted the land was, for there were no lights to be seen in any direction.

We found Zagossa to be a collection of only two hundred dwellings, not all of them occupied, housing about four hundred people. The place was illuminated by a single floodlight mounted high on a pole. (The lighting was the same kind as that in Cairo, only on a much smaller scale.)

Dalkayel lived in a house in the centre of the town with his wife, Leora. Like her husband, Leora was a mortal of about forty-five years of age. Aside from her, the house was empty.

"My children have gone south," she said. "Two boys and a girl. They live in Antarctica now."

Thanks to her children's absence, there was plenty of room for Kway, Jannet, Vallensel and me. It was nice to be able to pass the remainder of the night in warm, comfortable surroundings. It was even nicer to get ourselves and our clothes clean of vicuna's blood.

I felt we were re-entering civilization after a brief, and hopefully never to be repeated foray into pre-civilization barbarism. I hadn't liked being a cave-dwelling 'atavist' at all.

17

Come the morning, we could get a better idea of the geography of the locality. Zagossa was at the northern extremity of a wide, 'U'-shaped bay. The Pacific Ocean seemed to lie almost due south, but we were told this was not so. The bay was, in fact, a relatively small north-running indentation in a longer and wider bay running east-west with the Pacific Ocean lying a hundred kilometres west of our position.

If the sea was the most prominent feature to the south of Zagossa, the mountain was the most prominent to the north. We were told the parts of it visible from the house rose over a thousand metres, while the parts we couldn't see added another five hundred metres to the height. Dalkayel astonished us by saying he still climbed the mountain once in a while just to prove, as he put it, that he wasn't getting old.

I'm not getting old either, but a climb like that would have killed me. Once again, as I had been with Kway and Rivien, I was struck by Dalkayel's physical size. It was not easy to gauge under his clothing but I knew he was stronger than any of us on Koltetra. The explanation occurred to me that the restless, unharnessed energy of Earth's malcons found release in part through sheer hard work — work that was thoroughly pointless. There were special kinds of guide which could fly you up into the mountains if you wished to go there. No one needed to climb.

Aside from the mountain and the sea, Zagossa had little to commend it. It was uncomfortably squeezed between the two, a little cluster of duram houses separated from the moderately calm waters of the bay by the town's only access road. The road worked its way along both sides of the bay, one direction — the direction we had come from — taking you eventually towards Patagonia, the other running west for a while and then north to a town called Tres Rios, which was a hundred and thirty kilometres away by road (on account of the need to skirt the mountain) or eighty kilometres if you flew directly towards it.

Dalkayel and Kway set off early in the afternoon to make arrangements for our collection by the Antarctic Council. They could have done so from the house, but Kway decided to use another location. He was being cautious and anticipating the worst again.

I was becoming concerned about Jannet. She had been hostile to Kway — when he wasn't around! — while we were in the cave, and now extended that hostility to Dalkayel and Leora. She evidently didn't fear them as much as she feared Kway, and expressed herself in ways that might cause offence to less civilized people. For instance, she said she thought Dalkayel and Leora were stupid to live in Zagossa, asserting the place was practically moribund and the weather was awful.

Leora politely explained that her parents lived in Zagossa and that her husband liked the place. As for the weather, well, you got used to it. Climate control wasn't so good in southern parts of Latica.

Speaking to Vallensel and me privately, Jannet asserted that Kway was insane. Indeed, she went so far as to propose that we return to Ultima Salem, even if the Mayor was going to expel us.

"What can we possibly learn from these Antarctic clowns?" she said. "They're violent, destructive, full of the most ridiculous notions, and regressive. They're rebels against civilization and decency and a secure future, and it sullies us to be associated with them.

Koltetra will judge us harshly if we tarry with them much longer, now we know what they stand for."

"But *do* we know?" asked Vallensel.

"Open your eyes," Jannet retorted. "Look at them. If it's possible for the Tenth Civilization to harbour evil, they're it."

As always when listening to other people debating, I could see both sides. Vallensel thought we should give the Antarctic people a proper hearing; Jannet thought we'd given them hearing enough already.

It was an argument which went on for a long time, interrupted only by Leora bringing us refreshments and by our occasional individual absences to visit the bodily waste depository.

As the afternoon wore on, Jannet became openly critical of even Vallensel when the latter was out of the room. Vallensel was similarly, though more moderately, critical of Jannet. I found myself an unofficial confidant and referee to both of them. I could see I needed to make a peace between them, but they had adopted intransigent positions and I had no idea how to bring them together in some sort of agreement.

Kway and Dalkayel got back early in the evening.

"It's all been arranged," Kway reported. "You'll be on your way tomorrow night. And not a moment too soon. I'm in need of a rest after this operation."

It was some time later when Dalkayel entered the room. I knew immediately something was wrong. He looked scared.

"There's a sentinel-aircraft hovering some distance off to the east over the mountain road to Patagonia," he reported. "It seems to be waiting for something. And someone used my Mem terminal this afternoon. I've checked with Leora. It wasn't her. It was one of these three."

Kway's whole countenance changed in an instant. The way he suddenly looked wasn't just frightening; it was terrifying. "Which of you contacted Mem?" he demanded.

"It wasn't me," said Vallensel.

"Or me," I added hastily.

Jannet shook her head.

"I've a hideaway in the mountains you could use," said Dalkayel.

"Forget it," said Kway. "These three couldn't get up a hill without stopping for breath every few minutes. How many men do you know in Zagossa who'd be willing to do the Council a favour?"

"Twenty or so."

"I only need four. Send them up the mountain and tell them not to make themselves too hard to spot. The longer they can avoid being caught, the better are the chances I can get these ungrateful weaklings away from here."

Dalkayel hurried out.

"Whichever of you it was," Kway continued, "you certainly did a good job. They know we're in Zagossa. There'll be sentinels converging on the town along both the access roads. They'll block the exits. The sentinel-aircraft will follow them in, watching to see we don't leave by any other route. If we run they'll chase us. If we stay put, they'll search every house." He gave us a look of undisguised hatred. "I could have had you out tomorrow night. All quiet. No fuss. So one of you had to betray me. I don't know why I bothered with snivelling mice like you."

"What are we going to do?" asked Vallensel.

"You can go back to Koltetra for all I care."

"Can't you destroy the sentinels?"

"That works when they're not expecting attack. Not here. A sentinel is empowered to use minimum necessary force. Bearing in mind what happened when we got you away from the Culture Secretary, this lot are sure to be armed. If I shoot at them, they'll shoot back."

Leora came into the room and said: "I've found a friend who'll help. She's coming over with her guide."

"Let's go," said Kway.

We followed him outside. It was now dusk. The sentinel-aircraft, no longer stationary, was slowly approaching Zagossa.

The four of us got aboard Leora's friend's guide and it carried us to a house on the western edge of the town. The woman who had brought the guide led us inside.

Kway said to her: "Get away from here. Go back to Dal's. Leora will look after you. Leave the guide in case we need it. And thank you."

She nodded and left.

The window at the back of this second house commanded a view of the road running along the western side of the bay and thence towards Tres Rios. We could see two well-separated guides approaching along it.

"Now we wait," said Kway.

Dalkayel came into the house and announced the decoy party was on its way.

By now the trap was tightly closed. The sentinel-aircraft was hovering directly over the town, while, of the two guides coming along the western shoreline, one was very slowly approaching the outskirts. The other was keeping further away. Sentinels were already getting out of the latter. Kway drew his gun.

"Dear reason!" said Jannet suddenly. "Are we going to stand here and do nothing? He's mad. Can't you see he's mad?"

"Bitch!" said Kway. "Don't worry. We're leaving you behind."

"Stop this," she said, with more boldness than I'd

reckoned she was capable of. "All they'll do is send us back to Koltetra."

"One more word out of you and I'll stop *you*," Kway warned.

As we watched, the sentinel-aircraft began moving off eastwards.

"They've spotted the decoys," said Dalkayel. "Give them a hard time, lads."

One of the two sentinel-containing guides blocking the western exit from Zagossa — the one that had yet to discharge its passengers — continued to approach the town. Our best hope was that it would pass the house we were in and join the pursuit of the decoy party.

Jannet made a dash for the door of the room. She reached it before any of us could stop her. Kway raised his gun. For once, I moved with a speed I didn't know I possessed. I forced the weapon ceiling-wards.

"She's not a sentinel," I shouted. "She's a human being."

Kway wrenched the gun from my grasp. "She'll tell them where we are."

"Then she'll tell them."

Kway looked at Vallensel. "Are you with him?" he asked, meaning me, "or are you with us?"

"I'm with Felip on this one," Vallensel replied.

Jannet was now out of Kway's line of fire. Presumably she was making her way along the outer wall of the house. After that she had to turn right and thence down the road to the sentinels in the approaching guide. Certain detention for the rest of us was only minutes away.

"Bloody turds, the lot of you!" said Kway. He then rushed from the room after Jannet.

I remembered what I'd been told about Kway not allowing himself to be detained alive. And I knew in that instant that it was no sick joke, no exaggeration, but literal truth. Without thinking, I hurried after him. Vallensel called me back. I ignored him. Whatever Kway intended, he had to be stopped.

As I ran outside, Jannet, walking as one would on a stroll through a Koltetrian park, turned the corner, emerging from the cover provided by the house and onto the road. Kway was nearby but too far away to grab her and prevent her revealing herself to the sentinels in the approaching guide, which would not yet have passed the house, but must by now have been getting close to it.

Kway hurled himself onto the roadway. He appeared to trip and rolled over. His forward motion carried him into a crouching position. The gun discharged. It was a hasty shot using much more power than necessary. The shock wave and the crash of thunder momentarily checked me.

As I rounded the corner of the house myself, somebody gripped me from behind and pulled me back. It was Vallensel. He slammed me against the wall.

"No, Felip, no," he said desperately.

And then, like a living nightmare, the scene I had glimpsed before Vallensel's intervention overwhelmed me. I had seen the approaching guide, no more than a dark smudge, dissolving into a white-hot ball of ionized gases. A chunk of the road was vaporizing along with it. Jannet, to one side of the direct blast, had been caught by the shock wave and heat. Her clothes and hair had caught fire.

"Jannet," I muttered weakly.

Several flashes and accompanying thunderclaps tore the air. The sentinels from the second guide — the ones that had alighted a distance from Zagossa — were returning Kway's fire. The discharges were well over his head. Mere warnings. If Kway shot at them again, they'd be empowered to kill him. He turned and ran off into the town.

Vallensel peered round the corner of the house. "Back inside," he ordered, trying to manhandle me.

I resisted. "Jannet," I said again.

"Jannet's dead."

I allowed Vallensel to drag me indoors to where Dalkayel still watched and waited.

"Do you want to surrender?" Dalkayel asked.

"I want to meet the Antarctic Council," Vallensel replied.

"And you?" said Dalkayel to me.

I felt I had come so far; to give up now would mean throwing away all the sacrifices. I thought of Kerra telling me not to go twitchy because she had decommissioned a couple of sentinels, and made my decision. There was no time to dither, far less debate the issues. "I'm with him," I said, nodding at Vallensel.

"Right," said Dalkayel. "I don't think we have a hope of escaping, but keep your wits about you. Be ready to do anything I say."

We watched several sentinels rush past in pursuit of Kway. While he was amongst the houses, they couldn't shoot at him for fear of hurting people not involved. Unfortunately it was also harder for him to get a clear line of sight on any of them.

Once Kway's pursuers had gone by, we could see only two sentinels blocking the western exit from Zagossa. One was some distance away, standing in the middle of the road. The other was circumspectly approaching our house.

"When I shout, take a deep breath and hold it," Dalkayel commanded. "We have to get to the guide you came here in. You'll find it's outside, parked in a recess to the left. I'll tell you when."

Ten seconds later, a dart swerved through the open door and imbedded itself in the ceiling. Dalkayel shouted and I breathed in quickly, catching a faint whiff of Trangas as I did so. You want to be happy, I thought, just breathe normally. But my decision had been made. I wasn't even slightly tempted.

The sentinel could have been no more than a few metres from the entrance to the house. Dalkayel snatched up the table that would normally be used for meals.

"Now!" he shouted, and ran out of the door and into the open.

Vallensel was quickest to react, but I wasn't far behind. I saw Dalkayel had caught the neck of the sentinel with the edge of the table. I doubted the table was sharp enough to bring about complete decapitation, but the sentinel was plainly decommissioned nonetheless. I hastened to join Dalkayel and Vallensel on board the guide.

Dalkayel said to the guide: "Tres Rios. Velocidad maxima." And to us: "Just hope I didn't give that sentinel time to transmit a coherent message."

We turned onto the road. Jannet lay where she had fallen. Kway's energy bolt must have missed her by only a metre or two, for the left side of her body was mutilated. Half her head was missing. Her remains were still smouldering.

"What about that?" asked Vallensel, referring to the one remaining sentinel from the second guide which was still blocking the road.

"I'll try and run it down," said Dalkayel.

But before we were anywhere near close to it, it, and a stretch of the road where it was standing, vaporized, caught in a gun blast fired from some distance.

"Thank you, Kway," commented Dalkayel grimly. "A parting gift."

We surged away from the town. Our guide avoided the two gunshot craters in the road by taking briefly to the rough verge. As we passed the second of them, another clap of thunder reached our ears.

"Sweet reason!" I muttered wretchedly to myself.

Looking behind us, we had a clear view of Zagossa beneath its majestic mountain. Although it was getting dark, the floodlight had yet to turn on. As a result, the glow emanating from a location in the upper part of the town was that much more prominent. I guessed it to be a burning house.

The sentinel-aircraft, recalled from the false pursuit to the east, zoomed low over the buildings. As it drew level with the centre of Zagossa, it suddenly lit up. Its height increased violently and it tipped sideways. The air around it, turned into a plasma by Kway's energy bolt, blew outwards, producing a blue and white fireball of an explosion. The aircraft's panflector shielding protected it from vaporization but couldn't save it from being destabilized. It began falling out of the sky. Even then, despite being hit at close range and square on, it might have righted itself, but it was too near the ground. The side of it struck a roof. It dropped further and disappeared amongst the houses, flames and a pall of thick black smoke suddenly marking its location.

"One down," said Dalkayel.

The air was filled with thunder as the sound waves from Kway's shooting down of the aircraft reached our rapidly retreating guide. There were more flashes amongst the now distant houses.

"Do you think he might make it?" I asked.

Dalkayel looked at me but said nothing. Just the slightest shake of his head indicated his answer.

It wasn't distress I felt. More a kind of numbness born of the waste, the hopelessness of it all. "In the name of reason, why doesn't he surrender!" I shouted with frustration — frustration at my inability to stop the madness.

"Not him," said Dalkayel. "Not Kway Myer."

And then the flashes of light ceased. The glow from vaporizations and fires faded. The town's floodlight came on. We reached the headland of Zagossa's bay and turned west, following the coast towards the Pacific Ocean. Zagossa disappeared from sight.

I hardly noticed us travelling on in the gathering darkness. I was too lost in my thoughts, too shocked. As if one death wasn't dreadful enough to come to terms with, I now had to face up to two of them. There was no doubt in my mind about it. For the first time in his life, and I knew also for the last time, Kway's luck had failed him.

18

After a few minutes the road we were fleeing along turned northwards. We came to another 'U'-shaped bay and resumed heading west, travelling on its northern shore in the direction of the Pacific Ocean.

At last, Dalkayel broke the gloomy silence. "The sentinels will be after us soon," he said grimly. "Once they've run the diversionary party to ground and found the lads don't include you two, they'll realize you may have slipped out in the opposite direction."

"Surely Kway opening fire would have convinced them of that," said Vallensel.

Dalkayel didn't agree. "Quite the reverse. They'll think he was trying to divert them from the quarry they're hopefully still chasing up in the hills."

The road turned north again.

"There'll be other sentinel-aircraft called in for support heading this way now," said Dalkayel. "It comes down to a question of time. If the decoy party can evade capture for long enough, they may buy us the time to get to Tres Rios before the sentinels start searching the surrounding countryside."

The road changed direction yet again, this time to the east of north; the coast followed it in an irregular fashion. By then it was over thirty minutes since we had left Zagossa. Given the speed our guide was travelling at, that amounted to a hundred and twenty kilometres of road. An aircraft could cover a distance like that in less than ten minutes. But then they couldn't be sure we were actually on the road and had not taken to the adjacent moorland. That meant they'd have to scan the ground to each side of the road, as well as the road itself. That would slow the pursuit considerably. Vallensel and I both watched the sky around us nervously. We could see no sentinel-aircraft.

"Listen," said Dalkayel. "Assuming we make it to Tres Rios, I want you two to take to the open country this side of the town. I'll then travel on alone until the sentinels catch up with me. I'll probably be questioned, since they'll be aware you were sheltering in my house in Zagossa, but I'll blame that on Kway, saying he threatened Leora and me. As long as they believe that, I won't be detained and should be able to join you later. What you must do for the time being is this. You'll find Tres Rios is quite large for this part of the world. Most of the houses are occupied, but a few, particularly those highest above sea level, are deserted. Wait until it's totally dark, then start making your way past the town. Don't go into it. Skirt it by way of the hills to the east. That'll bring you to a valley. After you cross it you'll come to some outlying dwellings. I don't think any of them are lived in. Make yourselves comfortable in the one furthest from the town. Understand?"

We confirmed we did.

"Good. And remember. No communicating with Mem, no lights, and nothing else that might give your presence away. I'll try and get back to you before dawn."

Tres Rios, illuminated by two pole-mounted floodlights, came into view a few kilometres away. Architecturally it was like a larger version of Zagossa, and the geographical setting was also similar, except that the mountain lay to its east rather than to its north, and the sea lay to the west instead of the south.

Dalkayel stopped the guide to let us out. He gave some further broad directions concerning the route we should take, and left us. As instructed, we walked directly away from the road up a steep incline until we felt safe from detection. Then we began to work our way across the sloping ground overlooking the town.

I saw the aircraft first. I pointed it out to Vallensel, and we quickly crouched down among the rocks which were dotted about in the landscape. The sentinel-aircraft was illuminating the road and a wide strip of verge with a spotlight, but where we were it would be using infra-red imaging to detect anything of interest; i.e. us. Our idea was that by crouching down we'd be mistaken for grazing animals, of which there were many in the hills. That's if we were detected at all, which ideally we wouldn't be.

The sentinel-aircraft flew low over the town, just high enough to avoid striking the pole-mounted floodlights, and then proceeded along the road after Dalkayel. I estimated it would overhaul him within five minutes.

Once the aircraft was out of sight, we resumed our tramp across the hills. We got to the valley Dalkayel had spoken of after about three quarters of an hour, with no bones broken but with a few bruises, the ground being uneven and covered in wet, slippery grass; combined with the darkness, the terrain made occasional falls inevitable.

At the bottom of the valley was a stream several metres wide and a metre deep. We scouted around for a few minutes but could find no way to cross it other than the hard way. The water was fast-flowing and extremely cold, and it was quite an achievement that we both waded from one bank to the other without being bowled over. Nonetheless our legs hurt badly for some time afterwards from being severely chilled. I confess we said a few uncharitable things about Dalkayel in that connection.

By the time we entered the house — duram built — to which we had been directed, we were at the end of our tether. Our bodies, not yet recovered from the rigours of cave-dwelling in Patagonia, were aching and exhausted, and the unremitting wind had sapped our spirits (despite the thermaks we were still wearing). We sank down into the sheltered darkness with boundless relief.

After a time, revival was sufficient to check the house was indeed decommissioned, and subsequently to make ourselves as comfortable as possible. The town's lighting was almost ineffective where we were, some distance up the valley, but it was still bright enough for us to be able to see what we were doing. Once we'd made a few basic arrangements, including re-commissioning the house as far as possible without it being discernible from outside, we settled down, sitting against a wall, listening to the moaning of the wind, and to a steady low-pitched roar that we soon realized was the sound of the sea. Distant from the shore our house may have been, but the wind carried the noise of the waves straight to us.

(The sea was, in fact, the big difference between Zagossa and Tres Rios. Zagossa's bay is sheltered; Tres Rios's faces directly into the Pacific Ocean. The result is a roaring, pounding tumult of waves crashing endlessly against the latter's coastal defences.)

For all the external sounds, a great quiet came upon me. The gloomy twilight of the house seemed to fade and other pictures filled my mind. Sad pictures. Terrible pictures. Every one was a memory of Jannet. I watched the images pass before me with mounting misery, but also with complete acceptance.

"What are we going to tell them?" I asked Vallensel, partly as a means of combating my distress.

"Tell who?" he said dully.

"The people back home. About Jannet."

"We tell them the truth. That she lost her nerve. And in doing so made a couple of errors of judgement. The second error proved to be a fatal one."

"You don't think she was right?"

"Right? To think the malcons — or at least the ones like Kway Myer — are insane? Maybe. But to want to get away from them? No. We came to Earth on a voyage of discovery. You don't discover things by running away in the face of danger. You see it through. And that's what we've got to do."

"It's not right morally, though, is it? Jannet was a good woman."

"Yes, she was a good woman. She didn't deserve to die. But don't forget she imperilled our mission by her actions. My sympathy for her has limits. Anyway, awful though it is, what's done is done. We can't turn back."

"Paradise on Earth," I said sadly. "That it should have come to this."

I stretched out on the floor and tried to sleep. Jannet's burning body kept me awake for a long time, and roused me from my fitful slumbers several times during that longest of nights. Never had I felt so wretched.

*

Kerra was standing in front of me. She was hysterical. "I'll make you pay for Kway," she screamed. She swung the gun in a wide arc. The Mayor's residence, the Parliament building, the Yarway Pyramid, crumpled in a blast of irresistible energy. Koltetra's debating chamber was next in her sights. I begged her to stop, but some mysterious force prevented me from taking action. Kway began to shake me. "Felip! Felip!" he said quietly.

I let go of the ghastly nightmare with a strange mixture of relief and regret, for in its way the reality was as bad. I opened my eyes to the dark house and to Vallensel calling my name as he shook me gently by the shoulder.

196

"Dalkayel is here," he reported.

Dalkayel was over in a corner of the room, dumping stuff on the floor from out of a sack. It turned out to be food sufficient for a few days.

"I'm glad you're here," I said to him. "I was afraid you might be arrested."

"I'm a good actor. They stopped me not ten minutes after you took to the hills. That was a close call. Anyhow, who did they discover they'd caught up with but poor, innocent Dalkayel, so scared by the fighting he didn't even know where he was going. They told me not to worry about Kway Myer — that he was no longer a danger to anyone — and advised me to return home. So that's what I did. By the time I got there, every house had been searched looking for you. Since then they've been scouring the hills. Not in all my days have I known the Mayor to be so determined. Whatever have you Koltetrians done to make him this angry?"

"I wish I knew," I said.

"What will they do when they don't find us in the hills?" asked Vallensel, clearly learning fast about the advantages of anticipating the future.

"I don't know. It's such an unprecedented situation. My guess is they'll tighten the blockade in this part of southern Latica. Anything leaving the locality by road or air will be intercepted. Beyond that, they may search other towns than Zagossa, but it's unlikely. Invading privacy on such a scale would probably lead to Parliament being convened. Too much of a nuisance for everybody, including the Mayor."

"You mean we'll be safe while we stay inside this house, but not if we leave?"

"That's about it."

"So how are we going to get to Antarctica?"

"We'll let the Council worry about that. In which

connection," — Dalkayel took out of his pocket a disc like a call-button but bigger, being about six centimetres across — "I've brought you a present. It's a device made in Antarctica. If there's a Mem terminal nearby, this will pick up Mem information transmissions without Mem being aware of it. It operates on two channels. Press the green side and you hear Mem. A second press turns it off. Press the white side and you'll hear communications from Antarctica. The Council broadcasts operational messages to its personnel living, as I do, under the Mayor's authority, every six hours at one, seven, thirteen and nineteen hours, Salem Meridian Time. On good days when all is well with the world, there won't be any messages. On active days, two or three perhaps. Listen to those broadcasts because that's how the Council will tell us when and how you're to be got away from here."

"Just a thought," said Vallensel, "but what happens if the sentinels do search this town? Shouldn't we plan for that possibility?"

"If they start a search of Tres Rios while you're in it, your chances of escape are very slight. About the only advance plan you can have is to take to the hills now. In that case, you'd be at risk from sentinel-aircraft and exposure to the bad weather. On balance, your best course is to stay here. We'll worry about them searching Tres Rios when they actually do."

"Will you be able to decommission the sentinels if it's necessary?"

"What? And risk going out like Kway? No possibility. He made an awful mess of Zagossa: several houses destroyed, aircraft wreckage scattered all over the place, roads damaged. It's amazing none of the townspeople were killed. That's not my kind of action. Besides, just because I'm a malcon doesn't mean I carry a gun. In fact very few of us possess any kind of weapon. We want to build something better than the Tenth Civilization, not a blood-soaked reconstruction of the first seven."

"It sounds as if you disapprove of Kway," I observed.

"To some extent. But there are occasions when force is justified, and at those times people like Kway have a role to play. If anything, I don't disapprove of Kway so much as of the circumstances that give rise to his sort of person. It's a shame things are the way they are."

Dalkayel's opinion of firearms and his moderate attitude started me revising my view of Earth's malcon community. Kway and his comrades had convinced me they were the malcon norm. Dalkayel made me wonder if perhaps this was not so.

*

My first impression of the house at Tres Rios was that it was a passable place to stay. We were warm, sheltered and clean. And also well fed, for Dalkayel was able to visit us every other night with food and drink and various odds and ends for our comfort. Compared to the cave in Patagonia, we were living in luxury.

Second impressions were less favourable. That was because our only entertainment consisted of using Dalkayel's disc to listen to Mem's babblings, turning it over at the appropriate hours to hear operational messages from the Antarctic Council. On the first day there were none. On the second, there was a single announcement of a collection of some sort from the Sahara Reserve. Nothing was said about us. And so it was also on subsequent days. Boredom and frustration became our predominant emotions. As the house turned into more of a prison and less of a refuge, its suitability was called increasingly into question. There was nothing for us to do in it. A state of affairs like that is endurable for a day or two, but when there is no end in sight, one's patience is badly tried.

Dalkayel could counsel us only bleakly. The Mayor knew we were somewhere in the far south of Latica and had diverted most of his surveillance hybrimorphs to that area, with the result that we simply dared not move. It was plain the sentinels were waiting for us to make a run for it. We would be ill-advised to even show our faces at the windows. The authorities' vigilance in inspecting every vehicle entering or leaving the area was without parallel in Tenth Civilization history. Never before had they persisted for so long and been so thorough. Dalkayel assured us the people in Antarctica were doing their best to come up with a strategy. Covert supporters in the Mayor's domain had been asked to demand the convening of Parliament, the intention being to protest at the 'intolerable' and 'uncivilized' behaviour of the sentinels in southern Latica. The right of citizens to freedom and privacy in their movements was not being respected. So far, that idea had failed to bring Parliament into session or to persuade the Mayor to reconsider. Another idea was to make the Mayor think we had already escaped to somewhere else. No one, as yet, had found a convincing way of doing that. It was good to know we hadn't been forgotten, but our morale suffered nonetheless from the enforced captivity. We became fractious and argumentative.

19

Our house commanded a good view down the valley to the bay. We could follow the course of the large stream — the one we had had to wade through — to its confluence with two other similarly sized watercourses where the valley ended and the central, lowest lying parts of the town were sited. Thereafter, it was hidden by houses. Beyond the town we could see on clear days the restless ocean and the headlands on both the north and south sides of the bay. Clear days were, however, the exception. The view was more often obscured by rain or drizzle.

Which brings me to the subject of meteorology. Considering there was supposed to be a climate control system in operation, the weather was strangely bad. We'd arrived at the Tres Rios house on Segunday 31st, and over the following twenty days to Primaday 34th, I kept a record. (It was something to do.) There was no denying the weather was not what one would expect in a climate controlled environment. While there were sometimes sunny or starlit skies, more often there was either continuous cloud with rain, or broken billowy cloud with showers. The wind was ceaseless, predominantly from the west, with occasional changes to other directions, especially when it was raining. As for the temperature, that was impossible to judge from indoors except by the clothing the townspeople wore when they were out in the open. I saw no one not wearing a thermak, which meant it was definitely cold. After a starry night there were twice even faint traces of frost on the ground early in the morning, though that always cleared quickly within an hour or two of dawn.

Vallensel reckoned the climate control system was serving some purpose that we were unaware of. I disagreed simply because I could conceive of no purpose that would require persistent rain, strong winds and low temperatures. It gave us a topic to discuss, though it was not a pleasant dispute, we both losing our tempers.

The weather during the morning of the twentieth day in our Tres Rios hideout was typically poor. A gale howled in from the west, concentrating in the valley before rushing up towards the mountain tops to the east. The sea was as rough as ever, pounding the coastal defences relentlessly.

We listened, as usual, at 0600 local time for operational messages from Antarctica, of which there were none, and then switched Dalkayel's disc to Mem. It helped — though not much — to relieve the boredom.

The sort of information Mem usually transmits as part of its public information service is utterly uninteresting; news along the lines of 'yesterday Madam X did so-and-so' and 'today Mr Y will visit here-and-there'. Trivial stuff. Nothing ever changes on Earth, nothing new is begun or completed, there are no triumphs or disasters to report. Only rare deaths amongst the important mortal members of the populace suggest even the slightest hint of impermanence. It therefore immediately attracted our attention when Mem announced, in a seemingly routine fashion: "A climatic disturbance has developed centred at latitude sixty-five south, longitude one-one-five west, tracking north-east. Wind speeds in the vicinity of the disturbance are currently approximately one hundred and fifty kilometres per hour. It is not expected the climate control system will be capable of damping the disturbance down. Inhabitants of Latica south of latitude fifty are warned to expect a period of severe atmospheric turbulence and are advised to remain in shelter.

Anticipated arrival time on the western seaboard of Latica is sunrise tomorrow."

We were severely tempted to make enquiries of the Mem terminal. Both of us were of the opinion that a global climate control system never allows conditions to reach a stage where they are beyond being damped down. Certainly the one we were building on Koltetra was not expected to be flawed in that way. We wanted to know how common such a development was and what caused it. But remembering Jannet and speaking no Spanish, we didn't dare ask.

As the day wore on, Mem's commentary on the climatic disturbance increased in priority, also becoming more strident. Some of what was said made no sense to us. Mem stated, for example, that the ocean pumping stations moving warm water from the equatorial regions of the Pacific Ocean to Antarctica had been switched off, and that refrigeration plants in the path of the developing storm were operating at their maximum capacity. This was, we were told, intended to reduce the temperature difference between the ocean and the air circulating in the climatic disturbance to as small a value as possible. The implication was clearly that the storm owed its origin to a cool air mass in contact with the warm ocean. But where had the cool air mass come from? We remarked again the seemingly permanent cold that had assailed us throughout our time in the south of Latica. Vallensel now speculated that the climate control system was defective. I thought such a suggestion was barely credible.

By evening, Mem had changed its forecast. The storm was moving north-east less quickly than previously predicted, which had given it more time to acquire energy. Circulating wind speeds were now averaging two hundred kilometres per hour. A revised arrival time in Latica was given as mid morning tomorrow. Worse still, the storm was tracking further north than originally calculated. Instead of being safely out of its way, we were now directly in its path. Inhabitants of several towns, including Tres Rios and Zagossa, were warned that infrastructure damage was likely.

Naturally, we kept a watch on weather conditions outside the house, but they provided no intimation of what was coming. The sky had cleared in the afternoon and the wind had dropped. A calmness had descended on the scene, disturbed only by the crashing of waves sweeping in eternally from the Pacific Ocean.

Dalkayel turned up after dark. He was clearly very concerned about the storm. "I've never known a typhoon come this far north before," he commented.

"Is that what this is: a typhoon?" I asked.

"Typhoon or hurricane. Either word will do."

Asking Dalkayel what we couldn't ask Mem, Vallensel stated as an indirect questions: "You're saying there have been typhoons before? The expert we spoke to at the Climate Global Monitoring Centre didn't mention them."

"It's not something he'd want to confess to. But south of latitude fifty they get several every year."

"Several a year!" I exclaimed.

"About that. Why do you think the island of Tierra and the tip of mainland Latica give allegiance to the government of Antarctica? It's because nearly everyone who isn't a malcon has left those places for gentler climes."

"But what's the point of these typhoons?" I asked, baffled. "I don't see what they're for."

"They're not for anything. They're just what happens on the boundary between a controlled and an uncontrolled zone."

Vallensel gave me a 'what did I tell you?' look.

"Haven't you realized?" Dalkayel said, picking up on my incomprehension. "The climate control system no longer extends to Antarctica. It's decommissioned in that part of the planet."

I was prepared to be told the system was malfunctioning; I had never contemplated the possibility of being told it wasn't working at all. The global climate control system was the crowning achievement of the Eighth Civilization, its technological masterpiece, the product of a thousand years of human labour which had enabled humankind to repopulate the hitherto hyper-tropical Earth after the Warming. Without it, people would still be confined to, and struggling to survive in, the polar lands. Earth's example had inspired, and was still inspiring, generations of climatological engineers on the New Worlds. And here was Dalkayel telling us that the Tenth Civilization had failed to maintain and protect its most priceless inheritance. Had it not been for the cold wind that was once again blowing outside the house, I would have dismissed him as a liar or as someone in need of psychomedical help.

"How long has Antarctica been uncontrolled?" asked Vallensel.

"I don't know exactly," Dalkayel answered. "Well before my time. I'd guess about three hundred years."

"So it's decommissioned deliberately?"

"Yes."

"Why?" I asked in amazement.

"It's a malcon issue. The way it used to be, the polar regions had two seasons: a cool summer when the sun was in the sky between the two annual equinoxes, and a warm summer during the days of natural darkness when the sun was replaced by an array of heat-and-light Starfire lamps, placed in an orbit taking them over both poles. To give you some idea of their power, the lamps drew energy from about thirty solar flux converters. When they were working you could stand in the open in the far north of Greenland or at the South Pole wearing only the lightest of clothing without discomfort.

"But then the Starfire lamps experienced a system failure. It was bad luck that the repair was estimated to take at least a year. As a result, rather than face so much time in low temperatures, the inhabitants, both in the far north and in Antarctica, opted to be evacuated. With the falling population worldwide, there was no shortage of accommodation for them elsewhere.

"That was the cue for some of us malcons to get on the move. We weren't interested in the polar parts of Merica, Europa and Rossiya, but the south was a different matter: an entire uninhabited continent for the taking. We saw forming a primarily malcon community there as an opportunity to start something new — to get away from the torpor that goes with living up north.

"The Mayor disapproved. He regarded what we were doing as a form of rebellion, which I suppose it was, and called a halt to the Starfire repair work. He thought that would break us. He thought we'd give in. Well, he's still waiting. And as long as our defiance lasts, he's prepared to put up with a few typhoons every year."

"I've never heard of anything so ridiculous," I said. "If there's a dispute between the Mayor and the people of Antarctica, it should be settled by discussion. Carrying on like this is not only uncivilized, it's stupid. Both sides lose from having the Starfire lamps inoperative."

"It could be worse," said Dalkayel. "At least Antarctica's power stations are still allowed to draw on the solar flux converters; which means we can heat the buildings and keep the roads clear of snow and ice. Anyway, I don't agree with you when you say it's stupid. The general view in Antarctica these days is that the

Mayor doesn't really want the malcons living there to surrender. You see, Antarctica provides a neat way of segregating the troublesome elements of Earth's populace. If they returned to the Mayor's jurisdiction, they could go anywhere. And everyone knows they'd only cause trouble. It's better to leave them where they are."

"Then why not repair the Starfire lamps?"

"And be seen to give in to us? He can't do that. Besides, he'd have to make a decision. It's easier to leave things as they are."

I confess to not knowing what to make of Dalkayel's tale. It was too full of intrigue. My conviction was greatly reinforced that the Mayor was a totally unsuitable man to possess authority, but beyond that I could make nothing of what appeared to be a reprehensible situation. The people of Koltetra are going to find it awfully hard to believe this, I thought to myself. It didn't fit with any idea I'd ever had about the Tenth Civilization.

Dalkayel didn't return home that night. His wife was staying at her parents' to keep an eye on them, and had agreed it was more important for him to look after us. He was not inexperienced where typhoons were concerned and reckoned we'd be safe indoors, but he wasn't certain about that.

Neither was Mem. Around midnight, a short while after the artificial lighting had dimmed, Mem announced several towns, including Tres Rios and Zagossa, were to be evacuated 'within hours'. The full force of the typhoon was now expected to reach our location an hour before noon. Wind speeds had been revised up again to two hundred and fifty kilometres per hour, with gusts to an even more terrifying three hundred. It was about this time I began to get worried.

Evacuation was out of the question for Vallensel and

me. We couldn't leave with everyone else because we'd be recognized and detained. In other words, we had to stay where we were, regardless of the danger. Dalkayel was of the opinion the biggest threat was posed by the sea. At Zagossa the dwellings were sheltered to some extent from storm-driven waves by being at the top end of an inlet many kilometres from the Pacific Ocean proper. In contrast, Tres Rios was fully exposed to the fury of the ocean. He had no idea what damage the sea might do, nor how far inland it might penetrate. Our house, which was at least thirty metres above the high water mark and a kilometre inland, ought to be secure. But was it? The situation was highly disturbing. We tried to sleep, with limited success.

At four in the morning, the lighting over the town brightened to daylight intensity. Mem announced that, while the centre of the storm would pass some way to the south of Tres Rios, the winds along our stretch of coast, together with the accompanying sea swell, would do considerable damage and posed a threat to life. The Palatine of Latica had directed that those inhabitants in the path of the typhoon who wished to move to places of safety should prepare to do so immediately. Aside from being kept constantly informed about the situation, she had ordered (from the comfort of her residence in Brasilia) that her First Secretary personally direct the evacuation. He, poor man, was flying south from Santiago and would arrive within the hour. Also heading in our direction were other aircraft from the nearby beamway terminuses including Buenos Aires and Puerto Cothani. They would have on board fetchers to assist with carrying possessions and weak, elderly people. Mem informed us that the many aircraft would have to be away from the typhoon zone by eight o'clock.

After hearing these items of news, sleep became

impossible. The three of us watched through the windows of the house and listened to Mem's announcements being repeated over and over, in Spanish and in English.

As I waited fearfully for the approaching storm, I was struck by the irony of our situation. For twenty days we had thought Tres Rios a boring prison. For twenty days we had been wishing for something to happen. Well, our wish was in the process of being granted. And I, for one, was suddenly thinking a boring prison hadn't been so bad after all.

20

To some extent, while geography had condemned Tres Rios, it also helped, for the beamway connecting Santiago to Puerto Cothani ran only a few hundred kilometres east of the town. Aircraft could therefore travel most of the way to Tres Rios at high speed, quite unaffected by whatever winds might be blowing. Only those last few hundred kilometres had to be covered using chem-ion thrusters and at the mercy of atmospheric turbulence. The location of Tres Rios thus aided, as well as compelled, its evacuation.

From five o'clock onwards, aircraft began arriving, setting down in various open spaces around the town. Each discharged a number of fetchers, which were soon systematically calling at one house after another. They would disappear inside, to re-emerge a while later loaded up with possessions and escorted by the house's occupants. Then it was a short journey to the designated aircraft to wait for a full load.

The first aircraft to leave did so at six o'clock. I remember the time, for as it rose into the air we heard an operational message from the Antarctic Council.

The message stated: "We wish to warn our citizens living in the following towns," — a list including Tres Rios was given — "that a severe storm will pass over you within the next three to six hours. You are recommended to take advantage of the evacuations being offered by the Palatine of Latica. Any of you with personal reasons to prefer evacuation to Antarctica are advised to make your way as soon as possible to location *Field Yellow*. *Nereus* will collect you."

"That's us," said Dalkayel. "The storm may be a

misfortune for everyone else, but it's good news for you, my friends. They'll pick you up while everyone is out of the way."

"It didn't sound like a message specifically for us to me," said Vallensel. "More like for all the malcons in these parts."

"It's meant to. We don't want to give the Mayor any more help catching you than we have to. *Field Yellow* is the code word for a location designated by the Council at the time of the Zagossa business. I and a couple of colleagues are the only people who have been told where it is. So it's definitely a message just for you."

"You malcons think of everything," I said with admiration.

As if to prove the point, Dalkayel went on to tell us where *Field Yellow* was, in case, as he put it, anything unpleasant happened during the storm.

I was puzzled by what he said. *Field Yellow* was a cliff top forty kilometres away overlooking the Pacific Ocean. Surely weren't there much nearer places where an aircraft could land? Dalkayel just grinned and became very mysterious.

"You wait and see," he said. "I'll give you a clue, though. *Nereus* was the name of an ancient deity. Fourth Civilization, I believe."

Beyond that he wouldn't enlighten us. He was so clearly enjoying his secret, it seemed churlish to spoil his fun. We switched the disc receiver back to Mem and watched the activity outside.

As time wore on, the comings and goings became increasingly frenzied. Until about seven, the number of aircraft arriving continued to outstrip the number leaving. Small huddles of people could be seen scurrying this way and that, clutching bundles of one kind or another. Around most of the aircraft were a few individuals waiting for fetchers to get out of the way so that they could take their seats on board.

Several sentinels turned up and began calling on each house to ensure no one was unaware of the situation. They were no danger to us, because they made no attempt to force an entry. If their noisy presence was ignored, they presumably concluded the house was either unoccupied or had already been evacuated, and simply moved on to the next.

By this time, the weather had noticeably deteriorated. Although the town's lighting was still full on, the sky was no longer dark, to the extent that one could see it was totally overcast. The motion of the clouds was impossible to discern, they forming a featureless sheet of lowering grey. To the west, the two headlands on either side of the Tres Rios inlet were visible for a short while after the day broke, but were soon lost from sight as the spray from countless waves was lifted by the strengthening gale to form a kind of drizzle.

A number of people from houses near our own set off down the valley, leaning heavily into the wind. A laden fetcher went ahead of them, providing a small degree of shelter. Guides were remarkable for their absence from the streets; the wind was already too strong for them to be used safely.

Watching the last of the people from the valley literally pushing against the gale as they made their way towards the aircraft waiting in the flatter, lower reaches of the town, I said to Dalkayel: "We'll never get to *Field Yellow* in this." I was aware as I spoke that my voice was raised to offset the growing tumult from outside.

"No," he agreed. "We'll have to wait until the storm has started to die down."

Waiting was easier to talk about than to do. To the howling of the wind and the roar of the sea was added a new sound. It was one I had heard once or twice on Koltetra: the sound of duram creaking under stress. If the house collapsed, we'd be in bad trouble indeed. I had to constantly resist an impulse to make for one of the aircraft still being loaded in a pool of light below us in the town.

At half past seven it began to rain. Almost simultaneously, the first waves broke over the seawall that in normal weather conditions kept Tres Rios safe from flooding. Small cascades of foamy water could be glimpsed amongst the dwellings nearest the beach.

Aircraft stopped arriving. Every few minutes, one would rise into the air, almost but not quite steadily, and turn away to the east. Many passed over or near us, chem-ion thrusters blazing, as they made their way towards the mountains and the Puerto Cothani to Santiago beamway.

A sentinel came down the valley carrying an old man in its arms. Its speed was very erratic as the wind buffeted it. That old man and his rescuer were the last living things we saw.

At eight o'clock precisely, the final five aircraft took off, more or less together. They were quickly swallowed up by the grey monochrome cloud. We didn't hear them go. The howling of the wind, the creaking duram walls, and the beating of rain and spray against the house made that impossible. As I watched the aircraft disappear, the glow from their chem-ion thrusters outlasting their passing for a few seconds, I was filled with a sense of profound desolation. We were alone. Humanity had left this place. I and Vallensel and Dalkayel were beyond help. I fancied we should perish and no one, not the Mayor, not the Antarctic Council, not Roshan and Ruth, not Kerra, would ever know what had happened to us. If this was solitude, I could do without it.

By now the waves coming over the seawall were no longer small affairs, but huge sheets, dwarfing the nearby houses. The wind caught the great white columns of water and dashed them into the town, drenching the lower streets.

The floodlighting switched off. Tres Rios was plunged into twilight. It became difficult to make out the more distant parts of the town with any distinctness; the rain was too heavy. Soon we could see no further than the nearer parts of the valley.

We passed that morning in frightened suspense. Little was said, because we'd have had to shout to make ourselves heard. By degrees the rain grew more torrential and the wind grew more violent. Every moment we thought it can't get any worse than this, and every next moment it did. Uprooted bushes and shrubs bowled past us, heading for the mountains. Much more alarming, since we had lost sight of the sea and had no idea how far inland it was penetrating, were the bits of sea-foam. Soon they took on the appearance of a kind of turbid snow, sweeping up the valley in great flecks and covering the ground in a blotchy brown whiteness.

The worst moment came at eleven. A gust hit us which was so violent it sounded almost like thunder. One of the nearby houses appeared to go out of shape. A large crack extended down one wall. More cracks. A lump fell off the roof. Then quite suddenly the building fell to pieces. Several bits were hurled by the typhoon against a neighbouring dwelling, which disintegrated in turn. We fearfully surveyed our own walls for signs of collapse, but there were none. It was not reassuring. I, for one, was terrified.

And so the morning wore on. On and on. Endlessly. The noise and the fear induced a cataleptic state in us. It felt more like a nightmare than real life.

Around two in the afternoon, things took a turn for the better. The sky lightened, even to the extent that we could make out individual clouds scudding overhead. The rain eased, and the wind gradually blew less hard. The sea came back within the range of visibility, but by then the tide was out and there was nothing spectacular to observe. Eventually, faintly at first, but with increasing clarity, the two headlands returned to view. Finally — and it's hard to express how uplifting this was — patches of blue sky appeared in the far west.

By four o'clock the rain had stopped, and Dalkayel decided it was time we left. Outside, we found the wind was still a lot stronger than we had come to expect at this latitude, but was no longer life-threatening. We also found how close had been our escape. The outer wall of the house that had sheltered us was cracked in several places and was evidently unsafe.

Given that *Field Yellow* was forty kilometres south west of Tres Rios, we'd need a guide to get there. It would not be completely stable in the strong wind, but that was a risk we had to take. If we left it too late, the sentinels would have time to re-establish their presence in the area and we'd be back in captivity, one way or another. The great problem I could foresee was finding a guide that the storm hadn't wrecked.

Making our way down the valley with difficulty against the wind, we were amazed at the extent of the damage. I estimated up to a quarter of the buildings were in need of repair to some degree. A number of others had simply blown away. Much of the larger vegetation — Tres Rios had had no trees — had been uprooted. Of usable guides there were none. Every one of them had been blown over, or been pushed by the wind into a place it couldn't be manoeuvred out of, or been partially buried in debris.

Dalkayel was unperturbed. He didn't lead us into the centre of the town but took us along a narrow road running at an angle to the valley. It soon became a track rather than a road, ascending in a zigzag up towards the mountains. With the wind at our backs it was not an arduous climb.

A few hundred metres above Tres Rios we came to an ancient stone ruin, quite small, only two metres high and ten on each side. Dalkayel led us behind the building. There, sheltering from the wind, was the undamaged guide we were seeking.

"What a stroke of luck," he said, grinning broadly. "People leave their guides in the strangest places."

We got aboard. Dalkayel diagrammed our destination into the guide's delible memory. It set off at once, informing us, as was quite proper, that the wind was gusting above its stability limit. Dalkayel told it to go ahead anyway.

The guide made its way gingerly into Tres Rios, avoiding the obstacles that were littered everywhere. In the lowest parts of the town, which we had to detour to get past, nothing remained intact. Large boulders from the beach had been hurled by the waves right over the seawall and had demolished everything in their path. Many now stood in seawater-filled ponds that the storm had created. Even the seawall itself had several chunks torn out of it. Tres Rios's three streams had become swollen torrents, overflowing their banks and adding to the flooding and destruction. We were fortunate to find an intact bridge so that we could cross to the south side of the town and the road to Zagossa.

"Will this place be repaired?" I asked Dalkayel as we drove by.

"Possibly, but more likely not. The majority of those evacuated won't come back, and those who do probably won't stay for long. They'll never feel safe here in future. You may well have just witnessed a new extension of the Antarctic Council's domain. Only malcons will be prepared to live here from now on."

Once we had left shattered Tres Rios behind, we followed the road to Zagossa for a while. However, after roughly thirty kilometres we separated from the road and headed westwards, keeping approximately to the shoreline. The going was very difficult over the uneven waterlogged ground and the guide was compelled to travel slowly. Fortunately the storm had done little damage in these parts. There were only a few alpacas and some low vegetation to be blown about and both had survived unscathed.

At last we came to *Field Yellow*. The guide halted near the edge of a steep, rugged incline which descended into the sea.

"Wait here," Dalkayel said. He got out of the guide, walked right to the edge of the cliff, and waved slowly with sweeping movements of both arms at the sky to the west. But the sky was empty.

"They'll know we're here," Dalkayel told us as he returned to the guide.

"They will?" I said.

"It's done looking through a tube with mirrors," he said. He had that grin on his face again. There was plainly some private joke being had at Vallensel's and my expense. "Keep your eyes on the sea," he advised us.

I obeyed, but as I didn't know what I was looking for, it was an unhelpful instruction. And what a sea it was! Enormous waves crashed and foamed against the foot of the cliff, making the ground on which we were standing vibrate. Further from the shore, the waves were like an army of hills marching fruitlessly landwards. It was the roughest water I have ever beheld.

"There it is!" exclaimed Dalkayel, pointing out to sea. Naturally, Vallensel and I searched the sky in the indicated direction for an aircraft. We had no success. And then, almost at the same instant, we saw the island emerging from the waves. But this was like no island I had ever come across before. It was silver coloured and tubular in shape. Our view of it was oblique. There were two cylindrical towers on its upper surface, the larger one in the middle, and the smaller one at the end nearer to us. The thing didn't haul itself completely out of the water, but seemed to float there, partially submerged. I judged it to be very large on account of the swell having only a limited effect on it.

"What in the name of reason is that?" I asked, awestruck.

"It's a seaship!" Vallensel exclaimed in a flash of realization. "*Nereus* is a seaship."

"Impressive, isn't it?" said Dalkayel. "A Seventh Civilization invention, appropriately modified. As far as I'm aware, it's the only one of its kind in the galaxy."

As he spoke, the smaller tower opened, though it was too far away for us to make out any details. There was a brief sparkling about the aperture, and then a small magrider emerged, coming towards the cliff top. It landed twenty metres from us. There was nobody in it.

"How far away is that seaship?" asked Vallensel, more astonished than ever.

"About a kilometre at a guess," answered Dalkayel.

"I'm impressed," said Vallensel. "To throw a dissipating beamtrack that far without access to a flux receiver is quite an achievement."

I couldn't argue with that.

"Well," said Dalkayel, "we've made it. Once you're on *Nereus*, you're out of the Mayor's reach. Give my regards to Antarctica."

"Aren't you coming with us?" I asked.

He shook his head. "My wife will be worrying about me."

We walked to the magrider over the wind-ruffled vegetation.

"I'm sorry we didn't manage to get all three of you this far," Dalkayel said in parting. "And if you see her, let Kerra know she has my deepest sympathy. Kway is a loss to us all."

"We will," I promised.

Vallensel and I entered the magrider. Dalkayel waved in farewell, and we rose cleanly into the air. I turned my eyes from Latica to *Nereus*. The outward-bound part of our long, long voyage from Koltetra was at last about to be completed.

Part 4

An Act of War

<h1 align="center">21</h1>

We were greeted on our arrival in the tower structure by an old mortal who introduced himself as Captain Teksillar. He informed us he was in ultimate charge of the seaship.

"We've been waiting a long time for you," he said. "*Nereus* left port four weeks ago as soon as Madam Dyanie told us you were trapped in the south of Latica."

"I only wish we could have got here sooner," I replied. "The last three weeks have done my temper no good at all."

"I can well imagine. It must have been very frustrating to cross so many light-years of space and then be halted by a mere forty kilometres between Tres Rios and here."

I agreed that it had been.

"And now, gentlemen, you've got just two and a half thousand kilometres to go. Submerged, it'll take us about thirty-six hours. We'll be docking at Vostbrok in the morning, the day after tomorrow. Until then, make yourselves at home. I've a few matters to attend to, but after that I'll be free to show you around."

"You mean we've got to be escorted?" said Vallensel, somewhat out of turn.

"Not at all. You are most honoured guests aboard this vessel, as you will be in Antarctica. I think you'll find our treatment of you will contrast favourably with the Mayor's. Go as you please."

I expressed my appreciation of Captain Teksillar's attitude and assured him we would rather explore the seaship in his company than on our own. Vallensel followed my lead, and surprised me by apologizing for his inappropriate remark. I suppose it's hard for even the roughest malcon to be uncivilized in such manifestly civilized company.

It was odd to my ears that Captain Teksillar, on our guided tour of *Nereus*, persistently referred to his seaship without using the 'sea' prefix. In my vocabulary, a ship travels in space. It is a *sea*ship — an ancient mode of transport whose demise occurred in the early years of the Ninth Civilization — which travels on or through water. Listening to Teksillar speak, I soon realized why he did not make the usual distinction. It was simply that he was far more at home plying the oceans, both physically and in his imagination, than in journeying through space. The sea, in a sense, was his 'space'.

Nereus is three hundred and fifty metres long, twenty-five wide, and twenty high, excluding the two towers on its upper surface. The interior walls, as was to be expected, are largely made of duram. The hull, however — and this was only our first surprise — is made of a carbon-silicon-silver polymalloy. As with seaships, I thought polymalloys were obsolete before the advent of the Tenth Civilization. The material was apparently the best for the job. *Nereus* needed a hull that was not going to be corroded, that could withstand great pressure, and was not so brittle it would crack if the seaship suffered an impact. The last point was the most telling, for *Nereus* weighs a hundred and fifty thousand tonnes when travelling submerged. Polymalloys are much better at coping with impact stresses than duram; they can be mangled almost without limit, whereas duram fractures.

Another surprise concerned speed. I calculated that the vessel was only managing sixty-five kilometres an hour, which was awfully slow. Teksillar explained that *Nereus* had never been intended to be used as a rapid means of transport and that there are physical limits on how fast a 'ship' can move through water.

The final surprise was to learn what the seaship was for. After all, in a world laced with magrider beams, and with chem-ion thrusters able to fill in all the gaps, seaships are obsolete, aren't they? Not if you live in Antarctica, they aren't. Aside from facilitating the most sensitive activities of the malcons, as witness our extrication from Latica, *Nereus*'s prime role is to function as an embassy-cum-village. That is why it is so large. With the exception of the Mednean Sea, which is closed off by dams, there is no oceanic expanse of water anywhere on Earth where *Nereus* cannot go. Teksillar's seaship gives the Antarctic Council a claim to seventy per cent of Earth's surface. Its purpose is political more than anything else.

Perhaps the least surprising fact about the seaship was that it was an uneventful sort of place to spend time in (though not as bad as the house in Tres Rios). We travelled to Antarctica submerged and I passed a fair amount of the voyage asleep.

When the coast of Antarctica came into view, *Nereus* began travelling even more slowly and on the surface. Captain Teksillar called us up to the large central tower to show us our first view of what he described as 'the land of the future'.

First impressions were dreadful. There was an unbroken blanket of grey cloud above us, and though it wasn't raining it looked like it should have been. There was a bitterly cold wind at our backs and an air of bleakness over the scene which was worse than anything I had ever encountered on Earth or on Koltetra. Added to which, the vigorous swell imparted a noticeable up-and-down motion to the seaship now it was surfaced which made me feel distinctly queasy.

We watched 'the land of the future' extend slowly above and along the horizon. I did my best not to prejudge it. I've known coasts which appear barren from off-shore but which, on closer inspection, reveal inland a thoroughly fertile prospect. Distant views can be deceptive. Yet my heart sank as we drew nearer. Apart from the coastal fringe, the ground was covered in whiteness. Initially I took that to be frost such as had formed overnight in Tres Rios. But I soon realized it was snow. Snow not only on the mountain tops but on low ground! I was appalled.

Imagine, if you will, someone who has lived for all the life he can remember with the unquestioned belief that Earth has achieved perfection. One day he meets certain people who tell him faults have developed in the perfect system. Preposterous, he thinks, not because perfect systems don't ever become faulty, but because they always repair their faults. So he doesn't believe these people. Then they show him; let him see for himself. But still his brain resists. Our misguided hero sees and accepts, as he is required by logic to do, but always at the back of his mind he is looking for a way to deny the new position and reinstate the old. That's how I was. Every time a further facet of the perfect Earth's unrepaired faults was shown to me, I believed what I saw. Right, I thought, I accept I've been mistaken all my life. And then some new, even more damning evidence would come to light and I would be shocked, and know thereby that complete acceptance still eluded me. That's how I felt when I saw snow-covered Antarctica for the first time. Without climate control, Antarctica at the end of a winter would be snow-covered. It was obvious. But I was still taken aback by the reality. This time, I said to myself, I truly believe the Tenth Civilization is in decline. I will not be surprised in future by what I already know.

*

As planned, we arrived at the port of Vostbrok shortly before noon. The seaship had a kind of dock built for it, into which it fitted like a finger in a glove. We were able to walk from *Nereus*'s central tower directly onto the floor of its enclosure.

The welcome we received was a huge contrast to that given to us in Ultima Salem. An equerry of some sort led us away from the dock into a building, and thence to a fairly large hall, against the far wall of which was a raised stage. The body of the hall was packed with people. On seeing us, they all, as of one mind, began smacking their hands together, thereby producing a considerable din.

"How quaint," said Vallensel in my ear.

We proceeded through the only clear space in the room, leading to the stage. A woman rose to greet us. Her hair was grey, marking her out as a mortal, but her age I guessed at no more than forty-five. She seemed by the set of her face to be a benign person. As was clearly intended, Vallensel and I joined her on the stage.

My experiences in the debating chamber on Koltetra have given me a feel for audience numbers, and my estimate was that most of Antarctica's population was watching this ceremony. In a strange way I felt more nervous here than I ever had on Koltetra, where audiences were much larger. This event seemed somehow of far greater, even unique, importance.

The grey-haired woman raised her arms and the assembled hundreds physically present ceased their hand-smacking and became quiet.

"Gentlemen," she began, addressing Vallensel and me, "may I, as Chief Overseer of the Antarctic Council, welcome you to our continent. I speak for all my people, both here and in the northern lands, when I say we are most honoured to have you among us. I trust you will soon realize, if you do not already, that only now has your voyage from Koltetra reached its true end; that you are with friends who share your aspirations, and who will do their best to see your mission is brought to a successful conclusion.

"It is no exaggeration to say that we have followed your journey here from Ultima Salem with the greatest interest, and at times, I must add, with trepidation. I am sure we are as glad as you will be that it is over at last. We have much to learn from you, as you have from us, and I look forward in the coming days to an open exchange of information and opinions, as befits civilized people. Rest assured, you won't regret coming here. Welcome."

She embraced each of us in turn. The audience broke once more into hand-smacking, something I have since learnt is an ancient way of indicating approval.

Vallensel nodded to me; he was no speechmaker.

I said: "I extend on behalf of Vallensel and myself my gratitude that you are treating us to so warm and friendly a reception. It is all I could have hoped for. I can only echo your words, Madam Overseer, that we have much to tell and much to learn. It will be a privilege to discharge our civilized duty in that respect.

"I would also like to thank you for the efforts made by the people of Antarctica to enable us to get here despite opposition in certain quarters...."

The audience seemed to find that remark amusing, though I had not intended it to be so. It broke my verbal stride and I fell silent. The grey-haired woman took this to mean I had finished, and gestured with an outstretched arm for us to follow her. We walked from the hall to the sound of more applause.

After passing through an ante-room we found

ourselves in the open air. An oddly designed guide pulled up. We had to get down into it rather than up. Inside there was space only to sit, but, that said, the seats were very comfortable and well separated.

"Home," commanded the grey-haired woman, and the car set off.

"Now that the public welcome is over," she went on, "we can be more informal. No bothering with protocol in Antarctica. We leave that to the northerners. I'm Sheila Mress and, in case you haven't worked it out, I'm in charge down here."

"You mean your position is akin to the Mayor's, or Koltetra's Executive Director?" I ventured.

"More or less. I should think I have a closer resemblance to your Executive Director than I do to the Mayor. Old Mose should have been removed a long time ago. He's like a Sumatran sabre-toothed cat: king of his part of the world, but actually a relic whose time is past."

"Old Mose?" I queried.

Sheila leaned forwards conspiratorially. "Sometimes we southerners are a little disrespectful. 'Old Mose' is our name for the Mayor. Strictly speaking he should be called 'Mayor of Jerusalem, Warden of the Yarway Pyramid, President of Parliament, Justiciar Supreme, Constable Keeper of the Peace and Senior Palatine'. That's more respect than most of us can manage, so we settle for 'Old Mose'. 'Old' because he is, and 'Mose' because that's his name."

Outside the car, the duram houses of Vostbrok came suddenly to an end. The ground flanking the road became very rugged. To the left and ahead, the contours blocked the view near at hand; to the right we could see to a distant white mountain. The terrain was devoid of trees and bushes but not bare. A stumpy kind of heather covered it.

"I must admit," said Vallensel, pursuing the subject of Old Mose, "I don't know what 'Mayor of Jerusalem' means. It's a strange form of words."

Sheila explained: "The word 'mayor' was the name of an ancient office of government. It was a title given to the head of a town administration. As often as not, the job was mainly ceremonial. As for Jerusalem, it was the city they buried under the Yarway Pyramid."

"You're saying Jerusalem no longer exists and a mayor was a minor official. So why has the most powerful man on Earth got such a title?"

"It's a history lesson you want," said Sheila. "Okay. It happened like this. When the Ninth Civilization set up the global Parliament, they chose Jerusalem as its location. Within a short space of time it became clear Parliament needed someone to preside over it — someone the ancient parliaments used to call a 'speaker'. Every faction had its preferred candidate and hated everyone else's. Enter the Mayor of Jerusalem, who at that time was exactly that: the top official in Jerusalem. He had the advantage of being neutral and on the spot. Predictably, every faction didn't want to give him the position, but not as much as they didn't want to give it to any other candidate. So he got the job. He's had it ever since. At first it was just a conflict resolution role within Parliament, but by the time Ultima Salem was constructed and the Yarway Pyramid had set the seal on the Tenth Civilization, the Mayor's functions had grown to pretty much what they are today: the man who rules the planet."

The road we were driving along was gradually increasing in altitude. At first there was snow only in patches, but these soon merged to form a continuous covering. The black, snowless ribbon of road stood out starkly behind and in front of us. Overhead, the cloud was so thick it induced a twilight look to the landscape, though it was only early afternoon.

And so, in due course, we came to Merigast, capital of Antarctica, the city where Sheila and the Council live. It lies three hundred metres above and twenty kilometres inland of Vostbrok, and houses some two hundred thousand southerners. (In Antarctica, the people call themselves 'southerners' in preference to 'malcons', which latter word they regard as disparaging.)

What struck me most strongly as we passed along the wide, snow-cleared streets was the number of people going about on foot in the freezing air. There were hybrimorphs of one kind or another around, but very few compared to up north. I even saw grown adults carrying things. A few weeks ago I'd have doubted their sanity. Now I was keeping a more open mind. One tends to equate civilization with easy living. It occurred to me I couldn't think of any good reason why the two sides of the equation went together. Perhaps they didn't. Perhaps in Antarctica civilization was combined with hard living in a hostile climate. Like so much else about southerners, it was an idea that needed digesting.

To my surprise, Sheila Mress's residence was much like any other in the city, except that it was flanked by several annexes for the occasional guests visiting the woman-in-charge. The car pulled up outside the building and we had to walk through the cold to get indoors. Was that a civilized way to treat us? Just what does 'civilized' mean anyway?

Inside, the house was no bigger than my own on Koltetra. If anything, it was a little colder, though not unpleasantly so. There were no living organic items of furniture. Dead things, though, there were in plenty: wooden objects could be seen all around. Once again I wondered where all the hybrimorphs were. Sheila admitted to having only three: a cleaner, a chef, and the car outside. Everything else she did for herself. Even fetching things. I could hardly imagine life without a fetcher.

As I took in my surroundings, I fancied my view of life and the civilization I had always accepted without question in the past was shortly to be challenged as never before.

It turned out to be the safest bet I had ever made.

22

Sheila Mress, Vallensel and I spent the afternoon and the next three days talking about subjects of mutual concern, interspersing our discussions with official functions, such as the banquet held for us the first evening in Merigast, and the Direct Interaction concert on the second evening, when we were treated to a performance of Eleanor Bayley's latest work by the composer herself. It was a superb piece of music. I was pleased to note that audiences in Antarctica respond as they do elsewhere, by applauding with a collective melodic waveform. It was well deserved.

These public engagements aside, our talks with Sheila, which were, after all, what we had come to her continent for, absorbed all our waking hours. The contrast with Old Mose was as sharp as that of white with black. Only now that we had Sheila for comparison was it brought home to us just how stark and hostile our reception in Ultima Salem had been. Up north, for all its superficial familiarity, I had felt like an unwanted nuisance; in Antarctica, for all its superficial strangeness, I felt like a valued friend. It made a lot of difference.

The other eleven members of the Antarctic Council — Sheila being the senior-most of them — joined the discussions intermittently to add their own worthy contributions. I noticed there were never more than two or three of them present at any one time. This, they explained, was because they took the view that it would have been overwhelming for Vallensel and me to have to talk to all of them at once, not to mention a display of bad manners on their part. Such was the consideration shown to us. They may have forsaken some of the machinery of civilization, but their standards of conduct remained exemplary.

We spent roughly a quarter of the time telling Sheila about Koltetra. Her interest was not merely a case of being polite. She asked many perceptive questions, and proffered advice on how to deal with certain of Koltetra's problems which we could pass on when we returned there.

But it was Sheila's comments about Earth which provided the critical revelation for us. "Imagine," she said, "a world whose inhabitants have perfect knowledge; that is, they know everything it is possible for them to know, given the nature of the universe. Imagine also that they have perfect technology; that is, they can in principle do anything it is possible to do. Then give them virtually limitless energy; six thousand orbiting solar flux converters, each capable of delivering as much power as would have satisfied the needs of an entire palatinate in the heyday of the Seventh Civilization before the Warming. Finally, give them control over their own genome so that they can direct their evolution where they will. That is a description of a mature Tenth Civilization. It is a description of the state of affairs that humankind has laboured to bring about ever since the first humans decided they didn't like the world as they found it. They sought the knowledge and the power to enable them to fashion Earth to their liking. It was a long journey. From the dawn of the First Civilization on the Nile in the year 1, to the establishment of the Tenth Civilization five thousand eight hundred years ago, covers a span of seven thousand three hundred and fifty years. They were years of war and suffering and struggle. And then that ultimate goal was reached. It's the goal you're aiming for on Koltetra, and that every New World works ceaselessly to attain. Perfection.

234

"And so we created paradise on Earth. Unfortunately there's a slight qualification to be added to the description of this idyllic state. Because unpredictability is a fundamental part of all physical processes, it is not possible to avoid occasional accidents, breakdowns and failures. So what do you do? You build self-repair into your paradise. It becomes immortal. A paradise not just for the present, but forever. That too we have built on Earth.

"That leaves one other weakness to confront: human nature. If you have the technology to do whatever you like, sure enough two people will come along wanting to do mutually exclusive things. One must stand aside for the other. In practice, they fight. Sometimes they kill one another. Where's your paradise then? Too often, it's reduced to a pile of rubble. And, astonishing though it is to us, that's exactly what used to happen. Endless endemic conflict was the prime characteristic of the first seven civilizations.

"That's where genetic intervention comes in. This tool that was originally developed to remove genetic diseases at their point of origin can also be used to treat the 'disease' of human conflict. And disease it must surely be. For, having attained perfection, you realize as never before that all conflict must necessarily be destructive. When you are at the summit, every path leads downwards. Conflict becomes in all cases harmful, and therefore always abnormal, which means that any emotion which produces conflict must also be abnormal. A disease.

"So you begin collectively to use genetic intervention to alter the very structure of the human brain. You aim for no less than to purge human nature of its aggressiveness, and thereby to eliminate conflict. No coercion is needed. It's not in parents' interest to have rebellious and destructive children. The result is that over the millennia conflict becomes rare. Less and less does the anger of debate, far less the clash of arms, disturb the peace. And so it is on Earth.

"Regrettably there are a few people left out of the general beneficence. Dissatisfied immortals from an earlier age, and discontented parents who vent their frustration by deliberately conceiving aggressive children. This small dwindling minority, this last remnant of a bestial past, are to be pitied. And occasionally restrained from their troublesome acts of violence. They are the demon in paradise. But not to worry. The ultimate irony is that the system is designed to cope with malcons. Do you know what the philosophy is? Think of the worst possible damage the malcons might plausibly do, multiply it by ten, and ensure the self-repair capability of the system can cope with it. In other words, no matter how much damage we southerners do, paradise can always regenerate itself. It's indestructible.

"If you're one of the contented people, what I've said would sound like a fair account of how Earth is; and indeed of how it ought to be. It is, I would guess, how Koltetrians see it without exception. It's how the two of you saw it until you came here. Maybe it's true. Perhaps we southerners are a remnant: possessors of a kind of personality that has become redundant; an irrelevance.

"So. That's the world of the Tenth Civilization. What I'd like to know now is what you make of it. Let me have your opinions, gentlemen?"

Vallensel spoke first. "You're forgetting the decline in numbers. I've seen Chaytambeor. That's not paradise. From what I've heard, humankind up north is dying out. Where's the perfection in that?"

"I don't think falling numbers are that significant. Societal models indicate they'll stabilize eventually. As

236

for Chaytambeor and the other off-Earth settlements, who wants to live in them? It's nicer here."

"You sound just like Ruth," said Vallensel crossly.

My own reaction to Sheila was quite different. I know a philosopher when I hear one. She was giving us a matter-of-fact analysis, deliberately avoiding any emotional content. It was fascinating, not least because I was hearing my own amorphous views expressed methodically.

"What you've been doing is putting the case for the Mayor," I said. "Before I venture my own opinion, I'd like to know how *you* see it as Chief Overseer."

"I congratulate you on your perceptiveness, Felip. Okay, I'll put the Antarctic case before you tell me what you think. The way it looks to me, far from being a remnant, we southerners hold the key to the future. It is the Tenth Civilization that is a thing of the past. It has nowhere left to go. It is complete. It has become like its symbol, the Yarway Pyramid. Changeless. Where is the life in changeless things? Where is the humanity?"

"But surely," I said provocatively, "when the perfect state has been attained, change cannot but be evil, for it must destroy what is perfect. If you have a perfect world populated by happy people, to change it to something less is madness. You'd create a world of faults and misery. Is that what you advocate? Destructive change?"

"I think on balance it would be preferable to a world of bleating sheep, yes."

"How can you seriously say that? Make people unhappy and they'll fight. The old, mutually exclusive desires will resurface. You've only to look at history to see what that leads to. Wars and cruelty and pain. And with the weapons we could construct, humankind would probably turn Earth into a global ruin. Better a paradise for sheep than a world ripped to pieces."

"I see you're back in the debating chamber on Koltetra," said Sheila, smiling.

I smiled back. "True enough. I want to see it your way, but the fact is, when I return to Koltetra, what I'm saying to you is what will be said to me. And the case you've put so far, to be frank, won't alter Koltetra's course one bit."

"I take your point. Let me state it this way. You're immortal, are you not?"

"Yes I am."

"And happy to be?"

"Yes."

"Do you see yourself in individual terms in the same light as the Tenth Civilization? Both of you traveling changelessly into the indefinite future, both of you with perfect 'bodies' that repair themselves forever. Do you see that kind of identity between an immortal person and the immortal Tenth Civilization?"

"Yes, I suppose I do."

"Wrong, Felip," said Sheila forcefully. "Are you the same person now that you were a hundred years ago?"

"Yes," I replied cautiously, wondering where Sheila was leading.

"Physically, yes," she agreed. "But mentally you aren't. You've discarded old memories to make way for new ones. You're a different person. You're changing constantly. That's exactly what the Tenth Civilization doesn't do. There's no change up north. You told me yourself you became fed up with being a Congressman. That's change. It's part of being alive. Just think. If you were a totally changeless person, could you really consider yourself truly alive?"

Vallensel thought this was amusing, for it was a long time since I'd been taken by surprise in a debate.

"I don't think the question would even occur to me if I

was completely changeless," I replied, trying to sidestep. But there was no escape.

"Precisely. It doesn't occur to them up north. They're dead and they don't even know it. The paradise being built on Koltetra is no more than a cosy tomb. Living things, be they viruses or human beings or entire societies, are always changing. That is one of their defining characteristics. Do you realize the Tenth Civilization has been around on Earth longer than the first seven put together? Most people are proud of that. And I would be too if today's civilization differed from that of a thousand years ago. But it doesn't, apart from the few things that haven't been repaired and the smaller number of people alive. Otherwise it's exactly the same. It's moribund. That's why I'm living in this uncomfortable wilderness trying to build something new, instead of lazing on some Mednean Sea beach watching the time passing by all day."

"I accept what you say about change and life being closely related, but I don't think destroying the Tenth Civilization is rational. Your proposed cure is worse than the disease."

"Look, Felip. What's the point of climbing a mountain if all you do when you get to the summit is sit there doing nothing? The human, alive thing to do is select another summit somewhere else and set off for that. Certainly you have to descend a way, but you soon climb back up again."

"So you want to replace the Tenth Civilization with an Eleventh?"

"That's how we see it, yes."

"But you're doing exactly what the builders of the Tenth did. They disliked Earth how it was, so they changed it until it was perfect for them. That's what you're proposing: changing the world until it's perfect for you. Then you're right back where you started, with a perfect civilization. So why bother. Settle for the perfect planet you've already got and save everyone from the trauma of taking it all to pieces just to reshape it differently."

"That's a little too simplistic. Let me tell you my dream. It's a society perpetually rebuilding itself, pulling down old structures and putting up new ones; a society of continual change; a society always striving to reach a goal, but a goal which is forever moving its position. One could never be bored in a world like that."

"It's an interesting dream, but difficult to achieve. I can see endless conflicts about selecting the changing goals. I'm far from convinced it would turn out to be an improvement on the Tenth Civilization."

"To be honest, I'm not convinced either," said Sheila disarmingly. "All I can say is, let's go there and find out. Maybe it would be a big mistake; maybe not."

Vallensel had listened to this dialogue without comment. Now he said: "The way it seems to me, perfection itself is the problem. Build the perfect system and what have you got left to do but wait for death?"

"But if you don't strive for perfection, what else is there to strive for?" I asked.

Vallensel shrugged. "I don't know. But for me, fighting my way to a goal is fun, so when I've arrived I want to move on to the next goal and start all over again. I agree with Sheila, Felip, not you."

So for the most part did I. Perfection itself was the error. It was perfection that lay behind the apathy and the decay. The mystery of Earth that we had crossed fifteen light-years to investigate was almost completely solved. My unease that by contacting the malcons I had set in motion a sequence of events that had led to two deaths was much reduced. I knew I would never have discovered the truth without speaking to Sheila Mress.

Only two things continued to puzzle me. One was that the decision to drop out of the Galactic Information Grid had been taken positively. It wasn't a can't-be-bothered matter. Parliament had *chosen* to stop repairs. The second was why the Mayor had been so determined to prevent us getting to Antarctica. Sheila could enlighten us on neither of those things. I continued to wonder.

I also wondered about something else. How was I ever going to convince the people of Koltetra that the goal they'd been pursuing for the last six and a half thousand years was a disaster in disguise? The arguments simply weren't strong enough. Madam Magrit would tear me to shreds.

23

After three days of talks we had covered all that we wanted to say to one another and were in need of a rest. Sheila also had the business of returning us to our ship, and thence to Koltetra, to arrange. She didn't think it was going to be an easy matter.

"Here in Antarctica," she told us at one point in our conversations, "there is no space capability. After the climate control system failed, the space-capable vessels went north with the people. There were none for us to inherit when we moved in. And since then, the Mayor's rigorously kept spacecraft out of our hands. We do enough damage on Earth; the last thing he wants is for us to go doing it in orbit as well. In theory we could develop our own independent capability, but our resources are too constrained to permit it at the moment. So we can't get you to your ship. You need the Mayor's agreement, I regret to say."

"Can't we just return to Ultima Salem?" I asked. "Then Old Mose can expel us like he was going to anyway."

"That would be the ideal solution," Sheila agreed. "But you're forgetting you've been involved in criminal activities. Someone has been killed. If you were citizens of Earth, your freedom might be curtailed on that account. As foreigners, I don't know. There's no precedent to go on. I can't guarantee the Mayor won't send you off to a psychotherapy centre, so caution is called for."

This possibility was highly unexpected. I had become accustomed to the notion that the Mayor was straining every muscle to get us expelled. The thought that he might shift his policy through a hundred and eighty degrees was novel, to say the least.

"It makes a kind of sense," said Vallensel. "Old Mose wanted to stop us getting to Antarctica. That suggests he thinks we'll find out something from meeting the southerners that he doesn't want communicated to the New Worlds. Since he's failed to prevent us getting here, the only way he can ensure his dark secret stays secret is to stop us leaving."

"I could understand that if I knew what his dark secret is," I remarked angrily. "But I don't."

Neither Vallensel nor Sheila nor the other members of the Antarctic Council knew either. It was a frustrating mystery.

Sheila did her best to put our minds at rest on the subject of our departure from Earth. "Don't be too down-hearted. The Mayor and I don't exactly talk to one another, but there are channels of communication I can sound out. I'll ask for a promise of unmolested passage for you to your ship. You never know, Old Mose may be agreeable."

It was an unsatisfactory way to leave the matter, but the situation was not within our power to control. Sheila expected a reply to her enquiries within three or four days. I was not optimistic about what she'd be told.

*

Vallensel and I had been allocated separate annexes to Sheila's house in which to live, and were told we could be based there while we remained in Antarctica. We had the status of honoured guests and could do as we pleased.

That evening was the first free of official engagements, and I planned to spend it making a start on compiling a summary report of our talks. I reckoned it would need a lot of drafting and redrafting before I could seriously present it to the Ruling Congress of Koltetra. Vallensel concurred with my suggestion that he should draw up a similar document independently which we could compare with mine later.

I had just begun the task when I was summoned to the main entrance of the house. Someone wanted to see me. I found Kerra Dyanie waiting in the porch, her thermak over her arm. The sight of her provoked a thorough mess of conflicting emotions in me. I was pleased she had called, because there was something about her I found strongly attractive; yet I was also confused because I didn't know what to say, frightened lest she held me responsible for the death of her husband, and guilty because there were many ways during those last fatal minutes in Zagossa when I could have saved his life if only I'd 'anticipated'. I tried to say something sensible but the only word that came out was hello.

"Can you spare me some time?" she asked.

"Of course I can," I assured her. "Come in." I led her into the living room. "Kerra, I'm er...."

"Kway's dead, Felip," she said unemotionally. "I haven't come here to talk about that."

I looked at her, not knowing what to think. Just for an instant I saw something in her face that I didn't understand, but it quickly passed.

"You're supposed to offer me some hospitality, you rude man," she said.

"Right. Server!" I called out.

The server came trundling in. "Yes sir?" it said.

"What would you like?" I asked Kerra.

"Nothing for me," she replied.

I was expecting any answer but that.

She laughed. I had to admire her technique for breaking up the tension. It was worth a smile.

244

"Sorry, Felip. I couldn't resist. You were being so serious. I'll have a glass of sweet-milk, please."

"I'll have one as well," I instructed the server.

It went out.

"Well," she asked, "was it worth your while coming here?"

"Definitely yes. I think I've learnt enough to submit a coherent report to the Koltetrian Congress. Sheila Mress is an informative woman with some interesting ideas."

"You're very lucky. There can be few people who get the chance to change the course of history like you will on the New Worlds."

"I wish it was as easy as that."

"Why wouldn't it be?"

"I just don't think they'll listen. I know I took a lot of convincing that the Tenth Civilization isn't the answer to everything. And I've seen the contrary evidence first hand. How much harder for the people of the New Worlds, who'll only have my report and Vallensel's to go on."

"You seem to be rather defeatist, Felip."

"Oh, not really. I'll make them listen, even if it takes years. It's going to be hard work, that's all."

The server reappeared with our drinks. We took them and sat down facing each other.

"Talking of work," she said, "that's the reason for my visit tonight. I've got nothing to do at the moment. The Council won't send me up north because they're afraid I might behave unwisely. You know. Distraught woman wreaking vengeance. I've been advised to recuperate for a while. The trouble with that is it's not helping to take my mind off things. I need to be kept busy." She looked at me but didn't seem able to complete the line of reasoning.

I told her: "I've got a few days before Sheila can let

me know where Vallensel and I stand as regards the Mayor allowing us to return to our ship. If I can be of any service, you've only to ask."

"Then I'm asking."

I looked into her eyes. Try as I might, I could find no trace there of the woman who could callously decommission sentinels like it was a normal part of everyday life. Before me now was an unhappy human being who needed my help. It was my civilized duty.

"Antarctica's your continent," I said. "You know what there is to do here that could occupy us. Have you got anything in mind?"

"I could show you around. But then I thought, that's what the Culture Secretary did, and I don't want to be like her." She looked down at her feet for a few seconds. "Would you like to try something completely different?"

For a brief, and I'll confess rather alarming moment, I thought she was leading in a direction not appropriate for a widow of a mere four weeks. But it was my mind thinking carnally, not hers.

"Do you know what a horse is?" she asked.

"Of course I do. Koltetra isn't that primitive. We have herds of them. They roam freely and eat the vegetation."

"Have you ever ridden one?"

"Have I ever *what* one?"

"Ridden one."

"I didn't realize you could. Isn't it rather dangerous? How do you know where it's going to go?"

"If it's a wild one it'd be dangerous. But we have tame ones. They let you steer them."

"That's certainly something different," I agreed.

"Forget it if you'd rather not."

I had to admit it. She'd come up with a first rate way of occupying herself, so I said: "It's a great idea. It'll be something I can teach them on Koltetra when I get back."

246

She drained her glass. "Good," she said. "You know, Kway and I were always pretty sufficient company for one another. We didn't have many friends. And now he's gone — silly, isn't it? I thought he was indestructible — the few people I do know are either too busy, or they remind me of what I want to forget, or they try to smother me with sympathy. Then I recalled the gentleman Koltetrian. I didn't think you'd let me down, somehow. Just don't go condoling on me, okay?"

"Okay," I agreed.

"One other thing. Shall we invite Vallensel along as well?"

"I suppose we could."

"I'd be twice as occupied if we did," she remarked reflectively.

"Then we shall."

"I'm glad. I'm quite looking forward to it already. I hadn't better stay any longer. There'll be things to organize. Is it all right with you if we set off early tomorrow?"

I said it was. She stood up and I escorted her to the front door. She put her thermak back on.

"Goodnight then, Felip."

"Goodnight, Kerra."

She looked at me with a serious expression on her face, and said: "On second thoughts, would you mind terribly if we left Vallensel behind? I shall have my work cut out looking after one equestrian novice. Two might be a bit much."

"I can understand that," I replied, equally seriously. "It's up to you to decide about Vallensel."

"Yes, but would you mind if he didn't come with us?"

"Not really."

She nodded, said goodnight again, and walked off into the icy darkness. There was no sign of a guide. I concluded she was returning to wherever she came from on foot. And in that weather too! The people of Antarctica certainly seemed to have a liking for the hard life.

I tried to get back to report-writing, but I couldn't summon up the concentration. I looked up the meaning of 'equestrian' and went to bed.

*

Next morning, I woke early, full of anticipation, only to discover the penalty of a decommissioned climate control system. It had clouded over during the night and was snowing vigorously. Kerra called round to suggest we delay our departure, with the result that Vallensel and I spent the day writing our reports.

By nightfall, the two of us were in a position to compare what we had written and found we agreed surprisingly well. We also reached an understanding about going our separate ways for a day or two. He was very sympathetic where Kerra was concerned, but less so with me, cautioning me in a brotherly fashion against taking advantage of her. I assured him firmly that he had nothing to worry about. I am not an ignoble man.

*

The bad weather cleared during the evening, permitting Kerra and me to leave snowy Merigast late the following morning. Though it remained cloudy with a strong wind, it was nothing so unpleasant as to deter us. And the weather forecast was fairly good; i.e. no typhoons!

We made the flight of five hundred kilometres northwards above the clouds. Consequently I was unable to see the ground, but my companion showed me what I was missing using maps and pictures aboard the aircraft. The land below, I was told, is called the Pen — a long thin peninsular reaching to within about a thousand kilometres of Tierra. A sizable mountain range runs down it, now permanently snow-covered. To the west of the mountains there is little in the way of habitation, it being extremely windswept. The only west coast town of any significance is Vostbrok, which lies at the southern limit of the typhoon zone. Other than that, the shore belongs to seabirds. Indeed, someone had prevailed on the authorities to resurrect a number of extinct species from the archives and reintroduce them to the continent. After an absence of nearly eight thousand years, penguins once again nest on the icy, wind-swept fringe of Antarctica and hunt fishes in the sea.

The east coast of the Pen is, in contrast, much more hospitable. In the lee of the mountains it is often quite warm, especially in summer, thanks in part to the ocean pumping stations that keep the sea from becoming cold. There are many small towns along the coast; taken together they house about a quarter of Antarctica's population.

We landed among the eastern foothills of the Pen at an inland settlement called Ramska. I was relieved to find the place free of snow, though it was nonetheless very cold — slightly below freezing.

On arrival, it soon became clear I was rated an 'important person'. The citizens of the little town repeated the welcome accorded me earlier in Vostbrok. A sort of ask-and-it's-yours policy was put into effect. Kerra considered it very useful because it enabled us to open a number of metaphorical doors far quicker than would otherwise have been possible. And I found it gratifying to have strangers approach me with enquiries of what I thought of Antarctica, and of what I thought of this or that issue confronting Earth today. It was marvellous to be appreciated.

The enthusiasm of the locals was, at first, almost overwhelming. Kerra had brought quite a quantity of things with her and these were carried by willing hands. And when we called into the town's hotel, the owner, a far-sighted immortal who'd built the place when the first malcons began settling the continent, allocated us two of his best rooms.

We spent the remainder of the day wandering around the town and the nearby fields, and pouring over various maps of the area, deciding where we'd go. Kerra had been to Ramska before and knew the territory, so I was happy to let her make the decisions. It certainly kept her occupied.

And it gave me something unexpected to think about on my own account. I couldn't help noticing I was getting to like Kerra Dyanie. Quite a lot.

I didn't know what to make of that, really. After all, I would shortly be going home to Koltetra; and she would be looking to rebuild her life with a new southern partner. Even a short-term relationship between us was out of the question. Any such possibility would have been better not even occurring to me.

But it did....

24

When the next day got round to dawning — the nights are long at this latitude and time of the year — it was only the unpredictable weather that could have upset our plans, but our luck held. We were treated to a warm day (in the context of the locality and the fact that it was the end of winter) and a mostly blue sky.

We had our breakfast, and then Kerra gave me my first surprise.

"The stables," she said, "are a couple of kilometres out of town. We'll walk. It'll toughen you up a bit."

Privately I had no desire to be toughened up. Publicly, though, I made no protest. I could hardly begin the day by complaining. And while I didn't consider lack of toughness to be a trait needing a remedy, she obviously did, and I was not disposed to disappoint her.

Her second surprise was to expect me to carry things. She handed me a sort of shoulder harness possessing large pouches into which she stuffed various items of food. I watched her put hers on and followed her example. A rucksack, she called it.

Her third surprise was going too far. She buckled on a large belt containing a number of loops into which she fixed twenty or so Trangas darts and a small hand-launcher. She didn't propose I equip myself similarly, but I objected nonetheless.

"What *are* you doing?" I asked.

"Just a precaution, Felip," she replied.

"Against what?"

"Unfriendly people."

"Surely you don't think the Mayor will try and detain us down here."

"Not the Mayor. We'll have plenty of time to talk about it later. Just remember, it's only Trangas. I probably won't have to use it, and if I do it won't hurt anyone."

We set off from the hotel in the direction of the mountains, reaching the stables in about twenty-five minutes. I was quite pleased with myself for I didn't have to stop once, not even on the hill.

Our arrival must have been expected, since the people at the stables gave me the 'important person' treatment even before I'd been introduced. It took them some time to get around to what we had come for, namely a couple of horses. They led two beasts out from one of the rooms of the stables opening directly onto the courtyard.

When you see a horse at a distance, it looks large. (It is in fact the largest animal so far resurrected on Koltetra.) When you have one standing next to you that you're supposed to climb up on, it looks enormous. The horse presented to me had a kind of seat tied midway along its back, and some straps attached removably to its head. The whole contrivance looked awfully unsafe.

"Watch what I do," said Kerra. She put her foot into the footrest dangling from the seat, and with apparently complete ease rose lithely into a sitting position, swinging her free leg over to the far side of the horse as she did so.

Feeling severely daunted by what she'd made look so easy and which I was sure must be awfully difficult, I raised my left foot. My misgivings immediately came true. To get the foot into the footrest required not only that I balance on one leg, but that the other had to be contorted at a most difficult angle. Added to that, the head-straps I held in my hands seemed too insubstantial to haul myself up by, and I reckoned the horse might object if I did use them in that way. Nevertheless, I

252

refused to be defeated. (Did I have a choice?) By some miracle I got my left foot in place — then disaster! The horse decided to move, only a fraction it's true, but it was enough to make me lose my balance. Only my grasp of the head-straps kept me upright. I sort of half-twisted and hit the horse's flank with my shoulder. Hesitate now, I thought, and I'm lost. I gritted my teeth, put my foot back in place, and pulled on the head-straps, hopping up with my other leg at the same moment. The animal snorted and took a step backwards, but by then I was committed. To my surprise — and, I suspect, the horse's — I came to rest in roughly the correct position, my right leg dangling, my hands clutching the straps, and my arms partly wrapped round the horse's neck. From up on high, the animal felt most unstable, and it needed great resolve to lean back into an upright position. Then, very cautiously, I peered down the right hand side of the horse to find the other footrest. With that sorted out, I permitted myself to feel the relief that comes with the successful accomplishment of a dangerous task.

That, of course, was only the preliminary. Next came instructions on how to get the animal moving, how to stop it, and how to steer it in the interim. The guidance technique struck me as excessively primitive. I wondered no one had thought to incorporate into the horse genome a few genes that would provide horses' bodies with a lever or two for a rider to use. But then I suppose if you were doing that you'd also add a hollow body to shelter passengers in and either wheels or a lot more legs, until before you knew it you'd have redesigned the horse and turned it into a novel kind of guide.

We set off from the stables at a slow walk which, as my confidence grew, was increased to a faster walk. It wasn't so hard once you got the knack of it.

We kept on the level for the rest of the morning,

heading broadly north. The terrain we encountered was rocky and undulating in a craggy way, with mosses and heather underfoot. Lichen encrustations abounded where the ground was too steep for vegetation proper to anchor itself. Trees there were, but isolated, being in ones and twos. All of them were bare. There was no snow to be seen, except on the higher ground, but an unmistakably frosty chill hung in the air. The sun shone brightly, yet always remained very low in the northern sky, imparting little warmth. There was a bleakness to the scenery which contrasted adversely with what I had experienced up in the Mayor's part of Earth.

When I felt confident enough, we turned west and ascended a little way into the mountains. There we found a nice view with a north-easterly aspect and dismounted to look at it from a sheltered position. It was a good place to eat the food Kerra had stored in our rucksacks.

"This land has seen more changes in the last ten thousand years than any other place on Earth," she mused as we looked at the scene. She pointed out a small lake in the near distance, brilliant in the light of the wan sun. "Before the Warming, that would have been solid ice under a huge thickness of snow. All around here would have been a lethally cold wilderness. Then came the Warming, which turned it into a rocky desert where a few million survivors managed to keep the human species going. Climate control changed it yet again, giving the land long, warm summers. Woods sprang up. There were meadows and heat hazes and birds chirping and flowers. In terms of Earth's lifespan it lasted for so little time. A flicker of paradise before it reverted to this. Icy moorland. Given the rate at which Antarctica is cooling, it's predicted there'll soon be snow on the ground here all year round again."

I heard what she said but found it impossible to

visualize. A vivid imagination has never been one of my strong points.

"We have places like this on Koltetra," I said between mouthfuls. "Each time we extend our climate control system they get fewer in number."

"Don't you like wildernesses, then?"

"Not much. They aren't civilized."

"What nonsense. This is a beautiful place. I can feel at home here more than anywhere up north. What's civilization got to do with it?"

"You can't build civilizations in barren lands. Civilization goes with fertile soil, with environments that are friendly to humans. This place — and I agree it's beautiful — is not civilized. It's wild."

"Yes, it's wild, but we're successfully building a civilization here despite that. Being wild makes it harder, not impossible."

I shrugged. "Perhaps. Anyway, it's only my personal view. I suppose I just feel more comfortable in locations that are better organized. It's a matter of what you're used to."

"You mean a prejudice?"

"Yes." Which reminded me for some reason of the Trangas darts in her belt. "Talking of prejudice, what's the weaponry for? Who did you think you might have to tranquilize?"

"I take it Sheila didn't tell you about the bandits."

My look of astonishment told her she took it correctly.

"Surely," she said, "Sheila made clear there are divisions within our society."

"Yes, she did. She told me there are a number of factions in Antarctica. And she mentioned that some of them disagree strongly with the policies of the Council. And now I think about it, she did remark that one or two of these groups have taken themselves off into the wilderness. But she didn't say anything about bandits. Who are they?"

"Basically, they're an extreme form of opposition. That's the most intractable problem we face. A developing Tenth Civilization has its goal clearly defined and almost universally accepted. Disputes, as you must know from Koltetra, are about methods and priorities rather than ends, and are ritualized in a parliamentary system. But in Antarctica we have yet to agree on a goal, let alone the best way of getting to it. And we've still to come up with a means which is acceptable to all parties of resolving disputes. The result is that some elements in our society are unwilling to accept the wishes of the majority. They hold protest rallies from time to time — which is acceptable as long as they're peaceful. But occasionally they turn into riots. Obviously we do our best to, shall we say, discourage people who go that far, and they are the ones who sometimes 'take themselves off into the wilderness', as Sheila delicately puts it."

"And the Pen is where these outcasts live?"

"Most of them. The rest of Antarctica, except for the coastal fringes, is too cold for them to survive in, seeing as they have to keep away from built-up areas. Materially their existence is very precarious. That's why they resort to banditry. They rob anyone who gives them the chance. They even raid towns on occasion, especially during the winter."

I suddenly fancied there were bandits watching us from behind the larger boulders. An uncomfortable feeling affected the back of my neck.

"I'm appalled," I said. "There's no excuse for rioting. It's barbaric. And as for banditry! You'd be justified in imposing psychotherapy on people like that." (I hoped none of them were listening.)

Kerra shivered. "The Mayor's people would. But it's

256

not easy for us. Sometimes we're not even sure they're wrong. For instance, there's a group that wants the Eleventh Civilization to be a pastoral one, where men spend their days toiling in the fields and women look after and educate the children. They'd re-create every creature in the archives, even the parasites and the dangerous species. Their idea is to restore the Earth of long ago, decommissioning all the technology and giving humans a place within the natural world, rather than lording over it. Who's to say their wrong?"

"It doesn't appeal to me. The idea is too simplistic."

"It doesn't appeal to the majority of us either, which is why they're an opposition group. The trouble is, as I know well, opposition can be so very frustrating. A few of the no-hope minorities are driven to despair, and that can lead them to behave violently. But you see, in doing that, they're only reacting to the Antarctic Council the way most of us have reacted to the Mayor. It makes the imposition of psychotherapy on them impossible for us."

"It strikes me you'd be justified."

"What kind of man are you!" Kerra snapped in a sudden display of fury.

I took refuge in a stunned silence, feeling hurt.

"You think they're bad," she said more calmly, staring across the cold, bleak moor towards the lake. "I can tell you there's one faction that wants to hasten the collapse of the Tenth Civilization by the use of systematic destruction. In other words, by the waging of war. But even if I thought they were the most degenerate people on Earth, and I certainly think they're some of the worst, I still wouldn't impose psychotherapy on them."

I remained silent.

After a while, still looking into the distance, she said: "I'm sorry, Felip. I didn't mean to shout at you."

I regarded her. She was motionless, her hair ruffling

slightly in the chill wind. I wanted to touch her but didn't dare. "I don't mind," I said.

We sat for a long time, watching the shimmering lake and listening to the wind, each with our own thoughts, while the two horses waited patiently over to one side. I was profoundly troubled. I had seen the lethargy and decay of the Mayor's world. Now I was discovering the alternative, a dynamic society in which all the old human faults, the aggression, the endless quarrelling were being rediscovered. What a choice for humanity, I thought. What a choice for Koltetra. To spend one's days in endless sleep, or to spend them in endless pain — for that, it seemed to me, was the stark choice between the world of Old Mose on the one hand, and the world of Sheila Mress on the other.

Eventually we remounted our horses — I had less trouble with that the second time — and rode down to the lake. There were thin pieces of ice around its margin, and no sign of life in the water beyond a few bits of alga. By then the sun was only an hour from setting, so we made our way back to the stables, arriving just as the long twilight was turning into night proper. Having established from me that, weather permitting, I was happy to go riding again the following day, Kerra arranged for the same horses to be at our disposal on the morrow. Then we walked down into the town, and to the hotel, where we had an evening meal.

I can't speak for Kerra, but the day had left me exhausted. All I wanted to do was sleep. She agreed to make an early night of it.

Alone in my bedroom, I congratulated myself on keeping her well and truly busy. I also toyed with the idea of taking her back to Koltetra with me. It was an absurdly presumptuous notion. Even so, it was a nice fantasy to dream of as I settled down to sleep. Kerra and

Koltetra and homesickness. Then it was morning and reality was restored.

25

The next day began disappointingly. Ramska was blanketed in thick, freezing fog. We decided not to go riding until it cleared.

That created the problem of how to pass a few hours. Fortunately, the hotel had a story salon we could make use of, so after breakfast we settled down in there with some of the other guests.

The story on show was a fairly modern offering based on the formula of two men in love with the same woman, only in this tale there were two female friends, of whom one was a malcon and one wasn't. The malcon woman was being courted by two malcon men, and the contented woman was being courted by two contented men. The plot turned out to have a message in it. Both women selected one of their two suitors after a lengthy chase. The rejected contented man went off on a tour of Merica to put his sorrows behind him. The rejected malcon, contrastingly, took to drinking too much wine and ended up raping the malcon woman, murdering her newly-wed husband in a gory fight, and mangling several sentinels using a hundred-tonne fetcher he'd commandeered. Exit the evil malcon to a psychotherapy centre, just in time for the rejected contented suitor, cheerily returning from his tour of Merica, to pair off with the widowed malcon woman, who'd clearly decided she'd had enough of malcon men.

I found the story thought-provoking because if I fell in love with Kerra, as seemed possible, and she rejected me, I knew how I'd feel about it. I'm too civilized to stoop to rape and murder or even drunkenness, but I sure as anything wouldn't just shrug my shoulders and go sight-seeing in Merica. And yet, wouldn't I be happier if I could do that, and wasn't happiness all I really wanted from life? The story had obviously been created up north by somebody with no affection for malcons, but one nonetheless came away from it glad that the murderer had received psychotherapeutic treatment, not out of anger at him, but out of pity, as one would feel glad when someone in pain is relieved of that pain. The tale had me feeling sorry for malcons, and I was one! The Mayor possessed a skilful propagandist in that storyteller.

Kerra's reaction was quite different. She dismissed the thing as contrived and false. And the treatment meted out to the murderer, she said, made her despise northerners more than ever. I think she saw it as an instance of 'them' attacking 'one of us'. Whatever her viewpoint, she didn't wish to discuss it and went off to her room with a don't-you-dare-argue kind of grimace on her face. I was left to amuse myself for a while, distinctly nonplussed.

In late morning the fog cleared, leaving the landscape encrusted in a glistening frost. Kerra reappeared. We had an early lunch and set off for the stables.

By the time we arrived, the sun, which had thawed the ice off north facing surfaces, was being increasingly occluded by thickening high cloud. Kerra reckoned we were in for some snow.

Nothing daunted, we mounted our horses and rode west into the mountains. After climbing about three hundred metres we passed the snow-line, and had to steer the horses between irregular patches of crystalline ice. Experiment revealed the depth of some of these patches, especially on south facing slopes, to be over a metre. The freezing wind made my eyes water and my nose run. I was amazed that anyone, outcast or not, should attempt to survive outdoors in such a climate.

Our outward journey ended at the entrance to a deep,

wide valley facing south-east. The northern-eastern slope of it was thickly covered with snow which formed impossible-looking overhangs in places.

"Every year a little more snow settles in this valley than melts," Kerra commented. "Eventually, perhaps a thousand years from now, enough will have accumulated to form a glacier. Another few thousand years after that and there'll be icebergs from here floating in the sea. Icebergs, for the first time since the Warming!"

I tried to imagine how the valley would look a millennium hence, but I couldn't do it. All my mind kept returning to was the pointlessness of something that could so easily be prevented, if only the Mayor would deign to give the necessary orders.

Kerra went on to say that the process wasn't just happening here. Glaciers were forming all over the continent. Global sea level had already dropped by nearly a metre on account of the ice and snow now locked up on the land mass of Antarctica.

And glaciers weren't the only consequence of Antarctica being allowed to get so cold. There were the typhoons too. They arose because the only part of the climate control system that is out of order are the Starfire lamps which are supposed to keep Antarctica warm and lit in the winter. As a result, all the other parts of the system are forever channelling as much heat as possible southwards in an attempt to counter the continental cooling that is taking place. This has led to the formation of a large, stable mass of very cold air over the Antarctic heartland, surrounded by circulating warm water and air around the coast. It's a potent combination. Every so often, especially in late winter and spring, some of the very cold air from the South Pole flows out seawards. Depending on how much of it is involved, the southern latitudes experience dense fogs, snow-storms, and typhoons caused by the icy air's contact with the warm sea. (The typhoon when we were in Tres Rios was the first of the season, coming at the end of the southern winter.) Mostly these climatic disturbances skirt the coast, but occasionally, as we had witnessed, they track to the north. It seemed to me to be a heavy price to pay for the dubious benefit of keeping the malcons of Antarctica in their place.

We trekked at a leisurely pace back towards the stables and the isolated little town. As we did so, the wind dropped to almost nothing and the cloud became lower. By the time the stables came into sight, a few flakes of snow were falling.

We returned the horses to their owner and tramped down to Ramska. The snow set in heavily. Large flakes fell vertically in the still air, muffling the sounds of the world. We entered the hotel covered in white.

The question of how to spend the evening arose. We decided against another visit to the story salon, opting instead for quiet conversation in her room. It was a pleasant enough way to pass some time. Kerra seemed to want me to do most of the talking and I was happy to oblige, telling her about my life on Koltetra as far back as I could remember. Like Sheila, she made an interested and encouraging listener.

To my surprise, the reason for that lay partly with me.

"You know," she said at one point in the conversation, "I think you must love Koltetra very much. Your whole demeanour changes when you talk about it. Like you're more alive somehow."

"I'm a good ambassador," I said in reply.

The conversation flagged eventually and I decided to go, not wanting to outstay my welcome. However, before I could leave, Kerra started rummaging around in one of the bags she'd brought with her, and came out with two

Direct Interaction caps. She plugged them into each other to keep the interaction private, and handed me one of them.

"Are you any good at D. I.?" she asked.

"I play a bit," I replied. "I didn't know you were interested in that sort of thing."

"It depends who's making the music."

"Well, I don't know," I said doubtfully. "I'm not all that proficient."

"Go on, Felip. Give it a go."

I put the cap on. "Let me experiment first," I said.

She nodded, put her own cap on, and lay back with her eyes closed.

I began with a few scales, varying the tonal quality from one to another. I find each cap is slightly different from every other and responds to brainwaves in a distinct way that needs allowing for. Within a few minutes I felt I had the measure of this particular cap and was ready for something more serious.

"What would you like?" I asked.

"Something relaxing. Something that will make me think of my gentleman Koltetrian and his home world."

I started with the sound of a waterfall, gradually introducing high-pitched tinkling notes which cascaded lower and lower until they reached a base out of which blossomed a gentle melody. It was a melody I'd heard during the Eleanor Bayley concert in Merigast on my second night in Antarctica. I sat there looking at Kerra and let the music play itself. Wistful and forlorn it was.

The waterfall faded away to be replaced by a rippling down-rush of background notes. I closed my eyes in order to concentrate more on the melody. I played variations on it, intertwining it with different harmonies. Then I increased the tempo, making the music more exciting, until I recalled the lady wanted to be relaxed. I

264

almost literally put the brakes on, drawing back to a point where I could recapitulate Eleanor Bayley's opening tune.

Up to that moment, Kerra had listened without response. But now I detected a new accompaniment not under my control. It worked in with my own efforts beautifully. Our two inputs mingled. Hers somehow seemed to fly, and as it did so, pulled mine into the air with it. The duet became a song of light-heartedness that portrayed the moors and mountains of the Pen as if we were soaring and diving acrobatically above the icy land.

We continued in this fashion for some time. Eventually, at the back of my mind, though not in the music, a warning sounded. Something was wrong, but I couldn't place it. Perhaps the music had become a little too frenetic. I tried to calm it down without success. On and on we went. I perceived with some alarm that we were no longer just flying. There was a desperation behind Kerra's input. She was flying to get away. In an effort to reassert my control, I introduced a loud, intrusive trumpeting sound. I had to think the most concentrated music of my life to prevent her overwhelming me.

And then, like a suddenly exhausted bird, she plunged. The melody she had been driving (I can think of no better word) broke up, to be replaced by an appalling discord. It compelled me to silence. Out of it came a heavy, unbearably tense straining among base notes, a throbbing in which I had no part whatever to play. I struggled to escape. Only after several seconds was I able to open my eyes.

Kerra lay there, eyelids clenched shut, tears glistening on her cheeks. She was perfectly still. Scarcely breathing. Slowly the tension ebbed and the music faded, until at last I heard Eleanor Bayley's original melody repeated, played very slowly and in a minor key. On those last few notes hung more misery than I had ever known.

I watched until she opened her eyes, an age later. She looked unblinking at the ceiling. On impulse, I took the cap off my head and went over and sat beside her. And there I stayed, holding her lightly, while the widow of Kway Myer cried out her grief on my shoulder.

*

All storms take their course and die away, even emotional ones. In truth, I was to blame for Kerra's. Direct Interaction is a very intimate, deeply personal thing; I should have known better than to allow her to do it with me. In her mental state, however well hidden even from herself, it was asking for trouble.

I got up and fetched a cloth from the bathroom for her to dry her face on.

"That wasn't how you were supposed to keep me occupied," she said, pretending to smile.

"No," I agreed inadequately. I waited, feeling awkward. "Shall I stay, or would you like me to leave?"

"Take me away from here, Felip."

I thought she meant away from the hotel, which wasn't practical at that time of night. However, before I could say anything, she continued: "I hate this planet. I wish I could come back to Koltetra with you. Anything to get away from this dreadful world."

"Let's not think about that tonight. We can discuss it tomorrow. Tired minds make bad decisions."

"A truer proverb was never spoken," she said, and sighed. "I think it's time I had some sleep. I hope I haven't spoilt your evening."

"Not at all." I kissed her gently on the forehead. "I'll see you in the morning."

266

"I think you're pretty good at D. I.," she said as I turned to say goodnight at the door.

I smiled. "It beats Wagner."

She frowned.

"Goodnight, Kerra."

And with that I went to my room, though her distressing music echoed long in my head and denied me my sleep for some time.

*

The next morning greeted us under a blanket of snow fifteen centimetres deep. The sky had cleared overnight to dazzling effect.

We planned to take the flight south to Merigast in the afternoon, which left us with the morning to pass. Kerra took charge as usual, and led me on a hike of several kilometres up a ridge south-west of Ramska. I found the jaunt hard going, and made much worse by the snow, but I was definitely 'toughening up', for it scarcely made me ache at all.

From the top of the ridge, whose sides were steep enough to be scary in places, we had a good view to the east, the visibility being excellent. In the far distance, approximately forty kilometres away, one could just discern the sea. Between it and where we stood was a white panorama, broken by the black of occasional jutting rock faces, and in one place by a forest of conifers.

"Have you thought any more about me coming to Koltetra with you?" Kerra asked.

"Not a great deal. I didn't know whether you were serious."

"I think so. I considered it a lot last night; and it's been on my mind today. I'm sick of Earth. Your ship gives me a chance to get away. I know I'd always regret it if I didn't take that chance."

"I'll have to ask the others."

"I realize that. But with Jannet gone, you have the spare space, and there's also the point you made about the Koltetrians being hard to convince. Taking someone from Earth along, someone with first-hand experience of how things are here, should help you get the message across."

"That had occurred to me as well. I don't think the other three will object in the least."

"Good."

"You have to promise me one thing, though, Kerra."

"What's that?"

"No guns and no explosives. Not even Trangas darts."

"I can promise that, all right. It would be a relief not to have to carry them."

I could ask for no more than that.

"Are there views like this on Koltetra?" Kerra inquired, shading her eyes so as to better see the snowy landscape.

"In the polar latitudes, but they're getting fewer as we develop the climate control system."

"That's a pity. I shall miss the snow," she said, apparently taking for granted her forthcoming trip in Mother. "Earth can be so lovely. It's only people that spoil it."

"I think you're being a bit harsh."

"Am I? When was the last time a clod of mud or a tree or a bird made you unhappy? Only people do that."

I could see where she might be leading and decided not to encourage her. "People can make you happy too. I've been happier in your company than I ever would have been on my own."

"I suppose so," she said vaguely, and then continued

as if I hadn't spoken. "Do you know the worst thing of all? I'm one of the bringers of unhappiness. A wretched malcon."

Not for the first time, I was taken aback by this enigmatic woman. It wasn't the sort of remark I'd have expected from her. "We have to be true to our nature," I said. "We have to believe in ourselves. You do what you think is right. That's how it should be."

"Yes, but *is* it right? That's another thing I hate about northerners. They don't have any doubts. They're certain that what they've got, and how they live their lives, is pure and perfect. Complacent over-confidence, I know, but sometimes I envy them. To have doubts is a terrible thing."

Kerra's remarks could be so perplexing. I just don't think that deeply myself and I dislike having to. "Do you really, honestly, wish you were like the northerners?"

She looked at me for a moment and seemed about to tell me something confiding. But then she turned away. "No. I rather be dead," she said. She hunched her shoulders and shivered. "I get like this sometimes. It soon passes. Take no notice."

"Okay," I agreed, not completely honestly. "We'd better be getting back, otherwise we'll miss our flight."

We returned to Ramska, pausing now and then to admire the snow-covered scenery and to throw snowballs at one another.

Our leave of the hotel was accompanied by more 'important person' ceremony. It was the same at the aircraft. A number of people gathered and broke into their quaint, hand-smacking applause. I made them a short speech, expressing appreciation for their kindness and hospitality, and assuring them I would remember it always. Then we flew south, keeping above the clouds as on the outward journey.

As we neared our destination, I thanked Kerra for a lovely three days.

"I should be the one to thank you," she replied. "It was just what I needed."

"I'm glad. Maybe we'll do it again on Koltetra."

"I hope so, Felip," she said, touching my wrist.

"We could start a horse-riding school," I mused.

"Indeed we could. Welcome to my world," she said happily.

"Welcome to the future," I corrected. "And no more of this thinking you're a 'wretched malcon', okay? Because you're not."

"No more," she agreed.

26

The meeting of the Antarctic Council started straight after breakfast. Under the supervision of Sheila Mress, the continent's twelve most authoritative people came together especially to discuss the plight of the Koltetrians in their midst. The participation of Vallensel and myself in the proceedings was politely requested. Since our future was at stake, we'd have been unwise to decline the invitation.

The previous evening, as soon as Kerra and I had alighted from the aircraft bringing us from Ramska, Vallensel had greeted us with the news. Sheila's enquiry about returning us to our ship had confirmed for the Mayor that we two Koltetrians had reached Antarctica. Now he knew where we were, he was demanding our return 'within one week'. And threatening that if this demand wasn't met, he'd hold the entire continent responsible and order sentinels in to make arrests. In his view, Vallensel and I had carried out, or at the very least were implicated in, a number of serious criminal acts. The legal process would have to take its course. Only once that had been settled would our status on Earth be reviewed with regard to our returning to Koltetra. Until then, neither the people nor the hybrimorphs under the Mayor's control would assist our departure in any way.

Sheila's response had been to summon this urgent Council meeting. Considering all fourteen of us present reckoned the future of civilization on the New Worlds hung in the balance, nobody doubted she was right to do so.

Accustomed as I was to the formalities of the Koltetrian Congress, it was strange to me that the

Antarctic Council conducted its business in a rather disorderly way. Aside from a human secretary who took notes, the twelve were more like friends sitting about having a chat than leaders hoping to influence the fate of humankind.

Sheila began the meeting by giving a brief account of the situation, and ended by asking what we were going to do about it.

"It seems to me," said one of the other women, "that the problem hinges on whatever is motivating Old Mose. Does anyone have any idea of the reason why his treatment of these two gentlemen is so negative?"

No one spoke.

"I mean," the woman continued, "we all expected him to put up some resistance when Vallensel and Felip and Jannet took their leave of the Culture Secretary. But once it was clear to him they'd not been kidnapped, what did he have to gain by pursuing the matter? He's never reacted like this before to our activities. What's he think he's doing? If we understood that, we might be able to put his mind at rest or come up with a ploy to make him revise his attitude. All the time we don't know what's upsetting him, we're floundering in the dark."

"I don't think we can do anything about that," said one of the men, Conflict Management Superintendent Stegarthly. "He did his best to stop Felip and Vallensel getting here, and he's going to do his best to stop them returning to their ship. He's plainly not about to enlighten us on the subject of his motivation. So what it comes down to, given the Mayor won't relent, is what courses of action are open to us?"

"That's easy," said Sheila. "Either we surrender or we fight. And that is a question we must first get our guests to answer." She looked at Vallensel and me. "In principle, and I stress in principle at this stage, we can either accept the Mayor's refusal to let you return home or we can defy him. If we choose the former, it means complete submission to his authority and to his demands in this case. That includes agreeing to your returning up north and being subjected to the legal process, something which may result in psychotherapy being imposed on you."

"That would be absurd," said Vallensel angrily. "We're perfectly sane."

"That's not how it looks to northerners," said Sheila. "Anyway, it's beside the point. We can surrender or we can fight. Without going into practicalities, what would you have us do?"

"I'm inclined," I said in my best debating manner, "to the view that the Mayor should be defied."

Vallensel voiced his concurrence.

The Council discussed the matter amongst themselves for a few minutes. The verdict was unanimously in favour of taking action.

Sheila turned to us again. "Then we must give our consideration to practical issues. When we fail to hand you over, I am certain the Mayor will not be sending in sentinels to arrest us. That's a bluff. He will, however, impose sanctions against us. That means we cannot simply be patient and play a delaying game. Waiting, perhaps for years, until he forgets all about Koltetra, and then returning you covertly to your ship, isn't an option. Intentionally or otherwise, he is forcing us to act now. So once again I have to ask our Koltetrian friends for guidance. To send you on your way at this time means we will need to seize a space-capable vessel. Sentinels, and perhaps some people too, will be empowered to use minimum necessary force to prevent that happening. We will in turn be compelled to use force against them. Are you prepared for that to happen?"

"Do you mean people might be hurt?" I asked, frowning.

"That is a possibility," Sheila replied.

"Is there no other way?"

"The logic is unassailable. You need a space-capable craft to get to your ship. The Mayor controls them all and won't let you have one. Therefore we have to take one by force. What other way can there be?"

It was an impossible position. No civilization worthy of the name would condemn even a few individuals to face injury, and maybe death, in order to save itself. What business had I making such decisions?

"What would you advise?" I said weakly, to avoid having to reply.

"Stop tiptoeing, Sheila," said Conflict Management Superintendent Stegarthly. He addressed himself directly to me. "This isn't a decision we can make for you, Felip. It's your responsibility; yours and Vallensel's. But think of this. Is the Mayor's interference with your right to return home something you'd expect of a friend? If it was justified, one could see it as an act of love, even if it is painful for you. Do you regard it as justified? I think not. Nor does anyone else in this room. What's more, neither does the Mayor, for if he did he'd provide the reasons for his decision. Yet he remains silent in that respect. It is most definitely not an act of friendship. No, it is an act of hostility. Furthermore, if you attempt to exercise your legitimate right to go home and the Mayor uses force to stop you — as he implies he will — then that force constitutes an act of war against Koltetra. I repeat, *an act of war*. Is that what you would expect from a civilized man? What you and Vallensel must decide is whether your greater duty is to Koltetra, or to the ideal that violence is never justified. If you steal a spacecraft, and the Mayor undertakes an act of war to stop you, you must either surrender or wage war on Koltetra's account. War is by nature destructive of life. Are you prepared to accept that price?"

Once again there was silence. Stegarthly certainly didn't tiptoe. There was a lot of plain talk in that speech of his. Vallensel fidgeted at my side but said nothing.

"Are you saying," I said at last, "that the spacecraft would not be stolen for us to use, but that Vallensel and I would be the ones to steal it?"

"That is correct," said Stegarthly. "Surprise is crucial to success. Once Old Mose is aware we have a space-capable vessel, he'll lock up way-station six. You'd never get in. Or out. It has to be steal and escape in one go."

"Then there is a danger we ourselves might get hurt?"

"There is a danger you might get killed, Felip."

Paradoxically that made the decision easier. It is uncivilized to sacrifice others; it is quite the opposite to voluntarily risk sacrificing oneself. Unfortunately it wasn't that simple.

"What about Roshan and Ruth? They'll need to be with us. How are you going to get them here?"

"We aren't," said Stegarthly. "We have asked the Mayor to release them into our care, and he has absolutely refused. The alternative is to abduct them. It is unlikely any of our people could persuade your colleagues to go with them freely. What could they tell Roshan and Ruth? 'Come with us and we'll take you to Antarctica, from where you will mount a violent attempt to regain your ship'. Would they come? I doubt it. And that assumes we can get one of our people into their residence to talk to them. Even that would be difficult."

"I'm sure I could persuade them to join us," I said.

"Maybe you could. But do you think you could just walk in and lead them out? Again, force would be required. Efforts would be made to stop you. And remember, Malta, where they're still being held, is an island in the Mednean Sea, blocked off from the ocean at both ends. *Nereus* can't go there. You'd have to fly in and out. It would be a journey even more fraught than your journey here. Not to mention what happens if you fail and get detained. You'd be worse off than ever."

Stegarthly somehow reminded me of one of Antarctica's glaciers-to-be, unstoppably grinding its way to the sea. He continued: "What I'm saying is that rescuing Roshan and Ruth would be yet another act of war. Not only would it be much more hazardous than stealing a spacecraft, it would make the latter harder because the Mayor would be put on his guard. The consensus among us is that the two Koltetrians on Malta must be left behind."

There were murmurs of agreement from the other Councillors.

I was horrified. "And if I refuse to accept that decision?" I asked.

"Refusal isn't an option open to you. You need our help. If you insist on involving Roshan and Ruth, that help will not be provided. We cannot endanger the lives of our people on an operation unless there is a good chance it will be successful. I do not believe a rescue from Malta is viable. A surprise spacecraft seizure, yes; rescue from Malta, no."

Why, oh why, did I feel so often overwhelmed by my situation? These people were talking about the desertion of my friends and engaging in warfare. This was not civilization as I understood it, but a descent into brutality. I was dumbfounded.

Vallensel now said: "I can only express my personal view, but as I see it we came a long way, at great expense to Koltetra, on a mission that we now know to be vitally important to the future development of the New Worlds.

If it is unavoidably necessary that Roshan and Ruth are left behind, then so be it. As for waging war on the Mayor, he started it. I have no reservations about fighting back."

I mused sadly on how easily a civilized man lapses into atavism when 'unavoidable necessity' presents itself.

"What about you?" said Sheila to me.

"On the question of using force against the Mayor, it strikes me the man is behaving irrationally. When a society lets itself be led by someone like that, the victims of the irrationality may have legitimate recourse to aggression when all other means of redress have been exhausted. So I must ask this question: is there nothing else we can do, either to change the Mayor's mind, or to return to our ship without conflict if he remains adamant?"

The view of the Council, as I had expected, was negative. It was fight or surrender.

"Then I agree to the use of force," I said.

"And the two Koltetrians on Malta?" Sheila asked.

"If the Council considers that to retrieve them would imperil our escape from Earth to an unacceptable degree, then I will, with extreme reluctance, defer to the Council's opinion."

"It takes great courage to make such a decision, Felip," Sheila said consolingly. "It is a choice between two evils: to abandon your mission, with all the consequences that flow from that; or to abandon your friends. In these particular circumstances, I think your decision is the morally correct one."

Her words made me feel a little less bad.

With the key decisions made, the Council turned to a more detailed discussion of the means of our escape. Vallensel and I were mere observers of that part of the deliberations.

At the end, I made one final point: "Madam Kerra Dyanie, who the Council will be aware played a major role in bringing us to Antarctica, has asked if she might come with us to Koltetra. I have no objections myself. Nor do I have as spokesman for the people of Koltetra. I am confident they will accord her a warm welcome. I therefore seek your assent to her accompanying us."

"Strictly speaking, our assent is not required," said Sheila, "but obviously our cooperation would be a great help. I know of no reason why that should not be wholeheartedly given." She looked at the other Councillors. They all nodded. Sheila said: "You may tell Madam Dyanie she has our blessing."

That was no small compensation for the evil I had had to agree to participate in.

Kerra was waiting outside for news of what had transpired. When the meeting concluded, I gave her a full report. None of what I told her surprised her.

"I'm always glad once decisions have been made," she said. "Now we can get on with doing. Superintendent Stegarthly will draw up a plan. We have only to carry it out."

As simple as that!

*

When the one-week deadline for handing Vallensel and me over had passed, the Mayor didn't send in the sentinels. Sheila was right about that being a bluff. What he did instead was decommission the beamway between Puerto Cothani and Antarctica and, when that failed to produce the desired result, shut down the solar flux converter input to Antarctica's flux receiver power stations, though only for three hours. It was not a token gesture, but a clear warning there would be worse to come if the Council persisted in defying him. It meant Antarctica's people were starting to suffer because of our presence amongst them. Since handing us over was out of the question, the only other option was to return us to our ship and send us on our way urgently. Old Mose would then have no reason to continue with this particular quarrel with the southerners. Planning for our departure thus acquired a very high priority.

The plan took two weeks to draw up. As agreed at the Council meeting it explicitly assumed there would be only three escapees.

Further discreet enquiries were, in fact, made about Roshan and Ruth, but to no avail. All that came of them was bad news. We learnt Culture Secretary Annalivia had gone to Malta to give them a lurid account of the deeds which Vallensel and I had participated in. These included illicit terrestrial engineering near the main north-south road in Patagonia, the corruption of a number of citizens who gave us assistance despite knowing it to be contrary to the directions of the authorities, the shooting down of a sentinel-aircraft, causing it in turn to set several inhabited dwellings on fire, the vandalizing of two stretches of road outside Zagossa, the vaporizing of a house and numerous hybrimorphs and, dwarfing all of these crimes, the murder of Jannet. We had voluntarily disobeyed the Mayor in order to consort with a gang of regressive civilization-haters skulking in Antarctica. We were a disgrace to Koltetra and to the civilization which gave us birth.

I don't know how much of the story was believed by its audience, but the facts were undeniable, even if the interpretation accorded them was highly questionable. I had to admit, given what they had been told, that getting Roshan and Ruth to join us might well necessitate, as Stegarthly had predicted, abduction rather than rescue. I gradually became convinced they had to be left behind. I only hoped they would forgive Vallensel and me, and that Koltetra would not judge us too harshly.

The Antarctic Council attached great importance to our return to Koltetra, and not just for selfish reasons. (During the two weeks of escape planning, there was a second power cut, and it lasted longer.) Like me, they saw it as part of their duty as civilized people to communicate their information; and nobody could deny the information in question was potentially of the highest significance.

For this reason, when the plan was complete, Conflict Management Superintendent Stegarthly himself chaired the gathering called to explain it. Other participants were five planners who would not themselves be taking part in the operation, Captain Teksillar of *Nereus*, Rivien, who had been brought down from Fayoun to take active charge, three other subordinates to Rivien who would assist in getting us onto the spacecraft, and of course Kerra, Vallensel and me.

Although Stegarthly had, unusually, taken a direct involvement in what was under discussion, it was the senior of the planners, under his intimidating gaze, who explained the details using maps and diagrams and pictures. He informed us there were many ground-stations for spacecraft dotted all over Earth. In selecting one, they had gone for criteria of size and nearness to the sea. A large station would have sentinels on guard and be too complicated a proposition; one far from the sea would involve an increased risk of our being detected in transit. They settled on a site on the island of Sulawesi. The station there was now classed as smallish, though it had once been much larger in the heyday of space travel. Currently it handled a few flights per week, entirely by service hybrimorphs engaged in the maintenance of space facilities such as way-stations and solar flux converters. Location of the ground-station on the island was good: a mere one hundred kilometres inland, with the nearest parts of the coast readily accessible to *Nereus*. Another point in favour of Sulawesi was that it was sparsely populated, which meant fewer people for us to encounter by accident. A drawback, due to the lack of inhabitants, was that the roads were poor. We'd need to be equipped with a specially adapted guide. Even then, it was expected three hours would be required to cover the distance from shore to station, the terrain being very overgrown in places. We were also warned of a further drawback in the shape of a number of tigers, reconstructed from the archives by the Tenth Civilization, which inhabited Sulawesi. Although the animals had been given an instinctive fear of humans, they were nonetheless to be treated as extremely dangerous.

The station itself lay at the top of a sheared-off mountain and consisted of a perfectly flat surface of eighty square kilometres, plus some service buildings and hangars. It was a place visited by sightseers, with the consequence that our attack would need to be timed to minimize their numbers; we didn't want them getting caught up in any shooting that might occur. It was impossible to say where on the human-made plateau a suitable vehicle would be found, but it was considered very unlikely there'd be less than ten spacecraft capable of carrying three human passengers to way-station six, where Mother was still patiently waiting.

Next in the plan came the business of flying the stolen craft. It was explained how to ensure it obeyed us rather than any instructions it might receive from the ground. Basically, the technique was to 'block' its radio ears.

Getting into the derelict way-station was, the planners assured us, no problem. The vessel we stole was bound to have an operating key to signal the doors to open. There was a small risk the Mayor would try to obstruct the exit from the station before our ship could leave, but he'd need to be very quick to get another spacecraft into orbit after us that fast. The planners didn't think it was anything much to worry about.

Finally, Vallensel and I were told we needed physical training. The likelihood was that we could walk onto our chosen spacecraft from a distance of a few paces, but if anything went wrong, being able to run a kilometre or two might make the difference between success and failure. It was an instance of the anticipation much advocated by Kerra.

Five weeks we were given. Then everything would be ready and we'd be off.

Off to commit an act of war.

27

In a trivial kind of way, I found breaking the equation between civilized behaviour and indolent behaviour to be harder than almost any other. Vallensel and I, with Kerra along for encouragement — a neat psychological trick on the part of the planners — spent the five weeks running. First, short distances on flat ground; then long distances on uneven surfaces; (by 'long' I mean two kilometres or so); then uphill; then uphill wrapped in clothing that simulated the environment on Sulawesi. 'Humid, tropical' it was described as, and it was most unpleasant to exert in. Only my determination not to weaken or give up in front of Kerra kept me going. By the end of the five weeks I had just about managed to stop regarding exercise as a form of degeneracy. My leg muscles had grown to a size more on a par with the Antarctic male norm; my pulse rate was less prone to hitting a hundred and twenty beats a minute on the slightest physical provocation; and my stomach had adjusted to a diet aimed at assisting the formation of muscle tissue.

Altogether it was an entirely new kind of life for me, and I found it less disagreeable than I would have expected, due in large part to the increasing respect Kerra showed me, and to a growing intimacy between us. Vallensel was superbly considerate in that regard, contriving to be absent at just the right times.

For the final run of our training, we jogged up a steep hill east of Merigast. The wind was at our backs so it was cheating a little, but we covered the distance in fourteen minutes, and that was no mean achievement considering the snow was twenty centimetres deep and the hill was a hundred and fifty metres high.

At the top there was a small flat area from where we could observe the Antarctic capital. We sat down on some rocks, breathing heavily, and looked at the view for a while until our bodies had recovered from the effort of getting there. Vallensel then said he was as hungry as a starving crocodile and he certainly wasn't going to wait around for us. He set off at a slithery trot for Merigast. Kerra and I watched him shrink into the white distance, the cold wind blowing in our faces.

"I like Vallensel," said Kerra. "He's a good friend."

"That he is," I agreed.

We looked at one another and quite suddenly she had that harmless, wicked expression on her face that I'd come to associate with 'and now we're going to go on a run that's even harder than the last one'. This time her purpose was quite different.

"When are you going to tell me you've fallen in love with me?" she said.

"I em.... I didn't think it was appropriate just yet."

"What's 'appropriate' got to do with it? If it's true, it's true."

"Well, yes. But then, if you already know, why have I got to tell you?"

"Because you're dying to. And because I'd like you to. I don't think you should put it off or you may find you've left it too late."

"What do you mean?" I asked with hopefully concealed alarm.

She smiled. "It's not someone else. It's what the future holds. Every time you resort to force there's always a risk. Something may go wrong."

"If anything bad happens, I'll protect you. I promise. And I do love you. But I still don't think it's appropriate for me to say so."

"No. You're right. It isn't. When I wake up in orbit

over Koltetra, then it will be appropriate. Here and now, Kway is still too close, too much on my mind. I can't think rationally about another man until I can contemplate my husband in the past tense instead of the present. Yet.... Oh, I don't know. Life can be so complicated at times."

"It'll get simpler as the days go by."

"I hope so." She chuckled. "You know something? You remember when I first met you I thought you were a weak, timorous, unimaginative fool? I judged you were the sort of man, if you pushed him with a feather, he'd fall over. A typical northerner, bowled along by events. But now that I know you better.... Not a fool, not unimaginative, and" — she patted my thigh — "no longer weak. In fact, I don't think it ever was your character that was weak, so much as your body. A man lacking physical strength — or a woman, come to that — can't be expected to be assertive. Since you've put on weight, I sense a lot of determination behind that bland exterior of yours."

"Is that a compliment?"

"No. Statement of fact."

"Oh! I suppose you're right. But only to a degree. It's never seemed to me brute strength is particularly important. It's more a matter of what you believe. Beliefs can hold you in check and make you appear indecisive. After you've got to know Koltetra, you'll understand what I mean. When a person has spent all his life living to the set of unquestioned social standards there, he can't change overnight. At least I can't. That's why I strike you as bland. And timorous."

"Did I say you're timorous?"

"You haven't said I'm not."

"No. Well.... We won't know about that aspect of your character unless we come under fire on Sulawesi."

I shuddered at the thought, and remarked: "The fact is, being timorous doesn't count against you on a peaceful planet like Koltetra."

Then I added by way of friendly retaliation: "I have to say my people will consider *your* character to be very rough. You're going to have as much trouble adjusting as I've had here. No firearms, no outcasts, no dissent except through formal channels. When you get frustrated, you go and shout at your congressional representative. No decommissioning things."

"I don't think it will be all that difficult for me. I just need to belong to something that's going somewhere, like Antarctica is and the northerners aren't. I'll fit in all right on Koltetra. Your planet hasn't reached its destination yet."

"I know I haven't reached mine," I said, looking at her in a suggestive sort of way. "Come on. Vallensel will be getting lonely."

We ran back down the hill.

*

Our departure from Merigast could hardly have been more different from our arrival. Secrecy was judged to be essential. The Mayor was not to be given any reason for thinking Vallensel and I had left Antarctica. Consequently, we said farewell to Sheila Mress in private. Several other members of the Council, including Superintendent Stegarthly, were present. I thanked them for all their friendliness and for their invaluable assistance. They in turn wished us luck and gave us, in a rather touching ceremony, a message we were to present to the Koltetrian Congress with a view to its being transmitted thereafter throughout the New Worlds. To minimize the risk of loss, Kerra, Vallensel and I were each given an identical copy recorded on a standard call-button, adapted to be compatible with transfer to a visuary system such as Koltetra was known to possess. Also recorded on the call-buttons were copies of Vallensel's and my reports drawn up after our talks with Sheila. These call-buttons were each fused to a strip which was to be chemically adhered to our belts prior to our seizure of a spacecraft.

Once the message ceremony was finished, each of the Councillors kissed Kerra on the cheek and said nice things to her about their hopes for her future. We then set off for the coast.

We travelled to Vostbrok at midnight — an hour when hopefully nobody would notice us, and any who did would realize they were supposed to look the other way. It now being the middle of spring in the southern hemisphere, the sun was only a little below the horizon, the sky to the south being dim rather than dark, so the journey was made in a kind of nocturnal twilight.

On arrival in Vostbrok we went straight to the dock where *Nereus* was berthed. Captain Teksillar greeted us and showed us to the accommodation that had been allotted to us on board. It was suggested, bearing in mind the hour, that we might like to sleep, but we declined to do so. We were too unsettled. Also, *Nereus* was to leave its dock within a couple of hours and we wanted to witness the event.

The last humans to come aboard were Rivien and his team of three subordinates, an hour before departure. Each of them carried a gun.

The flurry of activity in which the seaship's hybrimorphs and their human masters were engaged, loading various items and checking this and that, subsided by imperceptible stages, until at four o'clock precisely Captain Teksillar, standing with his Koltetrian guests and Kerra in the central tower of the seaship, ordered the vessel to get underway.

The walls of the dock distended to release their grip, and *Nereus* slid very slowly into the open sea. For five minutes or so it reversed away from its home port. It was full daylight by then and the town could be seen clearly as we receded from it: a cluster of dwellings set in a snowy white landscape.

As *Nereus* switched from reverse to forward motion, the top of the sun's disc appeared, blood red, over the land to the south-east. I realized this was the last time I would ever see Antarctica; that sun illuminating the white hills made the perfect image to remember it by.

The seaship picked up speed. Soon a surge of water was washing over its upper surface and swirling round the base of the two towers. I gave my temporary southern home of eight weeks a final salute, and Captain Teksillar led us into the warm interior of the seaship, ordering that it proceed submerged.

By now, having been awake all night, I was feeling tired. I made my way to my cabin and my bed.

I was restless for quite a while. *Nereus*'s deep, never-changing hum and the many thoughts that ran round in my excited mind were not conducive to sleep.

Gradually, however, mental quiet came upon me. I got used to the seaship's sound, while the thoughts fell away until only one remained — one that clung on for a long time. When this escape of ours from Earth had been in the future, the thought had lain low. Now it reproached me with a vengeance. Again and again the question demanded an answer. How long would it be before Roshan and Ruth forgave us for what we were going to do to them? How long? How long?

*

The voyage to Sulawesi took a week to complete. We were not allowed to relax on *Nereus* during those seven days. The vessel had a gymnasium which we were expected to use. We also spent time going in great detail over the layout of the ground-station, and getting the plan of action and the part each of us was to play clear.

It was decided, with more approval from me than Vallensel, that only Rivien and his team would carry firearms. As Rivien explained, it was their job to dispose of any force that might be deployed to prevent our escape. Our job, on the other hand, was to return to our ship. He didn't want anyone getting their roles mixed.

"Besides," he added, "you're less likely to get hurt if you aren't armed. And that goes for you as well, Kerra."

To my surprise she didn't argue. I wondered if perhaps she was trying to impress me. I took it as a hopeful sign.

Nereus arrived at our destination — a bay on the coast of Sulawesi designated *Prime Beach* — in the early afternoon of Quinday 43rd. We waited there, submerged, until midnight. The four-day old moon had set by then. (The state of the moon had been a major consideration in the timing of our escape.) Captain Teksillar threw an expensive dissipating beamtrack ashore for us, enabling us to land on *Prime Beach* in comfort. Two journeys were necessary: the seven people first; the adapted guide second. While we waited for the guide, we sat on the sand in the hot, humid air, listening to the surf as it broke. I preferred that noise to *Nereus*'s humming, which was now conspicuous by its absence.

The specially adapted guide, which only just had room inside for its seven passengers, was certainly unusual. For one thing, it ran by means of an array of short legs instead of wheels, and for another it had several sets of arms which it moved in the manner of someone swimming. They were clearly intended to assist in pulling it through obstacles.

Once the guide was ashore, *Nereus* submerged. The intention was for the seaship to wait until the following night, when it would retrieve Rivien and his men from the beach and return them to Antarctica.

Our strange guide, its route programmed into its delible memory, set off up the beach. I had expected it to search for a path to follow, but it didn't. It simply forced its way into the dense wooded growth that began where the beach stopped. We inside received a lot of bumping as a result of this course of action, though it did at least have the advantage of movement in a straight line.

It soon became plain the guide's 'swimming' arms were immensely strong and were used not only to assist with pulling it through the vegetation, but also to force plants up to small trees in size out of its way. It managed a speed of fifteen kilometres per hour.

Eventually we came to a dirt road which enabled us to move much faster. We needed to resort to undergrowth-crawling thereafter only to avoid a couple of villages. When the road forked, we took the right hand option onto a more permanent surface. From then on it was a trouble-free journey as our guide ascended the two thousand metres to the plateau where the ground-station lay.

We arrived at the boundary of the place two hours before dawn. The guide was instructed to take us off the road into the adjacent forest. Two of Rivien's subordinates left us, heading around the perimeter of the ground-station in opposite directions. Their job would be to provide cross-fire if the need arose. It was that, I think, which finally brought home to me the awfulness of the action we were shortly to take.

The rest of us stayed with the guide, listening to the

sound of stridulating insects, and watching the ground-station. It was completely inactive. A few lights five kilometres away at the centre of the plateau were the only indication the station was in use.

The wait was long and tense. Eventually, the light of the coming dawn brightened the eastern sky. It was early enough to avoid any danger to human bystanders, of whom there should be none; and late enough for us to be able to see what was what.

Rivien directed the guide onto the plateau. The operation to seize our means of escape from Earth was about to enter its final, most crucial, and potentially most violent phase.

28

The guide, its arms folded out of the way along its sides, and its short legs giving the impression of a rhythmic front-to-back undulation, rushed forwards.

The surface of the plateau, which looked perfectly flat from a distance, and which undoubtedly had once been so, proved close up to be quite rough. Various small plants had insinuated their roots into the ground to make it decidedly uneven. Despite this, the guide managed a smooth sixty kilometres an hour.

Clustered in the centre of what was clearly a partially derelict station we could make out more than twenty craft. It seemed to take an age for us to get within identification distance of them. Several turned out to be for terrestrial or airborne use only. The majority of the remainder were integrated hybrimorphs with no passenger space. Only six were definitely spacecraft suitable for our use. We selected the nearest one and headed for it.

All this time a feeling of unreality hung over the scene. Our approach went undetected, or at least not responded to. Everything stayed quiet.

The guide came to a halt by our chosen spacecraft.

"Didn't need your physical training after all," said Rivien, with a grim expression on his face that failed to match the words. "Go."

We alighted and ran the few metres to the spacecraft.

Once inside we went straight to the control deck, where we activated the controls and ordered the pilot to take us to way-station six. It informed us it needed to be re-fuelled before that would be possible. There was nothing for it but to try another craft.

We returned to the open as quickly as we could and began jogging to the next nearest usable spacecraft, about half a kilometre away. Rivien and the guide had backed off, but he must have seen what we were doing.

The second craft proved to have the requisite amount of fuel. Kerra activated the device that would 'plug' the craft's ears to stop it being controllable from outside and gave it its instructions.

We heard the whine of chem-ion thrusters coming up to operational readiness.

"External monitors on please, pilot," Kerra commanded.

It should have been a nice tranquil view we saw. And it was, except for one thing: there was an aircraft, tiny in the far distance, apparently moving across our line of sight.

"Is that what I think it is?" Vallensel muttered.

"I'm not sure," said Kerra calmly. "It's presumably on a routine flight. We'll wait till it's gone by."

But it didn't go by. It altered course towards us.

"Damn it!" Kerra swore. "We must have been seen. Take us up, pilot. Rapid ascent."

In the three minutes we had so far been inside our second-choice spacecraft, Rivien had covered nearly two-thirds of the distance to the jungle from which we had come. I thought it likely he had yet to notice the danger.

Our spacecraft began to rise. I heard a machine-language blip, probably an instruction from Sulawesi space traffic control ordering our craft to return to the ground. The hybrimorph pilot, thanks to Kerra's 'earplugs', didn't get the message.

The vertical acceleration, which had begun quite languidly, suddenly forced us hard into our seats. I could barely move under the fierce linear gravitational field our ascent was generating.

The distant aircraft was still several kilometres away but now clearly heading straight for us. There was no longer any mistaking it: it was a sentinel-aircraft. Space traffic control would have told it we were engaged in an unauthorized flight. It would inevitably command us to return to the ground. When we didn't obey, what would it do? Using 'rapid ascent' meant we could outrun it. So it would only be able to stop us by opening fire. Would it do that? Would a measure that strong be allowed under the 'minimum necessary force' rule? Suddenly I was more frightened than I had ever been before in my life.

Even as I was fearfully asking myself these questions, I got my answer. I heard another machine-language blip. A few seconds after that, there was a flash of light from the distant sentinel-aircraft and instantaneously a dull explosion. We'd been hit — doubtless inflicting just enough damage to prevent us going into orbit. By this time we'd reached an altitude of four kilometres above the ground-station. The control deck lighting flared red. Had we been in space, we'd have been scrambling to get into spacesuits. Fortunately, the internal air pressure was not decreasing noticeably.

"Hull integrity has been breached," the pilot informed us, stating the obvious. "I cannot proceed. I am initiating an emergency descent."

The sound of the chem-ion thrusters changed. The feeling of acceleration died away, to be replaced by a sensation of weightlessness.

"Override. Continue," Kerra shouted furiously.

"Life is in danger. Override invalid. I cannot proceed," the pilot repeated.

The sentinel-aircraft, some way below us, had arrived over the ground-station.

"For reason's sake, shoot it down, Rivien," said Vallensel to himself.

"He can't," Kerra responded. "You need a narrow beam to bring down an aircraft. Hand held guns are not that accurate; five hundred metres at most."

We were in free-fall, but our altitude was still increasing on account of the velocity we'd acquired while under thruster power. The sentinel-aircraft gained height as it chased after us and was soon alongside.

Bearing in mind what Kerra had just said, I knew if Rivien was to stand any chance of shooting the aircraft down we needed to descend almost to ground level. There was no option but to let the spacecraft proceed with returning us to the ground-station.

Soon our upward velocity decreased to zero and we began falling to Earth. Some way into the descent, the thrusters came back on to slow us and bring about a gentle landing.

As we neared the ground, I could see Rivien was now at the edge of the forest. He and the subordinate who'd stayed with him were watching the disaster unfold.

Kerra seemed to go into shock. She slumped in her chair and said: "We're dead."

The terror in my mind cleared in that moment. My trembling ceased. Instead there came an overwhelming rage. For the first time in my life I hated someone. This Mayor, this disgusting, degenerate apology of a human being; this creator of all our misfortunes; this weak, tyrannical bully. What was he doing to us? To my Kerra? Weren't Jannet and Kway enough for him? I wanted to teach that man a lesson he'd never forget.

I had no confidence in Rivien's ability to rescue us; he was Kway all over again. Which meant if we landed at the ground-station we'd be detained. At worst, immediately; at best, before we could get back to *Nereus*. Kerra had said she'd rather die. I wasn't having that; I had promised to protect her. It followed logically we had to land away from the ground-station. Preferably far away.

"Can you still fly horizontally, pilot?" I asked.

"Yes," it replied.

"Then take us to Ultima Salem." It was a silly instruction, but I was momentarily obsessed with having a showdown with Old Mose.

Fortunately, the pilot had other ideas. "I have enough fuel to sustain a horizontal flight not in excess of two and a half thousand kilometres," it informed me.

"Then take us to...." I struggled to remember the name of some place around here that I had heard of.

"Rajalan!" shouted Vallensel. "Take us to Rajalan."

"That is not a legitimate use of my function," the pilot stated.

"Horizontal flight won't endanger our lives. Override. Do it!" I ordered.

By this time our pilot had brought us to within a few hundred metres of the ground.

"What about that?" said Vallensel, indicating the sentinel-aircraft hovering close above us.

I shrugged.

The thrusters changed their tone once more as the spacecraft started to accelerate horizontally. It was not something the sentinel-aircraft was expecting. We found ourselves leaving it behind.

"Not Rajalan," said Kerra quietly. "A walled city on an island full of dangerous prehistoric animals. It's about the worst place...."

She had no time to finish the remark. The sentinel-aircraft caught up with us again as we were passing over the perimeter of the ground-station. I had just enough time to register the direction we were travelling in had taken us by chance almost directly over Rivien and his subordinate. They were looking skywards, guns pointing at our enemy. And then there were two ferocious, almost simultaneous explosions. I knew instantly that a couple of energy bolts had been discharged at the sentinel-aircraft. We were close enough to it that our vessel jerked violently. I momentarily lost my senses. When I regained them, I found we were not only still alive, we were still flying. And I could make out no sentinel-aircraft on the external monitors.

My first thought was of Kerra. She became aware I was looking at her.

"I'm okay," she said. "I don't think we'll be going to Koltetra today, though."

I looked back to the external monitors. It was only then that I realized they weren't working properly. The panoramic view was fuzzy, and one section, on the side where the gunfire had hit the sentinel-aircraft, was blacked out. Despite this, I was able to make out the forests of Sulawesi still beneath us.

"Shall we reverse course and go back to the ground-station?" Vallensel asked.

"I think we should go on," I replied. "There are bound to be other sentinel-aircraft converging on that place now."

"I assume Rivien got the one that attacked us," Vallensel remarked.

"Safe assumption," Kerra replied. "Bringing down panflector-shielded aircraft is one of his skills."

"So what do we do now?" I asked. "Given Rajalan is a bad place to make for, where do we land?"

"The next island on our current course is Borneo," said Kerra. "That'd be our best bet."

I was just starting to feel optimistic about our immediate prospects when the pilot spoilt it all.

"I must inform you," it said, "that I am not airworthy."

The monitors appeared to show we were now no longer over land.

"Sweet reason!" I shouted at it. "We can't land here. We're over the sea."

"My external sensors are still within their working limits," said the pilot, "so I am aware landing is not viable. That does not alter the fact of my lack of airworthiness, which is due to my guidance system no longer functioning. I do not know where I am or what direction I am travelling in or how fast I am going."

"Are we still on course for Rajalan?" I asked in alarm.

"I do not know," it replied.

"You mean you're lost?

"That is correct."

"Do you even know if you're travelling in a straight line?"

"On the basis that output from my thrusters is balanced, and judging from the information supplied by my external sensors, I believe I am."

Kerra asked: "What about altitude?"

"I am not sure. Judging height optically is not easy for me. I estimate two thousand metres above sea level, but it could be five hundred metres higher or lower."

"We've got to land this thing urgently," said Vallensel. "It could fly into a mountainside and not even know it was doing it."

"I would know," the pilot corrected him. "The knowledge, unfortunately, would not be of any use, since I cannot control course alterations. However, for the same reason, the option of landing is not open to me. My knowledge of speed and height above ground are not sufficiently accurate for that."

"We can't just fly on till you run out of fuel and crash," exclaimed Vallensel.

"No," the pilot agreed.

"That's the trouble with hybrimorphs," commented Kerra. "Push them beyond their tolerance limits and they're useless."

As far as I could see, that left us without options. If we did nothing, we'd eventually crash. If we tried to land, we'd still crash, only sooner.

By looking at the external monitors closely, it was possible to identify a hazy red blob almost directly behind us — the rising sun. It confirmed we were still travelling westwards towards Rajalan. Below us, sea was replaced by greenery. I presumed we were currently over the island of Borneo.

"Have we got enough visual information on these monitors to talk the pilot down?" I asked.

"We'll have to have," said Kerra.

"In that case," Vallensel advised, "we should land straightaway."

Kerra had changed her mind about that. "Borneo has a low population density. It's like Sumatra but without the megafauna. I've no idea how far we'd have to walk to find habitation. And like Sulawesi, it's got tigers. If we see somewhere to land, we'll land. Otherwise we'd better keep going. There's a good chance we're still on a flight path that will take us to Rajalan. Better there than in a Borneo jungle."

"But we can't land in Rajalan," Vallensel argued. "This craft must look a mess, quite apart from it being space-capable. We'd hardly be inconspicuous."

"So we land a few kilometres short of the city," I said. "Then we run to it. We've trained enough for that sort of thing. When we reach the city's perimeter wall we can claim we got separated from a tourist party and would they please let us in."

"But the place is crawling with huge predators," Vallensel protested.

"Nonsense," I retorted. "We hardly saw any when we were there touring."

"They have an instinctive fear of humans," Kerra pointed out. "My worry is you two. If you enter Rajalan other than surreptitiously, you'll be detained. Which means you'll have to stay with the craft. I'll go to Rajalan alone. The authorities aren't aware I've committed any crimes so I'm safe in that respect. Once I'm in Rajalan it shouldn't be too long before I'll be able to arrange for the Council to get you out."

"I'm not having you walking around on Sumatra on your own," I said flatly.

"That's how it has to be," Kerra stated adamantly.

"No it doesn't."

"Don't argue."

"I'm not arguing. You're not going alone."

Fortunately Vallensel intervened before we got into a quarrel. He remarked: "Your debate is premature. We haven't landed yet. What happens after that we can talk about later. That's if we're still alive to discuss it."

We resumed scanning the ground below us for signs of habitation. Finding a village in Borneo to land nearby would solve many of our problems. However, from an altitude of two thousand metres and with defective external monitoring, we had no success. Kerra doubted there were any settlements for us to see anyway.

We flew on in silence until the green of Borneo was replaced by the blue of the sea.

"Pilot," I heard Kerra asking, "if Rajalan is due west of us, how long after we cross the Sumatran shoreline will it be before we reach it?"

"I cannot answer that question," came the reply. "I do not know how fast I am travelling."

"Assume a thousand kilometres an hour."

"Twelve minutes."

"That's the best we can hope for," she said to us. "We'll land eleven minutes after we cross the coast. If the speed's wrong or the direction's wrong, we could come down more or less anywhere on the island. Let's just hope I'm right. In that case, we should land no more than twenty-five kilometres from Rajalan."

The coast of Sumatra came into view. The poor quality of the external display made it difficult to distinguish very shallow water from dry land, so we were unclear when to start counting eleven minutes from. Time passed. As we progressed, the ground level gradually rose up to meet us. None of us knew whether there was any land on Sumatra higher than our altitude above sea level. We hoped, if there was, that the eleven minutes would be up before we flew into it.

When Kerra judged the time was right, she ordered the pilot to stop its lateral motion and take us down. We had to tell the poor thing when it seemed to be stationary as it had little idea itself. The craft had very roughly five hundred metres to descend. The pilot could only manage the manoeuvre by being given a continuous commentary from us on how well it was doing.

As we neared the ground, it became clear we had not picked a suitable location. There was a carpet of trees, unbroken in every direction. The pilot became aware of it at the same time we did, and warned us the surface was not suitable to set down on. We decided to proceed anyway. The truth of the matter was that flying nearly blind for two hours had frayed our nerves to the point where we were not prepared to endure any longer. The pilot continued to protest. It must have known it was unlikely ever to take off again.

The final stage of the landing was extremely difficult to judge. We had to cut out the thrusters as late as possible, but not so late we set the trees on fire. Fifty metres above the treetops was what we aimed for, and mainly by luck we got it about right. We fell freely for three seconds and then hit the trees. The control deck was filled with the sound of grinding as wood and duram mutually shattered one another. The spacecraft keeled over almost onto its side and decelerated to a stop with a thump which jarred me almost senseless. I was so stunned I couldn't breathe for a few moments. The craft tipped a little more, accompanied by further rending noises. And then there was silence.

We were down.

29

We scrambled outside with difficulty, having to jump three metres to the ground. Above us, birds wheeled and soared, screeching alarm cries. Everything else was still. There was no wind, and the air felt dry and warm, despite the early hour of the day.

Our landing had done a lot of damage. There were many broken branches littering the vicinity, and several trees had been forced over bodily to near horizontal angles. One corner of the spacecraft rested on a snapped-off but still upright remnant of one of these. We noted with relief that there was smoke wafting amongst the tree tops but no sign of flames.

I had expected the forest to be almost impenetrable, but I was wrong. The fuzzy view on the spacecraft's external monitors had been misleading. There was plenty of light penetrating the leafy canopy and a generous amount of room for ground dwelling animals to move about in.

"I take it we head west," I said. "Assuming the craft was on course, that's where Rajalan will be."

Kerra agreed. She advised us to equip ourselves with a means of defence before setting off, saying: "You want something straight, at least a metre long, thick, and preferably with a jagged end to it. Then, as long as we keep together, we should be able to deter anything undesirable."

It wasn't hard to find suitable implements amongst the debris produced by our arrival. Once small side twigs have been torn off, a broken branch makes a business-like weapon. At any rate, one felt a lot less vulnerable clutching one's big stick.

We set off. I noted with relief that Kerra made no attempt to raise again the idea of her going to Rajalan alone.

Once we were a reasonable distance away, we looked back at the spacecraft. It was certainly a mess: tipped at a steep angle, blackened where gunfire had oxidized the duram hull, and with two gashes in it. I wondered how visible it would be from the air.

"Too visible," was Kerra's verdict. But there was nothing we could do about it except get away from the vicinity as quickly as possible. And that's what we did.

Progress was far from ideal. The ground vegetation, at first no more than a minor irritation, became a troublesome impediment to our walking, making us fatigued much sooner than the distance covered would have led us to expect. In addition, the terrain was markedly hilly, which also tired us.

Kerra's training led her to believe we should head for the highest ground; one, because it might give us a view of where we were going; and two, because it reduced our chances of ending up in a dead-end gully. Unfortunately, we soon found the tops of the hills were as forested as everywhere else, with the visibility through the trees never exceeding a couple of hundred metres at most. And while we avoided gullies, we didn't avoid climbing hills only to come to a complete stop before precipices on their far sides. More than once we had to partially retrace our steps to get round obstacles of that kind.

As for megafauna, our luck — such as it was — held up. All we encountered that morning was a herd of five monstrosities, herbivores of some kind, a single one of whom, even on all-fours, was taller than any of us. They ignored us, which was a relief, since the branches we were carrying would have made little impact on them.

By midday, thirst and hunger and the fact we seemed

to be getting nowhere were spoiling our tempers. And then three things happened in quick succession to alter how we were feeling. Firstly, a sentinel-aircraft flew past us some distance to the north. It gave no indication of spotting us. Secondly, a Sumatran guide went almost vertically over us, heading east. Was it traveling directly from Rajalan? And thirdly, we annoyed an enormous deer with colossal spiked antlers. The beast came charging at us and stopped only a metre from us, head down, swaying its antlers from side to side and pawing the ground. We backed off hurriedly and it didn't pursue the matter any further. The encounter scared us badly. I, at least, realized that complacency about the megafauna was very unwise. That deer could have killed all three of us had it been minded to do so.

It was mid afternoon when we caught our first glimpse of Rajalan. We had ascended a steep hill and came to a north facing escarpment which dropped sufficiently steeply that no trees obscured our view in that direction. At first glance the scene was singularly disappointing; aside from a small lake, we could make out nothing but unbroken forest all the way to the horizon. And then I noticed what seemed to be three tightly-spaced stars in the far distance. At first I thought they were sentinel-aircraft, but Kerra said they never fly in formation. It also became clear they were motionless. It was Kerra who finally realized what they were: we were seeing Rajalan's night-time floodlights reflecting sunlight off their outer surfaces. The revelation was good news in one respect, for it meant we were no longer lost. But in another respect it was awful. I estimated their distance away to be anything from fifty to a hundred kilometres. Neither Kerra nor Vallensel disagreed with that assessment.

The conclusion was unsettling. On this sort of terrain

we could expect to achieve four kilometres an hour at most. Rajalan thus lay between, say, fifteen and thirty hours solid walking away. If you allowed for resting overnight and making detours to avoid unexpected obstacles, we were talking about trudging for several days through this megafauna-infested jungle. And the only prospects of water and food along the way were the lake in the distance and the berries and other fruits that Kerra happened to know were edible. Our chances of reaching Rajalan before thirst, hunger, exhaustion or even predation overcame us were not good.

Trying not to be intimidated by the trek ahead of us, we retraced our path off the hill and turned to the north.

We'd been going for half an hour when we came to a stream, which we thirstily drank from and then waded across. As we got to the far side a large cow-shaped animal raced through the water and ran off into the distance. And then, in hot pursuit, came a pack of dogs which weren't dogs: half our height, heavily built, with large fangs. They took no notice of us and quickly disappeared after their intended prey.

As evening approached, several Sumatran guides flew overhead on their way to the safety of the walled city. So also did a sentinel-aircraft, from which we hid by pressing ourselves against tree trunks.

We began to experience the instinctive fear of the dark that really has no place in a civilized environment. Our thoughts turned to caves. In contrast to Patagonia, regretfully we hadn't the option of making one. It was what we could find, or nothing. As we trod wearily on, 'nothing' looked increasingly likely. The ground simply wasn't the kind that had caves in it.

We continued for a while longer until our course brought us to an almost tree-less tract which we began to cross. We soon found ourselves in an area with dense undergrowth — mostly low bushes and ferns. Discussion of the merits of this area as a place for sleeping led us to decide we'd had enough for one day. There are limits to how far being 'toughened up' can get you. We agreed to go no further, and pass the twelve-hour night by taking it in turns to spend two hours awake and four hours asleep. I volunteered to stay awake first.

It was a lonely two hours. Kerra and Vallensel, once they had lain down in the undergrowth, were invisible to me, which was good. I sat with my own head below vegetation height, watching the sky darken and the moon set, all the while listening for sounds of danger. Occasionally I'd stand up to see what was happening, but mostly I sat.

At first I thought of practical things. The failure of the attack on the Sulawesi ground-station wasn't the end of everything. The Mayor had no reason to believe it had anything to do with Koltetra. With luck he'd think it was merely another bit of malcon vandalism. In that case we could try again.

And then my mind turned to dreamier subjects: Kerra; Koltetra; Mother, so close above our heads; killing (I am ashamed to admit) the Mayor. And eventually, ironically, I thought about the paradise I had strived all my life to help build on Koltetra; a paradise which, having found it completed on Earth, I was striving equally hard to get away from.

Soon it was fully night. I became aware of small animals scurrying in the undergrowth near at hand, and saw them from time to time when they came very close. But I couldn't identify them. They were just dark shapes moving around on the dark ground. They fled when I threw clods of earth at them, which reassured me that they at least could be persuaded to keep their distance.

The time came to awaken Kerra for the first of her

two watches, it having been decided she would take over from me when my two hour stint was up. I put it off for about half an hour out of consideration for her. After what she had been through that day it seemed cruel to disturb her. When I did wake her, my tardiness was not well received.

"Have you been asleep?" she whispered, unmistakably angry.

"No," I said, taken aback. "I didn't want to wake you."

"Well, I don't appreciate it. It's equal shares as far as I'm concerned."

It was too dark to read facial expressions but she knew she had upset me. The harshness went from her whisper. "If you do things like that, Felip, and I permit it, I shall become dependent on you eventually. I don't think that makes for a good relationship, do you?"

"No, I suppose not."

"Think about it. You'll understand." She moved towards me. "Kiss me goodnight."

It was the first time we'd kissed sexually, and it was a superb way of repairing my damaged ego. I was cheered up instantly. The utter sensuality of the woman was stunning. It was a happy man who fell asleep in the undergrowth.

The rest of the night was mercifully uneventful. Vallensel woke me for my second spell on sentry duty at midnight, warning me about the little animals in the undergrowth, which Kerra had told him were rats. (Not an animal we have on Koltetra.)

I woke Kerra for her second watch at exactly the appointed moment. That, it seemed, did not entitle me to another kiss. Kerra could be very perverse at times.

And so to the dawn. Vallensel kindly allowed us to sleep into the morning, which earned him a scolding from

Kerra. She pointed out we could have been that much nearer to Rajalan if he'd woken us when we'd agreed, and how ever did Koltetra manage if all the men on it were like him and me! His pained expression had my sympathy, though I hid it until Kerra turned away to survey the horizon, whereupon I caught his eye and winked. He grinned back.

Kerra took the lead and we resumed walking. In due course we came to the edge of the relatively clear ground and were about to re-enter the regular Sumatran forest. I paused to take stock of the scene, and saw nothing remarkable. But as I was about to set off after the others, something caught my attention on the edge of my field of vision. I turned my head and saw, charging towards us, an enormous bear.

I called to the others, saying: "Look," and pointing the creature out.

Kerra, as always, thought fastest. "The tree," she shouted. "Run!"

Vallensel and I took off after her. Either by training or instinct she knew the tree to make for. She began to climb into its branches. Vallensel and I followed her example. By the time the bear reached us, we were a good four metres up. We looked down at the bear. It looked up at us. Its supposed instinctive fear of humans didn't seem to be particularly effective.

We waited to see what it would do. It waited to see what we would do. A stand-off. We three lords of creation could do nothing but powerlessly, helplessly wait for this creature, at least twice the height of a tall man and with claws and teeth to match, to get bored and go away.

It did eventually, leaving us scratched and trembling. We returned warily to the ground and reacquired the big sticks which we'd had to drop in order to climb the tree.

When we were sufficiently convinced the bear wasn't going to reappear, we resumed our northward journey, conscious as we had not been before of our ever-present danger.

Shortly before midday we arrived at a lake, possibly the one we had espied the previous afternoon. It was an obvious place for large animals to congregate so we were inclined to avoid it. There had been sufficient surface water to drink on our route and we had no need to slake our thirst.

We were about to start making a detour when, to our surprise, a Sumatran guide, unmistakable with its shocking blue coloration, flew in over the trees and landed at the lakeside.

"About time," said Kerra. "You two will have to hide hereabouts for a while. I'll tell these people I got separated from my party. They'll take me to Rajalan. From there I'll get a message to the Council. They'll send one of our aircraft to retrieve you."

"If we don't starve or get eaten first," said Vallensel.

"You can come with me if you want to," said Kerra, "but you'll be detained if you do."

"I'm not ready to be detained," I said.

"Neither am I," Vallensel agreed.

Leaving Vallensel and me crouching in some long grass, Kerra broke from cover and hastened forwards to be rescued. She was half way to the guide before we realized she had made a serious error of judgement.

There was a movement in the undergrowth. It was one of those prehistoric crocodiles, a gryposuchus. And she was heading almost straight for it. I doubted she could run faster than the reptile, and I knew in that dreadful moment that any intervention by Vallensel and me, or by the Sumatran guide, would come too late.

Vallensel grabbed me and forced me to the ground,

slapping a hand over my mouth to stop me shouting a warning.

"No," he said as I struggled against him. "She knows."

I was driven to go to Kerra's assistance whatever the cost. Only Vallensel's weight on top of me prevented me sacrificing my life in vain. I could hear her screaming. Sweet reason, no! Please no.

Vallensel had his mouth very close to my ear. "Felip," he said quietly, "it's all right."

I felt his grip on me lighten. I raised my head to see the gryposuchus waddling in its crocodilian way towards the edge of the lake. My beloved Kerra was waving her arms and shouting as the Sumatran guide rushed to her rescue.

The shock I had experienced — imagination can so easily be infinitely more terrible than reality — coupled with the flood of relief that her 'screams' had only been shouts to attract attention, overwhelmed me. My body went limp and it was untold minutes before I could get my breathing and the shaking of my limbs under control.

When coherence returned to my thoughts, Kerra and the Sumatran guide were gone.

"That's one lucky lady," commented Vallensel. "I guess the crocodile wasn't hungry. When you're ready, we'd better find somewhere to hide until help arrives."

I got up, feeling weak and unsteady, and followed him towards the nearest trees.

We reckoned our best option would be to find a tree we could climb and in which we could settle ourselves with reasonable comfort. None in our immediate vicinity looked suitable, so we began to wander around the lakeside surveying the many candidates, all the while keeping our eyes open for unfriendly creatures lurking in the undergrowth.

At last we found a tree to our liking: sufficiently sturdy, easy to climb, possessing plenty of foliage to hide in, and with the kind of branches that offered the prospect of being less than excruciatingly uncomfortable to sit amongst. Vallensel went up for a preliminary look and reported it was acceptable.

I had been standing facing the tree and briefly forgot to look about me, relying on my hearing to warn of danger. Unfortunately, this particular danger was far enough away that I didn't hear it. Vallensel, his view obstructed by leaves, didn't become aware of it until after he had jumped to the ground. He straightened up and froze. Instinctively I turned. Behind me on the opposite side of the lake, and flying towards us, was a sentinel-aircraft. I froze too and hoped desperately that it hadn't seen us. As illusions go, it lasted for no more than a few moments. Probably it thought we were tourists in need of rescue. It was a nice gesture, but no thanks. The sentinels on board would certainly recognize us. In an instant we forgot all the other dangers; we forgot our tiredness; we forgot our hunger. We ran for our lives.

We ran and ran, not daring to pause to check on the pursuit, if indeed there was one. The strength slowly ebbed from our bodies. We slowed down. I dared to think sentinels from the aircraft were not chasing after us, or that we had eluded them. I staggered to a halt. So did Vallensel.

At that moment, there was a popping sound above my head. A dart bursting. Trangas. Breathing heavily from the running, I couldn't keep it out of my lungs. For a few seconds my brain fought against it. And then, like mist evaporating in the sunlight, a change seemed to come over the world. The urge to get away, the fear, the aggression lifted from my mind. The beautiful Earth, bathed in the balmy warmth of midday, lay before me, and I saw it for the first time. I was hot, streaming with perspiration, exhausted, but none of that mattered. I glanced at Vallensel. My own feelings were mirrored in his face. He radiated the happiness of a child whose every wish has been granted.

Just briefly, there was confusion in my thoughts. What had I been running from? And then I looked round. The sentinels from the aircraft were standing quietly, waiting. Those lovely, friendly hybrimorphs would sacrifice their lives to keep us safe. They were our guardians. Vallensel and I walked towards them. I felt like someone rejoining civilization after a mad foray into a barbarous land. It was wonderful to be at peace.

Truly I was in paradise.

30

The sentinels led us onto their aircraft, and once they had confirmed our identities took us, not to Rajalan, but to the big psychotherapy centre at Flinders, located on an island off the coast in the far south of Oz. It pleased me very much that they did this. As I reviewed the events of the preceding thirteen weeks, it amazed me I could have behaved in such an insane fashion. Only a lunatic would want to escape from paradise.

The radical change in my perspective both amused and fascinated me. I could no longer think what Koltetra had been concerned by. Yes, Earth had dropped out of the Galactic Information Grid. I supposed it merited a question, but surely not the mounting of an interstellar expedition. The fact that I had fervently supported such a mission suggested my judgement had not been entirely sound even on Koltetra. And having got to Earth and seen at first hand that all was well, why had I rebelled against it? Why had I fallen in with the malcons? My ability to identify with their kind had completely left me.

Only one thing clouded my new-found peace of mind: Kerra Dyanie. I longed to see her again; longed to bring an end to her suffering — as I now clearly saw it was; longed for her to join me at Flinders where she could get the 'wretched malcon' madness out of her head. We could be so happy and contented together. I felt sure I could persuade her to see reason.

Vallensel and I were examined over a period of ten days by a panel of psychomedics including three human doctors. They questioned us at great length and in great detail about our past, on Koltetra as well as on Earth, and about our attitude to life, to civilization, to ourselves, and to the way we saw those things relating. Neither of us could justify our earlier actions, but we did our best to explain how things had looked to us at the time. The psychomedical panel was well versed in such matters, for they had a clearer understanding of the way we had been thinking and feeling than we had ourselves.

When the examination was over, the panel went away to consider what treatment we required, or would be offered. Vallensel and I passed the next few days watching the world go by, waiting with a sense of pleasant anticipation for their verdict.

The Flinders psychotherapy centre was in no sense closed. People could come and go as they wished. Had the fancy taken us to fly to Antarctica, that dreadful land of snow and barbarity, we could have done so. We were unable to think of anything less desirable. Nobody in his right mind would seek the company of such a disagreeable bunch of scoundrels. We only wished all those pathetic malcons would have the sense to come to Flinders for treatment. They, and the world at large, would be far happier for it.

In fact we had no great desire to go anywhere much, passing most of the time either in the treatment centre or else in nearby Flinders town, which was very modern. All the buildings, including the warehouses, were organic; not a duram structure in sight. Being a coastal location, Flinders also boasted a fine beach. A wide creek had been excavated and filled with sand to produce a narrow 'U'-shaped bay around which people could laze. The more adventurous were able to go out in bather-hybrimorphs onto the sheltered tongue of water running down the centre of the creek. We went there several times, delighting in the blue sky, the blue sea, the freedom and the contentment. One day it would be like this on Koltetra. Truly, truly, we were in paradise.

One morning we were asked not to go wandering, as the psychomedical panel had reached their decision about us. The head of the centre, Dr Perris, would talk to each of us individually. This was verdict time and we awaited it happily. The love of humankind shown by everybody who had examined us left no room for doubt that they would only act in our best interests. To do otherwise would not be civilized, and these people were definitely civilized. I trusted them with my life.

Dr Perris saw Vallensel first in a private room at the centre. I waited outside for my turn, sitting in a home-grown organic chair. People passed by, exchanging friendly greetings with me as they went. Time was, I reflected, when a wait of this kind would have irritated me. Now I accepted it with benevolence. Life was too wonderful to waste on fretting.

When Vallensel came out, he was grinning. "It's all arranged," he said. "They're going to start tomorrow morning."

"Start what?" I asked.

"They'll tell you," he replied. "And be prepared for an incredible surprise."

I had no idea what he meant by that, so I was unsure what to expect when Dr Perris called me in.

The room where the doctor held his consultations was a comfortable size, entirely white in colour. Sunlight slanted in through the open window to create an impression of brilliant lightness. There were three seats arranged informally in the centre of the room, and two men standing by the window. One I recognized immediately as Perris. The other didn't register for a few seconds. When I realized who it was, I simply gaped. It was very rude of me. But this was one surprise I could never have been ready for. The second man was Kway Myer.

Dr Perris said: "I didn't tell you sooner, for I wanted to save the revelation until today. You believed Kway was dead. I'm sure you'll be delighted to see how wrong you were."

Yes, I was delighted for Kway the human being; I was less delighted for Kway the husband of Kerra Dyanie.

"Relax," said Dr Perris, who I'd told about my romantic involvement. "An unhappy malcon like Madam Dyanie won't have any interest in either of you now. Let's sit down."

He motioned to the three chairs. The way they were positioned gave none of us any disadvantage with respect to the other two. We sat.

"Now," Perris commenced, addressing himself directly to me, "I want to discuss with you this morning the arrangements to be made regarding your future happiness. The psychotherapy panel, after a careful investigation of your case, have concluded you would benefit from permanent neurosurgery to alleviate your over-developed aggressive drive. We are also convinced, as we are legally required to be, that society as a whole would benefit from your being made less aggressive. However, we do not consider your behaviour to be so deviant we can compel you to undergo treatment. The decision therefore rests with you."

Before I could give my impatient consent, Dr Perris held up his hand. "Not yet, Felip. We do not lightly interfere with a man's brain. I do not want you to decide until you know exactly what the situation is. There are, in fact, three options open to you. The first is that we withdraw the treatment you are currently receiving. The second is that we continue with it indefinitely. The third is the neurosurgery I've already mentioned. Let me explain each in turn.

"As you know, you are currently being given one and

a half micrograms of a drug called Philovitin every day. Philovitin is what we doctors call a selective neural anaesthetic. It binds to those cells in the brain responsible for negative emotions and puts them to sleep while leaving the rest unaffected. If we discontinue the drug, it will take about two days to clear from your body. Thereafter you will return to your former self. Your malcon nature will reassert itself. That is the first option, and it has the advantage that it is reversible. If you find, having tried option one, that you wish to reconsider the other choices, that possibility will always be open to you.

"The second option is for us to supply you indefinitely with Philovitin. Again, it is a reversible course of action; you can always change your mind later. What an indefinite supply entails is the use of a pseudo-parasite. These are genetically engineered and are based on tapeworms. They can secrete a range of drugs. In your case it would be a Philovitin-secreting worm, and we'd place it in your intestines. Once there, it will burrow into the intestinal wall and secrete Philovitin into your blood stream for as long as you live. We can kill it with a worming agent if you want it removed in the future.

"Third, there is permanent neurosurgery. This is irreversible, even in the regenerating brain of an immortal such as yourself. It is carried out by using the Philovitin worm in combination with a second drug-secreting pseudo-parasite. This latter one produces a substance that binds chemically to Philovitin and, in so doing, turns it from an anaesthetic into a neurotoxin, killing the anaesthetized brain cells. The disadvantage with this form of treatment is that you can't change your mind later. The advantage is precisely that it is permanent. You'll never have to worry in any way about your supply of Philovitin, whether ingested or supplied by pseudo-parasite. Once treatment is successful, we complete it by using a worming agent to remove both the Philovitin and the toxin pseudo-parasites from your intestines."

"The treatment is safe and painless?" I queried.

"Totally. And you can carry on living normally while the surgery is underway.

"Well, Felip, those are your options. Reversion, continued use of Philovitin, or surgery. You don't have to decide today if you'd like time to consider. In any case, I want you to talk to Kway before making up your mind. It is standard practice where neurosurgery is in prospect for the patient to speak to someone who has already undergone the treatment. Preferably it should be someone they know. Kway here was happy to have a word with you. If you wish, I'll leave you in private."

"I don't mind either way," I said.

"Stay by all means," Kway concurred.

The doctor leaned back as if to exclude himself from the conversation.

"I hardly believe it's you," I said to Kway. "You always used to look so angry. But now...."

"It's me all right. They cured me. And it must be a change for the better because I can see I don't frighten you any more."

"How did you know about that? I tried to keep it hidden."

"Fear shows in the eyes."

"Well, it was justified. You vaporized the head off a vicuna."

"That must have seemed really vile. The funny thing is, at the time I thought nothing of it. To see the truth, to see how a poor, sick malcon looks through normal eyes, you have to become normal. I was a monster."

"I wouldn't say you were that bad."

"I've murdered people, Felip."

"But Jannet was an accident."

"When someone dies as a foreseeable consequence of your deliberate actions, it's not an accident; it's murder."

"Yes, I suppose it is."

"And she wasn't the only one. There have been others. That's why they gave me no choice with the neurosurgery. They took me straight to the psychotherapy centre in Santiago and had me undergoing the procedure within hours. And I'm so glad they did."

"You honestly are glad?"

"Definitely. Why?"

"Kerra once told me you'd rather be dead; that you'd never let them detain you alive."

"That just shows how insane I was. That evening in Zagossa, when they'd cornered me, I put the gun to my head. I was that mad, Felip. Fortunately, a sentinel shot me with a stun dart at the critical moment. Those things work instantly. It saved my life. And do you know the maddest thing of all? At the time I thought I was sane." He smiled. It was a smile like Annalivia's. "So the question for you is: do you want to be cured like me? I guarantee you won't ever be sorry if you join me. It's so good to be happy."

Dr Perris returned to the conversation, saying: "One thing, Felip. If you'd like to come off Philovitin before making your decision, you're welcome to do so. You may view treatment differently in the absence of the drug. You must instruct me in this as I cannot take away your present happiness unless you ask me to."

The thought of returning to my old state was dreadful. Really there was no decision to make. "I wish to be cured permanently," I said. "If that means surgery, surgery is what I want."

The doctor nodded. Kway patted me on the shoulder. It was a good decision, wisely made.

There was little in the way of preparation before the surgery began. Early next morning Vallensel and I swallowed the first of the pseudo-parasites, the one that would secrete Philovitin into our bloodstreams. Twenty-four hours later, once it was certain the parasite was in place, we would swallow the second pseudo-parasite that would turn Philovitin into a neural poison.

That evening, Kway, Vallensel and I sat about talking together, laughing at our antics in Patagonia. For the most part our chatter was without significance except (with hindsight) for one thing.

Kway broached the subject, asking: "So how do you two stand now with regard to returning to Koltetra?"

"That's a good question," I replied. "I hadn't given it any thought. Where do we stand?"

Vallensel said: "We'll have to ask the Mayor about it, I suppose."

I suddenly felt uneasy. There was something at the back of my mind, some thought refusing to become conscious, or some emotion I couldn't place, couldn't put a name to. "I don't know I'm all that keen to leave Earth," I said. "There doesn't seem much point."

"It's our duty," Vallensel remarked.

"You could send Koltetra a message on your ship's soliton transmitter," Kway suggested. "That way you can do your duty without having to return home."

"That might be the best thing," I agreed doubtfully.

We left the subject at that, but like a persistent echo that refused to fade away, the mysterious unease in my mind kept coming again and again to me. At first I thought it might be guilt that my responsibility to Koltetra no longer had my full-hearted commitment. But that couldn't be it. I had done nothing wrong as regards

Koltetra. I would do my best to get a message to them. What was there to feel guilty about? Yet if it wasn't guilt that was bothering me, what was it? I went to sleep that night without finding an answer.

Treatment went according to plan. Next morning we swallowed the second parasite as part of our breakfast. Dr Perris told us that the surgery would take about four days to complete. After that, the aggression producing parts of our brains would be gone forever. It was like anticipating a homecoming. We were returning to the Tenth Civilization after a ridiculous dalliance with the regressive throwbacks of Antarctica.

Following breakfast we three comrades took a guide into Flinders and wandered about the warehouse district of the town, helping ourselves to some unusual fruits newly-arrived from East Asia. We returned to the psychotherapy centre for our midday meal, eating the fruits for dessert. Dr Perris looked in to check we were okay, but didn't stay.

Following lunch, we retired to Vallensel's room for a siesta. A tranquil discussion ensued about what we'd do when the surgery was complete. First move, we decided, would be to visit Roshan and Ruth, still living comfortably as far as we knew on Malta. That suggestion brought to my mind the same uneasiness that I had experienced the night before. And still it persisted in refusing to be identified.

While we were engaged in this talk of the future, the door of Vallensel's room opened and someone came in. It was nothing unusual; the psychotherapy centre was very relaxed where privacy was concerned. I was facing away from the door and so didn't immediately see who it was. She moved very fast. I had half turned towards her when she slapped me hard on the back. There was a sharp stab of pain.

At that moment, Kway leapt to his feet. "My love, you've come!" he exclaimed. His whole body radiated boundless joy.

I saw her face at last, and it was Kerra. She looked intensely absorbed as though engaged in a difficult task. I watched her rapidly move to Vallensel and strike him as she had struck me. And then that hidden emotion was there again. This time it filled my head. And I knew at last what it was. I looked at Kerra, that wild, sensuous, unhappy, wretched malcon, and I was ashamed. Ashamed! I didn't want her to see me how I now was. I didn't want Roshan and Ruth to see it. I didn't want those on Koltetra to see it. And I knew in that instant why the Mayor had treated us Koltetrians so badly. His dark secret was suddenly so plain; so obvious. The simple truth was that Old Mose too was ashamed; he and his Parliament.

I had no time to assimilate the revelation. Even as I felt it, the shame turned to anger, and the happiness cleared from my mind. It was as if a mental fog was suddenly dispersed to reveal the ugly, restless, aggressive reality. I knew the Philovitin-anaesthetized parts of my brain were anaesthetized no longer.

Kerra was embracing Kway like a mother cuddling her lost little boy. I did not like him.

She separated herself from her husband and scrutinized Vallensel and me.

Apparently satisfied by what she saw, she commanded us coldly: "Outside." When Kerra was like that we knew better than to argue. We obeyed. The door closed behind us.

For several seconds we waited, not knowing what to do. There was a bang. The door opened and Kerra came out, quickly shutting it again. I caught a faint smell that carried me back to Patagonia and the vicuna cooking on the fire. I looked uncomprehendingly at Kerra. She was crying silently.

Then she took my hand, as she had that other day on our way to Garden Island, and said: "Smile, Felip. We're going home."

And she led me, with Vallensel following close behind, out into the open air, and back to her sadder kind of reality.

31

It took me a long time to wake up. I seemed to be suspended in a dreamland of fleeting shapes, of strange and familiar voices, of comings and goings that I couldn't influence. But gradually my thoughts cohered and I opened my eyes.

The clock on the wall indicated it was four in the morning on Primaday 48th. It was daylight. My hospital room was empty except for a monitoring hybrimorph.

I tried urgently to work out how I felt. Was I the happy fellow of Flinders, or the malcon of Koltetra and Antarctica? I concluded that since I was desperately hoping the latter, my brain was still working in the way it always had before the sentinels captured me.

Recollections flooded my mind. I could see Kerra guiding Vallensel and me down to the beach where we were taken on board *Nereus*. Openly. It was an act of impudent defiance unprecedented in *Nereus*'s half-century of existence. Once underway we had informed Captain Teksillar of the neurosurgery that had been set in motion. That had brought about an immediate change of plan. *Nereus* had on board a supply of Anti-vitin — the antidote Kerra had injected us with that neutralizes Philovitin — sufficient for three days for the two of us. After that time, the Philovitin secreted by the first pseudo-parasite would take effect, and be made toxic by the second pseudo-parasite. As *Nereus* carried no worming agent, that meant we had three days to get to a health facility where the parasites could be eliminated from our systems. Unfortunately, Vostbrok, our intended destination, was over four days away by sea. So *Nereus* had altered course and made landfall on Auckland Island (an island lying to the south of Zealand) where there is a small malcon settlement. An Antarctic Council aircraft had picked Kerra, Vallensel and me up from there and flown us to the Merigast health maintenance clinic. We had arrived with twenty-four hours to spare.

The doctors had administered the oral worming agent, and to be extra safe, had put Vallensel and me into a coma. The resulting low metabolic rate, they explained, would make our brains more resistant to toxins. Then, only once they were certain the pseudo-parasites were gone from our bodies, would we be allowed to return to consciousness. Since I was now conscious and felt normally aggressive, I concluded the treatment to thwart the neurosurgery had been successful.

The hybrimorph monitor must have sent a signal, for after about ten minutes Kerra hurried into the room.

"I think the Flinders neurosurgery failed," I reported to her straightaway. (I knew that would be the thing uppermost in her mind.)

"That's what the medics reckoned," she agreed. "They tested a sample of cerebral fluid last evening. It would have shown up in that, apparently, if your brain had been damaged."

"I'm very relieved."

"So am I. I couldn't have faced you being like Kway." She took my hand and gripped it. "That was horrible."

"Did you...?" I was unable to complete the question. How do you ask the woman you love if she murdered her husband?

"We promised each other," she said quietly. "I would rather be dead than have them do that to me. Kway felt the same."

I wasn't so sure about the right and wrong of the issue, but I sensed this was not the time to start an ethical debate. "Is Vallensel okay?" I asked.

She nodded. "He came out of his coma half an hour ago. You were both very lucky, really. If I'd been a day later, the surgery would have caused permanent brain damage."

"A narrow escape."

"You don't know how narrow. The news got to Rajalan you'd been detained just before I was due to set off on my way to Antarctica. If I'd been in more of a hurry, I might not have heard it. It could have been many days before the news of your capture reached the Council via their unofficial channels. And that's not all. *Nereus* was the only means of rescuing you from Flinders, and that was at sea. Fortunately, Captain Teksillar's orders had been to return directly to Vostbrok from Sulawesi. Then the Council dithered over whether and how to rescue you. Superintendent Stegarthly thought the danger to our personnel was too great to justify mounting an operation. It took a lot of effort on my part to persuade him. He only agreed in the end so long as I was the only one at risk. Then *Nereus* had to be turned round: crew changed, stores taken on board, and so on. We didn't leave until late on Cuertaday 45th. It took five days to get to Flinders Island. They put me on shore during the night. The plan was for me to wait near the psychotherapy centre until you showed up, and extricate you. If you hadn't gone into the town to collect fruit that morning, I wouldn't have got you out of there in the afternoon. We had no idea it was so urgent. We should have known."

"You did all right."

"Yes, and about time. The second half of this year has been one disaster after another."

"Not quite," I said. I felt recovered enough to prop myself up on my elbows. "It could have been much worse. Do you remember the gryposuchus?"

"What's that?"

"You know. That huge crocodile you almost fell over on Sumatra."

"Oh that," she said, blushing. "One of my more appalling blunders."

"I thought it was going to kill you. That was the worst moment of my life."

She didn't say anything, but just looked into my eyes. I sat up fully and pulled her towards me. She didn't resist.

"I love you so much," I said, and kissed her.

It was a long kiss and would have been longer, but a medic came in and interrupted us. The embarrassed thing muttered that there was plainly nothing wrong with me, swept up a couple of invisible bits of dust off the floor, and left hurriedly.

It put me right off my stride. For her part, Kerra thought the situation was funny. Laughter being the infectious thing it is, I soon joined in. It was the first genuine laugh I'd had since leaving Koltetra. That too would have lasted longer than it did but for my not being fully recovered from the coma. I was overcome by a wave of giddiness and had to lie quietly for a few moments.

*

That evening, after a meal at the health clinic, Sheila Mress called round. She seemed uncharacteristically uncomfortable and formal, firmly requesting Vallensel and Kerra and me to speak to her together.

She began by asking about our rescue from Flinders, and was particularly interested in the effectiveness of Anti-vitin. "It's only been around a couple of years," she explained. "It reacts very strongly with Philovitin and renders it inactive. I'm sorry about the needle Kerra used. Clumsy affair, but she had to inject a large quantity quickly. The trouble is, in the absence of Anti-vitin you wouldn't have been able to make up your minds to do anything. People on Philovitin never can. And if they're forced, they resist."

"It worked out for the best," I said. "We've survived. We can make another attempt at escaping soon. Plus there's a bonus. I know the cause of Old Mose's behaviour towards us."

"What is it?" Sheila asked, though for some reason she wrung her hands when she spoke.

"Shame," I said. Kerra, Vallensel and Sheila listened as I explained my theory: that the Mayor and his Parliament were, consciously or otherwise, ashamed of what the Tenth Civilization had become. That was why Earth had dropped out of the Galactic Information Grid; they could no longer look the dynamic New Worlds in the eye. And when scrutiny had become inevitable with the arrival of the Koltetrian expedition, it was shame that had made the Mayor unwelcoming and uncooperative, and finally truculent. He was like a naked old mortal being exposed to study by vigorous young people. He had professed indifference, had snapped and snarled, had tried to chase us away; and when his efforts had proved in vain, was now doing all he could to stop us passing on what we had seen.

Vallensel had no doubt I was correct, admitting he had experienced the same emotion at Flinders as I had. Sheila was more guarded, though she agreed it was the best explanation she had yet heard.

"It's an interesting idea," she agreed, "but it's not why I'm here. There's a reason why I had to speak to you tonight; why it couldn't wait until tomorrow. It's bad news and I wanted you to hear it from me and not some other way." She took a deep breath. "You won't be going back to Koltetra. Your ship has left."

There was a stunned silence. I heard Kerra whisper: "Oh no."

"We pleaded with the Mayor to let you all leave together. Believe me, we pleaded. We knew he'd summoned Roshan and Ruth from Malta to his residence. The report we've received from one of our people claims he's accused you of crimes against civilization. He says that since you two had absconded you'd caused nothing but trouble; that you had been offered treatment and had responded by spitting in the doctors' faces; that he was no longer prepared to let you leave Earth under any circumstances; and that unless your two colleagues left immediately themselves, he'd have your ship destroyed. He gave them the choice of a limited failure of their mission or a total failure. They made the logically correct decision. The ship went four days ago. The Council only heard it had gone and got confirmation this afternoon."

"They left us behind," I said in disbelief.

"We would have done the same to them," Vallensel pointed out grimly.

"That makes it all right, does it?" I yelled furiously.

Sheila, her distress plain, remarked: "It's partly my fault. The message for the New Worlds you had fused to your belts wasn't exactly complimentary about the Mayor. The doctors at Flinders are bound to have passed it to him."

"And the reports we both wrote while we were in Merigast," Vallensel pointed out. "They weren't complimentary either."

There was nothing else to be said that would be listened to that evening. Sheila took her awkward leave of us. Vallensel too excused himself. I was alone with the woman I loved, the woman I had dreamt of taking back to Koltetra with me to start a new life. Now it was all in ruins. Everything I had fought for, everything I had worked for, everything I was looking forward to doing, destroyed. I was too distraught to speak, too distraught even to think. Try as I might — and sweet reason how I tried — it was too strong for me to fight down. I wept in Kerra's arms until I was too exhausted to weep any longer.

*

Once the Mayor had Vallensel and me in detention at Flinders, he had stopped the power cuts and re-commissioned the Puerto Cothani to Antarctica beamway. After we returned to Antarctica, it was feared at first that he would reinstate his sanctions, but it hasn't happened. He knows Vallensel and I will never report to the New Worlds, so he no longer has any interest in us. With our ship gone, we have ceased to be unwelcome, intruding foreigners and become merely two typical renegade malcons. Of course, we are aware he will molest us if we ever enter his domain, but confinement to Antarctica, once we got over the shock of being stranded, doesn't seem to be such a terrible thing. For me at least, there are compensations.

Kerra has a house about a kilometre west of Vostbrok. Two weeks after the awful news was broken to us, she invited me over to see it. It is a modest dwelling, isolated from any others — the nearest being three hundred metres away — and accessed by means of a dirt track. We got to it from the port on foot, which was good exercise.

The building is set in a field of tough, short grass. This vegetation is very attractive to a large number of rabbits who keep it cropped. They are a species modified specially to be able to withstand Antarctic winters. Their bodies are small and their fur is thick and white. They make a pretty sight bobbing around on the greenery and show great tameness, for they take food from our hands.

Inside, the house is austere, lacking most of the 'necessities' that people up north wouldn't dream of doing without. The view out of the windows, though, more than compensates for the austerity, if 'compensates' is the right word. To the south, beyond the lawn, one beholds a very rugged landscape, the higher ground permanently covered in snow, even at the end of summer. In the opposite direction lies the sea. There is a path over the gently sloping grass leading to a metal safety-rail. On the far side of that is a black cliff dropping almost vertically to a rock-strewn sandy beach, one which is covered only at high tide. Many jagged rocks can be seen beyond the tide-line.

The afternoon of my first visit to her home, Kerra showed me around the locality and then, as evening drew on, and I was tired from all the walking about, took me indoors for a meal. She prepared it herself. It is one of the most striking things about southerners, how much they do without hybrimorph assistance. Up north they have chefs. They could have them in Antarctica as well, and some people do, but not the majority.

Towards the end of the meal, our conversation turned to the New Worlds and their future.

"The only way we could have improved on today is to have done it on Koltetra instead of in Antarctica," I said.

"I know what you mean," she agreed. "We'll manage, though. We'll just have to come up with a new dream to replace Koltetra."

"I think we would have been happier."

"We're together. That's more important than which planet we live on."

"What a lovely thing to say. For the two of us, being together is indeed the most important thing. But as to which planet we live on.... well, it's not just we who are affected, is it? There are the colonies 'out there'. For them, our being on Earth instead of Koltetra will have a severely detrimental effect on their future."

"It will? You'd better explain that, or I'm going to start worrying I've got involved with an massive egotist."

I smiled. "I didn't mean that how it came out. It's not a matter of us as people, but of our message. Instead of what we would have told them, they'll get Roshan's and Ruth's message instead. As I see it, they'll state that Earth is the paradise they expected it to be except for two cultural developments. One — comparatively minor — is that perfection has led to a kind of lethargy setting in. That will be their explanation for Earth leaving the Galactic Information Grid. The other is the malcon issue. They won't be saying positive things about us. Malcons will be depicted as a major flaw in the perfect system."

"Which is what you thought to begin with?"

"Exactly. Roshan and Ruth never met a single malcon. All they have to judge malcons by is the attack you carried out on the road to Ashdod, and the negative opinions of the Mayor and his Culture Secretary. The report Koltetra receives will advise that malcons need to be tackled before they become the plague they are on Earth.

"And tackled they will be. It should be possible, by education most likely, but by coercion if necessary, to eliminate malcons before they become a serious nuisance. That's my prediction. Thanks to our expedition and the misinformed message that returns to Koltetra, the New Worlds will stop from developing the one thing that can save them from a blissful drift into extinction."

"Surely the New Worlds aren't that stupid," said Kerra. "If malcons are reported to be a problem, they'll be able to work out *why* we're a problem."

"I hope you're right, but I doubt it. Tragic, isn't it? It was such a trivial thing that that sentinel-aircraft should have happened to be passing the Sulawesi ground-station when we were there. And yet that one small mischance has sealed the fate of the New Worlds."

"If you're going to be like that, I don't want you around here," said Kerra crossly.

"Be like what?"

"Talking all this nothing-we-can-do rubbish. If you feel that defeated you should go and join Old Mose. He'd make a better companion for you than I can."

"You misunderstand me, my love. I said the outlook for the New Worlds, thanks to our disaster on Sulawesi, is grim. I believe that and I'll stand by what I say even if you don't like it. But I never implied there's nothing we can do. Quite the reverse. Think. If the future history of the New Worlds goes how I predict, that leaves us. Us here in Antarctica. History is repeating itself. When the Ninth Civilization sent out the great liners to found the New Worlds, they did it because they feared for the survival of humankind. They knew how close we came to extinction during the Warming, reduced to a few million survivors languishing here and around the North Pole. They wanted to ensure that if something like that ever happens again, there'd be humans elsewhere to carry on the human adventure. And we're now facing a different kind of disaster which looks set to produce the same result: the future of humanity depending on a few million southerners. People like Sheila and Rivien and you and me. That's an awesome responsibility. It makes me impatient to be underway because there's so much to do. For instance, we need to acquire a space capability so we can build our own transmitter and join the Information Grid on our own account. That way we may yet send a proper message to the New Worlds. And if we don't, we'll just have to go and recolonize them." I paused to get my breath back. "And that's just one thing that needs doing. I can come up with lots of others. Do you still think I belong with Old Mose?"

There was a strange expression on Kerra's face that I couldn't interpret. But she was looking straight at me, and clearly not with hostility.

"Oh Felip," she said, shaking her head slightly, "my strong, brave, imaginative, wise friend. Hearing you talk like that makes me so glad to be with you. You see things much more clearly than I do, and it's just what I need. A man to give me strength; someone to help me through my 'wretched malcon' moments. Kway did it with his outrage and anger. I think perhaps you can do it with your self-assurance.... and that hidden fire burning somewhere inside you, you gentleman Koltetrian."

"I hope so."

"I love you," she said.

It was the first time and it gave me a lump in my throat. I looked at her, the collar-length light brown hair, the beautiful gold-flecked green eyes, the slightly crooked but finely shaped nose, the pale-coloured skin, her almost overwhelming female attractiveness, and felt myself slipping away into a dreamy fantasy.

Getting back to the present with an effort, I said: "Talking for a moment of Kway, can I ask you one question that's puzzled me off and on?"

"You can ask. What do you want to know?"

"When you walked into that room in the psycho-therapy centre, did he know what you were going to do?"

She didn't answer straightaway. Then she looked at me with a sad smile on her face, and said quietly: "Kway died in Zagossa."

I left it at that.

*

After the meal, I walked alone down to the cliff top and leaned on the safety-rail. At my back to the south, the sun had dropped out of sight behind the distant mountains, but it never truly sets as this time of the year. All was quiet. The seabirds had ceased their squawking; the wind had dropped to nearly nothing; only the swell whooshing on the rocky beach fifty metres below broke the silence. There was a chill in the air.

I stood for a long time thinking of Koltetra. Of Jathra, and the Valley of Eternal Summer, and the Siren Hills, and my beloved Falls at Ikterun. Could it really be that I would never see them again? Homesickness is bad when you are away temporarily. How much worse when you are away forever. A great sadness came upon me.

For a time, I saw the world only mistily, while a couple of rabbits nibbled the grass at my feet. But I believe life is an undertaking of the present. One longs for what is past at the expense of the future, and I had too much future to risk ruining it with bitterness and regrets. If the beauties of Koltetra were beyond my reach, there were beauties on Earth to replace them. If there were challenges on Koltetra that were no longer mine to confront, there were challenges on Earth equally demanding of my attention. The Eleventh Civilization would be a long time in the building. There was so much to do. So very much.

As I sought peace in the tranquillity of my surroundings, I pondered that strangest irony of human history: that that very paradise, which, once finished, should have been a source of boundless pride, had instead become a source of shame. In attaining perfection, the people of Earth had left themselves without goals, without dreams, without hope. And thereby a little of their essential humanity had died. It was almost amusing in a macabre way that the only thing to revive the human dynamism atrophying inside the head of the Mayor of Jerusalem had been the need to hide from five harmless Koltetrians what he and his contemporaries really thought of themselves. Men and women had built the Tenth Civilization, but only weak and shallow, albeit happy, children could live there.

Gradually, as I watched the waves endlessly advancing and retreating on the beach below in the dim daylight, my thoughts became nebulous and finally ceased altogether. I was at peace with myself and the rest of the universe.

And there I stayed, unaware of the passage of time, unaware of the growing ache in my feet, unaware of the cold seeping into my body, until eventually the cries of my physical self made themselves heard, and my thoughts re-awakened to the unpeaceful lesser realities of my life on planet Earth. I turned to face the house. The light from its windows caught my breath, foggy in the frosty air. I shivered.

Slowly I walked back to my new home, and to the bed of Kerra Dyanie.

Epilogue

41 Years Later

APPENDIX

The following document has been appended to Felip Varrandoe's account, above, by unanimous order of the Antarctic Council, meeting in his absence.

DECLARATION BY THE MAYOR OF JERUSALEM AND THE CHIEF OVERSEER OF THE ANTARCTIC COUNCIL

We the undersigned honourably agree:

in the first part, that the boundary on Earth between the Mayoral Realm and the Southern Realm shall be the line of latitude 47 degrees 51 minutes south of the equator;
in the second part, that the Antarctic Council shall henceforth, with immediate effect and in perpetuity, cease all hostile and subversive activity directed against the Mayoral Realm;
in the third part, that the Antarctic Council shall direct all malcons/southerners living within the Mayoral Realm similarly to desist;
in the fourth part, that those malcons/southerners living in the Mayoral Realm deemed by the Mayor to be undesirable shall be accepted unconditionally by the Antarctic Council for resettlement in the Southern Realm;
in the fifth part, that any malcon/southerner guilty of serious crimes in the Mayoral Realm shall be offered,

at the Antarctic Council's discretion, permanent exile
to Chaytambeor in the Palatinate of Luna as an
alternative to psychosurgery;
in the sixth part, that access to the Mem system will
no longer be denied to the people of the Southern
Realm;
in the seventh part, that the two Realms will share the
facilities and the space-capability of the ground-
station on Garvie Mountain, Zealand;
in the eighth part, that the Southern Realm will be
permitted to restore the climate control system in
Antarctica to the extent desired by its people, and to
maintain it thereafter in commission;
in the ninth part, that henceforth the passage of time
will be the sole arbiter of the dispute between the two
Realms.

Whereupon we have set our hands this
Findelasemana 52nd, in the year of human civilization
13203.

I, the current Mayor of Jerusalem,

Shwa K'Pier

and I, the current Chief Overseer of the Antarctic
Council,

Felip Varrandoe.